3 9082 12476 2181

P9-CCU-507

THE FAMILY JENSEN
HARD RIDE TO HELL

AUBURN HILLS PUBLIC LIBRARY 50
3400 EAST SEYBURN DRIVE
AUBURN HILLS, MI 48326
(248) 370-9466

THE FAMILY JENSEN
HARD RIDE TO HELL

William W. Johnstone
with J. A. Johnstone

PINNACLE BOOKS
Kensington Publishing Corp.
www.kensingtonbooks.com

PINNACLE BOOKS are published by

Kensington Publishing Corp.
119 West 40th Street
New York, NY 10018

Copyright © 2013 William W. Johnstone

All rights reserved. No part of this book may be reproduced in any form
or by any means without the prior written consent of the publisher,
excepting brief quotes used in reviews.

PUBLISHER'S NOTE
Following the death of William W. Johnstone, the Johnstone family is
working with a carefully selected writer to organize and complete
Mr. Johnstone's outlines and many unfinished manuscripts to create
additional novels in all of his series like The Last Gunfighter, Mountain
Man, and Eagles, among others. This novel was inspired by Mr. Johnstone's
superb storytelling.

If you purchased this book without a cover, you should be aware that
this book is stolen property. It was reported as "unsold and destroyed"
to the publisher, and neither the author nor the publisher has received
any payment for this "stripped book."

All Kensington titles, imprints, and distributed lines are available at
special quantity discounts for bulk purchases for sales promotions,
premiums, fund-raising, educational, or institutional use. Special book
excerpts or customized printings can also be created to fit specific needs.
For details, write or phone the office of the Kensington special sales
manager: Kensington Publishing Corp., 119 West 40th Street, New York,
NY 10018, attn: Special Sales Department; phone 1-800-221-2647.

PINNACLE BOOKS and the Pinnacle logo are Reg. U.S. Pat. & TM Off.
The WWJ steer head logo is a trademark of Kensington Publishing Corp.

ISBN-13: 978-0-7860-3118-4
ISBN-10: 0-7860-3118-2

First printing: May 2013

10 9 8 7 6 5 4 3 2 1

Printed in the United States of America

First electronic edition: May 2013

ISBN-13: 978-0-7860-3119-1
ISBN-10: 0-7860-3119-0

BOOK ONE

Chapter I

The two men stood facing each other. One was red, the other white, but both were tall and lean, and the stiff, wary stance in which they held themselves belied their advanced years. They were both ready for trouble, and they didn't care who knew it.

Both wore buckskins, as well, and their faces were lined and leathery from long decades spent out in the weather. Silver and white streaked their hair.

The white man had a gun belt strapped around his waist, with a holstered Colt revolver riding on each hip. His thumbs were hooked in the belt close to each holster, and you could tell by looking at him that he was ready to hook and draw. Given the necessity, his hands would flash to the well-worn walnut butts of those guns with blinding speed, especially for a man of his age.

He wasn't the only one with a menacing attitude. The Indian had his hand near the tomahawk that was thrust behind the sash at his waist. To anyone watching, it would appear that both of these men were ready to try to kill each other.

Then a grin suddenly stretched across the whiskery

face of the white man, and he said, "Two Bears, you old red heathen."

"Preacher, you pale-faced scoundrel," Two Bears replied. He smiled, too, and stepped forward. The two men clasped each other in a rough embrace and slapped each other on the back.

The large group of warriors standing nearby visibly relaxed at this display of affection between the two men. For the most part, the Assiniboine had been friendly with white men for many, many years. But even so, it wasn't that common for a white man to come riding boldly into their village as the one called Preacher had done.

Some of the men smiled now, because they had known all along what was coming. The legendary mountain man Preacher, who was famous—or in some cases infamous—from one end of the frontier to the other, had been friends with their chief Two Bears for more than three decades, and he had visited the village on occasion in the past.

The two men hadn't always been so cordial with each other. They had started out as rivals for the affections of the beautiful Assiniboine woman Raven's Wing. For Two Bears, that rivalry had escalated to the point of bitter hostility.

All that had been put aside when it became necessary for them to join forces to rescue Raven's Wing from a group of brutal kidnappers and gunrunners.* Since that long-ago time when they were forced to become allies, they had gradually become friends as well.

Preacher stepped back and rested his hands on Two Bears's shoulders.

*See the novel *Preacher's Fury*

"I hear that Raven's Wing has passed," he said solemnly.

"Yes, last winter," Two Bears replied with an equally grave nod. "It was her time. She left this world peacefully, with a smile on her face."

"That's good to hear," Preacher said. "I never knew a finer lady."

"I miss her. Every time the sun rises or sets, every time the wind blows, every time I hear a wolf howl or see a bird soaring through the sky, I long to be with her again. But when the day is done and we are to be together again, we will be. This I know in my heart. Until then . . ." Two Bears smiled again. "Until then I can still see her in the fine strong sons she bore me, and the daughters who have given me grandchildren." He nodded toward a young woman standing nearby, who stood with an infant in her arms. "You remember my youngest daughter, Wildflower?"

"I do," Preacher said, "although the last time I saw her, I reckon she wasn't much bigger'n that sprout with her."

"My grandson," Two Bears said proudly. "Little Hawk."

Preacher took off his battered, floppy-brimmed felt hat and nodded politely to the woman.

"Wildflower," he said. "It's good to see you again." He looked at the boy. "And howdy to you, too, Little Hawk."

The baby didn't respond to Preacher, of course, but he watched the mountain man with huge, dark eyes.

"He has not seen that many white men in his life," Two Bears said. "You look strange, even to one so young."

Preacher snorted and said, "If it wasn't for this beard of mine, I'd look just about as much like an Injun as any of you do."

Two Bears half-turned and motioned to one of the lodges.

"Come. We will go to my lodge and smoke a pipe and talk. I would know what brings you to our village, Preacher."

"Horse, the same as usual," Preacher said as he jerked a thumb over his shoulder toward the big gray stallion that stood with his reins dangling. A large, wolflike cur sat on his haunches next to the stallion.

"How many horses called Horse and dogs called Dog have you had in your life, Preacher?" Two Bears asked with amusement sparkling in his eyes.

"Too many to count, I reckon," Preacher replied. "But I figure if a name works just fine once, there ain't no reason it won't work again."

"How do you keep finding them?"

"It ain't so much me findin' them as it is them findin' me. Somehow they just show up. I'd call it fate, if I believed in such a thing."

"You do not believe in fate?"

"I believe in hot lead and cold steel," Preacher said. "Anything beyond that's just a guess."

Preacher didn't have any goal in visiting the Assiniboine village other than visiting an old friend. He had been drifting around the frontier for more than fifty years now, most of the time without any plan other than seeing what was on the far side of the hill.

When he had first set out from his folks' farm as a boy, the West had been a huge, relatively empty place, populated only by scattered bands of Indians and a handful of white fur trappers. At that time less than ten years had gone by since Lewis and Clark returned from their epic, history-changing journey up the Missouri River to the Pacific.

During the decades since then, Preacher had seen the West's population grow tremendously. Rail lines criss-crossed the country, and there were cities, towns, and settlements almost everywhere. Civilization had come to the frontier.

Much of the time, Preacher wasn't a hundred percent sure if that was a good thing or not.

But there was no taking it back, no returning things to the way they used to be, and besides, if not for the great westward expansion that had fundamentally changed the face of the nation, he never would have met the two fine young men he had come to consider his sons: Smoke and Matt Jensen.

It had been a while since Preacher had seen Smoke and Matt. He assumed that Smoke was down in Col-orado, on his ranch called the Sugarloaf near the town of Big Rock. Once wrongly branded an outlaw, Smoke Jensen was perhaps the fastest man with a gun to ever walk the West. Most of the time he didn't go looking for trouble, but it seemed to find him anyway, despite all his best intentions to live a peaceful life on his ranch with his beautiful, spirited wife, Sally.

There was no telling where Matt was. He could be anywhere from the Rio Grande to the Canadian border. He and Smoke weren't brothers by blood. The bond be-tween them was actually deeper than that. Matt had been born Matt Cavanaugh, but he had taken the name Jensen as a young man to honor Smoke, who had helped out an orphaned boy and molded him into a fine man.

Since Matt had set out on his own, he had been a drifter, scouting for the army, working as a stagecoach guard, pinning on a badge a few times as a lawman. . . .

As long as it kept him on the move and held a promise of possible adventure, that was all it took to keep Matt interested in a job, at least for a while. But he never stayed in one place for very long, and at this point in his life he had no interest in putting down roots, as Smoke had done.

Because of that, Matt actually had more in common with Preacher than Smoke did, but all three of them were close. The problem was, whenever they got together trouble seemed to follow, and it usually wasn't long before the air had the smell of gunsmoke in it.

Right now the only smoke in Two Bears's lodge came from the small fire in the center of it and the pipe that Preacher and the Assiniboine chief passed back and forth. The two men were silent, their friendship not needing words all the time.

Two women were in the lodge as well, preparing a meal. They were Two Bears's wives, the former wives of his brothers he had taken in when the women were widowed, as a good brother was expected to do. The smells coming from the pot they had on the fire were mighty appetizing, Preacher thought. The stew was bound to be good.

A swift rataplan of hoofbeats came from outside and made both Preacher and Two Bears raise their heads. Neither man seemed alarmed. As seasoned veterans of the frontier, they had too much experience for that. But they also knew that whenever someone was moving fast, there was a chance it was because of trouble.

The sudden babble of voices that followed the abrupt halt of the hoofbeats seemed to indicate the same thing.

"You want to go see what that's about?" Preacher

asked Two Bears, inclining his head toward the lodge's entrance.

Two Bears took another unhurried puff on the pipe in his hands before he set it aside.

"If my people wish to see me, they know where I am to be found," he said.

Preacher couldn't argue with that. But the sounds had gotten his curiosity stirred up, so he was glad when someone thrust aside the buffalo hide flap over the lodge's entrance. A broad-shouldered, powerful-looking warrior strode into the lodge, then stopped short at the sight of a white man sitting there cross-legged beside the fire with the chief.

"Two Bears, I must speak with you," the newcomer said.

"This is Standing Rock," Two Bears said to Preacher. "He is married to my daughter Wildflower."

That would make him the father of the little fella Preacher had seen with Wildflower earlier. He nodded and said, "Howdy, Standing Rock."

The warrior just looked annoyed, like he wasn't interested in introductions right now. He looked at the chief and began, "Two Bears—"

"Is there trouble?"

"Blue Bull has disappeared."

Chapter 2

Blue Bull, it turned out, wasn't a bull at all, not that Preacher really thought he was. That was the name of one of the Assiniboine warriors who belonged to this band, and he and Standing Rock were good friends.

They had been out hunting in the hills west of the village and had split up when Blue Bull decided to follow the tracks of a small antelope herd while Standing Rock took another path. They had agreed to meet back at the spot where Blue Bull had taken up the antelope trail.

When Standing Rock returned there later, he saw no sign of Blue Bull. A couple of hours passed, and Blue Bull still didn't show up. Growing worried that something might have happened to his friend, Standing Rock went to look for him.

This part of the country was peaceful for the most part, but a man alone who ran into a mountain lion or a bear might be in for trouble. Also, ravines cut across the landscape in places, and if a pony shied at the wrong time, its rider could be tossed off and fall into one of those deep, rugged gullies.

"You were unable to find him?" Two Bears asked when his son-in-law paused in the story.

"The antelope tracks led into a narrow canyon, and so did Blue Bull's," Standing Rock replied. "The ground was rocky, and I lost the trail."

The young warrior wore a surly expression. Preacher figured that he didn't like admitting failure. Standing Rock was a proud man. You could tell that just by looking at him.

But he was genuinely worried about his friend, too. He proved that by saying, "I came back to get more men, so we can search for him. He may be hurt."

Two Bears nodded and got to his feet.

"Gather a dozen men," he ordered crisply. "We will ride in search of Blue Bull while there is still light."

Preacher stood up, too, and said, "I'll come with you."

."This is a matter for the Assiniboine," Standing Rock said, his voice stiff with dislike. Preacher didn't understand it, but the young fella definitely hadn't taken a shine to him. Just the opposite, in fact.

"Preacher is a friend to the Assiniboine and has been for more years than you have been walking this earth, Standing Rock," Two Bears snapped. "I would not ask him to involve himself in our trouble, but if he wishes to, I will not deny him."

"I just want to lend a hand if I can," Preacher said as he looked at Standing Rock. He didn't really care if the young man liked him or not. His friendship for Two Bears and for Two Bears's people was the only things that really mattered to him here.

Standing Rock didn't say anything else. He just stared back coldly at Preacher for a second, then turned and left the lodge to gather the search party as Two Bears had told him to.

The chief looked at Preacher and said, "The hot blood of young men sometimes overpowers what should be the coolness of their thoughts."

"That's fine with me, old friend. Like I said, I just want to help."

As they left the lodge, Preacher pointed to the big cur that had come with him to the village and went on, "Dog there is about as good a tracker as you're ever gonna find. When we get to the spot where Standin' Rock lost the trail, if you've got something that belonged to Blue Bull we can give Dog the scent and he's liable to lead us right to him."

Two Bears nodded.

"I will speak to Blue Bull's wife and make sure we take something of his with us."

Several of the warriors were getting ready to ride. That didn't take much preparation, considering that all they had to do was throw blankets over their ponies' backs and rig rope halters. Preacher had planned to spend a few days in the Assiniboine village, but he hadn't unsaddled Horse yet so the stallion was ready to go as well.

The news of Blue Bull's disappearance had gotten around the village. A lot of people were standing nearby with worried looks on their faces as the members of the search party mounted up. Two Bears went over to talk to one of the women, who hurried off to a lodge and came back with a buckskin shirt. She was Blue Bull's wife, Preacher figured, and the garment belonged to the missing warrior.

Two Bears swung up onto his pony with the lithe ease of a man considerably younger than he really was. He gave a curt nod, and the search party set out from the village with the chief, Standing Rock, and Preacher in the lead.

Standing Rock pointed out the route for them, and they lost no time in riding into the hills where the two warriors had been hunting. Preacher glanced at the sky and saw that they had about three hours of daylight left. He hoped that would be enough time to find Blue Bull.

Of course, it was possible that nothing bad had happened to Blue Bull at all, Preacher reflected. The warrior could have gotten carried away in pursuit of the antelope and lost track of the time. They might even run into him on his way back to the village. If that happened, Preacher would be glad that everything had turned out well.

Something was stirring in his guts, though, some instinctive warning that told him they might not be so lucky. Over the years Preacher had learned to trust those hunches. At this point, he wasn't going to say anything to Two Bears, Standing Rock, or the other Assiniboine, but he had a bad feeling about this search for Blue Bull.

Standing Rock pointed out the tracks of the antelope herd when the search party reached them.

"You can see they lead higher into the hills," he said. "Blue Bull followed them while I went to the north. He wanted to bring one of the antelope back to the village."

"Why did you not go with him?" Two Bears asked. "Why did you go north?"

Standing Rock looked sullen again as he replied, "I know a valley up there where the antelope like to graze. I thought they might circle back to it."

Two Bears just nodded, but Preacher knew that his old friend was just as aware as he was of what had really happened here. Standing Rock had thought he could beat Blue Bull to the antelope by going a different way. Such rivalry was not uncommon among friends.

"Did you see the antelope?" Two Bears asked.

Standing Rock shook his head.

"No. My thought proved to be wrong."

Two Bears's silence in response was as meaningful and damning as anything he could have said. Standing Rock angrily jerked his pony into motion and trotted away, following the same path as the antelope had earlier.

Preacher, Two Bears, and the rest of the search party went the same way at a slower pace. Quietly, Two Bears said, "If anything happened to Blue Bull, Standing Rock will believe that it was his fault for not going with his friend."

"He wants to impress you, don't he?" Preacher said. "Must not be easy, bein' married to the chief's daughter."

"He is a good warrior, but he does not always know that."

Preacher nodded in understanding. He had always possessed confidence in himself and his abilities, and he had learned not to second-guess the decisions he made. But he had seen doubts consume other men from the inside until there was nothing left of them but empty shells.

Eventually Standing Rock settled down a little and slowed enough for the rest of the search party to catch up to him. The antelope herd had followed a twisting path into the hills, and so had Blue Bull as he trailed them. Preacher had no trouble picking out the unshod hoofprints of the warrior's pony.

The slopes became steeper, the landscape more rugged. In the distance, the snow-capped peaks of the Rocky Mountains loomed, starkly beautiful in the light from the lowering sun. They were dozens of miles away, even though they looked almost close enough to reach out and touch. Preacher knew that Blue Bull's trail wouldn't lead that far.

The tracks brought them to a long, jagged ridge that was split by a canyon cutting through it. Standing Rock reined his pony to a halt and pointed to the opening.

"That is where Blue Bull went," he said. "The tracks vanished on the rocks inside the canyon."

"Did you follow it to the other end?" Two Bears asked.

"I did. But the tracks of Blue Bull's pony did not come out."

"A man cannot go into a place and not come out of it, one way or another."

Standing Rock looked a little offended at Two Bears for pointing that out, thought Preacher, but he wasn't going to say anything. For one thing, Two Bears was the chief, and for another, he was Standing Rock's father-in-law.

"Let's have a look," Preacher suggested. "We can give Dog a whiff of Blue Bull's shirt. He ought to be able to tell us where the fella went."

The big cur had bounded along happily beside Preacher and Horse during the search. He still had the exuberance of youth, dashing off several times to chase after small animals.

They rode on to the canyon entrance, where they stopped to peer at the ground. The surface had already gotten quite rocky, so the tracks weren't as easy to see as they had been. But Preacher noticed something immediately.

"Some of those antelope tracks are headed back out of the canyon," he said to Two Bears. "The critters went in there, then turned around and came out. They were in a hurry, too. Something must've spooked 'em."

Standing Rock said, "There are many antelope in these hills. Perhaps the tracks going the other direction were made at another time."

Preacher swung down from the saddle and knelt to take a closer look at the hoofprints. After a moment of study, he shook his head.

"They look the same to me," he said. "I think they were all made today, comin' and goin'."

He knew that wasn't going to make Standing Rock like him any better, but he was going to tell things the way he saw them to Two Bears. He had always been honest with his old friend and saw no need to change that policy now.

"What about the tracks of Blue Bull's pony?" Two Bears asked.

"He went on into the canyon," Preacher said. "Can't see that he came back out, so I agree with Standin' Rock on that. The way it looks to me, Blue Bull followed those antelope here and rode up in time to see 'em come boltin' back out. He was curious and wanted to see what stampeded 'em like that. So he rode in to find out."

"It must have been a bear," Standing Rock said. "Blue Bull would not have been so foolish."

"Blue Bull has always been curious," Two Bears said. "I can imagine him doing as Preacher has said." He looked at the mountain man. "As you would say, old friend, there is one way to find out."

"Yep," Preacher agreed. "Let Dog have Blue Bull's scent. If there's anybody who can lead us right to him, it's that big, shaggy varmint."

Chapter 3

Two Bears took out the shirt Blue Bull's wife had given him from the pouch where he had put it and handed it to Preacher. Preacher called Dog to him, knelt beside the big cur, and let Dog get a good whiff of the shirt.

"Find the fella who wore this," Preacher said. "Find him!"

Dog ran into the canyon, pausing about fifty yards in to look back at Preacher, and then resuming the hunt.

Preacher swung up onto Horse's back and nodded to Two Bears.

"He's got the scent. All we have to do is follow him."

They rode into the canyon, moving fairly rapidly to keep up with Dog. Now that they were relying on Dog's sense of smell rather than trying to follow tracks, they could set a slightly faster pace.

The canyon was about fifty yards wide, with rocky walls that were too steep for a horse to climb, although a man might be able to. Although there were places, Preacher noted, where the walls had collapsed partially and horses might be able to pick their way up and down as long as they were careful.

Preacher frowned slightly as he spotted a shiny place on a flat rock. The mark was small, barely noticeable. Preacher knew that the most likely explanation for it was that a shod hoof had nicked the rock in the fairly recent past. Blue Bull, like the rest of the Assiniboine, would have been riding an unshod pony when he came through here.

So another rider, most likely a white man, had been in the canyon recently. Preacher couldn't be sure it was today, but the evidence pointed in that direction. The antelope herd had started through the canyon, only to encounter a man on horseback. That had startled the animals into bolting back the way they had come from.

Then, Blue Bull's curiosity aroused by the behavior of the antelope, the Assiniboine warrior had ridden into the canyon as well, and . . .

Preacher couldn't finish that thought. He had no way of knowing what had happened then. Blue Bull could have run into the same hombre. There might have even been more than one man riding through the canyon.

This was Indian land, maybe not by treaty but by tradition, and the ranchers in the area had always respected that because of the long history of peace between the whites and the Assiniboine. They had never stopped white men from crossing their hunting grounds, as long as everyone treated each other with respect. It was possible some cattle had strayed up here from one of the ranches, and cowboys from that spread had come to look for the missing stock.

However, that bad feeling still lurked in Preacher's gut. It grew even stronger when he saw Dog veer toward a cluster of rocks at the base of one of those caved-in places along the canyon's left-hand wall. There was no hesitation about the big cur's movements. He went straight to the rocks and started nosing around and pawing at them.

"Your animal has lost the scent," Standing Rock said. "There is nothing there."

"We better take a closer look," Preacher said. He glanced over at Two Bears, who nodded. The chief's face was set in grim lines, and Preacher knew that his old friend had a bad feeling about this situation, too.

The search party rode over to the side of the canyon. Nothing was visible except a pile of loose, broken rocks, some of them pretty big, but the way Dog continued to paw at the stones told Preacher most of what he needed to know.

"Move those rocks," Two Bears ordered.

"But—" Standing Rock began. He fell silent when Two Bears gave him a hard look. Scowling, Standing Rock dismounted. He went to the rocks and started lifting them and tossing them aside. Several other warriors got down from their ponies and moved to help him.

They hadn't been working for very long before Standing Rock suddenly let out a startled exclamation and stepped back sharply as if he had just uncovered a rattlesnake.

Preacher leaned forward in the saddle to peer into the jumble of stone. He had a pretty good idea it wasn't a snake that Standing Rock had come across.

It was a foot.

Visible from the ankle down, the foot had a moccasin on it. The rest of the leg to which it was attached was hidden under the rocks.

The other warriors had recoiled from the grim discovery as well. Curtly, Two Bears ordered them to get back to moving the rocks. They did so with obvious reluctance.

Everybody knew what they were going to find. It didn't take long to uncover the rest of the body. It belonged to a young Assiniboine warrior. The rock slide that had covered him up had done quite a bit of damage to his features, but he was still recognizable. Standing Rock said in a voice choked with emotion, "It is Blue Bull."

"He must have been standing here when those rocks fell on him and killed him," one of the other men said.

"Why did he not get out of the way?" another man wanted to know.

"There must not have been time," Standing Rock said. "My . . . my friend . . ."

Deep creases appeared in Preacher's forehead as the mountain man frowned. He said to Two Bears, "Somethin' ain't right here. You mind if I take a closer look?"

"Go ahead," the chief said with a nod.

Preacher dismounted and approached the dead man. Standing Rock turned to face him. The warrior's stubborn expression made it clear he didn't want Preacher disturbing his friend's body. Like all the other tribes, the Assiniboine had their own rituals and customs for dealing with death.

"Standing Rock," Two Bears said. "Step aside."

"I won't do anything to dishonor Blue Bull," Preacher said to Standing Rock. "It's just that I don't think this is what it seems to be. Look at how he's layin' on his back with his head toward the wall and his feet toward the middle of the canyon."

"That means nothing," Standing Rock snapped.

"I think it does," Preacher said. "Let's say he came over here and was standin' facin' the wall for some reason. When those rocks came down on top of him, likely they would've knocked him facedown. If he heard the rocks start to fall and turned to try to run, not only would he be facedown, his head would be pointed toward the middle of the canyon."

"You cannot be sure about these things," Standing Rock insisted.

"Maybe not, but I think there's a pretty good chance I'm right. What it really looks like is that somebody dragged Blue Bull over here, then climbed up the canyon wall to start the rock slide that covered up his body."

Two Bears said, "He would have had to be unconscious or dead for that to happen."

Preacher nodded.

"Yep, more than likely. Maybe we can tell, if you let me take a good look at the body."

"He was my friend," Standing Rock said. "Stand back. I will do it."

"Sure," Preacher said. He moved one step back, but that was as far as he went. He wanted to be able to see whatever Standing Rock found.

Standing Rock knelt beside his dead friend and looked him over from head to toe.

"There are no injuries except the ones the rocks made when they fell on him," Standing Rock announced.

"Turn him over," Preacher suggested.

Standing Rock sent a hostile glance at the mountain man, but he did as Preacher said and gently took hold of Blue Bull's shoulders. Carefully, he rolled the body onto its left side.

A sharp breath hissed between Standing Rock's clenched teeth. Preacher saw what had prompted the young warrior's reaction.

A bloodstain had spread on the back of Blue Bull's shirt, just to the left of the middle of his back. In the middle of that bloodstain was a small tear in the buckskin.

"A knife did that," Preacher said. "Somebody stabbed him in the back, probably out in the middle of the canyon, and then tried to hide the body."

Two Bears said, "That would mean . . ."

"Yep," Preacher said. "This was no accident. Blue Bull was murdered."

The big man paced back and forth angrily. Despite his size, his movements had a certain dangerous, catlike quality to them. His hat was thumbed back over his blocky, rough-hewn face.

"Let me get this straight," he said. "You didn't have any choice but to kill the Indian."

"That's right, Randall," replied one of the men facing him. "He seen us. He might've gone back to his village and warned the rest of those redskins that we're up here in the hills."

The eyes of the man called Randall narrowed as he stared coldly at the two men he had sent out as scouts.

"There are several big spreads bordering the Indian land," he said. "And Two Bears doesn't mind if the punchers who ride for those ranches cut across the Assiniboine hunting grounds. You *know* that, damn it! We all do. So what in hell made you think that running into a lone warrior was going to cause a problem?"

The two men, whose names were Page and Dwyer, shuffled their feet uncomfortably. They didn't like being in dutch with the hardbitten ramrod of this gun-hung bunch that waited in the hills for nightfall.

Thirty men, along with their horses, stood around in

whatever shade they could find, watching as Randall confronted the scouts. The others were every bit as rough and menacing looking as their leader.

Page had spoken up earlier. Now Dwyer said, "You weren't there, Randall. You didn't see how spooked that redskin acted. He knew somethin' was up, I tell you. Page and me did the only thing we could."

"And we covered his body up good and proper," Page added. "Nobody'll ever find him."

Randall said, "You seem mighty sure about that. You know that as soon as the rest of his people miss him, they'll come looking for him."

"They won't find him," Page insisted.

Randall wanted to say something else. He wanted to cuss the two fools up one way and down the other. Instead, he just jerked his head in a curt nod and said, "You'd better hope they don't. Finding one of their own warriors stabbed in the back is likely to spook them a lot more than running across a couple of riders would have."

Earlier, when the two men had come back from scouting the approaches to the Assiniboine village, they had brought an Indian pony with them, trailing from a rope lead held by Dwyer. When Randall had demanded to know where the animal came from, they had hemmed and hawed around for a minute and tried to say they found it, but it hadn't taken long for his cold stare to get the truth out of them.

They had run into a warrior in a canyon that cut through a ridge several miles from the Assiniboine village. The Indian kept asking questions, the scouts claimed, so Dwyer had distracted him while Page got behind him and put a knife in his back. Then they had dragged him over to the side of the canyon and caved in part of the wall on him. Chances were they were right about nobody finding the body, at least not in time to have any effect on the mission that had brought Randall and his men to this part of the territory.

With the matter settled for the time being, unsatisfactory though it might be, Randall turned and stalked away to give himself a chance to control his anger. He looked up at the sky.

In a couple of more hours, it would be dark.

And once night had fallen, he and his men could ride down out of these hills and do what they had been sent here to do. That thought put a faint smile on Randall's rugged face.

The prospect of killing always did.

Chapter 4

Standing Rock and several of his friends carefully wrapped Blue Bull's body in a blanket and tied it onto one of the horses. It was a solemn group that left the canyon and started back toward the Assiniboine village.

"Do you have any idea who might have done this terrible thing, Preacher?" Two Bears asked as they rode at the head of the search party.

"I thought I spotted some sign from a horse wearin' shoes in the canyon," Preacher replied. "The ground's too rocky to be sure of anything, though. But I'd say there's a good chance Blue Bull ran into a white man. Probably more than one."

"Why more than one?"

"It ain't that easy for most folks to get behind somebody and stab 'em, unless the fella on the receivin' end of that knife is distracted somehow. If Blue Bull came upon two white men in that canyon, would he have stopped and talked to them?"

Two Bears looked over at Standing Rock, who was riding on his other side close enough to have heard Preacher's question.

"He would have talked to them," Standing Rock replied. "He would have asked them who they were and what they were doing on Assiniboine land."

"Would he have challenged 'em enough that they thought he might attack them?" Preacher asked.

"Blue Bull would never attack anyone without good reason!" Standing Rock responded.

Two Bears said, "Blue Bull's blood ran hot at times, like that of all young men. The white men might have believed they were in danger." The chief's voice hardened. "But that was no reason to murder one of my young men."

"No, it sure wasn't," Preacher agreed. "I think we're on the right track about what happened, though, regardless of the reason for it."

"Do you think you could track the men who did this, old friend?"

Preacher shrugged and said, "I could give it a try. There ain't all that much daylight left, but I can go up on that ridge and take a look around. If there really were some other riders in that canyon, they didn't come out either side of it. We would have seen the tracks at this end, and Standin' Rock probably would've noticed 'em at the other end when he went all the way through lookin' for Blue Bull."

"You saw no such tracks?" Two Bears asked his son-in-law.

Standing Rock didn't hesitate in his answer.

"I saw no tracks of any kind," he said. "Shod or unshod."

"There you go," Preacher said with a nod. He pulled back gently on Horse's reins. "I'll take Dog and have a look."

"I'm coming with you," Standing Rock declared.

Preacher started to say he wasn't sure that was a good idea, but he knew that if he did, Standing Rock would just be more put out with him. Besides, he supposed it wouldn't hurt anything to have the young man along. Preacher knew this country, but Standing Rock lived here and would know it even better.

"Sure, I'd be glad to have the company," he said. "Come on."

"We will take Blue Bull back to the village," Two Bears said as the two men turned their mounts. "Be careful."

That would be the smart thing to do, all right, Preacher thought, since there was at least one murderer on the loose somewhere in these parts.

He and Standing Rock rode back toward the canyon, which was only a couple of hundred yards away. As they approached, Preacher studied the ridge on both sides of the canyon mouth.

"I don't think we can get up there anywhere close, at least on horseback," he said. "We can leave our mounts down here, though, and check it out on foot."

"Perhaps my pony is more sure-footed than that beast of yours," Standing Rock said.

Preacher suppressed the annoyance he felt at the young warrior's bold statement. Here the fella's best friend was dead, and he still had to act like an ass.

"Maybe so," he said. "If you want to take a chance on rollin' down that ridge with a horse on top of you, I reckon that's up to you."

Standing Rock glared but didn't say anything else. When they reached the base of the ridge, he dismounted just like Preacher did. They took their rifles from saddle sheaths as they got ready to climb.

The ridge was rugged enough, with rocks jutting out

from it and hardy bushes growing here and there to provide handholds, that they had no trouble climbing the forty or fifty feet to the top. Dog found the going even easier and reached the crest first.

When Preacher made it to the top, he saw that the ridge was about half a mile wide. On the far side it dropped down into a narrow valley, and on the other side of that valley rose an even more rugged hill.

"We'll follow the canyon," Preacher said. "If there were riders down in yonder, they had to go down and come back out somewhere."

"There were riders in the canyon," Standing Rock said. His face was set in grim lines. "We know that because they killed Blue Bull."

"Somebody sure did," Preacher said. "Come on."

They walked along the side of the canyon, staying fairly close to the rim. Preacher saw several places where he thought men on horseback could get up and down the caved-in sides, but there were no hoofprints to indicate that any had done so recently. He didn't spot any footprints, either.

Then, when they weren't far from the place where they had found Blue Bull's body, Preacher stopped and pointed to the ground.

"Take a gander at those," he said.

The ground was pretty rocky up here, too, but there were stretches of dirt and scrubby grass. In one of those stretches, several prints made by a shod horse were visible.

Preacher knelt to study the tracks closer, and so did Standing Rock. After several moments, the warrior said, "They are only a few hours old."

"Yeah," Preacher said, "and they lead away from the canyon."

"There were two shod horses."

Preacher nodded, agreeing again with his companion. Standing Rock might be pretty stiff-necked most of the time, but he had a good eye.

"They have to be the men who killed Blue Bull," Standing Rock went on.

"We don't know that for sure"—Preacher held up a hand to forestall the protest he knew was coming from Standing Rock—"but I'd say the chances are mighty good that they are."

"We must follow them!"

"What if they're on their way back to a bigger bunch?"

"I do not care," Standing Rock said. "They killed Blue Bull. His death must be avenged!"

"Happens I agree with you. But we're liable to lose the light before we catch up to them. And we don't know what they're up to, but more than likely it ain't anything good. If they catch sight of us, they're liable to start shootin'."

"The Blackfeet call you Ghost Killer, do they not? They say you can turn yourself into a phantom and cut a man's throat without anyone knowing you were ever there."

"Reckon them days are a long time behind me," Preacher said wryly. "I ain't quite as stealthy anymore. But if we're careful, maybe we can get a look at them without bein' spotted."

"We must find more tracks—"

"Don't bother. Dog can show us where to go. Dog!"

Preacher made sure the big cur had the scent of the horses that had passed this way, and then once again he told Dog to hunt. Dog took off. Preacher and Standing Rock hurried after him.

Preacher had to call Dog several times to make sure he didn't outdistance them. Any kind of hunt always filled Dog with eagerness.

Preacher understood that. Even as old as he was, he felt the same way, getting caught up in the thrill of the chase. The fact that they were going after a pair of killers didn't really change that. This was far from the first manhunt Preacher had taken part in.

Dog led them down into the thickly wooded valley on the far side of the ridge. Preacher spotted more hoof-prints from time to time, but he relied more on the big cur's nose.

As soon as the sun dropped behind the mountains to the west, the light began to fade quickly. The two men could still see Dog ahead of them, though, so they kept going, trotting easily through the gray shadows of dusk.

Preacher didn't know how close they might be getting to their quarry so, instead of calling Dog, he let out a whistle that could be mistaken for the sound of a bird. Dog turned and trotted back to them.

"Why did you stop him?" Standing Rock asked.

"Keep your voice down," Preacher said. His own voice was little more than a whisper. "I don't want to go announcin' to those varmints that we're here. Thought I just caught a whiff of smoke."

He sniffed the air again. Smoke, all right, he thought. Not a campfire, though. Tobacco. Somebody had rolled and smoked a quirly not too far from here.

Something else suddenly caught Preacher's attention and made him take a sharply indrawn breath. Standing Rock heard it, too, and exclaimed, "Horses!"

"Yeah," Preacher said. The sound of hoofbeats drifted

through the darkening air. Quite a few riders were on the move. Twenty or thirty of them, Preacher estimated.

They were at least a couple of hundred yards away, too. Preacher stood there stiffly as he tried to track them by sound. As best he could determine, the riders were headed east.

The Assiniboine village lay in that direction. An icy finger trailed down the mountain man's back at that thought. Even though he didn't know who the riders were or what was going on here, his instincts told him that trouble was on the move tonight.

"Come on," he told Standing Rock. "We got to get back to the horses!"

"But those men . . . Who are they? Where are they going?"

"That's what we're gonna find out," Preacher said.

And if the uneasy hunch he had turned out to be true, he just hoped they reached the village before it was too late.

Chapter 5

Randall was a cautious man. He had to be in order to live as long as he had while following a dangerous profession. Most men who hired out their guns for any job where the price was right died at a pretty young age.

Randall had been at it for a while, though, and tonight was a prime example of how he had survived. In all likelihood, the Assiniboine brave Page had knifed in the back was still lying under those rocks. His people might have missed him by now, but the odds of anybody finding him were small. Randall still wasn't going to risk it.

So instead of using the canyon to cut through that ridge as he had planned, he led his men the long way around, riding north to a spot where the ridge petered out and going around it. That meant traveling several miles out of the way, but that didn't really matter to Randall.

They had all night to reach the Indian village and get the job done.

The sky was dark enough now that the stars stood out against the blackness like diamond pinpoints of light. When Randall glanced up at them, they made him think of real diamonds he had seen once, on a necklace stretched across black satin. That was in San Francisco, and the woman wearing the necklace was a beautiful redhead. Her name was Sherry.

Or was it Cherry? Randall wasn't sure anymore. Too many years had passed. He knew that the woman had wound up dead, though, because of him. An assassin working for one of the tongs had thrown a knife at him, and he had dodged it at the last second, so that it went right into the redhead's throat. Less than a heartbeat later, Randall had a gun in his hand and blew a slug through the murderous Chinaman's heart. The woman was dead, though, and it was a damned shame.

But he'd reminded himself that Sherry or Cherry— or whatever her name was—wasn't the first woman to die from being around him. Death just seemed to come natural for folks who got too close to him.

Well, a lot of years had gone by since then, he reflected as he rode across the rolling hills toward the Assiniboine village. He had done a lot of different things to earn his money, most of which involved guns and killing. Every now and then he used dynamite and blew somebody up. A little variety never hurt.

Most people weren't so casual about murder. He knew that, in his mind. He couldn't really bring himself to care, though. And as he glanced over his shoulder at the men riding with him, he knew that most, if not all of them, were the same way. As long as they got paid, they didn't care who died.

Randall didn't know exactly where the village was, but he had a pretty good idea. When he was sure they were getting close, he held up a hand and signaled his men to halt. When they had done so, he waved a couple of them forward.

"I'm going to take a look," he said. "Hold the men here. Keep it quiet. No talking, no horses stomping around. And no smokes. The smell of tobacco can carry."

"Injuns smoke pipes, don't they?" one of the men asked.

"Yeah, but they don't smell as bad as those cheroots some of this bunch favors," Randall said. "Just do as you're told."

"Sure, boss. No quirlies, no stogies."

Randall dismounted and handed his reins to one of the men.

"Here. Hold my horse."

He moved off into the darkness, trotting easily through the shadows. He blended into those shadows in his dark gray trousers, black shirt, and gray Stetson. In a matter of seconds, the rest of the men couldn't see him anymore.

Randall enjoyed moments like this. He was like a wolf gliding through the night in search of prey.

He had gone about half a mile when he heard the wailing. He followed the sound to the top of a hill, where he paused and knelt behind some brush. Parting the branches slightly, he looked down the slope.

The Assiniboine village was a couple of hundred yards away. Several fires blazed brightly among the lodges. Members of the tribe, men and women alike, were moving around. That sight brought a frown to Randall's face, as did the sorrowful cries he heard coming from down there.

Somebody was mourning, he thought. He supposed that another member of the tribe could have died during the day, but that possibility struck him as far-fetched since he *knew* that one of the Indians was dead for sure: the warrior Page had killed.

It looked like there was a good chance somebody had found the corpse after all.

"Those dumb bastards," Randall muttered. It didn't appear that the Assiniboine were all that alert, but they weren't sound asleep, either, and he had been hoping to have the element of surprise solidly on his side. Nobody could put up much of a fight if they were jolted out of a deep sleep and killed before they knew what was going on.

He would just have to deal with this, he told himself. The Indians still weren't expecting trouble. He knelt there and watched long enough, searching every shadow around the village, until he was convinced there were no warriors standing guard. He and his men could still hit them hard before they knew what was happening. They would just have to be more careful about their approach.

Satisfied that he had learned all he could, he backed away and then stood up. His unerring sense of direction meant that he had no trouble retracing his steps to the spot where he had left his men.

He paused and called softly, "It's me," before he came up to them. No point in giving anybody an excuse to get trigger-happy.

"Did you find those redskins, boss?" Dwyer asked quietly.

"I did," Randall replied. "I found something else, too . . . a village in mourning for someone who died."

Page said nervously, "Probably somebody who was, uh, gettin' on in years."

"Or a young man who was killed for no good reason," Randall said, without bothering to keep the caustic tone out of his voice.

Page was angry now. He said, "Listen, Randall—"

"Forget about it," Randall snapped. "It doesn't matter. We can still do what we need to do. Everyone dismount. We'll lead the horses. Quieter that way."

That brought a few mutters of complaint. Hired guns weren't that different from cowhands in one respect: They didn't like to walk. But they were being well paid and they would do what they were told.

"All right," Randall went on, "when we get there, we'll mount up and charge down the hill into the village. You can shoot all you want to, just make sure you aim high. There's to be no killing until I have the two we're after."

"But once you do?" one of the men asked.

"Kill anything that moves, for all I care," Randall said. "Let's go."

Preacher and Standing Rock ran back over the ridge. Even so, the distant hoofbeats of the fast-moving horses had faded away completely by the time the two men climbed down and reached their mounts.

"They are gone!" Standing Rock said as he swung up onto his pony's blanket-covered back.

"Yeah, but we got a pretty good idea where they're goin'," Preacher replied as he settled into Horse's saddle.

"And if we are wrong?"

"Then they ain't headin' for the village and there ain't nothin' to worry about."

"But we will lose them! Blue Bull's death will go unavenged!"

"Not necessarily," Preacher said, curtailing the impatience he felt. "We can pick up their trail later. With that big of a bunch, it won't be too hard."

He drove his heels into Horse's flanks and sent the big stallion trotting toward the Assiniboine village. Standing Rock kicked his mount into a gallop and dashed on ahead. The pony couldn't maintain that pace all the way to the village, though, so it wasn't long before Horse's ground-eating lope caught up to them.

Standing Rock looked over at Preacher and said, "You think they are going to attack my people."

"I don't have any idea why, because I don't know who they are, but that's my hunch, yeah," the mountain man said.

"They killed Blue Bull, and now they want to hurt the rest of the Assiniboine!"

It didn't make any sense, thought Preacher. This was pretty good grazing land hereabouts, and cattlemen always wanted to expand, wanted more range on which to run their herds. But as far as he knew nobody had been encroaching on the Assiniboine hunting grounds. The state of truce that existed between Two Bears's people and the neighboring spreads had been going on for a long time. Nobody wanted an Indian war.

He couldn't help but think that Standing Rock was right, though. For whatever purpose, those riders planned to attack the village.

And they had a pretty good lead on Preacher and Standing Rock, too.

Still, as the ground rolled past under the fast-moving hooves of the two horses, Preacher began to think they might have a chance to reach the village before any trouble broke out. If they could warn Two Bears to get ready for a fight, that might make a lot of difference in the outcome. But if the Assiniboine were taken by surprise . . .

Suddenly, Preacher threw a hand in the air and called

to Standing Rock, "Hold on!" He hauled back on Horse's reins and brought the stallion to a halt.

Standing Rock stopped, too, but clearly he didn't like it.

"What are you doing?" he demanded. "We must hurry—"

"Listen," Preacher told him. A moment earlier, he had thought that he heard something, but he'd had to silence their horses' hoofbeats before he could be sure.

Now he was sure, and he wished he had been wrong.

The roar and crackle of gunfire drifted ominously to them through the night air.

Chapter 6

With Randall at their head, the small army of gunmen thundered down the slope toward the Assiniboine village. Randall had given the order to attack a second earlier. He left his gun holstered for the time being. He had higher priorities tonight than wiping out some redskins.

His mind flashed back to the meeting in the Colonel's study, in the big mansion just outside the settlement of Hammerhead. That was where, as usual, the Colonel had given Randall his instructions for this job. . . .

"The chief's name is Two Bears. He's an old man, but I'm told that he's still dangerous. His daughter is called Wildflower. The boy is Little Hawk." The Colonel waved the well-manicured hand that held a long cigar. *"But you don't really need to know all that, I suppose. I have descriptions of the woman and the baby. The trader I employed to spy on the savages was able to supply me with that, as well as a map of the village, marked with the location of Standing Rock's lodge. That's the name of the warrior who's married to Wildflower. You should*

find her and the boy either there, or at Two Bears's lodge. I can show you where it is, too."

Randall wasn't surprised that the Colonel had all this information at his fingertips. Preparation had been one of the hallmarks of the Colonel's career, going all the way back to the days when he had commanded a regiment of Union cavalry during the war.

Preparation . . . and victory. The Colonel always won.

Lamplight shone on the Colonel's bald head as he put the cigar back in his mouth and leaned forward to spread out the map on the desk in front of him. A fringe of sandy hair that had turned mostly gray surrounded his ears. His face, once lantern-jawed and almost gaunt, had grown fleshier over the years of prosperity and comfort, but his pale blue eyes still burned with the fires of ambition that they always had.

The two men made a good team. The Colonel, the ruthless planner, and Randall, the blunt instrument charged with carrying out those plans.

Of course, the Colonel didn't think of them as a team. To him, Randall was just an employee. A valued one, to be sure, but still just someone who worked for him.

Randall knew that, but the Colonel's attitude didn't bother him. The Colonel paid well, and as long as Randall had plenty of money for gambling, good whiskey, and women, he didn't care what the Colonel really thought of him.

For the next few minutes, they went over the layout of the village, with Randall committing the details to memory so that he could find his way around without any trouble, even in the dark. That was when he preferred to attack, at night, so that no one would be expecting trouble. He had learned that in the war, too, riding for the Colonel.

"As for Wildflower, my source tells me that she's easily the most attractive woman in the entire village," the Colonel went on.

Randall grunted and said, *"That wouldn't take much. You know how Indian women are, Colonel. Every one I ever saw was short and squatty, with a face as round as the moon. They smell bad, too."*

"Well, I can't, ah, speak to how Wildflower smells, but the trader said she was quite beautiful. Slender, with long hair that she wears loose most of the time. Hair dark as a raven's wing." The Colonel chuckled. *"Appropriate, since that was her late mother's name. It wouldn't surprise me if Wildflower was the spitting image of her. That will make Two Bears value her life even more. That and the fact that she's the mother of one of his grandsons, of course."*

"And once you've got your hands on them, Two Bears won't have any choice but to give you what you want."

"Exactly," the Colonel said with a smile. . . .

These thoughts flashed through Randall's mind in the time it took for his horse to take two long strides down the hill. Up ahead, the Indians were running around the lodges, alarmed because they'd heard the horses galloping toward the village. They might be ignorant savages, but they knew that when strangers came charging out of the night, it meant trouble.

Behind Randall, the other men opened fire. Gunshots blasted out, and muzzle flames split the darkness. He hoped they were aiming high as he had ordered, especially since he was in front of them.

As he reached the outskirts of the village, a man dashed in front of him. Randall rode him down. The man's outcry was cut off abruptly as the horse knocked him down and iron-shod hooves smashed the life from him.

Randall didn't care how many of the savages died, especially the men. He just couldn't take a chance on having a lot of bullets flying around until he had secured Wildflower and Little Hawk. If both of them were killed by stray slugs, the Colonel's plan would be ruined.

He headed straight for the lodge occupied by Standing Rock and Wildflower. As he guided his horse around one of the crude dwellings, one of the warriors leaped up at him, trying to grab him and drag him out of the saddle.

Randall drew his gun with blinding speed, but instead of firing, he lashed out with the weapon and smashed it against the Indian's head. He felt the crunch of bone as the man's skull shattered. The Assiniboine warrior fell away limply.

For a second, that distracted Randall, and he wasn't sure where he was in the village anymore. That disorientation was over almost as soon as it began, though, as the long hours he had spent memorizing the map came back to him. He spotted his goal up ahead.

And just then, as if she were trying to cooperate with him, a young woman ran out of the lodge with a baby in her arms. Her head jerked from side to side as she looked around, obviously terrified.

Randall's heart slugged hard in his chest. Firelight lit the woman's face, making it appear even more coppery than it really was. Her movements caused her long dark hair to fly around her head, partially obscuring her features, but Randall could see enough to know that she was breathtakingly beautiful, just as the Colonel had described her to him. Her body was slender and lithe in a buckskin dress, and Randall felt an unaccustomed pang of arousal. Usually he didn't give a damn about women except as vessels in which to slake his occasional lusts.

This one, this Wildflower, she was different.

Randall shoved that thought out of his mind. It had no place in this night's work. He sent his horse thundering toward her. The woman saw him coming, screamed, and turned to run as she clutched the baby tighter against her.

Randall holstered his gun and swept toward her, leaning down from the saddle and reaching out with his left arm. It closed around her and jerked her off her feet. She screamed again as he lifted her onto the horse's back in front of him.

She didn't try to fight, though. She couldn't do that and hang on to the baby, too, and she seemed determined not to let go of the kid. That was good, Randall thought. Made his job easier. All he had to do was hold on to her, and he got the chief's grandson in the bargain.

"You'll be all right," he told her, raising his voice so she could hear him over the chaos that filled the village. "Nobody's going to hurt you!"

She squirmed and wiggled, but she was no match for his great strength. She must have realized that if she did manage to get loose and fell off the horse while it was running, she risked injuring not only herself but also her son. She stopped struggling, although her chest still heaved from fear and exertion. Randall's arm was clamped around her body just below her breasts, and he could feel them moving against it as she breathed.

He wheeled the horse around and headed for the edge of the village, wanting to get clear with his captives before the shooting started in earnest. The last thing he and his men needed was a bunch of angry savages on their trail, so the others knew to wipe out as many of the warriors as they could before they fled. That would slow down any pursuit.

Randall spotted Page and Dwyer up ahead, still firing into the air to maintain the confusion. As he galloped past them, Randall shouted, "Now you can kill them! Spread the word!"

Page whooped, and Dwyer shouted, "Kill 'em! Kill all the dirty redskins!"

From the corner of his eye, Randall saw both men lower their guns and start blasting away at the Assiniboine. The rest of the raiders did the same. Men, women, and children all fell under the deadly sweep of lead.

Suddenly, a couple of men on horseback blocked Randall's path. One of them was an Indian, which surprised Randall because he didn't think any of the Assiniboine had had a chance to get mounted. The other was an old man with a bristly white beard. Randall had never seen him before.

He jerked his horse to the side and went between two of the lodges. Fighting clogged his path. Ahead of him, the Indians dragged one of his men out of the saddle. The man howled for a second, then fell silent as they smashed the life out of him with tomahawks.

"Clear the way!" Randall bellowed at his men as he was forced to rein in. He tightened his grip on Wildflower as she renewed her struggle. "Clear the way! If I don't get out of here, the Colonel and his friends in the Ring will have our hides!"

That didn't really make sense—if they didn't get out of here, the *Assiniboine* would have their hides—but in the heat of the moment, Randall didn't care. He just wanted a lane through which he could escape the battle in the village.

That lane suddenly opened as several of his men sprayed shots through a line of warriors. As the savages collapsed with blood spurting from the bullet holes in their bodies, Randall jabbed his spurs into his horse's flanks. The animal let out a pained squeal and lunged forward, trampling one of those fat-faced Indian women Randall had mentioned to the Colonel. Randall never slowed down.

Suddenly he was clear. He ducked instinctively as a slug whistled over his head. With a twist of his neck, he looked back over his shoulder.

That whiskery old man was galloping after him, Randall saw to his surprise. He grinned.

He wasn't worried about some damned old codger.

Chapter 7

As soon as they heard the shooting, Preacher and Standing Rock got their mounts moving again. This time it was Horse that pulled ahead. The Indian pony simply couldn't keep up. Stubbornly, though, Standing Rock managed to stay only a short distance behind the old mountain man.

Preacher trusted the stallion to find the easiest and fastest route. He kept Horse's nose pointed in the right general direction, but otherwise gave him his head.

Horse responded as Preacher knew he would, gallantly summoning all the speed he possessed. It was like the stallion realized how urgent this situation was and and was determined to do everything in his power to help.

The ground flew past. Sometimes when they topped a hill, it seemed like they were going so fast they were about to take off and fly, Preacher thought. He clung to the saddle with all the agility and experience that long decades of frontier life had given him.

They left Dog far behind them, unable to match the speed of the horses except in short bursts, but Preacher knew the big cur would follow them and catch up as soon as he could.

Of course, it was dangerous to gallop flat out like this at night. A horse could step in a hole or trip over something, fall and break a leg. Break its rider's neck, too, more than likely.

Preacher was willing to run that risk because they were close enough now that he could hear the shooting even over the thundering hoofbeats.

The glow of fires came into view, marking the location of the Assiniboine village. Preacher aimed straight for it. As he rode, he checked each Colt and made sure the revolvers moved smoothly in their holsters. He didn't want either of them to hang when it came time to start swapping lead with those varmints who were raiding the village.

The questions of who they were and why they were attacking the Assiniboine still plagued him, but he could look for answers later.

Right now there was fighting to be done.

As Preacher reached the edge of the village, he saw a man on horseback gun down one of the Assiniboine warriors, who doubled over as the slug punched into his guts. The killer swung his horse to the side and started to draw a bead on a woman who was running away.

"Hey!" Preacher yelled.

The man jerked his head around just in time to catch a bullet from Preacher in his forehead. The slug bored into the man's brain an inch above his right eye, ripped through at an angle, and exploded out the left rear of his skull in a burst of blood and bone shards. In the firelight, the spray looked more red than pink. The man flew out of his saddle like he'd been hit with a giant sledgehammer.

By the time that man hit the ground, Preacher had found another target. He triggered again, and this time one of the raiders slewed around in the saddle, dropped his gun, and clutched his bullet-shattered shoulder. He managed to stay mounted, but his horse ran off wildly.

Standing Rock, with his Winchester in his hands, rode up beside Preacher. The rifle cracked, and another raider dropped his gun as the bullet creased him. Standing Rock worked the Winchester's lever.

Suddenly, Preacher spotted one of the strangers galloping toward them. He was about to cut loose his wolf again when he realized that the man had a prisoner. One of the Assiniboine women struggled to get free as the man held her in front of him like a human shield. Preacher held off on the Colt's trigger at the last second.

He sent the stallion surging forward, but the raider jerked his horse to the side and disappeared between a couple of lodges. As Preacher headed in the same direction, he heard the man shout an order for his companions to clear a path for him.

A fresh volley of shots almost drowned out the man's next words, but Preacher made out some of them.

"—out of here—Colonel—the Ring—"

Preacher didn't think anything about that. He was concentrating on catching up before the man got away with his prisoner, whoever she was.

He spotted the fleeing rider ahead of him, but several of the other men closed ranks and tried to block his path. Preacher put the reins between his teeth, guided Horse with his knees, and drew his other Colt. Both revolvers roared and belched flame as he charged toward the raiders. He couldn't tell how many of them he hit, if any, but they sure as Hades got out of the way of the old geezer with two guns who charged them like a madman.

Preacher reached the edge of the village. He saw his quarry again and fired a shot after him, aiming high because he didn't want to take a chance on hitting the prisoner. The man didn't slow down, but he did look back.

It was hard to tell in the uncertain light from the fires, but Preacher would have sworn that the varmint grinned at him.

Filled with fury, Preacher started after him. Horse had taken only a few strides, though, when another of the raiders suddenly angled in at them from the sides. The rider was too close, too quickly, and Preacher couldn't avoid him.

The stallion crashed into the other horse, and both animals went down. Preacher barely had time to kick his feet free of the stirrups so that when Horse fell, he was flung from the saddle. He hit the ground with stunning force that knocked the breath out of him.

Momentum made Preacher roll over a couple of times before he came up on a knee. Most men his age who took a spill like that would break multiple bones in their bodies. Preacher seemed to be made from whang leather and iron, though. He would be sore as blazes in the morning, but he could tell nothing was busted.

Not only that, but he had held on to both guns. He pointed them after the fleeing raider who had taken the woman prisoner, but with a grimace he stopped himself from firing. They were out of handgun range, and even if they hadn't been, it would have been too risky.

Anyway, he had more pressing problems, he realized as a bullet cut the air a foot or so from his head. He twisted and saw that the man who had run into him had managed to get up, too, and had taken that shot at him. The man fired again as both of Preacher's revolvers snapped up and roared.

The raider's second bullet came even closer than the first. Preacher felt its hot breath against his cheek.

But his shots were more accurate. Both shots slammed into the gunman's chest and drove him backwards. He ended up in a limp sprawl on the ground.

Preacher got to his feet, stumbling a little as he did so. Maybe that tumble had shaken him up more than he'd realized at first, he thought. He braced himself and looked around for Horse. He was worried about the stallion.

He shouldn't have been, he saw. Horse was standing up again and seemed fine. The other horse was still on the ground, flailing its legs and letting out shrill neighs of pain. The unlucky animal had a visibly broken leg.

Preacher ended its torment with a single well-placed shot and cursed the man responsible for the death of the innocent horse. He was glad he had blown the son of a bitch's lights out.

"Preacher!"

The shout made him turn around. Two Bears ran toward him, carrying a rifle. The chief had a streak of blood on his face but seemed to be all right otherwise. Standing Rock hurried along beside him.

"Preacher, are you all right?" Two Bears asked as he came up to the mountain man.

"Just shook up a mite," Preacher replied. "Nothin' to worry about. What's goin' on here?"

The shooting had stopped, but chaos and confusion still gripped the village. A couple of the lodges were on fire. As that garish light spread, Preacher saw that the raiders had all fled. The ones who could, that is. Half a dozen or so were still there, lying bloody and motionless on the ground.

"The men rode in shooting," Two Bears said. "We had no warning except when we heard their horses, and by then they were almost upon us."

Standing Rock said, "This must have something to do with the killing of Blue Bull."

The same possibility had occurred to Preacher. If the two men Blue Bull had encountered in the canyon were part of the group that had raided the Assiniboine village tonight, they might have been worried that Blue Bull would go back and warn the rest of his people.

"Maybe so," Preacher said in response to Standing Rock's theory, "but that don't tell us why they rode in here and started raisin' hell. Maybe they were slavers. I saw one of the varmints carryin' off a woman. Is anybody else missin'?"

"We will find out," Two Bears said. The three men started toward the lodges.

A number of Assiniboine men and women lay lifelessly on the ground, too. Preacher saw the deep trenches of grief in his old friend's face. Tragedy had come out of nowhere to strike these people today, and they didn't deserve it. Anger filled Preacher's heart.

No matter what it took, he was going to find out who was responsible for this atrocity and make them pay, the old mountain man vowed.

One of the women hurried to meet them. Preacher recognized her as one of Two Bears's other wives. Her dark eyes were wide with fear.

"Two Bears," she said, the words spilling rapidly from her mouth, "Wildflower and Little Hawk are gone!"

Two Bears and Standing Rock both stiffened in alarm.

"Gone!" Standing Rock exclaimed. "How? They must be here somewhere!"

The woman shook her head.

"No, we have looked everywhere. They are not in the village."

In a voice like flint, Two Bears suggested, "Perhaps they are among the dead."

"No," the woman insisted. "We looked. They are not here!"

"Hold on a minute," Preacher said. "The woman I saw who was bein' kidnapped by one of those varmints . . . she could've been Wildflower. I never got that good a look at her, but her hair was long and she wore it loose."

"My son," Standing Rock said raggedly. "Did she have my son with her?"

"Now, that I couldn't tell you," Preacher replied with a shake of his head. "I'm sorry. The light was bad, and everything was movin' too fast. I reckon she could've been holdin' a baby, but I can't say for sure."

"If the woman you saw was Wildflower, she would have my grandson with her," Two Bears said. "She would not have abandoned him in the midst of all this trouble."

"I must go to my lodge!" Standing Rock said. He ran off into the confusion.

Preacher and Two Bears followed at a slower pace. When they reached the lodge, they found Standing Rock on his knees outside the entrance, looking stricken.

He looked up at them and said in a hollow voice, "They are gone. My wife and son . . . gone."

"We will find them," Two Bears said. "We will bring them home safely." He looked at Preacher. "The woman you saw, she was unharmed?"

"Right then she seemed to be, as far as I could tell,"

Preacher replied. "There's no tellin' what happened after that fella rode off with her and the baby."

He was convinced now that Wildflower had had Little Hawk with her. That was the only thing that made sense.

"Who would have done this thing?" Two Bears asked. "Why?"

Preacher couldn't answer the second question, but as his mind went back to what he had heard the kidnapper shouting as he tried to get away, he drew in a sharp breath. He had heard the man mention a "ring," but at the time, in the middle of the battle, that reference hadn't meant anything to him.

Now maybe it did, and as a grim expression settled over his lined, weathered face, he muttered, "Aw, hell. Not *them* again!"

Chapter 8

Randall didn't call a halt until they had put several miles between themselves and the Assiniboine village. Even then, he didn't plan to stop for very long, just in case the Indians were able to mount a pursuit quicker than he thought they would.

Wildflower's struggles had subsided. She was too scared or too tired, or both, to keep trying to get loose from his grip. He felt a little tremor go through her body every now and then, but otherwise she didn't move.

The baby wasn't happy, kicking and squirming and crying. The noise was getting on Randall's nerves, so he told the woman, "Get that brat to stop squalling." Then he turned to the other riders and went on, "How many men did we lose?"

Somebody did a quick head count and reported, "Looks like we're down seven men, Randall. Plus we got three or four more wounded, but I reckon they'll probably make it."

Randall nodded in satisfaction. Those casualties were a reasonable price to pay for what they had accomplished. Nobody ever did anything worthwhile without suffering a few losses along the way.

Not only that, but his group was still large enough to fight off an attack if the Indians caught up with them. Randall didn't think that was going to happen before they got back to Hammerhead, but it made sense to be ready for trouble.

"Anybody have any idea how many of the savages we killed?" he asked.

"Had to be at least a couple dozen of them," Page said with a note of pride in his voice. "I accounted for four of the red heathens myself."

"Five if you count the one you stabbed in the back earlier," Randall muttered.

"What'd you say, boss?"

"Nothing," Randall replied with a shake of his head.

He had felt the prisoner shudder again as she heard how many of her fellow villagers had died. That told him she understood English. He hadn't known that for sure until now.

"We'll let the horses rest for ten minutes," he said. "A couple of you boys fall back a ways and make sure nobody's coming up behind us. If you see any signs of a rescue party, hotfoot it back here."

Two of the gunmen wheeled their horses and rode off into the night. Most of the others dismounted.

"Come here, Dwyer," Randall said. When the man walked over, Randall continued, "Here, take the girl. Hang on to her."

"Glad to," Dwyer said with a grin. He reached up and took hold of the prisoner as Randall slid her off the back of the horse.

The baby was still fussing but not crying as loudly and annoyingly as he had been. Randall swung down from the saddle and leaned close to the young woman, studying her face in the light from the moon and stars. He figured it would be a good idea to make sure she really was who she was supposed to be.

He hated to think about what might happen if he'd grabbed the wrong Indian.

"Listen to me, girl," he said in a harsh, commanding voice. "I know you understand English. Is your name Wildflower?"

She didn't answer him. Stubbornly, she kept her eyes downcast and wouldn't even look at him.

He reached out, took hold of her chin, and roughly tilted her head back so that she had no choice but to raise her eyes.

"I asked you a question," Randall said. "I want to know if your name is Wildflower. Are you Chief Two Bears's daughter?"

Her mouth twisted. For a second he thought she was going to answer him.

Then she spat in his face instead.

Without thinking, Randall backhanded her. She let out an involuntary cry and sagged in Dwyer's grip. She would have fallen if the gunman hadn't been holding her up.

"Damn, boss, take it easy," Dwyer said. "You told us yourself, we ain't supposed to hurt the gal and her brat."

"I didn't hurt her," Randall said as he wiped the spittle from his face. "I just let her know she'd better not try anything like that again." He reached for the baby. "We'll see how she likes having the kid taken away from her."

"No!" she cried as she tried to twist away from him. She couldn't do it as long as Dwyer was holding her.

"Because of what my big-mouthed friend here said,

you know I can't hurt this child," Randall told her. "But there's nothing saying that I have to keep the two of you together."

She fought him, but there was only so much she could do with Dwyer's hands clamped around her upper arms. Randall pulled the baby from her hands. The boy started wailing again as he was separated from his mother.

"I can fix it so you'll never see him again," Randall went on. "We'll split up, and I'll take the babe some place you'll never find him. He'll grow up not remembering you at all."

"No, no, no," the young woman babbled. "You cannot! He is my son!"

"Then tell me what I want to know."

"Yes! I am called Wildflower! My father is Two Bears!"

Tears ran down her cheeks as the ragged exclamations came from her.

"Yeah, well, maybe you're just telling me what you think I want to hear," Randall said. "Why should I believe you?"

"Because it is the truth!" She started crying harder. "My son! My son! Please—"

Randall silenced her by thrusting the baby back into her arms. She clutched him desperately. Randall nodded to Dwyer, who let go of her and stepped back.

"All right," Randall said, his voice quiet now. He reached toward her, and without really thinking about what he was doing, he stroked the long, midnight-dark hair. "I believe you. You were too upset to lie. Don't worry, you and your baby are going to stay together."

She raised her tear-streaked face to him again.

"You promise this is true?"

"It will be as long as I'm giving the orders," Randall said.

What he didn't tell her was that things could change as soon as they reached Hammerhead. When that happened, the Colonel would be giving the orders again, and if there was one thing Randall had learned, it was to not try to guess what the Colonel would do. The Colonel's thinking was always two or three steps ahead of everybody else's.

And if the Colonel were to decide that Wildflower and her son had to be separated or even had to die . . . well, that would be a damned shame, Randall thought as he looked at the beautiful young woman, but he would see to it. No doubt about that.

"Mount up," he told his men. "We need to get moving again. There's no telling how soon somebody will be coming after us."

"The varmints call themselves the Indian Ring," Preacher said as he sat in Two Bears's lodge with the chief and Standing Rock. "A few years back, when ol' Ulysses Grant was still runnin' things in Washington, there was another bunch known as the Indian Ring, but they was mostly just cheap crooks and politicians, which is two ways of sayin' the same thing as far as I'm concerned. The businessmen who were part of it paid bribes to government officials for the right to do business on Indian reservations. Sometimes they would pay off politicians to set aside certain treaties if they thought they could make some money out of it."

"What would such men want with my daughter and grandson?" Two Bears asked.

Preacher shook his head and said, "This ain't the same bunch. That first one got broke up after a while, mostly through political pressure. Oh, I reckon some of the no-good skunks who were part of it probably belong to this new Indian Ring, too, but they've changed their tune. It ain't just about graft and corruption anymore. Now they're out to steal everything that ain't nailed down, especially when it belongs to folks like you, Two Bears. They want all the land that's been reserved for the tribes, and they'll wipe out anybody who stands in their way."

"This is not a reservation," Two Bears pointed out. Standing Rock was still too upset to talk, but he was listening.

"Maybe not officially, but it's government land. Open range. The settlers around here haven't pushed to claim it and drive you and your people off, but maybe somebody else has got that idea. And if the Indian Ring is behind it, well, they wouldn't shy away from hirin' gun-wolves to grab Wildflower and Little Hawk so they can force you to do what they want."

"How do you know so much about this . . . Indian Ring?" Two Bears said the words as if they tasted bad in his mouth.

"Me and Smoke and Matt have come up against 'em a couple of times in the past," Preacher explained. "We've managed to bust up their schemes, but it took a heap of shootin' both times."*

"Smoke Jensen? I have heard you speak of him."

"Yeah, and Matt's a Jensen now, too. A real ring-tailed rannihan, too, just like Smoke." Preacher paused. "I reckon they're as close to family as this old codger has got."

*See the novels *The Family Jensen* and *The Family Jensen: Helltown Massacre.*

"And you think this Indian Ring has something to do with the attack on my village and Wildflower and Little Hawk being kidnapped?"

"I can't say that for sure," Preacher replied. "But I heard the fella who grabbed 'em mention some Colonel and a ring while he was givin' orders. Killin' Blue Bull like they done and then swoopin' down on the village in the night, murderin' folks left and right . . . well, trust me, Two Bears, that's exactly the sort of thing this new Indian Ring would do."

Standing Rock burst out, "Talk, talk, talk! We sit and talk while those men are getting farther away with Wildflower and Little Hawk! We should be pursuing them!"

Preacher understood how upset the young warrior was. If he'd been married and had a son, likely he would have felt the same way if they were captured. But there were other things that had to be considered.

"There ain't enough light to track them tonight," he said. "With a bunch that big, it won't be hard to pick up their trail in the mornin'. We'll go after 'em at first light."

"They could be miles away by then!"

"And they likely will be," Preacher admitted. "But that won't keep us from catchin' up to them."

"And what will happen to my wife and child in the meantime?" Standing Rock asked in a bitter voice.

Preacher scratched at his beard and said, "I been thinkin' about that. When the varmints first rode in here, did they start shootin' folks right away?"

Two Bears frowned in thought for a moment, and then said, "They were firing over the heads of my people. The killing did not start until they had been here for a few minutes."

Preacher nodded as if the chief's answer confirmed a theory for him.

"They were shootin' to keep everybody scared and confused while their boss went after Wildflower and Little Hawk. He didn't want to take a chance on either of them gettin' hit by a stray bullet. When he got his hands on them, though, and was carryin' them off, then it was different." Preacher's voice grew bleak and angry. "Then they could slaughter whoever they wanted to."

"I will find these men and kill them," Two Bears vowed.

"It's too bad all the fellas they left behind were dead," Preacher said. "If any of 'em had still been alive, we might've been able to make them tell us where the rest of the bunch is headed."

"Yes. We would have made them talk."

Hearing the cold hatred in his old friend's voice, Preacher didn't doubt that a bit.

He broached another thought, knowing that Two Bears wouldn't like what he was about to say.

"I don't think you should come along with us, Two Bears. I'll take Standin' Rock and some of your other young warriors, but you should stay here."

Two Bears drew himself up stiffly and said, "You think I cannot keep up with the younger men? Do not forget, you are older than I am, Preacher!"

"I know that, but your people have suffered a terrible blow tonight. They need their chief here to help them get through this time of tragedy." Preacher played his trump card. "Besides, there's somethin' else I need you to do."

Two Bears looked like he wanted to keep arguing, but he asked, "What is this thing you wish?"

"I'm gonna write out a telegram, and I need you to

go to the nearest settlement with a Western Union office and send it for me. The message is goin' to Smoke down in Colorado, and he can pass it on to Matt. He usually knows how to get hold of the boy. When they hear that the Indian Ring may be up to no good again, they'll come a-runnin'."

"Any of my warriors can do that," Two Bears said.

"I ain't so sure about that. This is mighty important, and I'd rather the chore be handled by the fella I trust the most in these parts."

Two Bears stared at him with narrowed eyes for a long moment, and then said, "I still think you believe I am too old to go with you . . . but I will do as you say. It is true my people will need me here. There is much to mourn."

"Still you talk!" Standing Rock said. "All this talk of telegrams and white men named Jensen . . . all of this will take time, time we do not have! We must pursue these evil men now!"

"Oh, we're gonna do that," Preacher assured him. "First thing in the mornin', like I said. But you can bet your warbonnet on this, Standin' Rock . . . if the Indian Ring and their hired killers are mixed up in this, the way I think they are, then we're liable to need all the help we can get. And there ain't nobody I'd rather have sidin' me in a fight than Smoke and Matt Jensen."

BOOK TWO

Chapter 9

Nothing was much worse than getting woken up out of a sound sleep and having to jump out of bed, Smoke Jensen thought.

Well, that wasn't strictly true, he corrected himself. Lots of things actually were worse than that, he supposed, and among them was being jolted awake and having to leave your nice warm bed when your nice warm wife was snuggled up against you.

But there were more important things to worry about right now. As he buckled on his gun belt, Smoke called through the closed door of his and Sally's bedroom, "Did we lose anybody out there, Pearlie?"

"Not permanent like," replied the foreman of the Sugarloaf ranch. "That young fella Steve Barstow you hired a while back got a bullet hole in his arm, but the bone ain't busted and I reckon he'll be all right."

"I'm glad to hear it."

Smoke turned back toward the bed. He would have pulled his clothes on hurriedly in the dark after Pearlie knocked on the door to wake him, but Sally, who had been awakened as well, had rose up into a sitting position and lit the lamp on the little table beside the bed. Its yellow glow lit up her face. Her drowsy expression and the way her dark hair was tousled from sleep made her prettier than ever, Smoke thought.

He went over to her now, leaned down, and kissed the top of her head. As he started to straighten, she said, "You wait just a minute, mister." She reached up, rested her hand on the back of his neck, and gently pulled him back down for a proper kiss.

When he stood up a long moment later, Smoke said, "You make it mighty hard to go off chasing rustlers in the middle of the night."

"Just giving you a reminder of what you've got waiting for you at home, so maybe you won't take any foolish chances," Sally said. "Although, that never seemed to do all that much good in the past, did it?"

"Who knows?" Smoke asked with a smile. "Without those little reminders, I might have done some things that were even more loco."

"I'm not sure that would be possible," Sally murmured. She pushed aside the covers and swung her legs out of bed. "You go ahead, Smoke, and let me know if I need to help with that wounded man. In the meantime, it's liable to be after sunup before you get back. I'll have plenty of hot food and coffee waiting for you and the boys."

Smoke nodded his thanks, went over to the door, and slipped out into the hall where Pearlie was waiting. The foreman held a lantern he had carried in from the barn when he came to wake Smoke.

"I told Cal to saddle your horse for you," Pearlie said as the two men left the house and headed for the big barn. "He knows to be careful not to let the critter take a nip out of his hide."

Smoke nodded. The big 'Palouse was pretty much a one-man horse, but he'd been around Pearlie and Cal

Woods, another of the Sugarloaf's regular hands, enough that he would tolerate being saddled by them, at least most of the time.

"Who brought the word about the rustlers hitting us again?" Smoke asked.

"Ollie Simms. He brought Barstow in to get that bullet hole patched up, too. Slewfoot, Dave Taggart, Billy Doyle, and Chet Burns are still out there, guardin' the rest of the herd in case the varmints come back."

Smoke shook his head and said, "Since they've already made one raid tonight, I doubt if they'll come back for more. They're bound to know that we'd be ready for them if they did."

The lanky foreman let out a disgusted snort.

"After raidin' the herd twice in the past month, you'd think they'd figure we were ready for 'em anyway. And we were. We had six men out there watchin' the critters, and still they got in, ventilated Barstow, and took off with nigh on to a hundred cows. Smoke, I ain't tryin' to tell you your business, but we got to put a stop to this!"

"We will," Smoke replied with a grim edge coming into his voice. "We're going to track them down and end it."

As Pearlie had said, this was the third time rustlers had hit the Sugarloaf herd in recent weeks. Each incident had escalated from the previous one. The first night, about fifty cattle had disappeared with no warning. No one had been riding night herd. There hadn't seemed to be any reason to, since everything had been peaceful lately. Anyway, wideloopers tended to avoid the Sugarloaf, since the ranch was owned by one of the deadliest gunmen in the West. Nobody with any sense wanted Smoke Jensen on his trail.

The second time the rustlers struck, shots had been

fired, but no one was wounded. The thieves had made off with about a dozen more cattle than they had stolen the first time.

Now, according to Pearlie, around a hundred head of stock had been driven off, and a man who rode for Smoke's brand had a bullet hole in him.

Neither of those things sat well with Smoke. He asked himself if he was getting soft for letting things go on this long.

If anybody had a justifiable reason for wanting to sit back and enjoy a quiet life, it was Smoke Jensen. Although relatively young in years, only in his mid-thirties, he had packed several lifetimes worth of living into those years. Fairly early on, he had known tragedy, losing first his father and then a wife and infant son. Falsely accused of crimes, he had ridden the owlhoot trail with every man's hand against him until he was able to clear his name. He had been shot, knifed, beaten . . . and he had given back even more punishment than he had suffered. Slugs from his guns had sent more badmen than he could count straight to hell.

So he could be forgiven for it if he had wanted to leave that wild, dangerous existence behind him and enjoy the life of a prosperous rancher with a beautiful wife and a circle of staunch friends.

Problem was he had lived for so long with the tang of gun smoke in his nose that the air didn't smell right without it. He had spent so many years as a fiddle-footed drifter with his old friend Preacher that he often got the urge to sit a saddle and go see what was on the far side of the nearest hill he could find. He had realized that, deep down, action and adventure were like water and air to him. He couldn't live without them.

A dozen men led horses from the barn before Smoke

and Pearlie got there. Smoke saw young Calvin Woods leading not only his own mount but also the big Appaloosa that Smoke normally rode. The 'Palouse tossed his head, clearly anxious to get out and stretch his legs on the trail.

The punchers were all wearing guns and had grim expressions on their faces. Smoke knew as he looked from each man to the next that they were all angry the rustlers had dared to strike at the Sugarloaf again.

"Where's Steve Barstow?" Smoke asked. He wanted to make sure Sally didn't need to tend to the wounded cowboy. Over the years she had had more than her share of experience at patching up bullet holes.

"I'm right here, Mr. Jensen," a voice came from the group. A couple of men moved aside, and a young freckle-faced, redheaded cowboy stepped forward. He had a bloodstained rag tied tightly around his upper left arm to serve as a bandage. "I'm ready to ride with you and the rest of the fellas."

"You don't have to do that, Steve," Smoke said.

"Yes, sir, no offense, but I reckon I do," Barstow insisted. "One of those no-good night riders put a hole in me, and I aim to do something about that. He made a bad mistake when he didn't kill me, or at least ventilate my gun arm."

Smoke had to chuckle at the young man's attitude. He said, "I don't blame you a bit for feeling that way, but you'd better be sure that you're up to some hard, fast riding."

"I'm up to it. If I ain't, I'll turn around and come back by myself. You won't have to waste a man by sendin' him with me."

"Fair enough," Smoke said. "Since you and Ollie

were up there tonight where the rustlers hit us, the two of you can lead the way."

Of course, Smoke knew where the herd was and could have ridden straight to it. He knew every foot of this ranch better than any man alive.

But he was also a natural leader of men and knew how they responded to challenges. At Smoke's words, Steve Barstow jerked his head in an enthusiastic nod and declared, "We sure will, Mr. Jensen."

"Let's mount up, then," Smoke said as he returned the nod.

The men swung into their saddles. They all carried handguns, and rifle butts stuck up from saddle sheaths strapped to every horse. They were armed for bear . . . or in this case, armed for rustlers.

When they left the ranch, they headed northwest, toward the mountains that loomed over the Sugarloaf. At this time of year, Smoke kept his herd in the high pastures that were thick with grass, vast parklike areas surrounded by stands of pine, juniper, and aspen. It was beautiful country, and never more so than when the deep green of those pastures was dotted with the darker shapes of grazing cattle.

After the rustlers had struck the first time, Smoke had sent a couple of hands up the slopes to stay at an old stone line shack that originally had been a trapper's cabin. Smoke had spent some time there himself, back in the early days when he had first come to this part of the country, before he was a successful rancher.

His hope was that the raid was a fluke, that some hardcases drifting through the area had come upon the cattle and decided to help themselves to a small jag. If that was the case, the loss of the stock angered him, but it was over and not worth tracking down the thieves, even though a part of him wanted to. Practicality and reason had prevailed on his mind for a change.

The two men keeping an eye on the herd hadn't been enough to keep the rustlers from coming back, but this time shots were fired. The two punchers were forced to retreat to the line shack and hole up there until the rustlers were gone. It was a bitter pill for them to swallow, but they were outnumbered three to one and Smoke wouldn't have wanted them to throw their lives away against those odds.

Smoke hadn't taken this second outrage lying down. He had taken Pearlie and several of the men and set out to trail the thieves. Unfortunately, a fierce thunderstorm had broken and washed out all the tracks before they could go very far.

Unable to find out where the rustlers had gone, Smoke had asked for six volunteers and had gotten twice that many ready to move up to the high pastures. They worked in shifts, two men sleeping in the line shack while the other four were out riding herd on the stock. That way they were able to keep someone with the cattle around the clock.

That hadn't worked, either. The rustlers had bush-whacked the night herders, wounding Steve Barstow and keeping the other men pinned down while the cattle were driven off.

While they were riding, Barstow told Smoke about what had happened and concluded by saying, "There had to be at least a dozen of 'em, Mr. Jensen. Probably more than that, considerin' how many were shootin' at us and how many it must've taken to drive off those cows."

"The gang's getting bigger every time," Smoke said, "just like they're getting more daring with each raid, too. If this keeps up, there'll be an army stealing our whole blasted herd."

"But it won't keep up," Barstow said. "Because we're gonna track down those varmints and give 'em their needin's."

Smoke chuckled and said, "That's right, Steve. We should've done it before now, I reckon. I'm getting too plumb peaceful."

Beside him, Pearlie let out a disbelieving snort and said, "Smoke Jensen, peaceful. That'll be the day. I'll believe it when I see it."

Smoke appreciated that sentiment from his foreman, but he knew there was some truth to what he'd said. The day would come when he would have to settle down some. Now, *Preacher* had never settled down, no, sir, mused Smoke, and that old mountain man had a lot of years on him. But Preacher wasn't married and didn't have a ranch to run, either. Responsibility and that old codger had always been strangers.

Of course, thinking about how things might be in the future assumed that he would live long enough to get there, Smoke reminded himself. The way bullets had a habit of flying wherever he was and whatever he was doing, that was a big assumption.

Wait and see, he thought. His life was a long way from peaceful and boring, and he didn't foresee that changing any time soon.

Right now, he had some rustlers to catch.

When they reached the high pastures, a voice called out from some trees in a challenging tone, "Who's there? Better hold it right where you are!"

Smoke would have answered, but before he could, Barstow said, "Take it easy, Dave. We've brought Mr. Jensen and some of the men from the ranch."

"Steve? Is that you?" A rider emerged from the shadows under the pines, holding a rifle. "Last time I saw you, you were bleedin' like a stuck pig."

"I'm fine," Barstow said. "I got enough blood left to go chase down those rustlers."

Smoke asked, "Did you see which way they went, Dave?"

"They headed north along Gunsight Ridge," Dave Taggart replied. "Slewfoot's trailin' the bastards."

Smoke drew in a sharp breath.

"By himself?"

"We wanted to go with him," Taggart said, "but he told us to stay here and keep an eye on the herd. Since he's been workin' for you longer than me or Billy or Chet have been, we figured we'd better do what he said."

Smoke understood that, but he didn't like the idea of Slewfoot going after the rustlers by himself. Clearly, the cattle thieves didn't mind shooting, and if they dropped off a couple of men to keep an eye on their back trail, Slewfoot might be riding right into big trouble.

Taggart went on, "We're coming with you now, though, aren't we, Mr. Jensen?"

"No, the three of you stay here," Smoke told him. "I don't want to leave the herd untended. We'll go after Slewfoot and maybe catch up to him before he gets himself into a fix—"

Smoke stopped short and lifted his head. He didn't have to go on, because all the men heard the same thing he did.

Drifting down from the north through the night air came the faint popping and crackling of distant gunfire.

Chapter 10

The cowboy called Slewfoot had ridden for spreads all over the West, but he had never found a better place to work than the Sugarloaf, or a better man to work for than Smoke Jensen. Any cowboy worth his salt rode for the brand to start with, but Slewfoot felt an extra level of loyalty to Smoke.

Not everybody would have taken a chance on a man most would have regarded as a cripple. It was true that when he wasn't on horseback, Slewfoot had a little trouble getting around. Years earlier, a horse had stepped on his right ankle and busted the hell out of it, and when the bones healed back together, they weren't in exactly the right places anymore. As a result that foot sat at a funny angle, and while he could still walk, he had to take it easy and his gait was a mite odd to see.

But put him in a saddle and he was as good as he ever was. He had to rig the right stirrup a little different, that's all. He could work just as hard as always, was still a sure hand with a lasso, and knew the ways of cattle frontwards and backwards.

He could shoot when he had to, as well, and if he got

any of those dadblasted rustlers in his sights, that was exactly what he intended to do.

He was tall and lanky, with a long face that reminded people of a horse. Stick a hat on his head and he looked like a beanpole wearing a Stetson. He paused now and took off that hat so he could scratch his head in puzzlement. He had been trailing those stolen cows by moonlight. A hundred head left a pretty big trail, one that could be seen even at night.

However, he had come to a place where the cattle seemed to have turned straight toward the ridge, and that didn't make any sense.

Gunsight Ridge loomed about half a mile to the west, a tall, blocky barrier with a V-shaped notch in it that gave it its name. That notch was distinctive, but it didn't serve as any sort of pass. It was too high for that, with no trail leading to it.

There *were* a few places where men on horseback could get over the ridge, but you couldn't drive a herd of cattle over it, even a small bunch like the one Slewfoot was pursuing. The closest place you could push a herd like that was still a good five miles ahead of him.

Yet there was no mistaking what he saw from the back of his horse. The rustlers were driving those cows straight toward the ridge.

Sugarloaf range ran all the way to the ridge. Slewfoot didn't think the thieves would hold those stolen cattle on Smoke's land. They would want to put as much distance as they could between them and Smoke Jensen, at least to Slewfoot's way of thinking. They ought to still be lighting a shuck north, the way they had started. There were some passes up there leading higher into the mountains, then down into the valleys beyond. Some of the isolated settlements in that direction were no better than outlaw towns, where the rustlers could dispose of those cows and get some quick cash in return.

Well, puzzling or not, that was the way the trail led, so Slewfoot hitched his horse into motion and commenced following it again. As he rode, he loosened the six-gun in its holster on his hip, and he checked the Winchester in the saddleboot as well. Those wideloopers were ruthless. They had proven that by shooting young Steve Barstow. Slewfoot hoped the kid was all right.

As he drew closer to the ridge, he kept a wary eye on the trees that grew thickly along its base. He wouldn't put it past those varmints to leave behind a couple of bushwhackers.

Because of that suspicion, Slewfoot was alert when his horse suddenly pricked up its ears and tossed its head a little. That told him the animal had caught the scent of another horse. Following his instincts, Slewfoot hauled hard on the reins and jabbed his heels into his mount's flanks, causing the horse to leap to the right.

At that instant, muzzle flame spurted from the shadows underneath the trees, accompanied by the sound of two rifle shots. Slewfoot wasn't hit, but he sensed the bullets slicing through the air not far to his left. He rode hard toward the nearest clump of trees that would give him some cover.

More shots cracked from the bushwhackers' position. Slewfoot leaned low over his horse's neck to make himself as small a target as possible. He pulled the Winchester from its scabbard, and when he reached the pines, he kicked his feet free of the stirrups and vaulted from the saddle.

He landed awkwardly but caught his balance right away. He knew he looked pretty funny when he ran, but right now how he looked didn't matter. Dragging his right foot, he scurried the few yards to the trees and dived behind them, even as more slugs whipped around him and chewed big pieces of bark from the trunks. The smell of pine sap seeping from those wounds was strong as he lay there in the darkness.

His hat had flown off when he went diving for cover. He edged his head around the tree and looked toward the growth at the base of the ridge. He saw several more muzzle flashes as the riflemen hidden there kept throwing lead at him. Bullets thudded into tree trunks and cracked through the branches around him.

Their mistake had been not waiting for him to get a little closer so they could make sure of him, he thought. Once his horse warned him, the bushwhackers had lost their best chance. For that he would always be grateful to the animal . . . for however long the rest of his life lasted, which was a pretty good question at the moment.

Those muzzle flashes gave him some targets. Lying on his belly, Slewfoot nestled the Winchester against his shoulder and drew a bead on one of the spots where he'd seen a spurt of flame. He waited until there was another orange flash, then pulled his own trigger. With a whipcrack of sound, the rifle kicked against his shoulder.

As soon as he fired, Slewfoot rolled to his right, moving fast. He wound up behind another tree and paused there. He heard slugs plowing into the ground near the tree where he had been a moment earlier. Both ambushers were still firing, he realized with a grimace, so either he had missed with his shot, or it hadn't done enough damage to put one of the riflemen out of the fight.

He was safe enough where he was, but he was pinned down in these trees. It was possible that one of the bushwhackers would try to keep him here while the other worked around for a better shot at him. That was what he would do if the tables were turned.

He had one bit of hope that lifted his spirits. Ollie Simms had headed for the ranch headquarters, taking the wounded Steve Barstow with him, to let Smoke know the rustlers had struck again. Slewfoot had a hunch that Smoke would hit the trail in a hurry. If Smoke hot-footed it up here and brought some of the Sugarloaf hands with him, that would change everything.

So now, Slewfoot thought as bullets continued to sizzle through the trees around him, all he had to do was wait for Smoke Jensen to show up. . . .

And hope that he could stay alive until then.

The gunshots they heard could have all sorts of explanations, but Smoke's gut told him there was only one that was likely.

Slewfoot had either caught up to the rustlers, or some of them had lain in wait for him. Either way, Smoke was convinced that was his rider trading shots with the varmints they were after.

He wasn't going to waste any time in getting to Slewfoot and giving him a hand. He shouted, "Come on!" at his punchers and urged the 'Palouse into a run.

The shots came from the north, the direction Slew-foot had gone. The dark, looming bulk of Gunsight Ridge to the west made it impossible to get lost, even at night.

Smoke couldn't let his stallion run flat out, although the 'Palouse would have been happy to. There was too much danger of the horse stepping into a hole or running into some unseen obstacle. Smoke kept his mount moving pretty fast, though, and the other riders trailed closely behind him.

Even though they were hurrying, time seemed to pass with agonizing slowness as they rode north. A few minutes could be an eternity in a gun battle. Not only that, but Smoke had to call a halt every so often to listen for the sound of shots. If the guns fell silent, that would send an ominous message indeed.

Every time he reined in and the other men followed suit, Smoke heard the crackle of rifle fire. The shots were coming at a slower pace now, instead of the furious volley they had been at first. That meant the fight had settled down to a standoff. Slewfoot was alive and still battling, but it was possible he was badly wounded.

Finally, when it seemed like they were getting close, Smoke signaled for the men to stop.

"Pearlie, pick four men to come with you and me," he said as he dismounted and pulled his Winchester from its saddle sheath. "Cal, you'll be staying here with the other men."

"Blast it, Smoke, I'd rather come with you," Cal objected.

"I know you would, but I want you here to take charge if we need you to come in and save our bacon."

Smoke's voice was firm and didn't allow for any argument. Despite Cal's youth, he had been smack-dab in the middle of plenty of trouble since coming to the Sugarloaf, and he was seasoned beyond his years.

"All right," the youngster said reluctantly, "but be careful."

"You're starting to sound like Sally," Smoke said with a quick grin.

"I just know how accident-prone this old pelican is," Cal said as he nodded toward Pearlie.

The foreman and former hired gun began, "It won't be no accident when you find yourself with my boot up your—"

"Let's go," Smoke said.

Pearlie quickly pointed out four men to come with him and Smoke. They started off on foot, moving quickly and blending into the shadows. The men who rode for Sugarloaf might not be professional fighters, but most of them were tough, experienced frontiersmen.

Now that the hoofbeats weren't drowning them out, the shots came loud and clear through the night. Smoke followed them, veering to the left so that he could approach under the cover of some trees. When he reached the edge of the pines, he stopped just behind one of the trunks and peered out across an open stretch of ground toward more trees at the base of Gunsight Ridge.

It took only a moment for the setup to become clear in his mind. A single set of muzzle flashes from a clump of trees to the right marked Slewfoot's location. Two riflemen, undoubtedly a pair of rustlers, were in the pines at the base of the ridge.

Pearlie eased up beside Smoke and took in the situation just as quickly. Quietly, he said, "If all six of us open up on those trees by the ridge, we'll skin those polecats quick as you please."

"Yeah, but I wouldn't mind taking at least one of them alive so we can ask him some questions," Smoke said. He pointed. "If you and I were to work our way around that way and get behind them, then the rest could open up and come just close enough to stampede them right into our arms."

Pearlie's teeth sparkled in the moonlight for a second like his namesake as a grin flashed across his rugged face.

"I like that idea," he said. "Ain't no guarantee those jaspers will cooperate in bein' took alive, though."

"All we can do is try," Smoke said.

He gathered the other four men around him in the shadows and explained the plan to them. They grasped it without any trouble, and Smoke knew he could count on them to do their part.

"We'll signal you with the hoot of an owl when we're ready for you to open the ball," he told them and received nods and murmurs of agreement. Satisfied that everyone understood, he said to Pearlie, "Let's go."

They catfooted through the darkness, using the cover of the trees as much as they could. When the trees ran out, Smoke dropped to hands and knees and motioned for Pearlie to do likewise. Flattening onto his belly, Smoke began crawling toward the ridge.

The grass was tall enough to conceal the two of them, and they moved slowly and carefully enough that the slight disturbance of the grass would be difficult to spot in the moonlight. Patience had never been Smoke's strong suit, but he had learned stealth from Preacher and the old mountain man had been a good teacher. The best possible teacher, in fact, since in his younger days Preacher had been able to creep into an enemy camp, slit the throats of several men, and get back without anyone ever knowing he was there until the next morning.

At last, Smoke and Pearlie reached the trees where the bushwhackers were hidden. When they were back safely in the shadows, they stood up. Smoke led the way to the very base of the ridge. They followed it toward the spot where the riflemen were holed up. The strip of trees was about twenty feet wide, so Smoke and Pearlie would have room to get behind the bush-whackers.

When the shots were so loud they sounded like they were practically in the laps of the men from Sugarloaf, Smoke stopped again. He stiffened as his gaze turned toward the ridge. The rock face was dark, but he saw an even deeper patch of darkness that had a faintly ominous look to it, as if it were the gaping maw of some hungry, primordial creature.

It looked for all the world like the mouth of a tunnel, but Smoke would have sworn there was no tunnel in Gunsight Ridge.

They could investigate that later, he told himself. Right now they had to deal with the men who were trying to kill Slewfoot. He tapped Pearlie on the shoulder to let the foreman know they were ready.

Then Smoke lifted his free hand to his mouth, cupped it around his lips, and waited until the rifles fell silent for a moment. When they did, he hooted like an owl.

A heartbeat later, gun thunder filled the night as the rest of Smoke's men opened fire.

Chapter 11

Before he and Pearlie had crept around here, Smoke had made it clear what his men were supposed to do. Some of their shots ripped into the ground just in front of the trees, while others smacked into the trunks and whistled through the branches overhead. They weren't missing by much, coming close enough with their slugs to make the two bushwhackers give up the standoff and beat a retreat. Smoke and Pearlie heard their boots thudding against the ground as they fled.

"Here they come!" Pearlie whispered.

"Split up and wait until they're close," Smoke ordered as he leaned his Winchester against the tree and drew his Colt.

Pearlie stepped over to one of the other trees and pressed his back against it so he couldn't be seen. The running footsteps came closer.

The bushwhacker who was in the lead raced past Smoke. With blinding speed, Smoke leaped out from behind the tree and struck, reversing his pistol so that the butt thudded against the man's head. The bushwhacker's hat softened the blow's force somewhat, but it was still enough to send the man tumbling off his feet with a pained grunt.

Smoke heard a rustle of movement as Pearlie tackled the second man. At the same time Smoke stepped forward and kicked away the rifle his man had dropped. He pressed the barrel of his revolver against the back of the man's head and reached down with his other hand to draw the weapon from the bushwhacker's holster.

"You're caught, mister," he said. "Try anything and I'll blow your brains out."

That was the last thing he intended to do, but the rustler didn't have to know that.

The thudding of knobby-knuckled fists on flesh made Smoke glance toward his friend. He couldn't make out any details in the shadows, but he saw the struggling shapes churning around. A gunshot roared, but Smoke could tell by the jet of flame from the muzzle that the weapon was pointed upward as Pearlie and the other bushwhacker wrestled over it.

A sudden smack sent one of the figures slumping to the ground. Smoke dropped to a knee beside the man he had captured, ready to lift his gun and fire if the other bushwhacker had been victorious.

Instead, it was Pearlie's voice that called softly, "Smoke?"

"I'm here," Smoke replied. "I got mine."

"Yeah, same here," Pearlie said.

Smoke took hold of his prisoner's collar and rose to his feet, hauling the man upright with him.

"Don't try anything," he warned. "My trigger finger is mighty itchy right now. Those are my cattle you stole tonight, and one of my men you shot."

The man swallowed with an audible gulp.

"You're Smoke Jensen?" he asked.

Smoke's voice was hard as flint as he answered, "That's right."

The prisoner started muttering something. Smoke couldn't make out the words at first, but after a few seconds he realized the man was saying a prayer.

"Save it," he said as he gave the prisoner a shove. "Anyway, where you're going, the fella with the horns and the forked tail is in charge."

The rest of the Sugarloaf men had stopped shooting. Pearlie raised his voice and shouted, "Hold your fire, boys." Smoke herded his prisoner out of the trees, while Pearlie took hold of the unconscious man's feet and dragged him into the open.

From the stand of pines to the right, a familiar voice called, "Mr. Jensen? Is that you?"

"That's right, Slewfoot," Smoke replied. "Come on out. Or do you need help? Are you wounded?"

The tall, skinny cowboy limped out of the trees carrying his rifle.

"Naw, I'm fine," he said. "Did you get those jaspers who had me pinned down?"

"They're right here," Smoke said.

Slewfoot came up and asked, "What're you gonna do with 'em?"

Smoke made his voice hard again and said, "The same thing any honest man would do with rustlers and murderers . . . string 'em up!"

"Murderers!" Slewfoot repeated. "You mean that Barstow kid who got ventilated . . . ?"

"Dead," Smoke said. He looked at Pearlie and the other men, hoping they could see him well enough in the moonlight to realize the ruse he was trying and not give it away.

Pearlie was quick on the uptake, as usual. He said,

"Yeah, the poor kid bled to death before anybody could get him back to the ranch house. That makes it murder, sure enough. Want me to fetch my lasso, Smoke?"

"That'll be fine," Smoke replied. "And bring mine, too. We'll find a tree with a good branch and have both of these bastards dancing on air before you know it."

The prisoner finally spoke up again, saying in a shaky voice, "You . . . you can't do that. We're entitled to a trial—"

"It just so happens I brought a dozen men with me tonight," Smoke broke in. "That's the right number for a jury. We'll have a trial if you want, and I'll be the judge and pass sentence when you're found guilty."

"Seems like a waste of time to me," Pearlie said. "I'll be back in a minute with them lassos and the rest of the fellas."

He trotted off into the night.

The prisoner swallowed again and went on, "Look, you don't have to kill me, Mr. Jensen. Just give me my horse and I'll ride on, and I give you my word I'll never set foot in this part of the country again. You can shoot me on sight if I do."

"I can shoot you right now if I want to," Smoke said, "but I'd rather see you hang."

"I didn't kill anybody, I swear it! I didn't fire a shot tonight."

Slewfoot said, "You were shootin' at me, damn it!"

"Well . . . I meant when we were driving off those cows. That's all I did. Some of the other boys handled all the gunplay. I'm not responsible for that cowboy gettin' killed!"

"You were part of it," Smoke said coldly. "To my way of thinking, that makes you just as guilty as the man who pulled the trigger."

"No . . . no, you can't . . ."

The man sounded like he was about to start bawling. Smoke didn't feel any pity for him, but the time had come to make a play.

"There might be something you can do—" he began.

The rustler didn't let him finish.

"Anything!" the man said. "Anything you want, Jensen."

"Tell me where the rest of the bunch was taking those cows."

The prisoner hesitated, saying, "I . . . I can't. The boss would—"

"Kill you? Is that what you were about to say?" Smoke asked. "What in blazes do you think is fixing to happen to you here? You can talk, or you can kick your life out at the end of a hangrope. The choice is up to you."

The rustler didn't say anything. His fear of the man he worked for had to be pretty strong to make him clam up in the face of a necktie party.

While they were waiting for Pearlie, Smoke drew Slewfoot aside. After warning the crippled cowboy not to show any reaction, he whispered the good news that Steve Barstow was actually still alive. Slewfoot looked relieved, but didn't do anything else except nod slightly.

Pearlie came back a few minutes later, along with the rest of the group from the Sugarloaf. The other riders all dismounted and formed a circle of grim faces. Now there were a dozen men surrounding the prisoners. The rustler who was conscious ran his fingers through his tangled hair and rubbed his face as he moaned in despair.

"All right," he said, the words seeming to bubble out of his mouth. "I'll tell you what you want to—"

The other rustler, who had appeared to still be out cold from the blow Pearlie had landed, must have been shamming, because he lunged up from the ground with no warning and rammed a shoulder into the nearest man. He yanked a six-gun from the cowboy's holster, tipped up the barrel, and fired.

The bullet wasn't aimed at Smoke or any of the Sugarloaf riders, though. Instead it slammed into the chest of the man Smoke had been questioning. The slug's impact made the rustler stagger back a step and collapse.

The gunman tried to swing the revolver toward Smoke and get off a second shot, but he was nowhere near fast enough. Smoke's Colt was already in his hand. Even if it hadn't been, his draw would have shaded the rustler's attempt. Smoke fired, aiming for the man's shoulder.

Two things ruined that plan. One was the poor light, and the other was the way the rustler swayed to the right just as Smoke pulled the trigger. The man must have been trying to avoid the shot, but he ran right into it instead. The bullet ripped through his throat and made blood spurt from severed arteries.

The rustler dropped the gun and clapped his hands to his throat, but there was no way he could stop the flood of crimson. His knees unhinged, and he dropped to the ground where he made a grotesque gagging sound and thrashed around for a couple of seconds before lying still.

Smoke knew the man was dead. He ignored the corpse and leaped to the side of the first rustler, dropping to one knee. The man had his hands pressed to his chest. Dark worms of blood crawled between his splayed fingers.

"Your partner shot you because he knew you were

about to talk," Smoke said. "But you can still tell me what you wanted me to know. Where will we find the cattle your bunch stole?"

"I didn't . . . didn't kill nobody. . . ."

"Don't worry about that now," Smoke said. "Just tell me where the rest of the gang went."

"Through . . . through the tunnel . . . Ah!"

With that sharp outcry, the man's back arched. A second later, he slumped again. His head fell to the side.

"He's dead, Smoke," Pearlie said.

Smoke nodded.

"I know. And I'd already figured out those stolen cows must have gone through the tunnel, so that doesn't really tell me where they wound up."

"We got a place to start lookin', though, wherever that tunnel leads to." Pearlie took off his hat and scratched his head. "Danged if I ever heard of a tunnel runnin' through Gunsight Ridge."

"Neither have I," Smoke said as he got to his feet. "While we're doing that, some of you fellas search these men. See if they have anything in their pockets that might tell us where they came from."

Pearlie, Cal, and Steve Barstow accompanied Smoke as he headed for the tunnel. When they reached the dark opening, Cal fashioned a torch from several broken pine boughs that he lashed together with a piggin' string he took from his pocket. He lit the makeshift torch with a sulfur match, and when the brand was burning brightly, he held it over his head to light their way as the men started into the tunnel.

The dark opening reminded Smoke more than ever of the mouth of a beast. He was about as icy nerved as a man can get, but he didn't like holes in the earth. They made him think about what might come crawling out from them.

This tunnel didn't go down below the surface, though. It bored straight through the ridge. Smoke told Cal to hold the torch close to one of the walls.

"I don't think this passage was man-made," he said. "I think an underground river used to run through here, before whatever earthquake thrust the ridge up, thousands of years ago."

"Why ain't nobody ever seen it before?" Pearlie asked. "I've ridden along this stretch of Gunsight Ridge dozens of times. I would've noticed it."

"Not if it was covered up and you weren't looking for it," Smoke said. "I think a rock slide must have plugged up the entrance, sometime in the past. Maybe far in the past. But then somebody came along, found the other end of the tunnel, followed it this far, and realized that if he could just break through the rocks, he'd have a back door onto Sugerloaf range that nobody else knew about."

Pearlie rubbed his chin. His fingertips rasped on the beard stubble that covered his lean, angular jaw as he frowned in thought.

"Pretty smart," he said after a moment. "So then the fella decided to use the tunnel to drive off stolen cows."

Smoke nodded and said, "That's the way it looks to me."

The tunnel was big enough for that. It was about thirty feet wide, and the arched ceiling rose about twenty feet. The floor was stone, so there weren't any tracks to prove that the rustled cattle had come through here, but they had the declaration of a dying man and the fact that there was no other place the cows could have gone.

The smoothness of the walls, ceiling, and floor was what told Smoke the tunnel had been formed by flowing water instead of being chipped out by tools in the hands of men. No telling how far back in the past that had been, he mused as he stood there looking around in the light of the torch Cal held.

"Reckon we can pick up the trail again at the other end?" Pearlie asked.

"That's what I'm hoping. Go back and get the other men and the horses. One more thing . . . Steve, I want you to ride back to the ranch."

Barstow had come into the tunnel with Smoke, Pearlie, and Cal. He said, "I been keepin' up all right, haven't I, Mr. Jensen? Why are you sendin' me back?"

"You've kept up just fine," Smoke assured the young cowboy. "But there's no telling how far this chase is going to lead us, and you'll need some rest if that arm is going to heal properly. Besides, I've got a couple of chores for you. I want you to tell Mrs. Jensen what we've found. She needs to know it may be a spell before we get back. Also, I want to get word to Monte Carson in Big Rock about this tunnel."

Monte Carson, who like Pearlie, had once been a hired gun who found himself on the wrong side from Smoke, had given up that life and become the sheriff in Big Rock, the nearest town to the Sugarloaf ranch. He and Smoke had been good friends for several years now.

Although Barstow still looked a little reluctant, he nodded and said, "I reckon I can take care of those things for you, Mr. Jensen. What do you expect the sheriff to do about this tunnel?"

"I don't think there's anything he can really do about it," Smoke said, "but he needs to know it's here. When we get back, I may do something about it, though. Some dynamite ought to close it up permanent like. I don't care for the idea of there being a hidden back door to Sugarloaf like this."

"Neither do I," Pearlie agreed. "It's too temptin' for thieves of every stripe."

"All right," Barstow agreed. "I'd rather come with you and settle the score with those wideloopers, though."

"It'll get settled, Steve," Smoke said. The flat, hard tone of his voice left no doubts in the minds of the men who heard it.

Chapter 12

Once Steve Barstow had started back to the ranch house with his messages for Sally and Sheriff Monte Carson, Smoke and the rest of the men led their horses into the tunnel.

They could have ridden—the ceiling was plenty high enough for that—but Smoke wanted to take it slow and easy as they made their way through the ridge. They could only see as far ahead of them as the flickering light from the torches they carried would reach, so there was no telling what they might run into. Smoke was confident that the passage ran fairly straight and true, but he couldn't be sure of that.

The darkness closed in behind them just as thick and stifling as it was in front of them, and as they went deeper into the tunnel, Smoke thought about the millions of tons of rock just above their heads. He didn't believe the tunnel was in any danger of collapsing. It had been here for thousands of years, after all. But that much weight looming over a man made him think, no matter how much he believed the path he followed was safe.

Smoke wasn't the only one who was a little nervous. Beside him, Pearlie muttered, "I don't much cotton to dark holes like this. They give me the fantods."

"There's nothing to worry about," Cal told him. "You're as safe as if you were sleepin' in your own bunk, back in the bunkhouse. Wait a minute. You've fallen out of your bunk while you were asleep before, haven't you?"

"Dadgummit, I was havin' a nightmare, and you know it. Don't go makin' sport of me about that, Cal."

"I remember it now," Cal said with a smile. "You were hollerin' 'Don't let it get me, boys, don't let it get me!' What was chasin' you, Pearlie? It must've been something pretty bad to have you running in your sleep like that. A bear, maybe? Or a mountain lion?"

"None of your doggoned business, youngster," Pearlie snapped. "My dreams is private."

"Yeah, and that's probably a good thing, too."

Their voices echoed against the rock ceiling. Smoke wanted to tell them to be quiet, but he realized Cal was nervous, as well, and was keeping himself calm by poking fun at Pearlie.

Anyway, anybody who might be waiting for them in the tunnel would hear the horses coming, so telling Pearlie and Cal to be quiet really wouldn't do any good. As long as they were inside this shaft, they wouldn't be sneaking up on anybody.

Chances were, the rustlers were long gone, along with the stolen stock. But they might have left someone behind to guard the far end of the tunnel, just as they had left bushwhackers to watch the end that opened from Gunsight Ridge.

"Stay alert," Smoke told his men. "We could be walking right into trouble."

"If we do, we'll give the varmints more hell than they figured on," Pearlie said.

Smoke had heard about tunnels like this one having bottomless pits in them. He didn't think that would be the case here. The rustlers wouldn't have been able to drive cattle through the tunnel if such a pitfall had been waiting for them. That would have resulted in a lot of cows plummeting to a bad end.

Even so, Smoke kept a wary eye out ahead of them as he led the group.

The half mile or so seemed much longer, and what felt like an hour passed before the men from Sugarloaf reached the other end. Smoke felt relief go through him as he spotted an irregular circle of grayish light ahead of them. That was starlight coming through the opening of the tunnel, he knew.

"Put out those torches," he told the men carrying the burning brands. "We'll wait a minute to let our eyes adjust before we step out of the tunnel."

The cowboys dropped the torches on the rock floor and stomped them out. What seemed like impenetrable darkness closed in around them like a shroud.

It didn't last long, though. Smoke's vision compensated for the lack of torchlight, and he was able to see the mouth of the tunnel even better now. He could even make out the tunnel's curving walls.

Murmuring a command to follow him, he started forward, still leading the 'Palouse. As he neared the entrance, he dropped his right hand to the butt of the Colt on his hip, but he didn't draw the weapon. He could do that quickly enough if he needed to.

When he reached the tunnel's mouth, he signaled a halt.

"I'll go out there and take a look around," he said.

"I'm comin' with you," Pearlie declared.

"No, you're not," Smoke replied. "You're staying here in case you need to take charge."

"You mean in case some of the skunks are waitin' out there and they kill you? That ain't never gonna happen."

Smoke chuckled and said, "I appreciate the vote of confidence, but I'm not bulletproof, Pearlie, and I've got the scars to prove it. Just stay here while I do a little scouting."

"Still say you ought to send somebody who ain't important," Pearlie muttered. "Like the kid here."

He nodded toward Cal as he added that last comment.

"Save the squabbling for later," Smoke said before Cal could respond to the gibe. He handed his horse's reins to Slewfoot. "I'll be back."

With that, he drew his revolver and glided out into the darkness.

Only it wasn't as dark now as it had been, Smoke noted as he left the tunnel. He glanced up at the sky, which was turning gray back beyond the ridge. The sun would be coming up in another hour or so.

The tunnel opened onto a long, brush-dotted slope that led down to a broad valley running north and south. Smoke had been over here on this side of Gunsight Ridge before, of course—he had been all over this part of Colorado—but to get here he had gone the long way around. The tunnel cut ten miles, maybe more, off the journey.

About fifteen miles north of here, the mountains that formed the valley petered out, dropping down to some broad flats with a small river flowing through them. A settlement known as Bitter Springs was located there.

It didn't amount to much—a general store, a couple of saloons, a blacksmith and a livery stable, and a few more businesses—but it was common knowledge that men on the dodge could stop there without having to worry about the law. The sheriff's office at the county seat was a long way off, and deputies hardly ever got up that way.

Buyers who didn't care too much about where merchandise came from could pick up some pretty good deals in Bitter Springs, too, Smoke knew. Cattle, horses, guns, wagons, mining equipment, anything with a value on it was traded there, and nobody asked any questions. It was a perfect place for the rustlers to dispose of the stock they had driven through the tunnel from the Sugarloaf.

As the light of approaching dawn grew stronger, Smoke ventured down the slope and studied the rocky ground. He saw tracks here and there, enough of them to confirm that the stolen herd had been driven down into the valley. Satisfied that they were on the right trail, he returned to the tunnel.

"No bushwhackers out there?" Pearlie asked as Smoke walked up to the entrance.

Smoke shook his head and said, "I didn't see any, and nobody took a shot at me. My hunch is that whoever is ramrodding those rustlers thinks that nobody else has any idea this tunnel is here."

"And I reckon he was right about that . . . until tonight."

"Yeah," Smoke agreed. "I found enough tracks to know that they drove our stock down into that valley below us. I don't know which way they went, but we ought to be able to follow them. I wouldn't be surprised if they were bound for Bitter Springs."

"That little wide place in the trail up north of here?" Pearlie thought it over and nodded. "Yeah, that makes sense. Plenty of hombres up there who'd be willin' to buy some stolen cattle and try to make some fast dinero on 'em."

The men mounted up. Smoke led the way down the slope toward the valley. They hadn't brought along any supplies, so they weren't equipped for a long chase. However, if the trail led farther than Bitter Springs, they could pick up some provisions there.

Smoke's instincts told him that wouldn't be necessary. He was convinced they would find the men they were looking for at the settlement.

When the cattle reached the base of the trail leading down from the tunnel, they had turned north, just as Smoke expected. The eastern sky continued to lighten, and eventually the sun peeked over Gunsight Ridge, flooding the valley with golden and rosy-hued light. The glow made the valley, which was rocky and choked with brush in many places, look more attractive than it really was.

This was mediocre rangeland, in contrast to the much better graze only a couple of miles away on the other side of the ridge. But people were always hungry for land, so several small outfits had been established here. Smoke and his companions passed some scrawny cows cropping at bunch grass, but didn't see any cowboys tending to them. Those animals would be allowed to run mostly wild in the brush until it came roundup time again.

A couple of hours after the sun came up, Pearlie pointed up a little draw to the left and said, "Looks like there's a house up yonder. Want to stop and talk to the folks, Smoke?"

"That's probably not a bad idea," Smoke said. "We might find out a little more about what we'll be facing when we get to Bitter Springs."

They turned their horses and rode along the twisting draw. After a hundred yards, a crude log cabin came into view. Smoke rose from the stone chimney at one end of the structure. That was what Pearlie had spotted. There was no barn, but Smoke saw a small shed and a pole corral off to one side of the cabin.

"Pearlie, Cal, you come with me," Smoke said. "The rest of you fellas wait here. It might spook whoever lives in that cabin if they see a whole gang of men riding up."

"We don't want nobody gettin' an itchy trigger finger," Pearlie agreed.

The three of them trotted their horses toward the cabin, slowing the mounts to a walk when they came within a hundred yards. Smoke's keen eyes searched the place. He hadn't seen any sign of movement so far. No dogs had come bounding out to meet them, barking and wagging their tails, as often happened when strangers rode up to a ranch.

Quietly, Pearlie said, "I ain't much likin' the looks of this, Smoke. Reminds me of a couple of times down in Texas when I come up on places where the Comanch' had been, but got spooked off for some reason 'fore they had a chance to burn the houses down. Everybody there was dead, though. Men, women, kids . . . they even killed the livestock."

"I don't see any bodies," Smoke said, "and it looks to me like there's a milk cow in the shed that's still alive."

"Yeah, I guess you're right. But if the folks this place belongs to ain't dead, where are they?"

He got his answer almost immediately, when one of the shutters over the lone window creaked open. Somebody thrust out a rifle barrel and fired, sending a bullet whistling menacingly over the heads of the three riders.

Chapter 13

"Damn it!" Pearlie exclaimed as he bent lower in his saddle. His hand reached toward his gun.

"Hold it," Smoke said sharply. He stretched out a hand toward Pearlie and gestured for him not to draw the weapon. The foreman stopped his draw with obvious reluctance.

All three of them had pulled their horses to a stop in response to the shot. A voice yelled from the cabin, "Don't come any closer, or the next one won't miss!"

"That fella needs to have a lesson taught to him," Pearlie said. "Somebody who owns a little greasy-sack outfit like this has got no right—"

"He's got every right," Smoke said. "The same rights we do. More, in this case, because this is his land, not ours."

"Well, yeah," Pearlie agreed grudgingly. "I reckon that's true. But I don't like bein' shot at! And I sure don't like bein' shot at and not shootin' back!"

"Just take it easy," Smoke told him. "You two stay here."

"You better not go any closer, Smoke," Cal warned.

"That hombre's liable to drill you next time, like he threatened. He sounded loco enough to do it."

Smoke shook his head and said, "I don't think so. Just because he's a little spooked doesn't mean he really wants to kill anybody."

"It doesn't mean he won't."

That was true, too, Smoke thought, but he wanted to talk to the rancher and he didn't feel like shouting his business all over the country. Again he told Pearlie and Cal to stay where they were, and then heeled the 'Palouse into a walk that carried him slowly and deliberately toward the cabin.

The rifle cracked again. This time the bullet kicked up dirt ten yards in front of Smoke's horse.

"We don't mean any harm, mister," Smoke called when the shot's echoes had faded away. "We just want to talk to you, that's all."

"I got nothin' to say to you dirty coyotes!" came the reply from the cabin. "We had a deal, and you busted it!"

"We don't have any deal," Smoke insisted. "We've never even met before."

He had kept the 'Palouse moving while he talked, and now he was within fifty feet of the cabin. He could see a narrow slice of face through the gap between the shutters. That didn't allow him to make out many details, but he thought he saw fear in the eye that peered over the rifle's barrel.

"Listen," Smoke went on, "I promise you we're not who you think we are, and we don't mean you any harm."

"You think I'm gonna believe that lie, after what happened to my Sara Beth?"

Smoke reined in and shook his head.

"I don't know what you're talking about, mister. It's

been more than a year since I've been in this valley. I didn't even know there was a spread here."

The man in the cabin didn't respond right away. After a long moment of silence, he said, "You ain't part of that no-good bunch who's been drivin' cattle up the valley to Bitter Springs?"

"They're the varmints I'm looking for," Smoke replied, letting a hard edge come into his voice. "If you have a grudge against them, then we should be friends, because so do I." He paused. "Those were my cattle they stole."

"Then you're—" The man stopped short for a second, then went on. "You just stay right there. Don't move."

"Fine," Smoke said, although he was getting slightly impatient with this.

The rancher withdrew the rifle, but he didn't close the shutter. Instead, he disappeared, but a moment later a different face peered out through the gap. Smoke couldn't be sure, but he thought this one belonged to a woman.

Sensing that she was studying him, he remained still in the saddle and let her take a good look. A minute or so went by, and then she withdrew from the window.

After another minute, the cabin door swung open and a tall, rawboned man stepped outside. He still had the rifle in his hands, but it was pointing toward the ground.

"My daughter says you ain't one of the polecats who chased her," the man said. "She couldn't see your friends back yonder quite as well, but she don't think they were part of the bunch, neither."

"They weren't," Smoke said. "I can promise you that. When did it happen?"

"Early this mornin', just before the sun come up. Our milk cow got loose and strayed off up the draw into the valley. She's done that before. Sara Beth went lookin' for her, and she saw a herd of cows bein' driven north. Three fellas who were with the herd spotted her and come after her on horseback, a-whoopin' and a-hollerin'. Vile, nasty things they yelled at her, too, and I ain't doubtin' for a second that if they'd caught her, they would've done everything they threatened to."

"You're probably right. I'm sorry that happened. My friends and I didn't have anything to do with it, though."

The rancher nodded slowly and said, "I reckon I believe you. Are you really Smoke Jensen?"

"I am," Smoke said with a faint smile.

"Well, come on in, then, and the rest of your bunch is welcome, too. We ain't got much, but I can have Sara Beth put on a pot of coffee and you're welcome to water your horses."

Smoke's friendly smile widened.

"We're much obliged to you for the hospitality, Mister . . . ?"

"Hannon. Ezra Hannon." The man tucked the rifle under his arm, clearly no longer interested in fighting. "Sorry for takin' those potshots at you."

"You were spooked," Smoke said. "Given the circumstances, I don't blame you. Likely I would have been, too."

Ezra Hannon shook his head and said, "With everything I've heard about you, I reckon it'd take the Devil his own self to spook you, Mr. Jensen." He paused. "And that's just what you're liable to find if you're headed to Bitter Springs."

* * *

A few minutes of conversation filled Smoke in on what had happened. Ezra Hannon, who had been operating this ranch for the past year with the help of his daughter, Sara Beth, and a single hired hand, a Mexican who lived in a *jacal* farther up the draw, had struck an uneasy truce with the rustlers. Hannon had encountereded them driving Sugarloaf cattle up the valley the last time they had struck Smoke's herd, and the men had warned Hannon that they would kill him and his daughter if he told anyone about what he had seen.

"But you're telling me," Smoke pointed out.

Hannon gave a disgusted snort.

"They said they'd leave me and Sara Beth and Pablo alone if we did like they told us," he said. "As far as I'm concerned, they broke the deal first. Anyway, now that you're on their trail, I don't figure I'll have to worry. You'll wipe that sorry bunch right off the face of the earth."

"I plan on getting my cattle back, that's for sure," Smoke said. He smiled at the young woman who handed him a cup of coffee. "Thank you, Sara Beth."

She wasn't much more than a girl, still pretty even though the hard frontier life was starting to put hollows under her eyes and lines on her face that shouldn't have been there on someone not yet out of her teens. She still looked shaken from her experience early that morning.

"How did you get away from the men who chased you?" Smoke asked her.

She cast her eyes toward the cabin's hard-packed dirt floor.

"I know a hidin' place," she said in a voice that was

little more than a whisper. "A little hole in the side of a gully. I pulled some brush over it and they couldn't even tell it was there."

"That was quick thinking," Smoke told her.

She glanced up at him, her eyes lighting with pleasure as she did so. In the hardscrabble existence she and her father lived here, she probably didn't get a lot of praise.

Smoke didn't want to encourage her to develop a crush on him, so he turned back to her father and asked, "How come you knew who I am without me telling you?"

"Shoot, you reckon there's anybody in this part of the country who ain't heard of Smoke Jensen?" Hannon said. "Probably everybody west of the Mississippi knows who you are, and plenty east of there, too. And when you get right down to it, we're neighbors."

Smoke chuckled.

"That's true. We've just got that big old ridge between us."

Sara Beth spoke up again, saying, "That ain't all, Mr. Jensen. When I was hidin' from those fellas this mornin', I heard 'em talkin' about you."

"What did they say?" Smoke asked.

"They were mighty pleased with themselves, rustlin' cattle from somebody famous like you. They said you'd never find out how they were gettin' the cows off of your range."

"That was mighty confident of them," Smoke said.

"How *do* they get those cows over the ridge?" Hannon asked. "I didn't think there was any way."

Smoke hesitated, but only for a second. Ezra Hannon struck him as an honest man, and Smoke prided himself on being a good judge of character.

"They didn't bring the cattle over the ridge," he said.

"There's a tunnel *through* it. An old underground river, from the looks of it. The far end of it was sealed off until recently, I'm pretty sure of that."

"A tunnel?" Hannon repeated. "I never saw anything like that."

Smoke used his thumb to point south.

"It's three or four miles back in that direction, at the top of a rocky slope."

"Well, that explains it. My range don't run that far, so I don't have any call to go down yonder." The rancher scratched his jaw. "Although I've been down there a few times, lookin' for stock that strayed. You'd think I would have seen it."

"You'd think so," Smoke agreed. "Maybe this end of it was covered up until recently, too."

Sara Beth looked at her father and asked, "Pa, you think this has anything to do with that blastin'?"

"You know, you might be right," Hannon said.

"Blasting?" Smoke asked. "Somebody was using dynamite down there?"

"Yeah, a couple of months ago. We heard the explosions. Sounded like thunder, but there wasn't a cloud in the sky."

"Did you ever see anybody, or have any idea who was doing it?"

"Nope. Just heard those big ol' booms."

That was something to think about, Smoke mused. An explosion on the western side of the ridge could have exposed this end of the tunnel.

The question was, who in these parts had been using dynamite a couple of months ago?

He had a hunch that when he found out the answer, he would also find the kingpin behind the rustling.

Chapter 14

Smoke and his men were on their way again before midday, leaving the Hannon ranch behind them.

"That Sara Beth gal is sort of pretty," Cal ventured as he rode beside Smoke and Pearlie.

The foreman hooted with laughter.

"Sweet on her, are you?" he asked Cal. "I'm sure her pa would let you marry her. He'd get an unpaid ranch hand out of the deal, to help him run that little greasy-sack outfit."

"Dadgum it, nobody said anything about gettin' married!" Cal's face flushed. "Anyway, I'm too young to get married. I've still got too many wild oats to sow. I reckon an old man like you wouldn't know anything about that."

"Son, I sowed more wild oats than you'll ever see in your life," Pearlie maintained.

They kept up their banter while Smoke thought about everything the Hannons had said. His instincts told him the answers were waiting for him in Bitter Springs.

It was midafternoon when they reached the flats and

not long after that when the buildings of the settlement came into view ahead. They formed a single block, scattered somewhat irregularly along both sides of what passed for a street.

As the riders entered the town, Cal looked around and started reading some of the signs aloud.

"McKendree's Mercantile and Trading Post. McKendree's Saloon. McKendree's Livery Stable. Looks like one family owns just about everything in town."

"Or one man," Smoke said. It wasn't unusual for the founder of a settlement to dominate its businesses.

The store was the biggest building. It and the two saloons all sported false fronts. The rest were drab, single-story structures built of weather-faded wood.

There was a café to the right, across from the livery stable, that didn't sport the McKendree name on its sign. BITTER SPRINGS CAFÉ, it read simply. Smoke angled his horse toward it, and the rest of the men from the Sugarloaf did, too.

A couple of men sat on a bench on the store's front porch. Smoke sensed their eyes following the newcomers. Over at the McKendree Saloon, a man rested his forearms on top of the bat wings in the doorway and peered over them as smoke curled from a thin black cigarillo clamped between his teeth. Smoke figured there were a number of other eyes watching them as they rode along the street, as well.

He dismounted and looped the 'Palouse's reins around a hitch rack that leaned like it would fall over in a strong wind. It wouldn't hold the horses if they wanted loose badly enough, but these animals were all well-trained and wouldn't stampede without mighty good reason.

"We all goin' in?" Pearlie asked as he and the other men swung down from the saddles as well.

"Why don't a couple of you stay out here and keep an eye on things?" Smoke suggested. "I know you're all hungry since we didn't have any breakfast or lunch, but I'll have somebody else spell you as soon as they've eaten."

Two of the men spoke, volunteering for the job. The others trooped inside, their spurs jingling and their boots thudding on the rough wooden floor.

The Bitter Springs Café didn't look like it did a lot of business. The windows weren't particularly clean, and the curtains that hung over them were dusty. Smoke saw a cobweb or two in the ceiling corners. Half a dozen tables covered with blue-checked cloths sat to the left, with a lunch counter and stools on the right. A board on the wall behind the counter had the menu scrawled on it.

Only one table was occupied. A youngish, sandy-haired man in a tweed suit and a string tie sat at it, but he wasn't eating. He had a lot of papers spread out on the tablecloth in front of him and was marking on some of them with a stub of a pencil.

Another man had taken one of the chairs from the same table and pulled it over next to the wall, where he sat with the chair tipped back and a Mexican sombrero pulled down over his face. He seemed to be asleep.

The third and final man in the café stood behind the counter. The apron he wore told Smoke he was probably the proprietor. Given the lack of business, he was most likely the cook, too, and swept out the place in the morning along with every other chore that needed to be done.

Which wouldn't be easy, because the man had

only one arm. The empty left sleeve of his shirt was pinned up.

He was stocky and florid faced, with gray hair and a mustache. He gave Smoke and the other men a nod and said, "Howdy, boys. You come for lunch? I don't get many customers this time of day, but I got a pot of stew still on the stove."

"Stew will be fine," Smoke said, "especially if you've got coffee to wash it down with."

"I sure do. Sit anywhere you want. I'll bring your food and coffee to you."

"Just set it on the counter," Smoke said. "We can get it."

"Suit yourself. Don't let the fact that I'm a cripple bother you, though," he added bluntly. "I'm used to it. Don't even think about it anymore. Cannonball took this left arm of mine clean off at Antietam, you know. Like to bled to death before they got me to the field hospital. Came pretty close to dyin' there, too." The man shook his head. "Nasty place, hospitals. Just downright nasty."

The man sitting at the table glanced up. Light from outside reflected on the lenses of the spectacles he wore.

"Joe has a talkative nature," he said. "Indicative of the fact that he doesn't see very many people. I think Esteban and I are his only regular customers these days."

"That ain't strictly true, Dr. Kingston," the counterman said. "There's a little mouse comes in here just about every day lookin' for something to eat. He ain't much for payin' his bill, though."

Smoke nodded to Pearlie and the other men, indicating that they should sit down. He went over to the table where Kingston sat and held out his hand.

"Name's Jensen," he said.

"Dr. Charles Kingston," the other man said as he

rose to his feet and shook hands. He was an inch or two taller than Smoke, with broad shoulders under the brown tweed coat. His grip had plenty of strength in it, too.

"You're a medical man, are you?"

"Oh, no," Kingston replied with a shake of his head. "I'm not that sort of doctor. I'm a geologist. I work for a mining company back East."

"This isn't really mining country," Smoke commented.

Kingston smiled.

"Not at the moment, no. But perhaps it will be, someday. My job is to search for areas that hold the potential for future endeavors."

"You think there might be gold or silver around here that nobody's found yet?" Smoke asked.

"Or copper or zinc or any number of other elements that might prove profitable." Kingston nodded toward the papers on the table. "I'll admit, though, that my reports haven't been promising so far."

Joe started setting bowls of stew and cups of coffee he had filled on the counter. Smoke's men helped themselves. Smoke said, "I guess I'd better get some of that food while there's still enough to go around."

"Why don't you come back and join me, Mr. Jensen?" Kingston invited. "You strike me as an educated man." He paused, and then added dryly, "There aren't an abundance of them around here. No offense, Joe."

"Oh, I ain't offended," the counterman said. "I can read and write and cipher, but the things you talk about are as far over my head as Pike's Peak, Doc."

Smoke got a bowl of stew and some coffee and

carried them back over to Kingston's table. He pulled out a chair with his foot and sat down.

"You're wrong about me being an educated man, Doctor, at least if you're talking about formal schooling," he said. "I've learned a lot from friends of mine, though. I used to know a fella who could quote for hours from Shakespeare and Homer, and if you wanted to talk philosophy or natural history, he was your man. Used to be a professor back East before he decided he liked fur trapping better. Not to mention the fact that I'm married to a schoolteacher." Smoke chuckled. "I reckon that's an education in itself."

Kingston smiled and said, "I expect you're right about that. Do you know anything about geology, Mr. Jensen?"

"Dirt and rocks, things like that?" Smoke shrugged. "Only what I've learned by riding over them, and sleeping on them some nights."

"It's a fascinating subject. You can find almost every different sort of geological formation here in Colorado."

"I imagine you can. The state's got all sorts of territory in it." Smoke sipped the coffee, which was strong and hot. "What do you do, go around digging holes?"

"Or blowing them out with dynamite," Kingston said.

That was exactly the question Smoke had been working his way around to, and he hadn't even had to ask it. Kingston had just volunteered the information.

"Then that was you doing that blasting about fifteen miles down the valley a while back?"

Kingston's smile turned into a frown.

"I didn't trespass on your land, did I? I was told that most of the valley is open range—"

Smoke held up a hand to stop the explanation.

"No, I just heard somebody talking about it," he said. "We're not from around here."

"I see. Well, in that case, yes, I did some excavating in that area." Kingston waved a hand at the papers. "But as I said, the results weren't promising."

"Uncover anything unusual, even if it wasn't gold or silver?"

"Not really."

Smoke nodded and started eating the stew. So far the conversation had been casual, but his brain was working furiously, considering the possibilities.

Dr. Charles Kingston didn't seem like the type of hombre who'd be running a gang of wideloopers, but Smoke thought there was a good chance Kingston had uncovered that tunnel through Gunsight Ridge with his blasting. That didn't mean he had to be tied in with the rustlers, because somebody else could have come along and found the tunnel mouth after one of Kingston's explosions revealed it.

On the other hand, the geologist might be the ringleader. Smoke had only known the man for a few minutes, so he couldn't really come to a conclusion about that either way.

If Kingston *was* tied in with the rustlers, or was even their boss, he would know who Smoke was and could easily guess that Smoke and the rest of the men from the Sugarloaf had trailed the stolen cows up here. In that case, Kingston would have to deal with the threat, which meant Smoke and his companions would be in danger as soon as Kingston got word to his gang.

If Kingston didn't have anything to do with the rustling, then Smoke wasn't risking anything by talking to him. But the only way to find out which of those various scenarios was true was to keep probing.

"Did you happen to see anybody bring a herd of cattle through here earlier today?" Smoke asked. There were no pens in Bitter Springs, so the stolen cows weren't being held here.

"No, but I haven't been here all day," Kingston replied. "Esteban and I just got back not long ago ourselves. I was checking out some hills to the east. Esteban's my assistant, by the way. He drives the wagon and helps load and unload the equipment."

Smoke glanced at the Mexican, who still appeared to be asleep. The man could have been pretending, of course.

The café's front door opened, drawing Smoke's attention. The man who came in was about as broad as he was tall. He gave that impression, anyway. His prominent gut extended in front of him like the prow of a ship. He wore a dusty black suit, but nobody was ever going to mistake him for a preacher. His moon-shaped face bore too many marks of dissipation and decadence for him to be a sky pilot. His head was bald under a black derby, and a red beard stuck out from his jaw like a brush.

"Well, well, Joe," he said in a rumbling voice, "this is the busiest I've seen your place in a long time. If you keep it up, you might last another two months before you go broke, instead of just one."

Joe had lost his friendly expression as he stood behind the counter. He said, "What can I do for you, Mr. McKendree?"

"You know what you can do for me. Sell out to me, like a reasonable man."

"If I do that, you'll be one step closer to owning the whole town."

"Why shouldn't I own it?" McKendree demanded, sounding offended. "I founded it, didn't I?"

"That doesn't mean you've got a right to own everything."

"That's exactly what it means," McKendree said. "Well, you'll come around eventually. They always do." The man's piggish eyes swung toward Smoke. "Who's this?"

"I didn't ask his name," Joe said.

Smoke got to his feet and said, "I'm Smoke Jensen, Mr. McKendree. My spread is on the other side of Gunsight Ridge."

"Jensen . . . Oh, I know who you are, Mr. Jensen. I know quite well. What brings you to our little town?"

"I'm on the trail of some stolen cattle," Smoke said bluntly. "The rustlers brought them here this morning and already sold them to somebody." Smoke's lips curved in a thin smile as he added, "You, maybe."

Chapter 15

McKendree's face turned dark red with rage, but his voice was carefully controlled as he said, "Do you know who you're talking to, sir?"

"The biggest man around these parts, I'm guessing," Smoke drawled.

"In more ways than one. I'm Oliver McKendree. Bitter Springs is my town."

"Then you must know everything that goes on around here. You're probably mixed up in it as well, neck deep."

"Be careful, Jensen," McKendree warned. "I don't take kindly to being accused of rustling."

"I don't take kindly to having my cattle stolen," Smoke said. "If you didn't have anything to do with it, you don't have to be concerned, do you?"

McKendree just glared at him without saying anything. Then he looked at the counterman again and said, "Remember what I told you, Joe. I'll pay you a fair price for this place, and you can start over somewhere else." McKendree's beefy shoulders rose and fell. "You could even stay on and run it for me, if you like."

"I don't reckon that's gonna happen," Joe said curtly.

McKendree shrugged again and turned away. With one last hostile glance at Smoke, he waddled out of the café.

When the town boss was gone, Joe said, "No offense, Mr. Jensen, but if I was you I'd saddle up and ride out of Bitter Springs. McKendree's got some tough hombres working for him."

Smoke looked at his men, smiled, and said, "So do I."

"Yeah, but I'm talkin' about professional gun-throwers. I've heard plenty about you. I know you're supposed to be mighty fast on the shoot, but *all* of McKendree's men are. Maybe not as fast as you, but probably faster than those fellas you've got with you. No offense."

Pearlie snorted to show that maybe he had taken a little offense at Joe's warning.

"What about those cows I was talking about, Joe?" Smoke asked. "Did you see them?"

The counterman sighed and nodded.

"Some fellas drove 'em up and held them a little way outside of town. A couple of shady cattle buyers hang around McKendree's Saloon sometimes, and one of them happened to be there. He made a deal with the men who brought in the cattle. Some of them went along with the herd, and the buyer hired a few local boys as punchers, too. They're on their way to Denver right now."

"What about the rest of the men who brought in the cattle?"

Joe looked like he didn't want to answer, but after a couple of seconds he said, "I reckon they're still over at the saloon."

"Thanks," Smoke said with a nod.

"You're goin' over there, aren't you? There's gonna be gunplay."

"That'll be up to the men I want to talk to," Smoke said. "If they tell me what I want to know, there doesn't have to be any shooting."

He figured the chances of that were pretty slim, though, and judging by the gloomy look on Joe's face, so did he.

"You, uh, wouldn't mind payin' for the meal before you go over there, would you?" he asked.

Smoke chuckled.

"We'll finish eating, and you'll get paid, Joe. Don't worry about that."

Charles Kingston started gathering up his papers, tapping them against the tablecloth to square up the edges.

"You're a brave man, Mr. Jensen," he said. "I've only been around here for a while, but long enough to know that Oliver McKendree is a bad man to cross."

"You're leaving?" Smoke asked.

"Going to my hotel room to double-check some of my calculations." Kingston smiled thinly. "Gunfire makes it rather difficult to concentrate on mathematics."

"Yeah, I reckon it would. I didn't know there was a hotel in this town."

"The proprietor of the Deluxe Saloon rents out a couple of rooms in the back. I'm sure Mr. McKendree will buy him out soon, too, and then the policy may change." Kingston looked over at the man in the sombrero. "Come on, Esteban."

The man stirred slowly, sat up, and thumbed back the sombrero, revealing a brown, dull-featured face. He nodded and said sleepily, *"Sí, señor."*

The two of them left the café. Smoke watched them

go, and then finished his stew and coffee, still wondering as he did so about Kingston's motives.

What happened in the next little while might tell him a lot, Smoke decided.

Pearlie sat down beside him and said quietly, "That fella Kingston is a mite suspicious, Smoke. He must'a been the one who uncovered the tunnel."

Cal joined them, turning a chair around so he could straddle it.

"Yeah," the young cowboy said, "but Mr. McKendree seemed a lot more like the sort of fella to be ramroddin' a gang of rustlers. I'm not sure a bunch of owlhoots would ever listen to somebody like Dr. Kingston."

They both had good points. Smoke nodded and said, "I'll take a stroll over to the saloon once everybody's finished eating. That might give us some answers."

"Or some hot lead, anyway," Pearlie muttered.

"You can tell a lot by who decides to shoot at you," Smoke said with a smile.

A short time later, all the Sugarloaf cowboys were finished with their meals. Pearlie said something under his breath about dying with full bellies, but Smoke ignored the comment. He paid the proprietor for the food and coffee, then said, "We'll be seeing you, Joe."

"I surely do hope so, Mr. Jensen," the one-armed man replied.

As the group stepped out of the café, Smoke said, "The rest of you boys stay here for a minute. I'll go over to the saloon by myself. If I make it there all right, you can come ahead then."

"You mean you're gonna slap a big ol' target right on your chest," Pearlie said. "You ain't goin' out in that street alone, Smoke. No disrespect, but that just ain't happenin'."

Smoke thought it over for a second and then nodded. Every so often, Pearlie got so stiff-necked it was just no use arguing with him. This appeared to be one of those times.

"All right," he said. "Let's go. Everybody keep your eyes open."

The two men stepped out of the shade of the café's awning and into the bright afternoon sun. Smoke's eyes narrowed against the glare. His vision adjusted quickly, though, and within a few steps he could see just fine.

That allowed him to spot a tiny reflection from the window built into the saloon's false front when he and Pearlie were more than halfway across the street.

"Smoke . . ." Pearlie said warningly.

"I see it," Smoke replied. "Better split up . . . now!"

They darted away from each other, Smoke going right and Pearlie going left. At that same instant, a shot rang out and powder smoke spurted from the window in the false front. Smoke heard the bullet whine between him and his foreman. It kicked up dust behind them.

If they had turned around and tried to make it back to the café, their backs would have presented easy targets for the bushwhacker. Since they were closer to the saloon, Smoke and Pearlie charged straight toward the enemy without having to talk about the tactic.

The saloon's front windows shattered, spraying glass over the boardwalk, as gunmen opened fire inside the building. Muzzle flame jetted over the bat wings as well.

Smoke drew his Colt as he ran and tipped the barrel up to fire from the hip. Three slugs smashed through the boards of the false front. The bushwhacker dropped his rifle through the opening as he rose up. Then he slumped forward and hung over the windowsill with his arms dangling.

Smoke dived toward the boardwalk. It was raised a couple of feet off the ground, and when he rolled up against it the thick planks offered him some protection from the would-be killers inside the saloon. A glance told him that Pearlie had done the same thing on the other side of the single step leading up from the street.

After the first few seconds, the men inside the saloon were too busy ducking to try to get a shot at Smoke or Pearlie, anyway. Cal and the other Sugarloaf punchers had opened fire, too, sending a volley of lead smashing into the front of the saloon. Some of them retreated into the café, while others took cover behind water troughs, barrels, and a parked wagon.

The men in the saloon weren't going to give up without a fight. As Smoke and Pearlie lay there against the boardwalk's base, scores of slugs sizzled through the air a few feet above them, going in both directions.

Smoke caught Pearlie's eye and pointed toward the corners of the building. The foreman nodded in understanding. He started crawling toward the corner on his side. Smoke did likewise on his side.

When he reached the corner, the angle was bad for the men holed up in the saloon. Smoke was able to leap up and dash along the side of the building. There was a door back here, and some horses tied up under a couple of scrubby trees. He was about ten feet from the door when it burst open and a couple of men charged out holding guns.

They were taking off for the tall and uncut, Smoke knew, since their ambush had failed and the men from the Sugarloaf were putting up a lot stiffer fight than they had hoped for. They forgot about fleeing when they spotted him hurrying along the side of the building, though. Instead, they twisted toward him and their guns came up spouting flame.

That was a mistake, because they were facing perhaps the deadliest gunman in the West. As slugs whipped past him, Smoke fired twice, putting the first bullet in the heart of one man and sending the second one into the belly of the other.

That emptied Smoke's Colt, so he stepped forward quickly and kicked away the weapons the two men had dropped when they collapsed with Smoke's lead in them. The one he'd shot in the chest was already dead, while the gut-shot man was too busy screaming in agony to care about anything else.

Smoke put his back against the wall of the building and thumbed fresh shells into his gun while keeping an eye on the door. No one else came out that way. He heard a couple of shots from the other side of the saloon and knew that Pearlie was doing some business over there.

Then all the guns fell silent.

Smoke waited. The ominous quiet continued for several long moments. Then Cal called from across the street, "Smoke! Smoke, are you all right?"

Smoke didn't answer right away. Instead, he went through the door into the saloon, ducking around the corner of it and going in low and fast with his Colt held ready to fire.

There was no need. Four men were sprawled on the floor in bloody disarray, including the one Smoke had seen watching them when they rode into town.

From a busted window on the other side of the room, Pearlie called, "You all right, Smoke?"

"Fine," Smoke replied. "You downed these men from the window?"

"A couple of 'em," Pearlie said. "The other two were already ventilated by our fellas across the street."

A quavering voice pleaded, "For God's sake, Jensen, don't shoot anymore!"

Smoke looked over and saw Oliver McKendree peeking at him over the top of the bar, where the town boss had taken cover when the bullets started to fly. Smoke smiled tightly and said, "Not so brave now that all your hired guns are dead, are you, McKendree?"

"They're not my hired guns! My men all took off when the shooting started. They said this wasn't their fight." McKendree got to his feet and wiped anxious sweat from his face. "I may have been mixed up in some shady business now and then in my life, but I'm not a rustler, Jensen. I swear it. And I didn't have anything to do with those men opening fire on you. Sure, I let 'em drink here, but what the hell else was I going to do?"

It was a little surprising, but Smoke found himself believing McKendree. Tough gunmen like the hombres scattered around the room in various attitudes of death usually drank wherever they damned well wanted to.

But if McKendree wasn't behind the rustling, that left only one real suspect.

Smoke went to the bat wings, but before pushing them open he called, "Cal, hold your fire! I'm coming out!"

By this time Cal and the other hands had emerged from cover and were gathered across the street. Pearlie waved them over, and they all joined Smoke in front of the saloon.

"I reckon we busted up this bunch of wideloopers, all right," Cal said with the exuberance of youth.

"We still have to round up the boss," Smoke said.

"It's not McKendree?"

"I don't think so." Smoke jerked a thumb at the saloon. "Go drag those bodies out. This town's too small to have an undertaker, so I reckon we'll have to plant them ourselves."

"Where are you goin'?" Pearlie asked as Smoke started walking toward the Deluxe Saloon, Bitter Springs's other drinking establishment.

"To finish the job," Smoke said over his shoulder.

He wasn't going in the saloon's front door. Instead, he headed around to the back. That was where those rented rooms Kingston had mentioned were located. That was where he expected to find the man he'd pegged as the ringleader of the rustlers.

He eased open a narrow door at the rear of the saloon. The short hallway just inside it was dim. Two doors opened on the corridor, one on each side. They were both closed when Smoke stepped in, but as a floorboard creaked under his weight, the door on the right was thrown open and a figure rushed out.

"Señor Jensen, look out!" a Spanish-accented voice cried. "Dr. Kingston, he is—"

Smoke was ready when Esteban jerked a knife from under the serape he wore and slashed at him. The blade would have ripped open Smoke's belly if he had been taken unaware.

As it was, he used the Colt's barrel to turn aside the knife and then stepped in to throw a punch with his other hand. The blow didn't travel very far, but it landed with all the power of Smoke's broad shoulders behind it. The impact drove Esteban's head around and fractured his jaw. He crashed against the wall, bounced off, and landed limply on the floor at Smoke's feet, out cold.

Smoke stepped over the sprawled form and looked into the room Esteban had come from. He saw Dr. Charles Kingston lying on the floor, and for a moment he figured the geologist was dead. He checked, though, and found that Kingston was still breathing. He had a good-sized lump on his head where Esteban had knocked him out with a gun or some other blunt instrument.

Pearlie stuck his head in the door and asked, "All over now?"

"Yep," Smoke said. "Except for trying to get those stolen cattle back."

By nightfall, Smoke had all the details. A sore-headed Dr. Kingston supplied most of them.

"Esteban had to boast a little before he hit me and knocked me unconscious," Kingston explained as they sat in the Bitter Springs Café. McKendree's Saloon was closed for repairs and probably would be for a while. "I never knew his last name until today. It's Larroca. Esteban Larroca."

"Sounds familiar," Smoke said. "He used to run with a bunch of outlaws down in Texas, I believe."

Kingston nodded and said, "That's right. Actually, he was their leader, until the Rangers got on their trail and he came up here to Colorado to lie low for a while. And those are the men he recruited to come up here and start rustling your cattle, Mr. Jensen. I'm sorry about that. But when I saw that old riverbed running through the ridge, it never occurred to me that someone might employ it for that purpose. I never even thought anything about it. I'd seen such formations before."

"But once Esteban explored it on his own and found

out that it ran all the way through the ridge, he figured out right away how to put it to use," Smoke guessed.

"Indeed. I honestly never thought he had the wits for such a thing."

"I imagine that's just what he wanted you and everybody else to think," Smoke said.

"What made you suspect him?"

"I just couldn't bring myself to believe that you were behind the rustling, Doctor." Smoke smiled. "No offense, but you're just too much of a tenderfoot."

"I'll, uh, take that as a compliment, I suppose. What are you going to do now?"

"McKendree was spooked enough after getting his place shot up that he was willing to give me the name of that crooked cattle buyer who took my herd to Denver. I plan to go after him and get either the cattle or the money and see the rest of the bunch behind bars."

"I suspect you'll do it, too," Kingston said.

From behind the counter, Joe asked, "You fellas need refills on your coffee?"

"That'd be good," Smoke said.

Before Joe could bring over the coffeepot, though, Pearlie and Cal came into the café, and they had a familiar figure with them.

"Monte!" Smoke greeted the sheriff of Big Rock. "What are you doing up here?"

"I practically wore out a horse getting here today after a rider from your ranch brought your message to me," Monte Carson replied. "Telegram for you came in early this morning, and I figured you'd want to see it right away."

The sheriff took a piece of paper from his pocket and held it out. Smoke took the yellow telegraph flimsy and unfolded it. He sat up sharply as he read the words printed on it in block letters.

Pearlie saw that reaction and said, "Trouble, Smoke?"

"You could say that," Smoke replied as a grim cast came over his face. "Pearlie, you take everybody but Cal and go after that herd. If you don't catch up to it by the time you get to Denver, you'll have to bring the law in on the deal."

"Sure, Smoke," Pearlie said with a nod. Smoke had every confidence in his foreman. Pearlie would bring back the cattle and see that justice was done.

"What about me, Smoke?" Cal asked. "Am I goin' with you, wherever it is you're goin'?"

"No, you're headed back to the Sugarloaf," Smoke said. "Don't think you've got an easy job, though. You'll have to tell Sally it looks like I'm going to be gone longer than I thought I would be."

"What is it, Smoke?" Monte Carson asked as Smoke stood up, folded the telegram, and stuck it in his shirt pocket.

"Preacher's in trouble," Smoke replied. "Looks like it might be the Indian Ring again."

Nothing more needed to be said.

The look on Smoke Jensen's face said it all.

BOOK THREE

Chapter 16

The two men on the box were wary as the stagecoach rocked along the road between Pine Knob and Buffalo Crossing, a couple of Wyoming settlements that served as stops on the line that ran from Laramie to Rock Springs. The jehu handling the lines had to watch the road and his team, of course, but even so his gaze darted frequently from side to side, on the lookout for trouble.

The shotgun guard beside him was even more watchful. The man sat stiff and straight, and his hands were clutched tightly around the Greener he carried. From time to time, he licked his lips nervously, tasting the dust that coated them.

These two men had good reason to be nervous. In the past six weeks, the stagecoach on this run had been held up three times. Another holdup attempt was due.

That wasn't the worst of it, though. In the first robbery the driver, riding alone without a guard, had been killed when he tried to fight off the bandits. The coach had had a guard on it when the robbers struck the second time, and he was shot and killed from an ambush before they stopped the coach. On the most recent occasion, the driver and guard had put up a running fight, and both men had been shot off the box and left to die in the dusty road as the outlaws chased down the runaway team and stopped it.

So it was clear that working for this stage line, at least on this particular run through some pretty rugged country, was a dangerous proposition. Some of the employees had already quit, in fact.

No passengers had been killed yet or even injured, just cleaned out of their valuables after the outlaws emptied the coach's strongbox and boot. But people were scared enough that the line's business had fallen off considerably. Most people didn't want to take a chance on what the road agents might do next.

The guard, a big, blond man who still looked young even though he was crowding middle age, turned his head constantly from side to side, watching the rough terrain on both sides of the road.

"I tell you I don't like it, Wes," he said. "There's a hundred places for those varmints to hide out there. They could be drawin' beads on us right now."

The driver was a grizzled old-timer whose wizened expression said that he had seen it all. He grunted and told the guard, "You worry too much, Tobe. If there's a bullet out there with your name on it, there ain't a damned thing you can do to stop it."

Despite Wes's fatalistic words, he kept almost as close an eye on their surroundings as Tobe did. He didn't want to die, either.

The coach started up a long incline. At the top was a pass between a couple of steep, rocky hills. On the other side of the pass, the road dropped down to a broad flat, and on the other side of the flat, about three miles away, lay the settlement of Buffalo Crossing. Once they made it that far, Wes and Tobe would turn the coach over to another driver and guard who would take it on to Rock Springs.

"We're almost past the worst of it," Tobe said as the coach rocked on its wide leather thoroughbraces. It was empty today, no passengers, which was becoming more and more common as news of the holdups spread. The box had a shipment of banknotes in it, though, bound for the bank in Buffalo Crossing, so the coach was still a tempting target for thieves, despite the lack of any passengers to rob.

"Dadgum it!" Wes burst out. "Ain't you never heard of a jinx, you lop-eared hog walloper?" As he guided the coach into the pass, he continued angrily, "When you might have people gunnin' for you, never say anything about being safe!"

"I never said anything about us bein' safe," Tobe replied. "I said we were almost past—"

The bullet came out of nowhere and smashed into his left shoulder, driving him back against the top of the stage. He cried out in pain and dropped the shotgun. The butt hit the floorboards hard enough to make one of the barrels discharge with a deafening roar. The load of buckshot went almost straight up into the air, narrowly missing Tobe and Wes.

Writhing from the pain of his wound, Tobe almost fell off the coach as Wes whipped up the team and shouted at them. The horses lunged forward, making the stagecoach lurch violently. Tobe was clutching instinctively at his injured shoulder, but he had to let go of it and grab hold of the seat to keep from tumbling off the side.

At the same time, a steadily growing rumble competed

with the thundering hoofbeats of the team. A couple of boulders rolled down from each side of the road. They smashed down into the trail, partially blocking it. Wes had to haul back hard on the reins to keep the team from running into the rocks.

If he'd had more time, he might have been able to steer around the boulders, he realized with sinking spirits. But he didn't have time, because masked men popped up behind other rocks on the hillsides and opened fire on the coach with Winchesters.

Wes dropped the reins and reached down to grab Tobe's shotgun that had fallen beside his feet. One barrel was still loaded. He brought the weapon to his shoulder and fired at the hillside to his right, where powder smoke puffed out from behind several boulders. He didn't know whether it would do any good, but he was going to put up a fight, anyway.

Dropping the now empty Greener, Wes came up in a half-crouch and swept aside his duster to claw at the butt of the revolver in an old holster at his waist. He got the gun out and had started to lift it when he felt a smashing blow against his chest. The impact knocked him down onto the seat again. He made another effort to raise the gun in his hand, but his strength seemed to have deserted him. His muscles wouldn't do what he asked them to.

The gun slipped out of his fingers as a black curtain fell over his eyes.

Beside him, Tobe struggled to draw his revolver, too. The pain from his wounded shoulder made his vision blur, and he couldn't really see much as he looked from side to side at the hills. He made out a couple of shadowy, blank-faced figures, and his brain tried to comprehend why the men had no faces.

It was because their hat brims were pulled down low and they had masks over the lower halves of their faces, he realized a moment later. He summoned up enough strength and determination to draw his gun and point it at one of the figures. The revolver was a single-action, and it seemed to take him forever to pull back the hammer. Finally, the weapon was cocked, and he squeezed the trigger. The gun roared and bucked against his palm.

Tobe had no way of knowing if his shot hit anything, because just as he fired, two more slugs slammed into him. He twisted from the impact and toppled off the seat, dead before he struck the ground beside the front wheel.

Wes still sprawled on the driver's seat, his head fallen lifelessly far to one side.

The outlaws stopped shooting. Echoes still bounced back and forth between the hills for several seconds before dying away.

Then the only sounds were the nervous stamping of hooves from the team and the clatter of small rocks down the hillsides as the outlaws descended toward their victims.

Buffalo Crossing wasn't a bad-looking little town, Matt Jensen thought as he rode into the settlement. Despite his young age, he had done a lot of drifting already and had seen dozens of towns about like this one, with its broad main street and its false-fronted businesses.

Some of the buildings were more substantial, though, including a hotel with two stories, several saloons, a big general mercantile, and an actual red-brick building that housed the bank. Unlike a lot of cowtowns that had an insubstantial look about them, as if they might have vanished completely if you rode back through the area six months later, Buffalo Crossing was beginning to develop a sense of permanence about it. He might stay here for a while, Matt mused.

But not for too long. Matt Jensen never stayed too long in any place.

He angled his horse toward the hitch rack in front of the fancily-named Hanrahan's Drinking and Gaming Establishment. Which, of course, meant that it was a saloon, and the name was really the only thing fancy about it as far as Matt could see. He swung down from the saddle and looped the horse's reins around the rack.

He was a tall, broad-shouldered young man in his twenties, wearing a black Stetson pushed back on his fair hair and a blue bib-front shirt. A Colt .44 double-action revolver rode easily in a holster on his right hip. On his left hip was a sheathed Bowie knife with a staghorn grip. Although both weapons had a bit of a polished, showy look about them, they weren't just for display. Matt could use both of them very well indeed, and had done so many times since he'd set out to become a wandering adventurer.

He had stepped up onto the boardwalk and was about to push through the bat wings into Hanrahan's place when a bit of fast motion seen from the corner of his eye caught his attention. Turning his head to look, he saw that a young woman had come out of the building next to the saloon and was pacing back and forth with an agitated attitude that said she was upset about something.

Matt liked to think he was in the habit of minding his

own business, but both his adopted brother Smoke and their mentor Preacher would have snorted in disbelief if they'd heard him say that. He supposed he was sort of curious about things; that was one reason he had become a drifter. When he saw something interesting he had a tendency to investigate it, even when that led him into trouble.

The girl who was moving around in the street was definitely interesting.

Matt had thought she was just a kid at first glance, but a closer look revealed that while she might be small, she was a full-grown woman with a woman's curves under the jeans and flannel shirt. Rich auburn hair fell in waves around her shoulders, and when she turned so that her face was toward him, he saw a light dusting of freckles across her cheeks. She paid no attention to the tall stranger standing in front of the saloon, but instead swung around and continued pacing.

Matt started to head on into the saloon, going so far as to rest his left hand on the bat wings to swing one side open. But then he stopped, giving in to an impulse, and went along the boardwalk.

The young woman turned again to come back toward him, and now that he was closer he could tell she had green eyes that went well with the freckles and red hair. She took more notice of him this time, frowning for a second before she turned away.

Matt read the lettering on the window of the building from which the redhead had emerged: LARAMIE STAGE LINE. In smaller letters under that was *Buffalo Crossing Station*. And in still smaller letters, *E.A. Hanrahan, Station Manager*.

He wondered if the Hanrahan who managed the stagecoach station also owned the saloon. It certainly seemed possible. If not, the two men were bound to be related.

Just past the office was a barn that no doubt also belonged to the stagecoach line. As Matt propped a shoulder against one of the posts holding up the awning over the boardwalk, a skinny old-timer in overalls and a battered hat limped out of the barn's open double doors and said, "Now, Miss Emily, there ain't no use in gettin' yourself all worked up into a state just yet. We don't know what your pa's gonna find out there. We got to hope for the best."

The redhead stopped and glared at the old man.

"We know good and well what he's going to find," she said. "The stage has been held up again." Her voice trembled a little from strain as she added, "We can only pray that Wes and Tobe haven't been killed."

Matt didn't like the sound of that. He straightened from his casual pose. The redhead's eyes darted toward him.

"Well?" she challenged. "Are you just going to stand there, or do you have something to say?"

"Didn't mean to eavesdrop," Matt said, "but I couldn't help but hear about your trouble, ma'am. I'm sorry."

"It's miss, not ma'am," she snapped. "Are you in the habit of going around offering condolences to strangers?" Before Matt could answer, she drew in a sharp breath and shook her head. "I'm sorry. I didn't mean to be rude. I'm just upset right now, that's all."

"Sounds like you've got a right to be," Matt said as he hooked his thumbs in his gun belt. "I've ridden shotgun on stagecoaches before. There's not much I hate more than road agents."

His words sparked an obvious interest in her eyes.

"You're a shotgun guard?" she said. "You wouldn't be looking for work, would you?"

"I'm afraid not," Matt told her. He still had enough money in his poke for supplies, and a little left over that he might be able to run into an even bigger stake in a poker game. Most of the time he didn't hire on to work for wages unless he really needed to.

"I'm sorry again," she said. "Clearly, you heard enough to know that we've been having problems with bandits. Several of our employees have been killed in gunfights with the outlaws. I had no right to ask you to risk your life like that when I don't even know you."

Matt took that as a cue. He took off his hat and said politely, "Matt Jensen, miss. It's a pleasure. I just wish I was making your acquaintance under better circumstances."

She cocked her head a little to the side as she looked at him for a second and then said, "Oh, you're a charmer, aren't you? I know your type."

"I didn't mean to—"

She stopped him with a wave of her hand.

"No need to apologize. I don't suppose you can help it. I'm immune, though. By the way, I'm Emily Anne Hanrahan. And yes, I know it rhymes."

"Emily Anne . . ." Matt repeated. He glanced at the window of the stagecoach station office. "As in 'E. A. Hanrahan, Station Manager'?"

"That's right. Do you have a problem with that, Mr. Jensen?"

He figured she would take offense if he told her she was too young, too female, and too blasted cute to be running a stagecoach station, so he just shook his head and said, "No, ma'am . . . I mean, Miss Hanrahan."

Besides, he told himself, judging by the intelligence

and the fire he saw in her eyes, those were unfair judgments anyway. He could tell just by looking at her that she was perfectly capable of running a stage station.

In hopes of distracting her from her current troubles, at least for a moment, Matt inclined his head toward the saloon and went on, "I reckon you're related to whoever owns Hanrahan's Drinking and Gaming Establishment? Or do you run it, too?"

"It's my father's," she said. "He owns this building and the barn, too, and has the contract with the stage line, but he's given me free rein to run the station. Not that any of this is your business, Mr. Jensen."

"No, it's not," Matt agreed. "I was just curious, that's all." He shrugged. "Some folks might say it's one of my failings."

Before Emily could respond to that, the old-timer who had come out of the barn said excitedly, "Here comes the stage!"

Matt and Emily both turned to look toward the eastern end of town, where a big Concord stagecoach was rolling toward the station with a saddle horse tied to the back and trailing along behind it. The coach was painted red with yellow trim and brass fittings, although the thick layer of dust that coated it muted the colors and dulled the shine. A large, beefy man in a brown tweed suit was on the box, handling the team. He wasn't wearing a hat, which revealed that he had thinning gray hair.

"Oh, no," Emily said in a hollow voice. "I don't see Wes and Tobe."

"Now, that don't have to mean nothin'," the old hostler said. "Could be they're ridin' inside."

"They wouldn't be riding inside unless they were hurt," Emily said. "And even if he was hurt, Wes wouldn't let somebody else handle his team unless . . . unless . . ."

She couldn't go on, but Matt knew what she meant.

The coach drew quite a bit of attention as it came along the street. Several people trotted after it on foot. Men called out questions to the driver, who just shook his head and didn't reply. He guided the coach directly to the station and brought the team to a halt in front of the barn.

"Seamus?" Emily asked in a hesitant voice. "What about Wes and Tobe?"

The man jerked his head toward the passenger compartment. The old hostler sprang over to the coach's door with an agility that belied the limp Matt had seen earlier and twisted the catch to open it.

When he did so, an arm fell out and dangled limply. Matt could see where blood had run down over the hand at the end of that arm and dried, leaving a grim trail.

"Tobe . . . ?" Emily whispered.

"Aye," said the big man on the driver's box. "And Wes is in there, too, lass. Both gone."

For a second, Matt saw tears shine in Emily's green eyes. But then she gave a determined shake of her head, and the tears were gone. Although her fair complexion was a bit paler than it had been a moment earlier, her face was composed and determined.

The big man climbed down wearily from the box. When his feet hit the ground, he seemed to notice Matt for the first time. His eyes, deep-set in pits of gristle, narrowed with suspicion, and he barked, "You! Did you have anything to do with this? Because if ye did, I'll tear ye limb from limb, as the Good Lord is my witness!"

Chapter 17

The man's hostility took Matt by surprise. He frowned and said, "Why would you think that?"

"Because I don't know you, mister, and it'd be just like the spalpeens behind this outrage to send somebody into town to spy on us and make sure nobody's on to 'em!"

The man clenched big, blocky fists and took a step toward Matt. Emily laid a hand on his arm and said, "Take it easy, Seamus. This fella just rode into town, and he didn't seem to have any idea what's been going on around here."

"Aye, and that's just what the villain would want you to think, isn't it?" Seamus demanded with a snort of derision.

Matt remembered what the old-timer had said about Emily's father going to check on the stagecoach. Seamus appeared to be alone, so that had to be him despite the fact that Emily called him by his first name.

"Listen, Mr. Hanrahan," Matt said, taking a guess on the man's identity. "Your daughter is right. I had no idea you were having trouble with outlaws. I just found out about it when I heard her talking to this old fella."

"Name's Ezekial," the hostler said. "Like the hombre in the Bible."

Seamus Hanrahan ignored him and poked a blunt finger against Matt's chest.

"Give me one good reason why I should believe you, boyo," he said.

Matt ignored the impulse to grab hold of the finger Hanrahan had just used to jab him and break it. Instead, he said, "I don't have any reason to lie. I just got here, like your daughter said."

"And we have no proof of that, now do we?" Hanrahan insisted.

This argument was futile and appeared destined to get even more so, but at that moment the crowd that had gathered around the stagecoach parted to let a newcomer through. The man was medium height and stocky, with a gray mustache. A badge was pinned to his vest.

"What happened, Seamus?" he asked. "One of your coaches get hit again?"

"Aye," Hanrahan rumbled. "A puncher rode into town and told Emily that he'd seen the coach stopped up in Tomahawk Pass. Said it looked like there'd been trouble. So I rode out to check."

Emily said, "I should have gone. It was my responsibility. I knew the coach was late."

"Blast it," the lawman muttered. "Why doesn't anybody come and tell *me* about these things? I'm supposed to be in charge of keeping the peace around here."

"Well, when it comes to these holdups, ye haven't

done a very good job of it lately, have ye?" Hanrahan asked, which made the star packer flush angrily.

Hanrahan didn't wait for the lawman to answer. Instead, he waved a hamlike hand at Matt and continued, "If ye really want to do something, ye'll arrest this fellow and make him talk. He's part of the gang."

The utter conviction of Hanrahan's words made Matt grunt in surprise. He said, "That's the first I've heard about it. Why have you got it in your head that I'm an outlaw?"

"Because I don't know ye, and ye come sniffin' around my daughter, tryin' to worm information out of her like a no-good spy!"

"You've jumped to a conclusion that's all wrong, Mr. Hanrahan."

The lawman turned to Matt and said, "I don't believe I've seen you in Buffalo Crossing before, mister. Mind telling me who you are and what you're doing here?"

For a second Matt wanted to be contrary and refuse to answer the man's questions, but that would just make matters worse, he supposed. He said, "My name's Matt Jensen. As for what I'm doing here, I'm just passing through. This looks like a nice little town and I was thinking about spending a few days here before I drift on, but now I'm not so sure. Place doesn't seem quite as friendly anymore."

He cast a meaningful glance toward Seamus Hanrahan.

"Matt Jensen, you say?" the lawman asked in an interested tone.

"That's right."

"You know the name, do ye, Sheriff?" Hanrahan demanded. "The young scut's wanted by the law, isn't he?"

"On the contrary," the sheriff answered briskly. "As far as I've ever heard, Matt Jensen's always been on the side of the law. He even received a commendation from the governor of Colorado a while back for rescuing a young woman and busting up an outlaw gang. Am I remembering that right, Mr. Jensen?"

Matt shrugged and said, "Close enough." His natural modesty wouldn't let him boast about it.

"Not only that," the lawman went on, "but his brother is Smoke Jensen."

That started some murmurs in the crowd. Most people on the frontier had heard of Smoke. Even Hanrahan obviously recognized the name.

The burly saloonkeeper wasn't ready to admit defeat, though. Instead, he blustered, "That's all well and good, but we got no way of knowing this young scalawag is tellin' the truth about bein' Matt Jensen."

"That's how he introduced himself to me before you got back to town," Emily said. "I'm not sure why he would have had any reason to lie about it."

Her father glowered at her for a second.

The sheriff said, "I remember seeing pictures in the paper when they had that celebration down in Denver I was talking about. This is Matt Jensen, all right, Seamus, and I doubt very seriously if he's mixed up with a gang of stagecoach robbers and killers."

"Maybe not," Hanrahan muttered with ill grace, "but what was I supposed to think when I come back into town and find a stranger talkin' to me daughter?"

"He could tell I was upset, and he asked me what it was all about," Emily explained. "That's all, Seamus."

As pretty as Emily was, Matt thought, Hanrahan ought to be used to young men trying to talk to her by now. Maybe that was part of the problem. Maybe Hanrahan was tired of trying to fend off a bunch of suitors for Emily's affections.

The lawman said, "All right, now that we've got that settled, tell me what happened, Seamus." His face was grim as he looked through the coach's open door. "I see they got Tobe and poor old Wes."

Hanrahan heaved a heavy sigh and said, "Aye. Wes was still on the driver's box, and Tobe was lyin' beside the coach. Both dead. Shot up pretty bad. I found the strongbox on the ground nearby, empty. They'd busted the lock off it with a shovel or a pick, something like that, the filthy buzzards."

"What about the passengers?"

"No passengers on this run," Hanrahan replied with a shake of his head. "And thank the Lord for that, although for the company's sake I hate to see folks afraid to ride the stage."

A man in the crowd said, "You can't really blame them for feeling that way, Seamus. With those killers on the loose, it might be worth a man's life these days to ride the stage. If I was married, I sure wouldn't let my wife and kids ride it, either."

Several men called out their agreement with him.

"Were they carrying something valuable in the strongbox, Seamus?" the sheriff asked.

Hanrahan glanced around at the bystanders as if he didn't want to answer that question in front of them . . . which in a way was a pretty plain answer, Matt thought. There had been something in that strongbox worth stopping the stage and killing two men for, all right.

"I'll come to your office and make a full report, Thomas," he said. He took hold of the dead man's dangling arm and lifted it carefully to place it back inside the coach. "First, though, I have to see to havin' these poor lads tended to properly."

"Sure," the sheriff said with a nod. "Come to the office whenever you're ready." He turned to Matt and went on, "In the meantime, Mr. Jensen, it'd be my pleasure to buy you a drink."

Matt was thirsty after spending a dusty day on the trail. That was why he'd headed for the saloon in the first place.

Besides, having a drink with the lawman would be a good way of finding out exactly what was going on around here, and his curiosity was still aroused.

"And it would be my pleasure to accept, Sheriff," he said with a nod.

A few minutes later the two men were sitting at a table in Hanrahan's with mugs of beer in front of them. The sheriff thumbed back his hat, took a long swig, and sighed.

"We haven't been formally introduced," he said. "My name's Thomas Blocker. Been sheriff around here for a while. And like I said out there, I know who you are."

"I appreciate you speaking up for me," Matt said. "Mr. Hanrahan was bound and determined that I was part of the gang holding up his stagecoaches."

"Seamus Hanrahan is a good man, but his head's like a block of stone in more ways than one," Sheriff Blocker said with a chuckle. "Once he gets an idea in it, you almost need dynamite to blast it out." He paused. "Just for the record, you *aren't* a spy for the gang, are you?"

Matt shook his head and said, "Like I told both Hanrahan and his daughter, I just rode into town a little while ago and didn't know anything about the robberies until I heard Miss Hanrahan talking about them."

"Emily Hanrahan," Blocker said. "Quite a girl. Always has been. Seamus raised her by himself, you know, and she's a handful. Grew up in a tavern back in New York City, until Seamus came out here for his health. You wouldn't know it to look at him, the big bruiser, but Seamus's lungs aren't the best in the world. He needed drier, cleaner air. And when he got here, what else was he going to do except open a saloon?"

Matt glanced around and said, "It looks like a good one, too."

That was true. Hanrahan's Drinking and Gaming Establishment wasn't the fanciest saloon Matt had ever been in, but it was certainly clean and well-appointed. The brass rail along the bar shone from diligent polishing, as did the banister on the staircase that curved up one side of the big room. Crystal chandeliers sparkled overhead. The floor had sawdust sprinkled on it, as was common, but somehow it seemed neater than in most saloons. In a nod to Hanrahan's Irish heritage, shamrocks were even painted in the corners of the front windows.

"It's a nice place, all right," Blocker agreed. "When Emily got old enough, she wanted to help him run it. Seamus wasn't having any of that. He made a deal with the stagecoach company to locate a station here, and he put Emily in charge of it so she'd have something else to do. She's done a fine job, too. You can't blame those holdups on her."

"I'm a little surprised she's not married," Matt commented. "I suppose her pa runs off any young fellas who come around. He seems the type."

"Yeah, he does," Blocker said with a grin. "But mostly it's Emily's idea. She's pretty picky, from what I hear. After a few of the cowboys who ride for spreads around here came into town and tried to court her, only to go limping back to their bunkhouses with their hides cut up by that sharp tongue of hers, the other young fellas sort of got the idea they'd be wasting their time."

That drew a chuckle from Matt. He had spoken with Emily for only a short time, but he could well imagine that what the sheriff was talking about was true.

"So you're just drifting," Blocker went on.

"That's right," Matt said, nodding.

"Don't suppose you'd care to sign on for a deputy's job, would you? I've heard that you've packed a star from time to time."

"That's true," Matt admitted. "But I'm not looking for a job of any sort right now."

"Can't blame a man for trying. I could use some help tracking down those outlaws. Seamus may not think I'm trying to put a stop to the robberies, but I'm only one man and I've got a lot of territory to cover. I've tried to trail them, too." Blocker shook his head. "This is rugged country with plenty of places to hide. I've lost their trail every time I've gone after them."

Matt thought it over and said, "If you want to try again, I could ride out there with you to . . . what was it Hanrahan called the place?"

"Tomahawk Pass. It's about three miles east of here."

"It's probably too late today to start," Matt went on, "but we could ride out there in the morning and take a look around. Maybe pick up the outlaws' trail."

"And you'd be acting in an unofficial capacity, not as my deputy?"

Matt shrugged.

"That's the way I'd prefer it." He took a sip of his

beer. "Lawmen have to follow too many rules. There's too much paperwork, too."

Blocker laughed and said, "That's the truth. But if you want to do that, Matt, I'd sure be glad for the help. Maybe you've got a better eye than I do. I'd like to think I'm a decent tracker, but I know there are better ones than me."

"I learned from two of the best," Matt said quietly, thinking about Smoke and Preacher. It had been a while since he had seen either of them, and he wondered how they were doing.

As ancient as Preacher was, most folks who hadn't seen him in a long time would be wondering if he was still alive. Matt didn't have any doubt about that. As rawhide tough as Preacher was, Matt wasn't sure but what the old mountain man would outlive them all.

Sheriff Blocker drained the last of his beer and set the empty mug on the table.

"Reckon I'd better get back to the office," he said. "Seamus will be coming in to tell me why those owlhoots went after this particular coach. My guess is that there was something valuable in that strongbox. Money for the bank, maybe. Alton Farnsworth, the president, gets shipments from the bank in Laramie sometimes."

"That makes sense," Matt agreed. "But the outlaws would've had to know it was there."

"Not that big a problem," Blocker said with a wave of his hand. "You may not be a spy for the gang, Matt, but I'll bet they have 'em. All it would take is paying off somebody who works in the bank here or in Laramie."

Matt nodded slowly. He knew the sheriff was right. Outlaws generally had ways of finding out where the most tempting targets were.

Blocker heaved himself to his feet, nodded, and left

the saloon. Matt thumbed his hat even farther back on his head, leaned back in his chair, and stretched his legs out in front of him. He had nursed his beer for about ten minutes when a voice beside him asked, "Would you like some company, cowboy?"

He glanced up, about to politely tell the saloon girl that he wasn't interested right now, when he saw that it wasn't some painted gal in a low-cut, spangled dress who had asked the question.

It was Emily Anne Hanrahan.

Chapter 18

She must have seen the surprise on his face, because she went on, "Don't get excited. Isn't that what women always say to men in saloons?"

"Not women like you," Matt said as he got to his feet. "Of course, I'm not sure I've ever seen a woman like you in a saloon before, Miss Hanrahan."

"Sit back down," she said as she pulled out one of the empty chairs at the table. "And don't bother trying to be flattering. I told you, I'm immune."

She sat down before Matt could help her with the chair. With a mental shrug, he resumed his seat as well.

"I suppose you and Sheriff Blocker gossiped about me," she went on. "He told you all about how my father arranged to have the stage station here so I could run it, didn't he?"

"He may have mentioned it," Matt admitted cautiously.

"Seamus thought I needed something to keep me busy. He knows I'd never be happy sitting around doing needlework and baking pies. Although, I *can* bake a very good pie."

"I'm sure you can, Miss Hanrahan."

"Don't make poems out of my name," she snapped. "It's annoying."

"I didn't mean to," Matt said. "It just sort of came out that way."

"There's nothing you can say to me that I haven't heard before, all the way from 'Girls shouldn't be running stagecoach stations' to 'Gosh, I'd shore admire to marry up with you, Miss Emily Anne.'"

Matt had a hard time not laughing. Emily had sounded just like some lovestruck young cowboy.

"I don't plan on saying either of those things to you," he told her. "You can run all the stagecoach stations you want to, as far as I'm concerned, and I don't have any plans at the moment to marry you or anybody else."

"Good," she said, and she sounded like she meant it. "Now that we have all that straight, I want to ask you again if I can talk you into signing on as a guard. You said you've had experience doing that, and from the way Sheriff Blocker talked about you, you're supposed to be hell on outlaws."

"Sorry," he said. "I've already got a job."

"Doing what?"

He glanced around. Nobody in the saloon was paying any attention to them. A pretty little redhead in jeans and a man's shirt might be an uncommon sight in a saloon as far as he was concerned, but the people of Buffalo Crossing were probably used to seeing Emily in here since she was the proprietor's daughter. Confident that no one was trying to eavesdrop on their conversation, Matt said, "I'm going to help the sheriff try to track down those road agents."

"You're going after the robbers?" Emily's auburn eyebrows arched in surprise as she asked the question.

"That's right. Sheriff Blocker and I plan on riding out to Tomahawk Pass first thing in the morning."

"Then you're going to be his deputy."

Matt shook his head.

"Nope. I'm lending a hand just as a citizen. I told him the same thing I told you, I'm not looking for a real job."

"All right," she said with a sigh. "But the return run from Rock Springs to Laramie will be passing through here in a couple of days, and right now I don't have a driver or a guard to take it. My father can drive if he has to, but I'd hate to send him out there alone."

Matt knew she was trying to play on his sympathy. Unfortunately, it was working. He said, "Let me think about it, if you've got a couple of days before the stagecoach comes back through."

"Sure." She smiled. "I suppose I could ride along with him. I can handle a shotgun."

"Now that's not fair," Matt said, returning the smile.

"I don't worry about playing fair, Mr. Jensen." Emily got to her feet. "I worry about winning."

She strode out of the saloon. Matt watched her go, thinking that she was certainly a spitfire, all right.

But it was all a pose, he sensed, at least to a certain extent. Under that hard-edged exterior, Emily was frightened, and he didn't blame her. The way things were going, her whole world might be on the verge of falling apart around her.

Matt had a hunch he wasn't going to be able to ignore that.

After finishing his beer, he took his horse to a livery stable and made arrangements to leave it there. He went ahead and paid for a week's rent on the stall, figuring there was a good chance he would be around Buffalo Crossing at least that long.

With that taken care of, Matt got a hotel room for himself. The clerk had heard about him—most hotel clerks knew everything that was going on in a town, somehow—and asked, "Are you going to be with us for very long, Mr. Jensen?"

"Don't know," Matt said. "I reckon we'll just have to wait and see. Where's the best place around here to get some supper?"

"That would be Henderson's Restaurant, on the other side of the street in the next block."

"Much obliged," Matt said with a nod.

He had left his saddle at the stable, but he still had his war bag and rifle with him. He put them in his room on the hotel's second floor and then came back downstairs, planning to find the restaurant and get something to eat.

A man was standing at the desk in the lobby, talking to the clerk. As Matt reached the bottom of the stairs, he saw the clerk nod toward him, and the man standing in front of the desk turned toward him.

"Matt Jensen!" he said.

Out of habit, Matt's hand was close to the butt of his Colt. There were already enough men out there with a grudge against him that he never knew when somebody might want to settle a score with him.

This man didn't look like a gunman or an outlaw, though. He wore an expensive-looking charcoal gray suit, a black vest, and a white silk shirt. His cravat had a diamond stickpin in it. His longish brown hair was lightly touched with gray. He managed to be slender and look well-fed at the same time. He was obviously well-to-do.

The man extended a hand and came toward Matt.

"It's an honor to meet you, Mr. Jensen," he said. "My name is Radcliff. Nicholas Radcliff."

Matt hesitated before gripping Radcliff's hand. He didn't see any signs that the man was trying to trick him. If Radcliff did try anything funny, Matt could get his Bowie knife out almost as fast as he could draw his gun, and Radcliff was close enough that Matt could gut him in a hurry if he needed to.

The man didn't do anything except smile and give Matt a hearty handshake, though. He went on, "I own the Artesian Saloon. I was hoping I could buy you a drink."

"I appreciate the offer, Mr. Radcliff," Matt said. "Do you make it to every stranger who rides into Buffalo Crossing?"

"Not at all. But not every stranger who rides into Buffalo Crossing is as famous as Matt Jensen."

"I'm not that famous," Matt said with a shake of his head.

"Don't underestimate your notoriety. You may not be as well-known as your brother, but I assure you, there are plenty of people around who know who you are."

"You know Smoke?" Matt asked.

"I've never had the pleasure. But now I'm acquainted with you. How about that drink?"

"Sorry," Matt said. "I was just on my way to get some supper at Henderson's."

"Even better!" Radcliff said. "I know George Henderson quite well. I'll make sure you get the best table and the best meal in the house. Come along, it's my treat."

Radcliff took hold of Matt's left arm. If it had been his gun arm, he would have jerked free and stepped back quickly, just in case this was a trap. Since it was his left arm, he disengaged it firmly from Radcliff's grip, but without acting like he was being ambushed. He didn't like the saloonkeeper and didn't particularly want to eat supper with him, but he figured the man was just pushy, not a real danger.

"All right," he said, his natural politeness winning over his dislike, at least for the moment.

"And then we can go to the Artesian and have that drink."

"We'll see," Matt said.

They left the hotel and crossed the street, then went along the boardwalk to Henderson's Restaurant. It was a nice place with curtains on the windows and white linen tablecloths, a far cry from the posh eateries Matt had visited in San Francisco but not bad at all for a Wyoming cowtown.

George Henderson, the owner, was a balding, rotund little man who greeted Matt and Radcliff effusively and showed them to a table in a corner next to a potted palm. The location was a bit secluded from the rest of the room.

"Two of your finest steaks with all the trimmings, George," Radcliff said. "And the best bottle of wine you have."

"Sure thing, Mr. Radcliff," Henderson said. "I'll be right back."

"Seems like you're pretty well-known in these parts," Matt commented to Radcliff.

The man waved a hand.

"The Artesian is the best saloon between Laramie and Rock Springs," he said. "That's what people really know." He took a cigar from his vest pocket and offered it to Matt, who shook his head. Radcliff raised his eyebrows and asked, "You don't mind?"

"Go right ahcad," Matt told him.

Radcliff bit the end off the cigar and lit it with a lucifer. When he had it going, he clamped it between his teeth and said, "I have a proposition for you, Mr. Jensen. Or may I call you Matt?"

"Call me whatever you want," Matt said, "but if you're about to offer me a job, the answer is no."

Radcliff grunted in surprise and took the cigar out of his mouth.

"How did you know I was going to offer you a job?" he wanted to know.

"It was just a guess, but two people have already wanted me to work for them since I rode into town, so I figured maybe you were going to make it three."

"I was," Radcliff said. "I could use a man like you."

"Doing what? Tending bar?"

"That would be a waste of your particular talents, wouldn't it?" Radcliff puffed on the cigar again and then went on, "No, I'd be hiring your gun, Matt."

Putting his hands on the table, ready to push himself to his feet and leave, Matt said coldly, "I'm not a hired killer."

"Of course not. What I had in mind was hiring you to protect me. You see, there's someone in Buffalo Crossing who wants me dead. He's already made several tries, and it's only a matter of time until he gets me . . . unless I can hire you to make sure that doesn't happen."

Matt still didn't like Radcliff, but he had to admit he was somewhat intrigued by the man's story. It wasn't what he'd been expecting.

"Just who is it that wants you dead?"

"Oh, you've met him," Radcliff said. "His name is Seamus Hanrahan."

Chapter 19

A disbelieving retort started to spring to Matt's lips, but he caught himself before he could say anything. Seamus Hanrahan hadn't struck him as the sort of man who would send hired killers after anybody, but he had met Hanrahan only an hour or so earlier, he reminded himself. He didn't really know what Hanrahan was capable of, and the fact that the man had an attractive daughter didn't mean a blasted thing.

Henderson came back with the wine and glasses and poured while Matt thought over what Radcliff had just said.

"I'll have those steaks out here in just a few minutes," the restaurant owner said.

When Henderson had gone away again, Matt said, "You must rate pretty highly in this town to get such personal attention from the owner."

"Like I said, George and I are friends," Radcliff replied. "Also, I own stock in the bank, and it holds the note on this place. I'm sure George would treat me and my friends well anyway, but that doesn't hurt."

"No, I don't reckon it does."

Radcliff lifted his glass.

"To an arrangement which will benefit both of us," he said.

"I haven't agreed to work for you," Matt pointed out.

"No, but you didn't refuse outright, either, so I still have hopes that we'll be able to conclude a deal. However, if you'd prefer, we'll simply drink to your health for now, Matt."

Matt nodded and clinked his glass against Radcliff's.

The wine was good, he thought, although he was far from an expert on the subject. As he set his glass down on the table, he said, "I have a hard time believing that Seamus Hanrahan would try to have you killed."

"Why? The man's from the roughest section of New York. I'm sure he was something of a shady character back there, before he came west. He has the second-most successful saloon in this town, and he wants to be first. What better way than by getting rid of the competition?"

"Wait a minute," Matt said. "I thought you looked a mite familiar, and now I recall where I've seen you before. You were in that crowd around the stagecoach Hanrahan brought in this afternoon."

"Guilty as charged," Radcliff said. "Along with half the other people in town."

"And you were the fella who made that comment about it not being safe to ride on the stagecoach these days."

"Well, that's true, isn't it? There have been eight men killed in four holdups, for God's sake. *I'd* certainly be nervous if I had to go anywhere on that stage. Wouldn't you?" Radcliff answered his own question. "Well, probably not, now that I think about it. You're Matt Jensen, after all. But we were talking about Hanrahan trying to put me out of the picture—"

He stopped because Henderson came up, trailed by a waiter carrying a platter with several plates of food on it.

"I hope it's all to your liking," Henderson said as the waiter placed the food in front of Matt and Radcliff. "Let me know if there's anything else I can do for you."

"Certainly, George," Radcliff murmured.

When Matt smelled the steak, he realized how hungry he was. It had been a long time since he'd chewed some jerky and eaten a stale biscuit from his saddlebags for his lunch. He picked up knife and fork and dug in, and Radcliff did likewise.

They ate in silence for several minutes. The food was just as good as the wine, Matt thought, and steak *was* something he knew a little about.

Radcliff was obviously eager to get back to their discussion, though, and eventually he said, "A week ago someone took three shots at me as I was leaving the Artesian one night. I was just lucky they missed."

"You don't have living quarters in the saloon?" Matt asked.

"No, I have a small house on one of the side streets. I like to get away from business concerns at least part of the time."

"Did you report the shooting to the sheriff?"

Radcliff made a face and said, "I did. Thomas Blocker is fine for breaking up fights between rowdy drunks, but that's about all he's good for. He said he would investigate the incident, but if he found out anything, he never told me about it. I'm not sure he even tried."

"Are you sure the shots were aimed at you? Maybe it was just some liquored-up cowboy letting off steam."

"The first one practically parted my hair," Radcliff said, "and the other two bullets came almost as close. I was pretty shaken up by the whole thing." He took another sip of his wine. "But that wasn't the end of it."

"Go on," Matt told him.

"A few days later, someone tried to burn down my saloon. One of my bartenders caught a whiff of the smoke in time, thank God. We were able to put out the flames before they could spread very far. But you could smell the coal oil in the alley behind the building where it started. There's no doubt in my mind that the fire was deliberate."

If coal oil was involved, that was a pretty easy conclusion to draw, Matt thought. In a way, that attempt was more serious than the bushwhacking Radcliff had described. Fire was at the top of the list of things that frontier folks feared, especially those who lived in towns. A blaze could get out of control quickly, and when it did, an entire settlement could burn to the ground.

"If Hanrahan was behind that, he was risking his own saloon, too," Matt pointed out. "Once a fire starts burning, you can't be sure where it's going to go, or how fast."

"I'm sure he thought he was safe because his place and the Artesian are at opposite ends of town. He was counting on the fire being put out before it could reach him . . . but after it destroyed my saloon."

"Maybe. Has anything else happened?"

"Two nights ago, someone threw a knife at me when I

stepped out onto the porch of my place. It barely missed. I can show you the spot in the wall where it stuck."

Matt shook his head and said, "That won't be necessary."

"Then you believe me?"

"What I believe is that this settlement isn't nearly as peaceful as I thought it was when I rode in earlier today."

"All little towns have their secrets, I suppose."

Matt went back to eating. After another few minutes had gone by, he asked, "Did you tell Sheriff Blocker about the fire and the knife?"

"He knew about the fire, of course. It caused quite a commotion. I told him I was convinced it was set deliberately. And I told him about the knife, as well, and suggested it was thrown by the same man who took those shots at me. He promised to look into it."

The note of scorn in Radcliff's voice made it clear that he didn't expect anything useful to come from the sheriff's investigation.

"So what about it, Matt?" Radcliff went on. "Will you help me stay alive and perhaps get to the bottom of this?"

"Here's the thing," Matt said. "I've already promised the sheriff that I'd lend him a hand."

Radcliff looked surprised.

"Doing what?" he asked.

"Tracking down whoever's been holding up Hanrahan's stagecoaches."

"You won't change your mind about that?"

"Once I give my word, I don't go back on it."

Radcliff shrugged and said, "I suppose I wish you luck, then. The trouble the stage line is having is bad for the town, and that means it's bad for my business, too.

But under the circumstances I'm not going to pretend to feel any sympathy for Hanrahan." He paused. "I do feel a little sorry for that girl of his, though. He's saddled Emily with quite a problem, and she doesn't really deserve it."

Matt nodded toward the remains of the meal and said, "I can pay for my own supper, if you want, since I turned down your job offer."

Radcliff laughed.

"Of course not! My invitations were made in good faith, and they still stand. I'd like for you to come down to the Artesian and have that drink with me."

"Thanks, but I reckon I'll pass. I was on the trail for a long time today, and what I really want is to get some shut-eye."

"I understand. Another time, perhaps."

"We'll see," Matt said.

Radcliff drained the last of the wine in his glass and said, "Once you've handled that other chore, if you're still around town, I'd like to talk to you again about my problem." A grim smile touched his lips as he added, "If I'm still alive, that is."

"It's a deal," Matt said.

Matt took a while to fall asleep. The conversation with Radcliff had given him a lot to think about. But when he finally dozed off, he slept well and was up early the next morning. After having breakfast in the hotel dining room, which was simpler and not as good as Henderson's food but still passable, he went to the livery stable and saddled his horse. The hostler gave him directions to the sheriff's office.

Sheriff Blocker was standing on the front porch of the squat stone building that housed his office and the jail, sipping from a steaming cup of coffee. He raised the cup in greeting as Matt walked up leading his horse.

"I figured you'd want to get an early start, Matt," he said. "All right if I call you that?"

"Sure," Matt agreed. "But I reckon I'll call you 'Sheriff.' I was raised to respect my elders."

Blocker chuckled.

"I fit that description, all right. Hard to believe you've done as much as you have, as young as you are."

"I got an early start," Matt said dryly. Like Smoke before him, violence had come early to his life, and he'd had to learn how to stay alive and deal with his enemies.

Blocker upended the coffee cup to get the last drop, and then said, "My horse is in the shed around back. I'll be ready to ride in a few minutes."

He was as good as his word, and five minutes later the two men were on their way out of Buffalo Crossing, heading east toward the hills where Tomahawk Pass was located. Along the way they passed Seamus Hanrahan's saloon, which was open but apparently deserted at this hour, and the stage station, which appeared to be closed.

"Did the westbound stage go on to Rock Springs?" Matt asked.

"Yep," the sheriff replied. "There's been no trouble between here and there, so one of the few drivers Seamus has left agreed to take it."

"All the robberies have been between here and . . ."

"Pine Knob," Blocker said. "That's the next town to the east. It's about twenty miles, over some pretty rugged country most of the way. Like I told you, lots of places for outlaws to hide, and plenty of good spots for ambushes, too."

"What happens if Hanrahan and Emily keep losing drivers and eventually nobody will take this run anymore?"

Blocker shrugged and said, "I reckon Seamus will have to forfeit on his contract with the stage line. It'll be a bitter blow for him and Emily both. I'd hate to see it happen."

"So would I."

"How come?" Blocker asked. "Seamus was pretty rough on you yesterday when you came into town."

"He had a lot on his mind," Matt said. "Besides, he's in the habit of chasing off any young men who come around Emily, like we talked about in the saloon. Put those two things together, and of course he didn't cotton much to me right off."

"And yet you're out here trying to help him."

"I don't cotton much to outlaws," Matt said.

They rode on toward the hills, drawing closer until Matt could see the pass between them clearly. It was about three hundred yards long, but quite narrow, no more than about forty feet at its widest point. Matt studied the twin hills, which were dotted with boulders, scrub pines, and clumps of brush, and commented, "You know, if it wasn't for the rocks and trees, those would look like . . ."

"Yeah," Blocker agreed with a grin, "we'd be calling them the Grand Tetons instead of those mountains up in the northwest part of the territory. As it is, they're called North and South Tomahawk Peak, but don't ask me how they got the names. It's been that way as long as I've been around these parts."

Rugged ridges stretched away from the hills on both sides, making Tomahawk Pass the best route through here. Matt could see why the road ran where it did.

As they approached a couple of large boulders in the trail, he pointed at them and said, "Those are the rocks the bandits rolled down the hill to stop the stage?"

"That's right. Seamus was able to get around them, but he said it was pretty tricky. Old Wes never had time to, I reckon. There was probably plenty of shooting going on by then." Blocker waved a hand toward the hillsides. "They were hidden up there, I'm guessin', on one side, maybe both. Must have opened fire right after they started those rocks rolling. Wes and Tobe never really had a chance, the poor varmints."

"Hanrahan said they busted open the strongbox. Let's take a look and see if we can find any boot prints. Sometimes that's as good for identifying somebody as a picture of them."

"Good idea," Blocker agreed. He reined in and dismounted. Matt did likewise. Leading their horses, they walked over to where the stagecoach had been stopped. They could tell the location from the boulders still in the trail and the welter of hoofprints where the team had come to a sudden halt.

Blocker rested a hand on one of the big rocks and said, "I'm gonna have to come back out here with a team of mules and haul these out of the road."

"Did Hanrahan tell you exactly where he found the strongbox?" Matt asked.

"He said it was about ten feet north of the trail, empty, with the lid busted open. Probably somewhere around there," Block said, pointing.

Matt handed his reins to the sheriff and went over to the spot. He hunkered on his heel to take a closer look at the ground. The surface was pretty hard here, but after a moment he saw a faint impression in the dirt, an irregular shape that might have been part of a boot heel. It had an odd, half-moon mark in it where a piece had been gouged out of the heel, almost like the mark on an outhouse door. . . .

Matt had just leaned forward to take a closer look when something whined past his ear like a giant bee and smashed into the ground in front of him, throwing up dirt.

"Bushwhack!" the sheriff yelled.

Chapter 20

Matt flung himself to the side as he heard the whipcrack of another rifle shot. He didn't know where that bullet landed, but it didn't hit him. He hit the ground on his shoulder and rolled quickly toward the nearest boulder blocking the trail. The shots were coming from the hill on the south side of the road. The big rock would give him some cover.

As he came to a stop, he glanced over and saw Sheriff Blocker crouched behind the other boulder. The lawman had his gun in his hand, but he wasn't trying to return the fire. Matt understood why. The shots sounded like they came from a pretty good distance up the hillside, which put the bushwhacker out of effective handgun range.

"You all right, Sheriff?" Matt called as he climbed to his feet but stayed low behind the rock.

Before Blocker could answer, a slug spanged off one of the boulders and ricocheted with a high-pitched whine. It was a nerve-wracking sound that Matt had heard all too many times in the past. This was hardly the first time he'd been ambushed.

"Yeah, I'm not hit," Blocker answered. "But we're pinned down."

It was true. Blocker had let go of the horses' reins when the shooting started, and both animals had run off down the road. Matt's horse was accustomed to gunfire, so he hadn't spooked as badly, coming to a stop about fifty yards away to crop at the grass growing along the side of the trail.

Matt looked at his Winchester sticking up from the saddle sheath and wished he could get his hands on it. That would have helped even the odds.

"At least they're not on both sides of us," he told the sheriff. "If they had us in a crossfire, we'd be in a bad fix."

"Yeah, but whoever it is can sit up there all day, and if we take a step out from behind these rocks, he's got us."

Blocker was right. Matt knew that if he hadn't leaned forward just when he did, that first shot might well have blown his brains out. It hadn't missed by much.

Matt lifted his hand and placed a couple of fingers in his mouth. He gave a piercing whistle that made his horse jerk its head up. The horse turned to look toward him, and Matt whistled again.

With a shrill whinny, the horse tossed its head, then broke into a gallop and headed back up the road toward them.

The hidden rifleman changed his aim and started shooting at the horse. Bullets kicked up dust around the animal's flashing hooves.

Matt burst out from behind the rock and dashed as fast as he could toward the slope. The bushwhacker must have realized that the horse was just a distraction, because he opened up on Matt again. Matt felt as much as heard a slug rip past his ear, and then he left his feet in a dive that carried him into a small stand of scrubby pines.

The tree trunks gave him enough cover that the odds of the bushwhacker hitting him were low. Also, he was at a slightly worse angle now for the hidden rifleman to draw a bead on.

That didn't stop the bushwhacker from trying. Bullets thudded into the trees near Matt.

The duller boom of a six-gun came from the road, telling Matt that Sheriff Blocker was getting in on the fight, even though the odds of him hitting anything were small. The shots served as another distraction, though, as Matt began working his way up the slope.

He used every bit of cover he could find, including trees, rocks, and clumps of brush. After a few minutes, during which time he climbed probably a hundred feet, he paused and looked back down. He could see the boulders in the trail and realized with a slight shock of surprise that Blocker was looking around the side of one of them at him. The sheriff motioned toward Matt's right.

Matt took that to mean the bushwhacker's location was more to his right. He nodded and angled in that direction as he started moving again.

The pace of the rifleman's shots had slowed considerably, although a slug still ripped through the brush on the hillside now and then. The man was firing blindly, Matt thought. Not only that, but the shots also gave him something to steer by. He could tell that he was getting closer and closer to the gunman.

He came to an open stretch where there wasn't any cover. As he knelt at the edge of the brush, he heard another shot and saw powder smoke rising from behind a jagged upthrust of rock about twenty yards above him. He was within revolver range now but couldn't see his enemy from where he was.

Forcing himself to remain patient, Matt waited. After a few minutes he saw movement as a rifle barrel was thrust over the top of the rock. It tracked toward him and he crouched lower, thinking that the bushwhacker had spotted him.

The rifle stopped. Flame erupted from the muzzle as another shot cracked. Matt knew then that the bushwhacker hadn't seen him. The man was still firing blindly, sweeping the slope with lead in the hope of hitting something.

Matt calculated the odds of leaping from cover and charging up the slope before the rifleman saw him and adjusted his aim. They weren't very good, he decided. He needed something to buy himself more time.

After a moment of looking around, he found a broken piece of pine branch about as long as his arm from the elbow to the wrist. It was fairly thick and heavy. He balanced it in his hand for a moment and decided it would do. Straightening quickly, he drew back his arm and threw it. The broken branch spun through the air, rising above the rocks where the bushwhacker was hidden before it dropped back down among them with a loud clatter.

Matt launched into a run while the branch was still in the air. He heard the racket as it landed, and then a sudden flurry of shots broke out. None of them came toward him, though. He could tell that from their sound. The bushwhacker had heard the branch fall and jumped to the conclusion that someone had snuck up behind him, which was exactly what Matt hoped would happen.

But that bought him only a couple of seconds. He counted them off in his head as he bounded up the slope, then jerked to the side and kept running. Another shot cracked. Matt weaved the other direction. Another leap brought him to the side of the rock. He caught a glimpse of a man's leg and fired on the run.

The bushwhacker yelped in pain. Gravel clattered as he moved hurriedly. Matt angled in toward the rocks. The rifle barrel jabbed into view, but he was ready and fired twice more, sending the slugs sizzling past the Winchester. The rifle flew into the air as its owner pitched backwards.

The man landed on the far side of the upthrust and rolled down the slope. Matt dropped to a knee and covered him, but he had a pretty good idea that the bushwhacker was no longer a threat from the loose-limbed way the man's body was moving.

When the bushwhacker came to a stop and didn't move again, Matt circled behind the rocks where the man had been hidden, just to make sure no one else was back there. The hillside was empty except for the empty shell casings that littered the ground. The bushwhacker had fired more than fifty rounds without scoring a hit. Some of that was due to Matt's skill and experience, but good luck had been on his side, too.

"Matt!" Sheriff Blocker called from the road below. "Matt, are you all right?"

"Yeah, this fella's done for, Sheriff!" Matt shouted back. But just in case that wasn't true, he kept his Colt trained on the sprawled bushwhacker as he carefully approached the man.

The rifleman had come to rest lying on his back. Matt was close enough now to see the pair of bloodstains on the man's shirt, as well as the one on his leg where Matt's first shot had struck him in the thigh. The man's eyes were wide open, staring sightlessly at the morning sky.

Matt had never seen him before.

He recognized the type, though, from the hard-planed, beard-stubbled features. He had swapped lead with enough owlhoots to know one when he saw him.

Blocker came puffing up the hill, still holding his gun. When he reached Matt and the dead man, he stopped to catch his breath.

"You know this varmint, Sheriff?" Matt asked.

Blocker studied the man for a moment, then said, "I don't know his name, but I've seen him around the settlement."

"Any particular place?"

Blocker shook his head.

"Not that I recall. In the saloons, more than likely, maybe in the hash house. But I couldn't say that he hung around any one place. You think he's a member of the gang that's been holding up those stagecoaches?"

"That's the most likely explanation," Matt said. "Could be that the gang left a man here to keep an eye on the scene of the latest robbery to discourage anybody from trailing them."

Blocker grunted and said, "He was tryin' to discourage us pretty permanent like, seemed to me." He looked around. "We'd better find his horse and take him back to town."

"He's not going anywhere," Matt said. "We ought to see if we can pick up the trail of the rest of them."

"You mean leave him here for the buzzards and the wolves?"

"Only until we're on our way back to town anyway." Matt's voice had a hard edge to it as he added, "When somebody tries as hard to kill me as this fella did, I don't worry too much about what happens to him."

"No, that makes sense, all right," Blocker agreed. "We'll see if we can find the signs left by the rest of the gang."

That proved to be a futile effort. Matt and the sheriff ranged all over the pass and the area around it but failed to find any tracks they were sure had been left by the gang's mounts. The road was just too well-traveled, and the surrounding countryside was too rocky.

Not only that, but the first shot that had gone past Matt's ear had struck the ground right where that partial bootprint he had seen was located, obliterating it.

That didn't really matter, he told himself. The way that print looked was etched in his mind, and he would know it if he saw it again. Of course, there was no way to be sure the boot that had left it belonged to one of the stagecoach robbers, but at least there was a chance.

Other than surviving the ambush, they hadn't really accomplished a thing. The incident had stiffened Matt's resolve, though, and by the time they got back to Buffalo Crossing at midday, leading the bushwhacker's horse they had found tied at the top of the hill, Matt's mind was made up.

The bushwhacker's body was lashed facedown over the saddle, and Matt left the sheriff to take the dead man to the undertaker's while he rode toward the stagecoach station. Bringing in a corpse like that caused quite a sensation in town, but the crowd followed Sheriff Blocker and left Matt alone.

Emily Hanrahan was behind the desk in the office when Matt walked in. She must have heard the commotion in the street outside, but she had ignored it. Several ledgers were open on the desk in front of her, so Matt figured she had been going over the station's accounts and didn't want to be distracted from the task.

He distracted her anyway, his entrance causing her to look up from the ledgers. A long lock of auburn hair fell appealingly in front of her face. She brushed it back and asked with a note of impatience in her voice, "What can I do for you, Mr. Jensen?"

"If that job offer's still open," he said, "I'm ready to ride shotgun on that stagecoach of yours."

Chapter 21

Emily set aside the pencil she'd been using. Matt could tell she was surprised by his decision, but she controlled that reaction and sounded only mildly interested as she asked, "What made you change your mind?"

"I rode out to Tomahawk Pass with the sheriff this morning."

"Why would you do that?"

"Just to take a look around and see if we could pick up the trail of those robbers," Matt said. "We didn't . . . but we did get ambushed."

Emily couldn't keep a look of concern off her face. She asked, "Are you all right?"

"Fine," Matt told her.

"What about Sheriff Blocker?"

"He wasn't hit, either. We got the bushwhacker, though. The sheriff's taking him down to the undertaking parlor."

"Then that was the commotion I heard a few minutes ago." Emily leaned back in her chair. "The man's dead, I suppose, or he wouldn't be going to the undertaker's."

"I would have preferred capturing him so we could

ask him some questions," Matt said with a shrug, "but there wasn't really time to worry about that while he was trying to kill us."

"Did the sheriff recognize him?"

"Only as somebody he'd seen around town a few times."

"You mean the outlaws have been coming right into town? That's pretty brazen."

"I reckon they figured it was safe enough."

Emily nodded slowly and said, "Several of the survivors from the holdups mentioned that the bandits wore masks and had their hats pulled low. They knew it was unlikely anybody would recognize them. I ought to go down to the undertaker's and have a look for myself, though."

"Are you sure that's a good idea?"

"I've seen dead men before," she snapped. "A couple of them just yesterday who were friends of mine, remember?"

Matt nodded and said, "It won't hurt to take a look, but I don't expect you'll recognize the fella."

He didn't say anything about the boot print he had seen. He wanted to keep that to himself for the time being. Besides, at this point he didn't know if it really meant anything.

"So that ambush is what made you decide to accept my offer?" Emily asked.

"I don't like it when somebody starts shooting at me," Matt said. "That bushwhacker won't ever do it again, but I'd like the chance to meet up with some of his pards. I reckon riding shotgun will give me that chance."

"Well, I don't know what to hope for. I don't want them holding up any more of our stagecoaches, but at the same time I'd like to see them brought to justice for what they've already done. I think you're the best chance for that to happen, Mr. Jensen."

"Call me Matt," he told her with a smile.

"All right, Matt. And I suppose you can call me Emily, as long as it doesn't give you any ideas."

"You've made it pretty plain that I'd be wasting my time if I did get any ideas."

"Yes, you would." She stood up. "Come on. Let's go tell my father. It looks like he's going to be driving the stage."

"I'm not sure how he'll take the news," Matt said. "He doesn't like me very much."

"He'll like you better once you're sitting on that driver's seat next to him with a shotgun."

As Matt predicted, Seamus Hanrahan was cool to the idea of him going along on the stagecoach's next east-bound run, but Emily said, "You put me in charge of running things, Seamus, and I'm hiring Matt."

Hanrahan didn't argue with that, although it was evident from his expression that he wanted to.

A couple of days passed without much happening. Matt spent some time in the station office talking to Emily, and while she seemed to warm up to him a little, she still kept her distance emotionally. That was fine with Matt. He was looking for outlaws at the moment, not romance.

He also spent some time in Hanrahan's saloon and took advantage of the opportunity to get to know the crusty saloonkeeper better. He hadn't forgotten about Nicholas Radcliff's accusations against Hanrahan.

The big Irishman got more voluble when Matt

worked the conversation around to his early days in New York.

"Aye, it was a rough time there in Hell's Kitchen," Hanrahan said as he leaned an elbow on the bar and talked to Matt. "When I was but a wee lad, the gangs put me to work runnin' errands and carryin' messages for 'em. My da was dead, and 'twas the only way I could help me poor old ma. I shudder to think about some of the things I saw in them days. There was this fella called Big Bill, and since he worked as a butcher he always had this meat cleaver with him, and one time he . . . No, never you mind, I don't want to even think about it.

"When I got older and married Emily's ma, God rest her sainted soul, I was runnin' a tavern that the gang had set me up in, but I knew I had to get out. That was no place to raise a family. As it turned out, Emily's the only family I had, since her ma departed this world bringin' her into it. That just made me more determined to leave New York. I saved up enough to get us train tickets and some left over to start a business out here." Hanrahan waved a beefy hand at their surroundings in the saloon. "And ye can see the results. I started off small, with barely a hole in the wall, and expanded as the years went on."

"You've done well for yourself," Matt said.

"Aye. It hasn't been easy. And goin' into the stage-coach business . . . well, 'twas quite a risk, let me tell you, lad." Hanrahan heaved a sigh. "If I have to forfeit me contract with the line, I don't know what it's gonna do. I might lose everything."

"Maybe if there were fewer saloons in Buffalo Crossing, you wouldn't have to worry about that," Matt suggested.

Hanrahan let out a derisive snort.

"The competition doesn't worry me. No other saloon in these parts can hold a candle to mine. No matter what happens, we'll muddle through somehow, Emily Anne and me. I'll do whatever it takes to make that true."

Matt could tell that Hanrahan was making an effort to sound confident, but the man actually was worried. The question was how far he would go to protect his businesses.

While he was waiting for the stagecoach run, Matt also kept an eye open for a boot heel with that peculiar gouge out of it. He couldn't go around asking men to show him their boots, not without arousing a lot of suspicion and getting some unwanted questions, but anytime he saw a man with his feet propped up somewhere, he took an unobtrusive look at the heels of the hombre's boots.

So far that effort hadn't paid any dividends, and he didn't really expect it to. The chance that he might find the man he was looking for was a longshot at best, but it didn't cost him anything to try.

Sheriff Blocker looked Matt up a couple of days after the ambush and reported, "I went through all of my wanted posters and didn't find that fella who jumped us. That doesn't really mean anything, though. There are plenty of owlhoots out there who don't have paper on them. Or maybe he does and I just never got that particular reward dodger."

"He wasn't shooting at us by mistake, that's for sure," Matt said. "He couldn't have missed that sheriff's badge of yours, shining in the sun the way it was."

"I'm just glad he didn't use it for a bull's-eye," Blocker said.

The day that the eastbound stage from Rock Springs

was scheduled to arrive at eleven o'clock, Matt was at the station early, carrying his Winchester.

Emily looked at the rifle and said, "We've got a shotgun for you to take along."

"I know that and I'll be glad to have it," Matt told her, "but I'm taking this repeater of mine with me, too."

"When there's a chance you'll run into outlaws, you can't have too many guns, I suppose."

Emily was visibly nervous. Matt asked, "The gang hasn't hit two runs in a row before, have they?"

"No, but that doesn't mean they won't. Things are getting pretty desperate for us, Matt. If we're held up again, the company might go ahead and cancel our contract, especially if there are significant losses. They had to make good on the bank shipment from the last time, and they weren't happy about it."

"So there *was* money in that strongbox."

Emily was standing at the window, looking out. At Matt's question, she turned and nodded.

"That's right. You're working for us now, so I guess it's all right to admit it. Mr. Farnsworth, the bank president, was having some cash shipped in from Laramie."

"Is there going to be anything like that in the strongbox this time?"

"I don't know," Emily said. "Nobody's told me anything about it if there is, but it's possible."

Seamus Hanrahan came in a short time later. The big man had traded his usual tweed suit for gray wool trousers and a butternut shirt. He was hatless, but he had a huge, long-barreled revolver tucked in the waistband of the trousers.

He fastened a glare on Matt and said, "If ye be thinkin' of tryin' a double-cross, boyo, know that the first shot from this old hogleg o' mine will blow a hole right through ye."

"Seamus, we decided to trust Matt, remember?" Emily said. "We have to trust *somebody*."

"How come you call him Seamus?" Matt asked. "He's your father."

"Well, I called him Da when I was little."

"'Tis because she's a rebellious, thankless child," Hanrahan said, "and that's her way of showin' her disrespect for her poor ol' da."

"Ha! Just look at him. How could anybody call a big, hulking brute like him Da?"

Matt grinned. The deep affection these two felt for each other was obvious, no matter what they called each other or how many sharp words they exchanged. That was just their way, he understood.

Old Ezekial, the hostler, came into the office and said, "I see the dust from the coach outside of town. She'll be here in a few minutes."

They all went outside to wait. Matt saw the dust cloud rising west of town, too. In a moment, a dark shape was visible at the base of it, and that shape quickly resolved itself into a Concord stagecoach being pulled by a team of six horses. The coach attracted the usual attention from the townspeople as it rolled to a stop in front of the station.

Emily coughed a little as the dust cloud swirled over the four of them waiting in front of the station. When it blew away, Matt saw the driver and the guard climbing down from the box.

"Any trouble, boys?" Hanrahan asked them.

The driver shook his head and said, "Nary a bit. We didn't see anything out of the ordinary, Mr. Hanrahan."

"May the Good Lord let it stay that way," Hanrahan said. "Jake, give that Greener to Jensen here."

The guard handed the double-barreled weapon to Matt and asked, "You're ridin' shotgun from here to Pine Knob, friend?"

"That's right," Matt said.

"Better you than me!"

The driver looked just as relieved as the guard to be leaving the stage. Both men took off their hats and slapped dust from their clothes.

Emily opened the coach door and said, "There'll be a ten-minute stop here, folks, while the teams are changed. You'll find hot coffee in the office, if you'd like a cup."

So there were passengers on this run, Matt thought. He watched with interest as a couple of men and a woman climbed out to stretch their legs. All three were well-dressed. The two men bore a definite resemblance to each other. Father and son, Matt decided. Judging by the possessive way the younger man took hold of the woman's arm as they went into the station, she was his wife.

The older passenger looked at Hanrahan and said, "I know you, don't I?"

"That ye do, Mr. Baxter. I'm Seamus Hanrahan. I'll be handlin' the team between here and Pine Knob."

"I thought you owned a saloon."

"I do. But me daughter's the manager of this station, so I'm helpin' out by drivin' the coach."

The man sniffed.

"You'd better keep us safe. We've heard that road agents have been stopping these coaches. If my son and

I didn't have to be in Laramie on business, I wouldn't be making this trip right now."

"Ye'll be perfectly safe, sir. I guarantee it."

Baxter gave him a curt nod and went on into the station. Hanrahan turned to Matt with a shake of his head.

"'Tis a bit of bad luck," he muttered. "Claude Baxter is a rich man. Owns a piece of several gold mines. And 'tis well-known in this part of the country that he always carries a lot of cash on him. If those bandits know somehow that he's on this coach . . ."

Hanrahan didn't have to finish the sentence. Matt knew exactly what he meant.

Claude Baxter might be too tempting a target for the outlaws to resist, not just because of the money he might be carrying, but also for the ransom he would bring if they kidnapped him, his son, and his daughter-in-law.

The run to Pine Knob had just gotten even more dangerous.

Chapter 22

The stage rolled out of Buffalo Crossing on schedule carrying the three passengers. Before it left, Emily drew Matt aside and said quietly, "I overheard Mr. Baxter talking to his son. They've got ten thousand dollars in gold in the strongbox to buy some mining equipment in Laramie."

"Your father was worried about something like that," Matt told her. "Don't worry, we'll get them through."

"I hope so," Emily said. "If anything happens to that gold, we're ruined. Claude Baxter will see to that."

As the settlement fell behind them, Matt looked ahead to Tomahawk Pass. He said to Hanrahan, "What do you think the odds are they'll hit us in the same place as the last time?"

"They might," Hanrahan said. "But there are plenty of other places along the route where they can set up an ambush."

"You were right about Baxter. He's got ten grand with him."

"Saints preserve us," the big man muttered. He

slapped the reins against the backs of the team. "The man's a fool. That's just askin' for trouble."

Matt agreed. But there was nothing they could do about it now except try to get Baxter and his gold safely to their destination.

His nerves were drawn taut as they entered the pass. Sheriff Blocker had done like he said he would and brought mules out here to drag the boulders out of the road. The trail was clear ahead of the stagecoach. Hanrahan whipped up the team and went through the pass in a hurry, while Matt's eyes intently scanned the hillsides searching for any sign of an ambush.

Nothing happened except for Claude Baxter yelling up from the passenger compartment, "Hanrahan! Why are you going so fast? You're bouncing us around in here like a bunch of beans!"

"Just tryin' to get you where you're goin' on time, sir!" Hanrahan replied.

"Well, slow down a little! We're not in that big a hurry."

Hanrahan slowed the coach, but only after they were through the pass. The road entered a long series of bends curving between more hills that weren't as rugged as the two Tomahawk Peaks. There were still plenty of places the gang of road agents could hide, but none that were set up quite as well for an ambush. Matt stayed alert anyway. He didn't plan on relaxing and heaving a sigh of relief until they reached Pine Knob.

Several miles rolled by. They came to a broad, shallow creek that flowed over a gravelly bed. Hanrahan started the team across the ford.

There were no hills close by to provide hiding places for the outlaws, but quite a few aspens and cottonwoods grew along the stream's banks. Matt cast a wary eye toward them and suddenly stiffened as he saw sunlight reflect off something.

"Better whip up the team, Seamus—" he began.

The sharp crack of a rifle shot interrupted him. One of the leaders threw up its head and screamed in pain, then collapsed. That forced the rest of the team to come to an abrupt halt, leaving the coach halfway across the creek.

"Get down!" Matt yelled as he grabbed his Winchester from the floorboards and threw himself off the box to the left. He landed in the stream with a splash and rolled underneath the coach.

Hanrahan's bulk created an even bigger splash as he jumped into the water. The big man scrambled under the coach.

"Are you hit?" Matt asked.

"No, but the devils came close, damn their eyes!"

Both Baxters, father and son, were shouting and cursing, and the woman screamed as shots continued to ring out.

"Get down and stay there!" Matt called to them. "They're not shooting at you!"

He hoped that was true. From what he had seen so far, it seemed to be. Bullets smacked into the creek around the coach and some of them thudded into the big wheels, chewing splinters from them. Matt figured he and Hanrahan were the real targets. The outlaws would want the Baxters alive.

The water was cold, since the creek was fed by deep underground springs and snow melt. Matt ignored its icy grip flowing around him and thrust the Winchester's barrel between the spokes of the nearest wheel. He spotted a muzzle flash and instantly returned fire. A man flopped limply out from behind the tree where he had been hidden.

"Ye got one of the scoundrels!" Hanrahan said.

"Yeah, but there's plenty more of them," Matt replied, "and there's not enough cover here."

He looked around and spotted a long, gravelly sand bar that stuck up a couple of feet from the water, about twenty yards to their left. No shots were coming from beyond that spot, so Matt thought it might provide enough cover to give them a chance. That would mean leaving the passengers, but Matt hoped they would be safe enough. They were worth a lot more in ransom as long as they were still alive.

Matt pointed out the gravel bar to Hanrahan and said, "Make a run for it, Seamus! I'll cover you!"

"No, lad, I'm too big and slow," Hanrahan insisted. "Ye go first, and if ye make it, I'll give it a try."

Matt was going to argue, but he realized Hanrahan was right. He said, "Did that old horse pistol of yours get too wet to fire?"

"Not a bit! I kept it out of the water."

"All right. Keep 'em busy!"

As Hanrahan opened fire with the big revolver, Matt lunged out from under the coach and sprinted toward the gravel bar. He heard bullets whining around him, but none of them touched him in the few seconds it took him to cover the distance. One last bound took him behind the long mound of gravel and sand. He threw himself down behind it and twisted back toward the stranded stagecoach.

"Come on, Seamus!" he yelled as he opened up on the trees with the Winchester, firing as fast as he could work the rifle's lever.

Hanrahan clambered out from under the coach and

launched into a lumbering run. Matt groaned inwardly as he saw how slowly the big man was moving. He remembered what Sheriff Blocker had said about Hanrahan having bad lungs. The man huffed for breath as he stumbled along.

With a sudden cry, Hanrahan went down. Matt yelled, "Seamus!"

Hanrahan struggled to get up, and then went still. Matt bit back a bitter curse. Emily would never forgive him for letting her father get killed. He liked the big Irishman, too, and was filled with rage toward the men who had cut him down.

Loud splashing drew his attention away from Hanrahan's body. He looked upstream and saw several riders galloping along the creek bed toward the coach. They wore masks and had their hats pulled low. One of them fired, and the other leader in the team screamed and went down.

Matt realized what they might be trying to do, but before he could react, a storm of lead tore into the gravel bank from the riflemen who were still hidden in the trees. As dirt and chips of stone sprayed over him, he had to duck as low as he could to avoid the barrage.

When he dared to raise his head again, he saw that the outlaws had cut loose the two dead horses. A couple of them were on the box now, one handling the reins. He backed the surviving members of the team, then lashed them with the whip and sent them pulling around the bodies of the slain leaders.

They weren't just robbing the strongbox this time, Matt told himself in amazement.

They were stealing the whole damned coach . . . and the passengers inside it!

Before leaving Buffalo Crossing, Matt had filled his

pockets with shotgun shells and cartridges for the Winchester. The shells were useless now after being soaked in the creek, but the rifle rounds would be just fine. He dug out as many as he could and thumbed them through the Winchester's loading gate as the outlaws drove the coach out of the stream.

Lunging to his feet, Matt raced after the vehicle. As he ran, he sprayed slugs toward the trees. He didn't care if he hit anything as long as he kept the men hidden there busy ducking instead of shooting at him. His long legs flashed as they carried him out of the creek. The outlaw handling the reins and the whip urged the team on to greater speed.

The Winchester clicked as it ran out of bullets. Matt tossed it aside, unwilling to carry its weight. His boots weren't made for running, but he poured on all the speed he could as he came up behind the coach.

The other outlaws yelled warnings at the men on the box, but they didn't seem to hear over the thundering hoofbeats of the team. The rest of the gang couldn't shoot at him, Matt realized, without endangering their own men, as well as the passengers. They didn't want to risk that.

Knowing that he would have only one chance at this, Matt leaped. He put all his speed and strength into the jump, which carried him onto the back of the coach. He grabbed at the canvas covering of the rear boot.

His hands slipped and he felt himself falling. Twisting in midair, he reached up and made one last desperate grab.

His fingers caught hold of one of the dangling ties used to keep the boot closed. He hung on as tight as he could as he hit the ground. The strain on his arm and shoulder were tremendous as he was dragged along. It felt like his arm was about to be ripped right out of its socket.

Grimacing with effort, Matt pulled himself up and reached with his other hand for the flapping canvas. He got it on the second try and hauled himself upward. The lower half of his body bounced and scraped along the ground, but he ignored the pain and grabbed for a higher grip.

Slowly, laboriously, he lifted himself until only his feet were dragging. He kicked and got a foot on the boot. That took some of the weight off his aching arms. Teeth clenched, he pulled himself higher.

A moment later, Matt had both feet on the boot and was standing there rocking back and forth as the coach careened along. He looked down at his side and saw that his Colt was still in its holster. That was a stroke of luck.

A brass rail ran around the top of the coach. Matt reached up and grasped it with one hand, then the other. With a firm grip, he started to climb.

The two outlaws on the box hadn't noticed him until now, but the shift in weight as Matt pulled himself halfway onto the coach roof made the one who wasn't driving glance back and yell in alarm. The bandanna tied over the lower half of his face twitched from the gust of air his shout produced. The man twisted on the seat and clawed at the gun on his hip.

Matt got his Colt out first and fired before the outlaw could get off a shot. His bullet struck the man in the shoulder and knocked him backwards. That made him topple off the front of the box. With a scream that was abruptly cut off, he fell under the slashing, pounding hooves of the six galloping horses.

The other outlaw ducked as Matt fired again. He dropped the reins. They fell free, slithering off the box.

Crouched on the floorboards, the man yanked his gun from its holster and triggered a shot. Matt threw himself flat on the coach roof as the slug whipped over his head. His Colt roared again.

A red-rimmed hole appeared in the center of the remaining outlaw's forehead. His eyes went wide and glassy as the bullet bored through his brain and exploded out the back of his skull. He fell to the side, already limp in death, and sailed off the driver's box.

Matt holstered his gun and pulled himself forward until he spilled over onto the seat. He saw the reins flying loosely between the legs of the racing horses. There was no way he could reach them.

The runaway team had to be stopped, though, and Matt saw only one way to do that. He held on to the seat with one hand, balanced for a second on the edge of the footboard along the front of the box, and then leaped out into empty air.

Chapter 23

Matt landed on the back of the left-hand wheeler. The horse jerked under him, but he grabbed its mane and hung on. When he was settled on the horse's back and confident that he wouldn't fall off, he took hold of its harness and leaned over to grab the right-hand wheeler's harness with that hand. He hauled back, slowing them, and that gradually slowed the other horses in the team as well. After a couple of minutes, the coach lurched to a halt.

Matt slid off the horse and ran back to the door. He twisted the catch and yanked it open, worried about what he might see inside.

Three pale, terrified faces stared out at him from huddled shapes on the floor. The younger Baxter had a pocket pistol clutched in his hand. Obviously thinking that Matt was one of the outlaws, he thrust it out and started to pull the trigger. Matt grabbed his wrist and shoved his arm up just as the pistol went off with a loud popping sound. The bullet flew harmlessly into the air, well over Matt's head.

Matt wrenched the gun out of the young man's hand

and said, "Hold on, damn it! I'm not part of that bunch. I just saved you from them!"

"Where . . . where are the rest of them?" the elder Baxter asked. All his bluster was gone now, scared right out of him.

Matt looked around, thinking that he might see the other outlaws galloping toward him, ready to wipe him out and take the Baxters prisoner again, but he didn't see anybody.

He heard shots coming from the direction of the creek, though.

A smile tugged at the corners of his mouth. From the sound of the gunfire, somebody had come along and pitched in to give him a hand.

That help might have come too late for Seamus Hanrahan, though.

"Let me turn this coach around," he said. "You folks will be all right now."

"Turn the coach around!" Claude Baxter repeated in disbelief. "Absolutely not! I insist you take us on to Pine Knob as scheduled, young man."

It sure hadn't taken the mining magnate long to get his arrogant attitude back once he realized he was safe, Matt thought. Luckily, he didn't give a damn about Baxter's attitude.

"Sorry," he said curtly. "We're going back."

He slammed the door without giving them a chance to argue with him.

Ignoring the angry shouts from inside the coach, Matt gathered up the reins, climbed onto the driver's box, and turned the stagecoach around. He sent it rolling back toward the creek, and by the time they got there, all the shooting had stopped.

Matt saw a number of bodies sprawled in the trees

and along the creek banks. A dozen men on horseback sat their saddles nearby, holding rifles. Matt recognized some of them from Buffalo Crossing.

He recognized Sheriff Thomas Blocker as well, who was kneeling next to a man propped up against the trunk of a cottonwood. Matt's spirits leaped as he looked at the soaked, bloody, but very much alive Seamus Hanrahan.

"Saints be praised!" Hanrahan said as Matt brought the coach to a halt and jumped down from the box. "You're alive, lad. I didn't think I'd ever see you again after that crazy stunt you pulled."

"And I thought you were already dead when I went after the coach," Matt said.

"No, a fellow as slow as I am has to be canny. When I got hit, I decided I'd better go down and stay down. I figured if the scalawags thought I was dead, they might stop shootin' at me. I kept me nose barely above water, just enough to get some air. Like to froze to death in that creek before the sheriff and his posse come along, but I'll warm up sooner or later."

Matt looked at Blocker and said, "You didn't tell me you were going to be following the coach, Sheriff."

"I didn't tell anybody until I was ready to ask for volunteers and ride out," the lawman replied. "It's not that I didn't trust you, Matt. I just didn't want to take a chance on word of my plan getting around before the stagecoach left. I have a hunch somebody in Buffalo Crossing is tied in with this bunch. I figure the man you killed a couple of days ago was in town getting orders the times that I saw him earlier."

Matt nodded and said, "I agree with you. Did you take any prisoners?"

Blocker shook his head regretfully.

"They put up too much of a fight for that when we hit them. There wasn't time to be careful."

"Well, maybe we can get around that. Let me take a look at the bodies. First, though, are you going to be all right, Seamus?"

"Aye," Hanrahan replied. His voice was fairly strong. "I've got a pretty deep crease in my side, but the cold water kept it from bleedin' too much. Give me a week or so and I'll be as good as ever!"

Matt nodded. He left Sheriff Blocker wrapping a makeshift bandage around Hanrahan's torso and went to look at the dead outlaws.

He checked their boots, and when he got to the fourth corpse, he found what he was looking for.

"Anybody know this man?" he asked the posse members who were sitting on their horses nearby.

One man spoke up, saying, "I've seen him before. I'm not sure where, though. Maybe in the saloon where I do most of my drinkin'."

"Which one is that?"

The man glanced toward Hanrahan and said quietly, "Don't tell that big Irish madman, but I'm talkin' about the Artesian."

That answer didn't surprise Matt. He said, "You wouldn't happen to know the fella's name, would you?"

The posseman rubbed his jaw and frowned in thought for a moment before saying, "I think I heard one of the saloon girls call him Dave."

"That'll do," Matt said with a nod. "Much obliged."

He went back over to Blocker and said, "I could do with the loan of a horse, Sheriff. It'll take you a while to gather up all these bodies, and I need to get back to town right away."

Blocker jerked a thumb toward the coach and asked,

"What about those three? Claude Baxter and his boy are yellin' their heads off about getting to Pine Knob so they can go on to Laramie."

"Maybe you can get a couple of volunteers to take the stage the rest of the way," Matt suggested.

"I'll pay good wages," Hanrahan put in. He had gotten to his feet. He was still pale but seemed steady on his feet. "Or rather, I should say that Emily will pay good wages. I got to learn to stop buttin' into the girl's business."

Matt didn't really care about any of that now. He said to Blocker, "What about that horse?"

"Take mine," the sheriff offered. "It's that roan over there. If you're bound on the errand I think you are, though, I really ought to be doing it myself."

"Trust me, Sheriff. I can handle this job."

"Never entered my mind that you couldn't," Blocker said.

Matt's clothes had dried in the warm sun by the time he got back to Buffalo Crossing. He had found his hat and the Winchester and recovered them. The rifle was fully loaded, as was the revolver on his hip.

He rode past the stagecoach station and Hanrahan's saloon without stopping. He was bound for the large building on the far side of the settlement that housed the Artesian Saloon.

Although he still had some unanswered questions, there was no doubt in his mind that Nicholas Radcliff was the mastermind behind the stagecoach robberies. Rather than Seamus Hanrahan wanting to put Radcliff out of business, it was the other way around. Radcliff had chosen to do that by going after the stagecoaches, knowing that if Hanrahan lost his contract with the line it would bankrupt him all around, including the saloon.

Matt wasn't sure why Radcliff hadn't just hired some hardcase to bushwhack Hanrahan and kill him, but he supposed Radcliff had his reasons. Everybody's own motives seemed sane to them, even if they were completely loco to anyone else.

He hadn't been in the Artesian before, but he knew where it was. It had big, fancy windows and a corner entrance. Matt dismounted, tied the sheriff's horse to one of the hitch racks, and stepped up onto the boardwalk to push through the bat wings. He found himself in a large barroom that bordered on elegance, especially for one that was located in a frontier settlement like Buffalo Crossing.

What he didn't see was any sign of Nicholas Radcliff.

Matt went over to the bar. A bartender in a red vest came up to him and asked, "What can I do for you, friend?"

"Is your boss here?" Matt asked.

"Mr. Radcliff? No, I haven't seen him for a while. Maybe I can help you—"

"No thanks," Matt broke in. He swung around and left the saloon.

After hurrying back to town, it was a letdown of sorts not to find Radcliff at the Artesian. He wasn't sure what to do now. He supposed he ought to go back to the stage station and let Emily know what had happened. If she had seen him ride by, she was bound to be worried about her father.

He swung up into the saddle and trotted along the street, passing Hanrahan's saloon. The doors of the barn next to the stagecoach station were open. Matt rode through them, figuring he would leave Sheriff Blocker's horse here with Ezekial.

He called the old hostler, but Ezekial didn't answer. Puzzled, Matt dismounted and started to look around.

It took him only a moment to spot a booted foot sticking out of one of the stalls.

Matt drew his gun and hurried over. Ezekial lay sprawled on his back in the empty stall. A bloody lump on his head showed where somebody had hit him. Matt figured he knew who that someone was.

He dropped to a knee to check and see if Ezekial was still breathing. The old-timer was. Feeling a little relieved by that, Matt started to stand up.

"Just stay where you are, Jensen," a familiar voice ordered. "If you try anything, I'll kill the girl."

Matt controlled the impulse to spin around. Instead, he slowly turned his head and saw Radcliff standing in the doorway that opened between the office and the barn. He had Emily in front of him with his left arm looped around her waist, while his right hand held the point of a small but deadly knife pressed into the soft hollow of her throat.

"You're not even going to make me go to the trouble of tricking a confession out of you, are you?" Matt asked.

"What would be the point?" Radcliff said. "You've already figured it out. When I saw you come riding back into town, I knew it had all gone wrong. You were supposed to be dead by now, and the Baxters were supposed to be in the hands of my men, along with that ten grand in gold."

"It didn't work out that way. The sheriff turned out to be smarter than any of us gave him credit for, I reckon. He followed the stage with a posse and jumped your gang while they were trying to kill Seamus and me."

Matt saw alarm leap into Emily's green eyes. She couldn't say anything because of the knife at her throat, so he went on, "He's fine. He was wounded, but he'll be all right."

"In a way, that's a shame," Radcliff said. "I'm sure he would have preferred dying to coming back here to town only to find his daughter dead and both of his businesses burned down."

Matt's eyes narrowed.

"Those attempts on your life and that fire set behind your place were all phonies, weren't they?" he guessed. "You were trying to frame Hanrahan and make it look like he was trying to kill you, rather than the other way around."

"I didn't want any of the blame ever getting back to me. You see, Jensen, I'm a very cautious man. I came up with several different ways to get rid of Hanrahan or put him out of business, and in none of them would any of the guilt ever fall on me."

"But now you're going to murder his daughter and burn down his place?"

"It's awfully crude, I know," Radcliff said with a shrug. "But I've run out of patience. You know the railroad's going to be here in another year or two. When it arrives, the man who owns the best saloon in town will make a fortune. An absolute fortune, Jensen. And that's going to be me."

Matt didn't say anything, but he shook his head.

"You don't think so?" Radcliff snapped. "What's going to stop me? I cut the girl's throat, I kill you, I set fire to the hay . . . Hell, I won't even need any coal oil for this one."

"Problem is that once you've killed Emily, there won't be anything stopping me from killing you. You really think you can get me with that knife before I put two or three slugs in you? My gun's already in my hand, you damned fool. You don't have a chance in hell, and you know it."

Matt was right, and as that awful realization dawned in Radcliff's eyes, the man stiffened. Insane hatred twisted his face, and Matt knew he was about to kill Emily out of sheer spite.

Matt moved as fast as he ever had in his life, uncoiling from his crouch and bringing his gun up in a smooth, blindingly quick motion. The Colt roared, flame licking from its muzzle.

Radcliff's head jerked back. His hand opened, and the knife fell to the hard-packed dirt at Emily's feet. Radcliff let go of her and toppled backwards. Both eyes were wide open, and the bullet hole looked almost like a third eye in the center of his forehead.

Matt stood still for a second, a thin tendril of smoke curling from the Colt's barrel, before he lowered the gun. Emily stared at him, her skin as pale as milk. A shudder went through her. Matt figured she was about to faint, so he said, "It's a good thing you're so blasted short. That way he couldn't hide behind you very well."

Her nostrils flared as she drew in a sharp, deep breath.

"Short, am I?" she demanded, the instinctive anger she felt acting to brace her and calm her fear. "You could have killed me, you know."

"Not likely. I was too close to miss."

"Ezekial? Is he—"

"Knocked out, but I reckon he'll be fine when he wakes up, except for a headache."

"And my father . . ." Emily's voice dropped to a whisper. "He's really all right?"

"He's really all right," Matt assured her.

"Good. I . . . Ohhh . . ."

Blast it, he thought. He had given it a try, but she had gone and fainted anyway.

Two days later, the westbound stage returned from Pine Knob. Now that the gang had been broken up, men were willing to hire on as drivers and shotgun guards again. When the coach rolled to a stop in front of the station, Matt, Emily, and Ezekial were waiting for it.

Ezekial and the driver got started changing the teams while the guard climbed down and dug something out of a pocket that he extended to Matt.

"Got a telegram here for you, Mr. Jensen," he said. "It got sent to Laramie. Then a rider carried it to Pine Knob, and we picked it up there."

"Somebody must really want to get in touch with you, Matt," Emily commented as Matt unfolded the paper.

"Yeah, I—" Matt stopped and stiffened as he read the words printed on the form.

"That looks like trouble," Emily said with a worried frown.

"Yeah. It's from Smoke. Preacher needs our help." He took a deep breath. "So I've got to be riding."

"So . . . so soon? I was hoping that . . . well, that you might stay around here for a while."

He smiled faintly as he looked at her.

"You sound like you're disappointed," he said. "I thought you were immune to my charms."

"Damn you, Matt Jensen," she said as anger sparked in her eyes. "Don't you make fun of me. Don't you— Oh, the hell with it."

She came up on her toes, threw her arms around his neck, and pulled his head down so she could kiss him.

After a long moment, she took her lips away from his and murmured, "Guess I'm not as immune as I thought I was." She buried her face against his chest. "Do you really have to go?"

"I do," he said quietly.

"Then I won't try to hold you." She sighed. "It's not like I don't have plenty to do, running the stage station *and* the saloon until Seamus is back on his feet. But if you're ever back in this part of the country . . ."

"I'll stop and see you," Matt promised.

"You'd better," she said, and then she kissed him again.

It was a promise he might not be able to keep, Matt thought as he rode away a short time later. Any time he got together with Smoke and Preacher, the air was always thick with flying lead. When the Indian Ring was involved, it was even worse.

Matt was well aware of that, but there was a little smile on his face anyway as he heeled his horse into a faster pace.

BOOK FOUR

Chapter 24

As Preacher had promised, he, Standing Rock, and fifteen Assiniboine warriors left the village of Two Bears's people early the next morning after the raid, riding out in the same direction the attackers had taken the previous night when they fled.

It wasn't hard to pick up the trail. That many men couldn't move as fast as they had been moving without leaving plenty of sign.

Following them might not continue to be that easy, however, and Preacher knew it. Once the men put some distance between themselves and the village, they might slow down and start being more careful about covering their tracks.

That was when the real challenge would begin.

Standing Rock was still in an agitated state. Preacher supposed he couldn't blame the man. Standing Rock's wife and son had been kidnapped, after all. Naturally, he was upset.

That could cause a problem, though, once they caught up to the raiders. As they rode along, with Preacher and Standing Rock in the lead, the mountain man commented, "You know, an old friend of mine named Audie used to quote all the time from books he'd read. One time he come out with a sayin' that makes a lot of sense: 'Revenge is a dish best served cold.'"

"What does that mean?" Standing Rock asked with his habitual scowl.

"It means that I know your blood's all heated up right now because you're mad as hell at those jaspers who stole your wife and boy. But when we catch up to 'em . . . and we *will* catch up to 'em, believe you me . . . it'll be better if you can cool off a mite. You'll think straighter and stay alive longer if you ain't burnin' up with rage."

"The men who took Wildflower and Little Hawk will all die! They will scream and beg for an end to their agony!"

"See, that's what I mean," Preacher said. "We both want the same thing, but we got to be smart in the way we go about it. If we just go chargin' in with all guns a-blazin', that's liable to be bad for us. More important, it might put the gal and the little boy in even more danger. You think on that while we're trailin' those varmints. That's all I'm askin' you to do, Standin' Rock."

For a long moment, the warrior didn't make any reply. Then he said, "I will think on it. But when the time comes for vengeance, do not try to stop me from claiming it, Preacher. This is *my* warning to *you*."

Preacher didn't say anything. He didn't know if he had gotten through to Standing Rock. All they could do now was to keep following the kidnappers' trail. . . .

And hope that Standing Rock wouldn't do anything so loco that it got them all killed.

* * *

Randall kept the bunch moving fast all night, except for brief stops to rest the horses. In the morning, he called a longer halt so that they could brew some coffee and eat some jerky and biscuits. While his men were taking care of those chores, he rode to the top of a nearby ridge and dismounted to look back over the way they had come.

They were pretty high, and he could see for miles from up here. Staying in the shade of a tree so the sun wouldn't reflect off the lens, he took a telescope from his saddlebags and opened it. With the precision of the former military man that he was, he scanned the countryside below him, searching for any signs of pursuit. He moved the telescope slowly and carefully, covering the grid that he laid out in his mind.

He didn't spot any riders, even in the haze along the far distant horizon. Satisfied that no one was in sight, he closed the telescope and replaced it in his saddlebags.

But just because he couldn't see anyone, he thought, that didn't mean they weren't back there. He was confident that the Indians would come after them. He didn't know how many of the warriors he and his men had killed, but if any of the savages were left alive, they would be coming.

It didn't really matter. Randall didn't think anybody could catch them before they made it to Hammerhead, and once they reached the Colonel's town, it wouldn't matter anymore. The Colonel's house there was as good as a fortress.

He rode back down to the place where he had left the others. Before riding to the top of the ridge he had told Dwyer to keep an eye on Wildflower and the baby. When he saw Dwyer hunkered on his heels next to a small fire, pouring coffee from a battered pot into a tin cup, anger welled up inside Randall.

"Where the hell are the woman and the kid?" he demanded as he strode up to Dwyer. He suppressed the urge to kick the careless son of a bitch in the head.

Dwyer was smart enough to know that Randall was mad. He said quickly, "Take it easy, boss. They're right over there. I've had my eye on 'em the whole time."

He nodded toward the little creek where some of the men were watering their horses. When Randall looked in that direction he saw Wildflower sitting on a rock in the shade of an aspen, a short distance away from the other men. She had Little Hawk cradled against her. Something went through Randall when he realized that the baby was at Wildflower's breast, feeding.

"The kid was hungry," Dwyer went on. "She asked if she could have a little privacy to take care of him, and I didn't figure it would hurt nothin'. I told her to stay close and warned her that I'd be watchin' her the whole time. She didn't try to get away or anything like that, Randall."

"She could have," Randall snapped.

"If she did, she wouldn't have made it fifty feet before I caught up with her."

Randall knew Dwyer was right, but that didn't really lessen his anger. Something about the woman put him on edge. He didn't like the feeling.

"Should I have told her not to do it?" Dwyer asked.

"No, that's all right," Randall forced himself to say with a shake of his head. He supposed Dwyer's decision was reasonable enough. He was just mad because Wildflower had gotten under his skin.

He left Dwyer at the fire and walked toward Wildflower and Little Hawk. She glanced up and saw him coming, but she didn't stop nursing the little boy, nor did she try to cover up the smooth, reddish-brown breast on which the baby fed. Little Hawk worked enthusiastically at her nipple.

"You'd better not be thinking about trying to run away," Randall warned as he came up to her.

"The only thing I am thinking about is feeding my son," she said coldly. She wasn't looking at him now. She stared off into the distance across the creek instead.

"Well . . . the next time you need to do that, ask me about it instead." Randall knew his words sounded awkward, and that knowledge irritated him.

"You were not here, and Little Hawk was hungry."

"I'm not arguing with you, I'm telling you," Randall snapped. "Are you about done there?"

"Little Hawk will decide when he is finished."

"We need to get moving again pretty soon, you know."

She didn't say anything. Her features were serene and composed, and maddeningly beautiful. Randall turned away from her with a muttered curse.

"Did you see my husband when you looked behind us?" she asked his back. "He will come, and when he finds you, he will kill you."

"Nobody was back there."

"He will come," Wildflower said with supreme confidence.

"If he does, then he'll be the one to die," Randall said harshly. He stalked off without looking back.

If things had worked out differently in his life, he thought, he might have stood and watched his own wife nursing their child and been filled with love for both of them.

But they weren't different, and such a thing would never be.

And the regret that went through him at that moment was truly painful . . . until he tamped it down and covered it up with hate.

Wildflower glanced toward Randall as he walked off, but carefully so that no one could tell she was watching him. She had been listening carefully ever since she was captured, even when it appeared she was too stunned to know what was going on around her. But, even so, all she knew was his name and the fact that he worked for someone he called the Colonel.

That and the fact that there was grief buried somewhere deep inside him. She had seen a flash of it in his eyes as he turned away. Perhaps she could make use of that, she thought as she looked down at her son's head while he continued to suckle.

She had never been as stunned and full of despair as she appeared to be. There was too much anger in her for that.

But if these white men believed that she had given up hope, there was a chance they might not watch her as closely. At the first opportunity, she intended to get away from them and take her son with her. They might be many miles away from her village when the time came, but that didn't matter. She would walk for weeks or even months if she had to in order to get back home. Whatever it took for the two of them to return to Standing Rock and the rest of their people, she would do.

Little Hawk lifted his head from her breast. He

looked sleepy and content now. She pulled her buckskin dress closed as she cradled him against her. She stroked his midnight-black hair and hummed softly as he snuggled into her warmth.

Protecting her son was more important than anything else, more important even than her freedom. She would kill anyone who threatened to harm Little Hawk, kill them with her bare hands, if necessary.

"All right, let's get mounted up!" Randall called. "Put that fire out, Dwyer." He turned and came closer to her again. "Let's go."

Wildflower stood up, keeping Little Hawk cradled in her arms. She walked toward the men, eyes downcast as usual. Let them think she was cowed. The time would come when they learned the truth.

"Let me give you a hand there, ma'am," the one called Dwyer said as he came up to her. "I can hold the baby while you mount up."

She didn't like Dwyer any more than she liked any of her other captors. He had a narrow, wolflike face, and he was friends with the one called Page, whose cold, ruthless eyes reminded her of those of a snake. But Dwyer had at least tried to treat her kindly at times. He might look at her with lust, but at least his gaze didn't have rage mingled with it, as Randall's did.

"Thank you," she said softly. She started to hand Little Hawk to the man, hating to let go of her son and yet knowing that it wouldn't hurt to make Dwyer believe she trusted him, at least a little.

Before she could do that, Randall came up and took Little Hawk out of her arms. She forced herself not to fight. It wouldn't have done any good, anyway, against someone as big and brutal as Randall.

"Get on my horse," he told her. "I'll hand you the kid."

Wildflower climbed onto Randall's mount, conscious of the way her dress rode up and exposed her bare legs. She ignored the shame she felt as the men's eyes followed her. Randall lifted Little Hawk, and she took him and held him tight against her. He was fussing a little now because he wanted to sleep and people kept moving him around and disturbing him.

"It is all right, little one," Wildflower murmured to him in their language. "It is all right. Sleep now."

Randall swung up behind her, slipped his left arm around her waist, and lifted the reins in his right hand. He heeled his horse into motion and led the way as the men rode away from this temporary camp.

Wildflower tried to reach out with her heart and feel Standing Rock behind them, coming after them to free her and their son. It was a futile effort. She couldn't sense him. Did too much distance separate them, she wondered. . . .

Or had he been killed in the fighting when Randall and the others attacked her father's village?

She tried not to think about that, but she couldn't banish the grim possibility from her mind.

If that was true, then it was one more reason the man called Randall had to die.

Chapter 25

Preacher and Standing Rock kept the rescue party moving fast over the next few days, but they made frustratingly little progress. As Preacher had expected, the men they were following began to take more pains to cover their tracks. Even with his skill as a tracker, sometimes he lost the trail and had to spend long hours looking for it before picking it up again. In some instances, without Dog's keen sense of smell to guide them, they might not have been able to find the way they needed to go.

The men they were following were professionals, Preacher mused as he rode along. And professionals wouldn't have attacked Two Bears's village and carried off Wildflower and Little Hawk unless they were paid to do so. That brought up the interesting question of who would have hired those killers to do such a thing.

Preacher intended to get an answer to that question before this was all over.

Several days into the chase, Preacher ranged ahead of the rest of the group. He had spotted a fairly large hill up ahead, and he thought that if he climbed to the top of it, he might be able to spot their quarry.

With Dog loping along beside him, Preacher sent Horse up the slope until it got too steep for the stallion. At that point, Preacher dismounted and went ahead on foot. He was breathing a little hard by the time he reached the crest.

He tipped his hat back and let a cool breeze wash over his leathery face. From here, as he gazed northwest, he could see miles and miles of mountains, hills, and valleys. It was a spectacularly beautiful expanse large enough to hide an army in, and he was looking for a couple of dozen men on horseback. The odds against spotting them seemed to be impossibly high.

Preacher had the eyes of an eagle, though . . . and the patience of a buzzard. He stood there with his gaze searching the landscape, motionless except for the slow turning of his head. He knew that movement caught the eye quicker than anything else, so that was what he watched for.

He saw birds darting from tree to tree. He saw a moose lift its antlered head high. He saw a bear lumber across a grassy park in search of a rotten log full of tasty bugs. He saw more birds soaring suddenly into the sky. . . .

His gaze dropped sharply, backtracking the birds' flight. At first he couldn't see anything except the rocky face of a cliff, perhaps three miles away across a valley.

Then the old mountain man grunted softly as he detected movement against the backdrop of that cliff. It was too far away for him to make out any details, but he could judge the speed of whatever was moving over there. It matched the pace of a group of men riding along on horseback.

"Got you," Preacher whispered. Beside him, Dog let out a little whine as if he understood.

Preacher stood there watching until the distant riders disappeared from view. He knew it was possible the men he had seen weren't the ones they were looking for. But this region was pretty rugged and not that well-populated, so his instincts told him those were the kidnappers. It was good knowing that they were still on the move, that they hadn't reached their destination and forted up.

Preacher went back down the hill to where he had left Horse. He mounted up and hurried to rejoin the Assiniboine warriors. As he trotted up to Standing Rock and reined in, he said, "I saw 'em."

Standing Rock leaned forward excitedly and asked, "Are you sure? You are certain it was the men who took Wildflower and Little Hawk? How far ahead of us are they?"

"About three miles, I reckon," Preacher replied. "And no, I ain't sure. I wasn't close enough to make 'em out. But the bunch was the right size and headed in the same direction as the ones we been followin', so I'm confident it was them."

"We must hurry—"

Preacher lifted a hand to stop Standing Rock before the warrior could kick his pony into a run.

"Hold on, hold on," the mountain man said. "We could run these hosses right into the ground, and we still wouldn't catch up to 'em by nightfall. We still got to be patient."

"Patient!" Standing Rock repeated with obvious disgust. "Would you be patient, Preacher, if it was your woman those animals had carried off?"

Preacher's eyes narrowed as he said, "There was a

time when your wife's ma was captured by a bunch of evil varmints. She might've been my woman, if things had worked out a mite different. Before that, there was a gal called Jenny . . ." Preacher shook his head as he forced those thoughts far back in his memory. "Never you mind," he rasped. "I know how you're feelin' right now, son. You can trust me on that."

It was obvious from Standing Rock's glare that he wanted to argue some more, but with a visible effort he forced himself to nod and said, "We will be patient . . . for now. But soon my patience will run out, Preacher, and then blood will be answered with blood."

"And I'll be right there with you doin' the answerin'," Preacher said.

Wildflower's frustration had grown stronger during the days that passed, as no opportunity for escape presented itself for her to seize. But her determination to get away from these men grew stronger as well.

She was running out of patience, though. If they weren't going to give her a chance to escape, she would just have to come up with one on her own.

With that thought in mind, she began smiling at the one called Dwyer.

She had considered trying to win Randall over to her side. It was obvious that he was attracted to her, and it was a deeper attraction than the mere desire that the other men felt for her.

But she sensed that there was too much bitterness inside Randall for that to ever work. She could never pierce that layer to get to his core. Dwyer, on the other hand, might be manipulated.

They were making camp every night now, and as

they settled in one evening after several days on the trail, Wildflower went over to Dwyer and said, "Would you hold Little Hawk for me while I tend to my needs?"

"You want me to hold him?" Dwyer asked, sounding surprised. Usually Wildflower took the baby with her when she went into the brush. Randall had given orders that someone watch her at all times, but they gave her a little privacy at moments like that, standing near enough that they could hear if she tried to get away.

"Please," Wildflower said, and again she ventured a faint smile.

"Well . . . all right, sure."

Dwyer held out his hands for the little boy. It tore at Wildflower's heart to hand him over voluntarily like this, but she forced herself to do so and kept the smile on her face.

"You will come with me? I would rather you guard me than any of the others."

"I, uh . . . of course I will. Happy to help."

Dwyer held Little Hawk with an awkward unease, but Wildflower didn't think he was in any danger of dropping the baby. Little Hawk reached up and caught hold of Dwyer's hat brim, tugging down on it. The gunman chuckled.

"Little varmint likes to play," he said.

"That means he feels you are a friend," Wildflower said.

"Yeah, I reckon. Cute little rascal, ain't he?"

As they walked toward a clump of brush, Wildflower asked, "Do you have children of your own, Mr. Dwyer?"

"Naw. At least not that I know of. Never really had a chance to settle down. When I was a kid, though, I sort of helped raise my little brothers and my sister.

I was the oldest, and we didn't have no pa after he died of a fever. When that happened, Ma had to go to work in a crib. . . . Ah, hell, you don't want to hear about all that. It ain't a pretty story."

"You have had a difficult life."

"No worse than a lot of other people, I reckon," Dwyer said. "Things are tough for you right now, too, but don't worry. You and the boy are gonna be fine."

"I pray to the Great Spirit it is so."

Wildflower went into the brush. While she was there, she heard Page call jeeringly to his friend, "Hey, Dwyer, you turnin' into a squaw? I see you got you a little papoose there!"

"Shut up," Dwyer muttered. "I'm just tryin' to give the lady a helpin' hand, that's all."

"Lady?" Page repeated. "She ain't no lady. She's a redskinned heathen!"

Some of the other gunmen joined in the gibes. When she was finished and came out of the brush, Wildflower took Little Hawk back and said to Dwyer, "I am sorry your friends mock you because you are nice to me."

"Aw, shoot, don't worry about them," Dwyer told her. "They're just jealous, that's all. And they're a bunch of ignorant sons o' bitches, to boot."

Randall hadn't been making any jokes. Wildflower felt his cold eyes on her and Dwyer as they talked, and she hoped she hadn't made a mistake by reminding him of things he had either lost or had never had. She was relying on his professionalism and his desire to carry out the job that the Colonel had given him.

Another day on the trail went by. Whenever she could, Wildflower looked behind them, as if she could make Standing Rock appear by the sheer force of her longing for him. That didn't do any good, of course, but she did it anyway.

That evening when they made camp, Dwyer was quick to come over and offer to help her any way he could.

"Thought you might need me to keep up with the tyke again," he added.

"Of course," Wildflower said. "Thank you." She gave Little Hawk to him, and he seemed more at ease this time when he took the baby.

They had stopped beside a creek. Wildflower nodded toward it and said, "I would wash. The trail has been a long and dusty one."

"Ain't that the truth? Well, I suppose it would be all right."

"Should you ask Randall?"

That question brought the response it was calculated to provoke. Dwyer snorted and said, "I don't have to clear everything with Randall. Come on, darlin'. We'll go downstream a little ways. You don't want all these varmints starin' at you while you're tryin' to clean up."

That was exactly what Wildflower wanted him to say. The timing was good, too, because Randall was having some trouble with his saddle and didn't seem to be paying any attention to them. After all this time on the trail with no trouble, even the most cautious of men could grow careless.

Some of the other gunmen watched them walk along the creek bank, but their expressions told Wildflower they were jealous, not worried. They thought it should be them spending time with her, not Dwyer. Except for Page, who just looked suspicious. He might prove to be a problem, she thought.

She kept going, and Dwyer didn't tell her to stop.

Soon they had gone around a bend and were out of easy sight of the camp, even though the other men were less than twenty yards away.

"This will be fine," Wildflower said. She held the skirt of her dress up and waded out into the water while Dwyer stood on the bank holding Little Hawk.

He watched her avidly as she bent, scooped up water, and splashed it over her face and arms. She bent lower and went all the way under so that when she came up again the buckskin clung to her body. She ran her fingers through her wet hair, pushing it back away from her face and wringing some of the water from it. The sun had set and the light was fading, but the shadows weren't thick enough yet to keep Dwyer from getting a good look at her.

He swallowed hard and licked his lips as he watched her.

Wildflower looked up at him and smiled again. Her eyes dropped to the gun on his right hip and the knife sheathed at his left side. Quickly, she lifted her gaze to his face again, hoping that he hadn't noticed where she was looking.

"Feel better now?" he asked in a voice hoarse with emotion.

"Much better," she said. She came to the edge of the water and stepped up onto the grassy bank. "Why don't you . . . put Little Hawk down for a minute? I'm sure he will be fine."

She didn't want her son to get any blood on him.

Dwyer swallowed again and said, "All right." He bent over and set the little boy on the ground. Little Hawk sat up, cooing as he pulled at stalks of grass with his pudgy hands.

Dwyer took a step, and that brought him within

inches of Wildflower. He said, "I don't reckon I've ever seen anybody as pretty as you, Wildflower. I don't care if you *are* an Injun. You're a beautiful woman."

"And you are a good man, Dwyer." She wondered suddenly if she could persuade him to help her and Little Hawk. If she could convince him to betray his companions . . .

But then his lean face turned even more wolfish, and he said, "I ain't that good."

As if to prove it, he grabbed her and jerked her against him, pressing the hard length of his muscular body to her. His mouth came down savagely on hers. Whatever true feelings of sympathy and affection he might have possessed, if any, had just been overwhelmed by the brutal lust that gripped him.

Wildflower did the only thing she could. The gun would draw too much attention, so she grabbed the knife, ripped it from its sheath, and plunged it into his side.

Chapter 26

Wildflower had hoped to kill the white man quickly and quietly, take his gun, pick up Little Hawk, and steal away along the creek before the rest of her captors realized that she and the boy were gone.

But as she shoved the knife into Dwyer's body as hard as she could, she felt the blade grate against a rib and turn aside before it penetrated the heart. Dwyer howled in pain and flung up his left arm, backhanding her across the face.

"You Injun *bitch!*" he bellowed.

The blow was awkward, but had enough force behind it to knock Wildflower back a step. She was about to fall in the creek when she caught her balance and lunged toward him again.

The knife was still stuck in Dwyer's side. He was pawing at it, trying to get it out, when Wildflower barreled into him. He was between her and Little Hawk, and nothing was going to stop her from reaching her child.

Dwyer went over backwards. Wildflower darted past him and scooped Little Hawk from the ground. She whirled around and dashed back into the creek. Water sprayed around her calves as she ran. She had always been fleet of foot, and that was her only chance of salvation now.

And if she failed to get away this time, she could always try again later, she thought wildly. None of them would ever trust her again after this, of course, but she might get a lucky break. . . .

"Come back here, damn you!" Dwyer shouted. "Redskin whore! Come back here!"

Over the pounding of her heart, Wildflower heard him splashing through the water after her. The creek was shallow, no more than six inches deep along the edge, and the bed was gravel so it wasn't too hard to run in it. Trees closed in ahead on the banks. If she could duck into those trees, the shadows might be thick enough to hide her as she slipped away. It was worth a try—

The sound of the shot was deafeningly loud. A terrible impact between her shoulder blades knocked her forward. She tried to hang on to Little Hawk as she sailed through the air, but he slipped from her grasp. Wildflower cried out, more from the terror of losing her son than from the horrible pain blossoming inside her.

It seemed to take forever for her to land facedown in the stream. She was aware of the water closing around her head, but by now an awful numbness was blotting out the pain. Numbness and nothingness, black, black oblivion that washed over her. She clung for a second to a feeling of disbelief that this could be happening, and then that was gone, too.

The last thing she heard was the angry wail of her son.

* * *

When Randall heard Dwyer yell, he jerked away from his horse and the balky cinch fastening with which he'd been struggling. Even in the fading light, a quick scan of the campsite told him that he couldn't see Dwyer or the woman.

Randall bit back a curse as he started to run. He never should have allowed Dwyer to get friendly with her, he told himself. It had been easier to ignore his own feelings, though, when there was somebody else around to deal with her all the time.

Randall reacted faster than the other men and his long legs carried him around the bend in the creek ahead of them, although several of them were trailing behind him. He heard Dwyer yelling at Wildflower and knew without being told that she was trying to get away. That fool hadn't been paying close enough attention to her, Randall was sure of that. Wildflower had lulled him into carelessness with her smiles.

Randall caught sight of them in the fading light. Wildflower was running in the creek with Dwyer hobbling along after her. He had his left hand pressed to his side. The dark stain on his shirt had to be blood. She had wounded him somehow.

In Dwyer's right hand was his gun.

Randall saw Dwyer bring up the revolver and opened his mouth to yell for him not to shoot. Before Randall could make a sound, the gun roared and flame stabbed redly from the muzzle, splitting the dusk. Wildflower flew forward under the bullet's impact.

"Noooo!"

Randall's shout was too late. Wildflower lay facedown in the creek, not moving. She had dropped the baby. Little Hawk landed in the water, rolled over, and came to a stop sitting up. The boy started to cry.

Dwyer stumbled to a halt several feet short of where Wildflower had fallen. Randall had stopped as well, stunned by what he had seen. He stood on the bank, about fifteen feet behind and to one side of Dwyer.

Still holding his wounded side, Dwyer looked around in apparent confusion. He saw Randall and turned slowly toward him.

"Boss, I . . . I'm hurt," he said. "The bitch stabbed me. I don't know how she got hold of a knife. . . ."

Randall knew. She had played up to Dwyer and gotten close enough to grab his knife. That was the only explanation that made any sense, and the empty sheath on Dwyer's hip was all the proof Randall needed.

"I n-never thought she'd try anything," Dwyer stammered. He looked afraid now as Randall stared down at him with a terrible expression of fury on his face. "Reckon I lost my head 'cause I'm hurtin' so bad. I knew I needed to stop her, any way I could—"

Randall didn't let him say anything else. Randall's gun was already in his hand. It came up fast and smooth and gouted flame. The bullet smashed into Dwyer's chest and flung him back in the water. A dark stain began to spread around him, matching the one that had formed in the creek around Wildflower's body.

"Randall, you—"

The strangled words came from Page. Without turning around, Randall said, "If you're thinking about it, Page, you'd better kill me with your first shot. If you don't I'll see to it that you're as dead as your stupid friend."

A couple of seconds of tense silence ticked past. Then Page said, "I ain't thinkin' about nothin', boss. I reckon Dwyer dug his own grave, and I don't aim to climb into it with him."

"That's showing some good sense," Randall said. He was shaken by this unexpected development, but his brain was beginning to work again. "Go out there and get that kid."

Page stepped down from the bank into the water and waded past the bodies to get to Little Hawk, who was soaked, cold, and bawling ferociously by now. The boy didn't quiet down any when Page picked him up. He kicked and squirmed, but the gunman held him tightly.

"Take him back to camp, dry him off, and sit by the fire with him until he warms up," Randall ordered.

"I ain't no damn wet nurse, Randall."

"No, but you can do that much. Get moving."

Page hesitated, but only for a second. The stony, menacing tone of Randall's voice didn't allow for much argument. He carried Little Hawk toward the fire. The rest of them, all of whom had gathered now to see what had happened, parted to let them through.

"Some of you get those bodies out of the creek," Randall went on. "We've got some burying to do. I want you to find a good place where the graves won't be found for a long time, if they ever are."

"But, Randall," one of the men said tentatively, "the Colonel's orders were to bring both the woman and the kid to him."

"I know that, damn it. But her corpse won't do him any good. There's no point in hauling it the rest of the way to Hammerhead. And if we make sure the Indians who are coming after us never find where she's buried, they won't know she's dead, will they?"

Several of the men muttered agreement as they saw what Randall was driving at.

"The boy is Two Bears's grandson," Randall went on. "The Colonel can still use him for leverage. And as long as they don't find out about Wildflower, the Colonel can pretend that he's holding her hostage as well. He'll still be able to get what he wants." Randall drew in a deep breath. "The Colonel always finds a way to get what he wants."

But *he* wouldn't, he thought. Not that there would have ever been any real chance, anyway. He had been fooling himself to think that there might have been even a shred of hope.

No, his life, his destiny, was the same as it had always been, Randall told himself: to follow the Colonel's orders, to bring death and destruction to the Colonel's enemies. For nearly two decades, that was really all he had known, and all he ever would know.

"Move, blast it!" he snapped at his men. "We've got work to do."

Randall took charge of the baby himself after that. Two more days would bring them to Hammerhead. Little Hawk couldn't go that long without eating. He was old enough to eat little pieces of biscuit that Randall soaked in sugar water. Randall soaked a rag in sugar water, too, and let the kid suck on it when he got too fussy. Maybe that would be enough to keep him alive until they reached the settlement. Unless they came across a woman somewhere who was nursing— pretty damned unlikely in this rugged wilderness—that was all he could do.

Their route angled north along the mountains until they came to a pass. They turned west there, and as they did, Randall saw evidence that the Colonel's surveyors and excavators had already been at work through here, laying the groundwork for what would come later. The approach was the key now, and the Colonel was taking steps to secure that.

On the other side of the pass, they descended into a broad, green basin that was some of the prettiest country Randall had ever seen. It was thickly grassed and well watered, and it would do for both farming and ranching, and under the Colonel's firm, guiding hand both industries would develop here without the bloody violence that had broken out between them in other places.

Peace was easy, Randall reflected, when one man controlled everything.

But the basin would never blossom into the paradise it could be without the railroad. There was already a burgeoning settlement, Hammerhead, that would serve as the supply point for all the new growth, but everything that had been brought there had to be freighted in by wagon and the mountains made their route go a couple of hundred miles out of the way. Wagons could never reach the pass that Randall and his companions had used . . . but a railroad could.

Building that railroad would be a monumental task, but if anyone was up to the challenges of such a task, it was Colonel Hudson Ritchie.

Hammerhead was visible from the outer slopes of the basin, sprawled on the banks of the Silvertip River. Smoke rose from its chimneys. Randall could hear hammering when they were still a mile away as men nailed together new buildings to house all the businesses that would flock here once the railroad was built. Some people might say that the Colonel was getting ahead of himself by establishing a town before there was even a good way to get to it, but he knew what he was doing. Randall had always believed that, and he still did.

The Colonel's mansion was one of the first things that had been built. It was at the western end of the settlement on a slight rise, so that it looked east along the main street. That was the way the town was designed, so the Colonel could step out onto his verandah in the morning and watch the sun rise over what he had made, the creator surveying his creation in all his god-like power.

Randall knew that people were eyeing him and his companions warily as they rode along the street toward the big, three-story mansion. There were plenty of reasons for that wariness. The riders were lean from the trail, covered with dust, hard-bitten faces stubbled by a week's worth of beard. They looked like a pack of wolves, Randall thought, and that's exactly what they were: the Colonel's gun-wolves.

The fact that their leader had a baby cradled in his arms just added a touch of confusion to the towns-people's reactions.

They reined to a halt at the wrought-iron gate between two stone columns that sat in front of the mansion. Holding the baby carefully, Randall swung down from the saddle. He looked up at the other men and said, "That's it. You've done your job. I'll see you later with your pay."

Page said, "Now that we're back, I don't mind tellin' you, Randall . . . you didn't have to kill Dwyer."

"If you think you've got a score to settle with me, Page, we can take it up later."

Page shook his head and said, "I didn't say I had a score to settle with you. I'm just sayin' you didn't have to kill him. You shot him because you wanted to. Because he shot that squaw."

Randall drew in a deep breath.

"Leave it alone, Page."

"Sure." Page lifted his reins. "But you know what you did, and why."

He turned his horse away. One by one, so did the other men.

Randall swallowed the anger that tried to come up his throat. He recognized its bitter, sour taste. He turned to the gate, opened it, and went up the flagstone walk to the house.

The door opened before he got there. A woman stood there, fair-haired, serenely beautiful, seemingly younger than the strands of gray among her blond hair said she really was. She smiled and said, "Welcome back, Mr. Randall."

"Mrs. Dayton," he said with a curt nod. "The Colonel's expecting me."

"Indeed, he is. He's waiting for you in the library." She moved aside to let him pass, adding, "He's expecting you to have the young woman with you as well."

"It's a long story," Randall said.

A long, ugly story.

But the end was in sight now.

Chapter 27

Colonel Hudson Ritchie wore a cream-colored suit, the sort of getup that Southern plantation owners wore, but that was the only thing he had in common with those Confederate sons of bitches. He had put many of their homes to the torch, back when he was wearing the blue of the Union cavalry, and as far as he was concerned, they deserved all the devastation that he had brought upon them.

He was a good-sized man, medium height but broad-shouldered, with some of the vitality of youth remaining to him despite the fact that he was getting on in years. A fringe of gray hair worn long remained around his ears and the back of his head. Otherwise his scalp was smoothly bald. His forehead bulged slightly, which he had always taken as a sign of his superior intelligence. His brain was so large that his head wasn't quite big enough for it.

He stood at the window in the library with a snifter of brandy in his hand. Since this room was at the back of the house, it didn't have a view of the town—*his* town—but from it he could see the mountains on the far side of the basin and all the rich landscape in between. He was already a rich man, but this basin, along with the help of his friends and associates back in Washington, was going to make him wealthy beyond compare.

That wealth would open the doors to even more power. In a few years, he would be in Washington himself, he thought. It was only a matter of time. And once he was there, there was no limit to what he might achieve. Even, if he dared to think about it, the White House. . . .

A door opened, but it was the one leading into the library, not the corridors of power in the nation's capital. Mrs. Dayton said, "Mr. Randall is here, Colonel."

Ritchie turned away from the window. He set his brandy on the desk, where the volume of Machiavelli he'd been reading earlier lay closed. He stood ramrod straight as the big man came into the library carrying a baby.

Ritchie almost called his subordinate "Lieutenant." Randall had carried that rank by the end of the war, and some days the Colonel had trouble remembering that those days were so far in the past.

Randall stiffened as well, and Colonel Ritchie knew the man's first impulse was to come to attention and salute. Such formality was no longer required, of course, but once something like that had been ingrained in a man, it was hard to forget.

"Colonel," Randall said. "It's good to see you again."

"And you, Randall," Ritchie said in his smooth, powerful voice, a voice meant for making speeches. "I see you have the lad." Right to business, as always. "Where is his mother?"

Randall drew in a breath. His back stiffened even more. He said, "I'm sorry to have to tell you, Colonel, that I don't have the woman. She was killed on the way here."

Anger boiled up inside Ritchie. He knew better than to let it control him, so he suppressed it and said, "Your orders were to bring both the woman and the child to me, Mr. Randall."

"Yes, sir, I know. I made my best effort to do so. Her death was . . . unavoidable."

The Colonel sensed that Randall was lying to him, or at least shading the truth. That was unacceptable. He snapped, "Tell me exactly what happened, in detail. Start at the beginning. I'll decide whether or not your failure to follow orders was unavoidable."

For the next few minutes, Randall gave him the same sort of report he would have expected about a military campaign. That was the way the Colonel planned his operations, and that was the way he expected them to be carried out. The raid on the Assiniboine village sounded like it had been conducted properly, but when Randall told him how the Indian woman called Wild-flower had died, it was all the Colonel could do to keep his rage from exploding.

In an icy voice, he said, "You were derelict in your duty, Randall. You should have kept a close personal guard over the woman at all times, and if you were unable to do so, you should have delegated that assignment to a man who could be trusted."

"Yes, sir," Randall said. "You're absolutely right. I take full responsibility."

"As well you should." The Colonel forced himself to move past his anger. "However, all is not lost. Thanks to the precaution you took of making sure the woman's body isn't discovered, we can proceed almost as planned. You're certain the body won't be found?"

"We buried her at the bottom of a ravine and then caved in the bank on top of the grave," Randall said. "No one will ever know what happened."

"Very good. I'll dispatch a fast rider immediately. Within a week's time, my demands will be delivered to this Assiniboine chief Two Bears. If he wishes to see his daughter and grandson again, he and his tribe will vacate the land they currently occupy, title to which will be transferred from the government to the railroad so construction can begin."

Randall looked down at the child in his arms, then raised his head and asked, "Sir, why didn't your associates in the Ring just use the army to run off those redskins? Why go to the trouble of kidnapping the woman and the little boy?"

"I'm not in the habit of explaining my tactical decisions to subordinates, Lieu— Mr. Randall." The Colonel picked up the brandy snifter from the desk and drained what was left of the smooth, fiery liquor. "However, since you and I have been together for so long, I'll make an exception this time. The same strategy occurred to me. The Assiniboine weren't even granted that land by treaty, so there wouldn't be a problem of breaking it. But they've been friendly with the white settlers for many years, and with the army as well. My associates believed that it would look bad in the public eye to force them off the land that is traditionally theirs." Scorn dripped from the Colonel's voice. "You know it's politicians making the decisions, not soldiers, when the first consideration is how something *looks*. But after the scandals of a few years ago, they're leery of appearing too greedy, I suppose. They'd rather pull strings behind the scenes." The Colonel's brawny shoulders rose and fell in a shrug. "I'm a practical man, Randall. I have to cooperate with those who can assist me in achieving my goals. The Assiniboine will leave their land seemingly of their own free will, and the boy will be restored to his grandfather."

"What happens when Two Bears finds out he won't be getting his daughter back?"

"By then construction of the railroad will already be underway. The only way for the Assiniboine to reclaim their land would be by going to war against the United States, Randall." The Colonel smiled. "Some ragtag band of redskins against the combined might of this great nation? The very idea is ludicrous. We've crushed all the Indian opposition so far, and we'll continue to do so."

"They'd be the ones who'd look like they turned hostile," Randall mused. "Nobody would care if the army wiped them out."

"Precisely. And so progress continues, as it was ordained."

Randall nodded slowly and said, "Thanks for telling me all this, Colonel. That's pretty much the way I had it figured, but it's nice to know for sure. What do I do with the baby?"

"Give it to Mrs. Dayton. She'll care for it."

"Him, Colonel. Little Hawk's a boy."

"What? Yes, of course," Ritchie said peevishly.

"He's still nursing. You'll need to find a woman whose tits have milk."

"Don't be crude, Randall. I leave everything to Mrs. Dayton. She'll handle the situation."

"Yes, sir," Randall said.

The Colonel gave him a nod of dismissal. Randall started to turn away, then paused.

"Colonel, again, I'm sorry for what happened."

"We'll make the best of it," Ritchie said. "And we'll succeed in achieving our goals."

"There's one more thing. . . ."

"Well? Spit it out, Lieutenant." The Colonel didn't bother to correct himself this time.

"Even though they never caught up to us, it's possible that some of the Indians trailed us here. They might still cause trouble."

The Colonel smiled and said, "There's a simple way to handle that problem."

"Sir?"

"If you see one of the filthy red heathens, Randall, just kill him. That's all. Just kill him."

Preacher leaned forward in his saddle to ease stiff muscles and looked out over the basin spread before him. It was a beautiful place, and he remembered riding through here a number of times in the past, starting in his fur-trapping days as a young man. He hadn't visited these parts in seven or eight years, though.

There was one very important change since the last time he'd been here.

"There's a doggone town down there now," he said to Standing Rock. "That's new."

"White men are everywhere," Standing Rock said. "Like lice."

Preacher grunted.

"That's one way to look at it, I reckon. But the trail leads straight toward that settlement. That's bound to be where those varmints took Wildflower and Little Hawk."

For the past couple of days, Preacher and Standing Rock had been pushing the rescue party hard. Even at that faster pace, they hadn't been able to catch up to the kidnappers. The gunmen just had too big a lead.

Preacher was confident that they would have caught up sooner or later . . . but now it looked like the kidnappers had reached their destination. The whole thing still made no sense to him, but he had a hunch all the answers could be found in that settlement he hadn't known existed until now.

Standing Rock said, "We will ride in and force the white men to tell us where my wife and child are. Someone there will know."

"Hold on, hold on," Preacher said. "You can't just ride into a settlement, start grabbin' folks, and demandin' answers."

Standing Rock lifted his rifle.

"That is exactly what I mean to do," he said.

"Yeah, and you'll get yourself killed mighty quick-like, too. For one thing, if the men we're lookin' for are there, and I'm bettin' they are, they'll be on the lookout for us. For another, if a bunch of Injuns go in there actin' hostile, folks won't take the time to find out why you're upset. They'll just commence to shootin'. You've got enough sense to know that, Standin' Rock."

"Then what do you think we should do, old man?" the warrior asked.

Preacher scratched at his beard and said, "I'll tell you what we're gonna do. We're gonna find a good place to camp that's still a ways outta that town, but not too far off. Then you and your men are gonna squat right there for the time bein'. Stay outta sight and don't let anybody know you're around."

"And what will you be doing while we do that?" Standing Rock asked, sounding doubtful.

"Why, I figured I'd take a look into that town and see

if I can find out what's what," Preacher replied. "Those varmints don't know I was there when they attacked your village, and they don't know I been trailin' 'em with you." A grin stretched across his whiskery face. "Besides, who'd ever suspect a harmless ol' geezer like me of lookin' for trouble?"

Chapter 28

Irene Dayton was waiting outside the library doors when Randall came out with the Indian baby. She'd been eavesdropping, of course. She always did. She considered that part of her job because it helped her take care of the Colonel.

Randall said, "The Colonel told me to give him to you."

"Of course," Irene said with a nod. "I'll take him."

She held out her hands, but Randall hesitated and didn't give her the baby just yet. Instead, he held the little boy under the arms and lifted him so he could look into the youngster's round face.

"He's a fighter," Randall said. "Yells all the time, and if you try to do something he doesn't like, he'll kick you."

Irene smiled and said, "All babies are like that, Mr. Randall. Well, most of them, anyway. If a baby is too quiet and docile, it's a sure sign there's something wrong."

"This one's fine, then. I wouldn't call him quiet and docile, not by a long shot."

He handed over the child, adding, "His name's Little Hawk."

"I know." Irene brought the baby close to her, her right arm around his bottom, her left hand supporting his head. "When did he eat last?"

"It's been a while. I've been giving him pieces of bread soaked in sugar water."

"He needs more than that. There's a Mexican woman, the wife of one of the laborers, who gave birth a couple of weeks ago. She should have more than enough milk. I'll send for her."

"Fine," Randall said with a nod. "Thank you." He started up the hall toward the front door, then paused and looked back. "Take good care of him."

"Of course, Mr. Randall," Irene said with a smile. "Don't worry. He'll be fine. I know how important he is to Colonel Ritchie."

Randall just grunted and went on out of the house.

Irene headed for her quarters. The Colonel had expected to keep the Indian woman and the baby together and had a room set aside for them on the third floor where they would have been under guard around the clock.

However, Irene liked to prepare for any eventuality, so she had taken the liberty of preparing a place for the child in her room. True, it was only an empty crate with the lid pried off, half-filled with blankets so it would be nice and soft. A crude, makeshift excuse for a cradle, to be sure, but she thought the baby would be comfortable enough in it. At this age, they didn't care about much except getting enough to eat and having a good place to sleep. Irene would see to it that Little Hawk had both of those things.

Randall had gotten attached to the baby while they

were traveling here from the Assiniboine village. Irene had been able to see that in the big man's eyes. Well, it came as no surprise. Even the most hardened gunman's heart might melt slightly after being around a child.

She wondered if having the baby around might melt the Colonel's heart, even the tiniest bit.

"Oh, no," she said aloud as she asked herself that question.

Nothing could melt Colonel Hudson Ritchie's heart.

Preacher could tell that the settlement hadn't been there for very long. Six months, maybe. No more than a year, for sure. Many of the buildings looked new. The weather had hardly faded the raw lumber.

Some of the buildings along the main street were still empty, too, and Preacher could tell by looking that they had never been occupied. They were waiting for businesses to move in.

The houses and cabins along the side streets were different. They had people living in them. Smoke rose from their chimneys. It took a lot of citizens to build and run a town of this size, and unless some disaster happened, likely it would just get bigger. Once ranchers and homesteaders moved into this lush basin, there would be plenty of support for the town.

One thing was missing, though, and Preacher's eyes narrowed as he thought about it.

"Howdy, old-timer!"

The friendly voice calling to him broke into his musings. He looked over and saw a man standing in front of the bat-winged entrance of a saloon. Unlike some of the other buildings in town, this one was occupied and open for business.

The man who had hailed Preacher sported a derby hat and a rusty handlebar mustache. He waved at the mountain man and continued, "Come on over, friend. You look like you could use a drink. I know a thirsty man when I see one, or my name ain't Archibald Ingersoll!"

Preacher angled Horse over to the hitch rack in front of the building. A freshly-painted sign hanging from the awning over the boardwalk read: EMERALD PALACE SALOON.

"Your job is drummin' up business for this place, is it?" Preacher asked the mustachioed man.

"It's worse than that, amigo," Ingersoll replied with a grin that revealed a couple of gold teeth. "I own this drinking establishment!"

"Well, it ain't ever'day I'm invited in by the boss his ownself." Preacher swung down from the saddle and looped the reins around the hitch rack. "First drink on the house?"

"Sure, why the hell not?" Ingersoll agreed. He glanced at Dog and added, "Your, uh, wolf will have to stay outside, though."

"He ain't all wolf. Just the mean part, with the fangs." Preacher looked down at the big cur. "Stay, Dog."

"He's well-trained," Ingersoll said as Dog sat down beside the stallion.

"Yeah, until he gets the smell of blood in his nose. Then I wouldn't want to be around him."

"I'll, uh, remember that." Ingersoll held out a hand toward the bat wings. "Go right in. Tell the bartender I said to set you up with a drink on the house. Just don't be too loud about it. Wouldn't want the rest of the customers to get any ideas, you know."

Preacher grunted and pushed through the bat wings. He stepped into the saloon's cool, shady interior.

The Emerald Paradise was new enough that the usual odors of stale beer, tobacco smoke, and human sweat hadn't had time to seep into the walls, floor, and ceiling. All those smells were present, but they were mixed with the tang of fresh-cut wood and weren't overwhelming.

The long hardwood bar was to Preacher's right; tables were to his left, poker tables, a roulette wheel, and a faro layout along the wall, and in the back of the room a small open area and a stage. It looked like the saloon planned to offer live entertainment, although nothing along those lines was going on now.

The place was fairly busy, though, with half a dozen men at the bar and that many again scattered among the tables. A poker game with four players in it was going on at one of the green-covered tables. A couple of women in glittery dresses delivered drinks to the tables while a bartender in a white apron handled the trade at the bar.

A staircase in the back corner of the room led upstairs. Preacher figured those gals did more than haul drinks around. They probably hauled ashes, too, and handled that chore in the rooms upstairs.

He went to the bar and stood there until the apron came over and asked, "What can I do for you, oldtimer? We're not lookin' to hire a swamper."

An angry retort started to well up in Preacher's throat. Here he stood with a Bowie knife and two holstered revolvers, and the varmint thought he was looking for a swamper's job!

Preacher didn't want to draw too much attention to himself as soon as he rode into town, though, so he said, "I ain't lookin' for work, friend. The fella outside, calls hisself Ingersoll, said for you to draw me a beer and make it on the house."

The bartender glanced through the front windows to the boardwalk, where Archibald Ingersoll was still exhorting passersby to step into the saloon and have a drink. The man sighed and said, "The boss is gonna give away all the profits, but if that's what he wants to do I reckon it's his business."

The man filled a mug with beer and slid it across the hardwood to Preacher. The old mountain man took a long swallow and then used the back of his other hand to wipe away the foam that clung to his mustache.

"Not bad," he admitted. "Cuts the trail dust just fine."

"Been riding a long time?" the bartender asked. Like most members of his profession, he couldn't resist the urge to talk, at least when he wasn't busy serving drinks.

"Long enough," Preacher said. "Say, what do they call this settlement? Last time I rode through these parts, this basin was empty."

"This is Hammerhead," the bartender replied.

"What sort of a name is that for a town?"

The bartender shrugged and said, "I couldn't tell you. You'd have to ask the Colonel."

"The Colonel?" Preacher repeated. He recalled hearing the man who'd grabbed Wildflower using that title. Clearly, this colonel was the one who had paid to have Wildflower and Little Hawk kidnapped. He was the one possibly tied in with the Indian Ring.

"Colonel Hudson Ritchie," the bartender supplied. "He founded the town. It was all his idea."

"That'd make him like the mayor, I reckon."

"Hammerhead doesn't have a mayor," the bartender said with a laugh. "It doesn't need one. We have the Colonel instead. He owns the whole place."

"I thought this saloon belonged to Ingersoll."

"The furnishings and the fixtures do. He rents the building from the Colonel."

"Sounds like this here Colonel's got himself a pretty good deal. He starts a town, gets folks to come in and live and work in it, and still owns everything to boot."

"I guess that was his plan all along," the bartender said. "That and to bring the railroad in here. Once he does that, this basin is really going to boom. You mark my words, old-timer."

"Oh, I believe you, I believe you," Preacher muttered. He thought back to the look around the settlement he'd taken as he rode in. "I'm guessin' the big house at the end of the street belongs to the Colonel."

"Biggest house in town for the biggest man in town."

Preacher nodded. He might have tried to pump the talkative bartender for more information, but at that moment one of the men farther along the bar called for a refill, so the bartender headed in that direction, leaving Preacher to stand there and sip his beer.

The old mountain man looked like he didn't have a care in the world, but in reality his brain was working quickly. On the way into the basin he had noticed that the place had everything it needed to blossom except a railroad, and now he knew that this Colonel Ritchie intended to bring one in. Preacher couldn't connect that up with the kidnapping of Wildflower and Little Hawk, unless somehow the Assiniboine stood in the way of the Colonel's plans. That was hard to figure, because Two

Bears's village was a good hundred miles away from here. . . .

But every railroad had to start somewhere, Preacher mused. With all the mountains around here, there were only certain ways that a railroad could run. Preacher's eyes narrowed as he called up a mental picture of the territory. Like using a finger to trace a trail on a map, his brain sketched a possible route onto that mental image, starting here at Hammerhead and working his way back to—

His hand tightened on the half-full beer mug. There it was, right in front of him in his mind's eye. The route would work, angling here, bending there, curving down through the hunting grounds of the Assiniboine to hook up with the tracks already laid by the Northern Pacific.

That didn't explain everything, though. If Colonel Ritchie was involved with the Indian Ring, it would have been more their style to use political and financial pressure to force the Indians off land that traditionally belonged to them. Maybe they had changed their way of doing things since the last run-in he and Smoke and Matt had had with them. Could be they had sort of left the Colonel to deal with the problem on his own, promising him their support if he could clear the way for the railroad without involving them.

All that could be hashed out later, Preacher told himself. Right now the important thing was to find Wildflower and the little boy.

He figured he knew the first place to start looking: that big fancy house at the end of the street.

Preacher lifted his mug to finish off the beer as the bat wings flapped open. He didn't look around, but in the mirror behind the bar he caught a glimpse of the man who had just come in. A shock of recognition went through the mountain man.

The last time he had seen that big jigger was in Two Bears's village, when the hombre had Wildflower in front of him and was trying to get out of the village while the killing went on all around him.

Chapter 29

The memory of that night was etched clearly in Preacher's brain. As long and violent a life as he had led, it would seem like all the desperate gunfights ought to start blending together, but they didn't, not really. At least they didn't for him.

So if he remembered that big fella, there was a chance the man might remember him, too. Scowling, Preacher looked down into his empty mug as he set it on the bar. The broad brim of his hat would obscure his features at least partially if the man glanced into the mirror at his reflection.

Several of the men at the bar turned to greet the newcomer. A couple of others stood up from one of the tables and moved over to join them. The big man looked around and asked, "Where's Page and the rest of the bunch?"

One of the men he addressed pointed upward with a thumb and said, "Gone to visit the gals already, Randall."

"I'm surprised they had enough money left for that," the man called Randall said.

"Page has always got the price of a poke on him. Claims he never lets himself get so broke he can't afford a woman."

"All right. The others can collect their pay later, I suppose. Come on."

Carefully, Preacher watched what was going on in the mirror. Randall went over to one of the poker tables, took a leather pouch from his pocket, and opened it, spilling coins onto the green baize. He spread them out with his other hand, and the men began picking up the gold pieces.

One of them bit into a coin he picked up. That brought a laugh from Randall.

"Really, Garth?" he asked. "You really think the Colonel would try to pay you with phony money?"

"No offense, Randall," Garth said. "I trust you and the Colonel about as much as I trust anybody . . . which ain't a whole hell of a lot, I admit."

"You satisfied these double eagles are real?"

"Yeah, I'm satisfied," Garth replied as he pocketed his payoff.

Blood money, Preacher thought angrily, his jaw clenching. Every one of the coins those men were picking up was stained with Assiniboine blood and earned by slaughtering innocent men, women, and children. On top of that, they had carried off a young woman and her child. Every one of the bastards deserved to be horsewhipped and then hanged. Preacher would have handled the whipping, gladly.

What he had just overheard tied everything up with a nice, neat bow. Colonel Ritchie was behind the raid on the Assiniboine village, and the only reason for it

that made any sense was that he wanted their land for
his railroad. Like Cyrus Longacre, the unscrupulous
railroad magnate with whom Preacher, Smoke, and
Matt had clashed a while back,* the Colonel believed
he was a law unto himself.

He would learn different, Preacher vowed, maybe
even before Smoke and Matt got here.

He had no doubt that the two younger men would
follow him. They would respond to the message he had
sent them, and starting at Two Bears's village they
would follow the same trail that had led him here. There
was no telling how long it would take them to arrive,
though, and Preacher was in no mood to wait. He
wanted to get Wildflower and Little Hawk out of the
Colonel's greedy hands as soon as possible.

His ears perked up as he heard one of the men ask
Randall, "What'd you do with the kid?"

"What do you think I did with him? I left him with the
Colonel's housekeeper. She'll take good care of him."

That confirmed Preacher's guess that the little boy
could be found at the Colonel's mansion. But why no
mention of Wildflower? That question made a worried
frown appear on the old mountain man's face.

The bartender came along and asked, "You want a
refill on that beer, old-timer?"

"Uh, no, I reckon not."

"Somehow I'm not surprised. You get your free
drink, but you don't want to spend anything after that."

"I got things to do," Preacher snapped. "Don't get
uppity, son, and I might come back later."

"Yeah, you do that."

*See *The Family Jensen: Helltown Massacre.*

The bartender drifted off again. Randall and the other hired guns were still standing around the poker table, talking. Preacher didn't want to risk being in the same room with them any longer, so he turned and ambled toward the entrance, being careful to keep his face angled away from Randall so the man wouldn't have a chance to recognize him.

He didn't sigh in relief until he'd pushed through the bat wings and was on the boardwalk outside. As an added precaution he kept his head down as he went to the hitch rack and untied Horse's reins. He led the stallion away. Dog followed them.

Preacher's brain ran rapidly through his options. He didn't have a large enough force to launch an outright attack on the Colonel's house. Clearly, Ritchie had plenty of hired guns available to defend him. Not only that, but if Standing Rock and the other warriors galloped into Hammerhead and attacked the mansion, there was a good chance most of the citizens would grab their guns and put up a fight without ever knowing the truth of the situation, seeing the Assiniboine only as marauding redskins.

No, this problem called for stealth, Preacher decided. Standing Rock and the others would wait where they were until they heard from him. If he could get into the mansion, grab Little Hawk and Wildflower—assuming she was there—and get out again without being discovered, they could rejoin the rescue party and make a run for it. With enough of a lead, they could stay ahead of any pursuit, just the way Randall had stayed ahead of the rescuers during the long chase to Hammerhead.

So it was up to him, he thought as he raked his fingers

through his beard, and the only ally he would have was darkness. A glance at the sky told him there were a couple of hours of daylight left.

Once night fell, he would take a look around that mansion and see about getting inside. Until then, he needed to lie low so there wouldn't be any chance of Randall spotting him and recognizing him from the Assiniboine village.

Leading Horse, with Dog padding along beside him, Preacher headed for the nearest livery stable.

The man who ran the stable wasn't as old as Preacher, but he was getting pretty long in the tooth. After exclaiming over what a fine-looking animal Horse was, he led the stallion into a stall, where Preacher unsaddled him.

The stablekeeper, whose name was McFarland, made sure Horse had plenty of grain and water, and then said to Preacher, "How'd you feel about a game of checkers?"

That was just like these old codgers, thought Preacher, not including himself in that category, always wanting to sit around and play checkers and run their mouths.

In this case, though, that might come in handy for him. He smiled and said, "I'd plumb admire to, friend."

They went into the stable's office. Dog had to stay outside, McFarland said. He had a big yellow tomcat, and he didn't think the critters would get along.

Preacher took one look at the scarred old feline and agreed. He asked, "What do you call him?"

"I've always just called him Cat."

Preacher thought that was a pretty poor excuse for a name, but he kept that opinion to himself.

McFarland already had a checkerboard set up on the desk, where he had obviously been playing a game against himself. He cleared it off and set up the pieces again, and he and Preacher settled down to a new game.

Preacher concentrated on his moves for a few minutes, long enough to tell that McFarland wasn't a very good player, and then said, apparently casually, "I've heard a lot about that Colonel fella who runs things around here."

"Colonel Ritchie? Yeah, he founded the town. Wouldn't be a blamed thing here if it wasn't for him."

"Lives in that big house up at the end of town?"

"Yep."

"Probably got a bunch of guards around. Rich men usually do."

"I wouldn't know about that. Wouldn't surprise me, though. All I know for sure is he's got a housekeeper. Handsome woman, too. Miz Dayton, she's called. Nice as can be, always smiles at me when I pass her on the street."

That was the woman Randall had given the baby to, Preacher thought. He supposed she was devoted to her employer.

"What about a fella called Randall?"

McFarland frowned slightly and asked, "Where'd you hear about him?"

"Oh, I don't know," Preacher said casually. "Here and there, I reckon. Somebody said he's the Colonel's right-hand man."

"Yeah, you could say that, I guess. They been together since the war. Randall rode in the Colonel's cavalry regiment and was his chief scout. Reckon he'd do just about anything the Colonel ordered him to."

Including killing a bunch of innocent people and stealing a woman and her baby.

"Of course, that's just rumor," McFarland went on. "Randall don't talk about himself or the Colonel or those days back in the war. Fact is, most of the time he don't say much of anything. It makes me a mite nervous just to be around him. Big, cold-eyed galoot like that, you never know what he's gonna do. Sort of like bein' around a mountain lion, I guess."

Preacher knew what McFarland meant. Randall gave off an air of menace that seemed to come natural to him.

A man could be mighty dangerous, though, without appearing to be. He figured he was a good example of that himself.

He moved a checker and said, "Things'll be different here when the railroad comes in, I reckon."

"They sure will. There'll be a lot more people, a lot more business, and a lot more money ridin' those rails into the basin. Right now there's barely enough to get by, but those of us who got here first will stand to make a fortune when the railroad arrives."

"And the Colonel will make the biggest fortune of all."

"Well, sure. That's only fittin', ain't it?"

It would be, Preacher thought, if the man had gone about things the right way, without resorting to murder and kidnapping. He had seen men of Ritchie's stripe before, though, former military commanders who had never gotten over the power they had wielded during the war. They regarded anybody who got in the way of their plans as an enemy to be destroyed, just the same as they had destroyed their enemies during that great conflict.

McFarland chuckled and said, "You ain't payin' enough attention to your moves, friend." He jumped one of Preacher's checkers and picked it up.

"Yeah, I reckon not," Preacher said. He reached out and jumped all five of McFarland's remaining checkers, ending the game.

Too bad it probably wouldn't be that easy getting what he wanted from Colonel Hudson Ritchie.

Chapter 30

The dining table was big enough for twenty people, but the Colonel sat at it alone, a plate full of roast beef and potatoes in front of him. A glass of fine wine was at his elbow as he ate. Mrs. Dayton stood by, ready to refill the glass if need be or provide anything else he wanted.

After eating in silence for several minutes, the Colonel asked, "Where's the child?"

"Sleeping, sir."

He wasn't sure why he asked. The child's welfare was of no real concern to him. As long as Two Bears *believed* that he had both hostages in his power and did what the Colonel wanted, the ultimate fate of Wildflower and Little Hawk didn't matter at all.

Idle curiosity had prompted the question, he supposed. There had never been a baby in this house before. In all likelihood there never would be again. He was much too old for fatherhood, and the prospect never really interested him, anyway. Family responsibilities would just get in the way of all the great things he was meant to accomplish.

However, that thought made something stir in his brain. Earlier he had been pondering the possibility of someday residing in the White House. All the presidents except one had been married, the Colonel realized with a slight frown, and that one—James Buchanan—had been an incompetent boob. The public expected the nation's leader to have a wife, a First Lady who would serve as the hostess for all the important state functions held in the White House.

His gaze turned speculatively to Mrs. Dayton. She was an intelligent, attractive woman. Her late husband had been an officer who served under his command. A bit of a dullard, but a competent officer. Following the man's death, she might have been destitute had it not been for the Colonel taking her into his service, so she had always been exceedingly grateful to him. His eyes narrowed as he considered the possibilities.

She noticed him studying her. She always noticed things. That was one of her talents. With a smile, she asked, "Do you need something, Colonel?"

He gave a brusque shake of his head.

"No, no, everything's fine," he said. "I was just contemplating something. Forgive me if I was staring. You know how absorbed I become with my thoughts, Mrs. Dayton. Often I don't even see what I'm looking at."

"Yes, sir," she said. Her smile faltered slightly. "I know."

"Perhaps some more wine . . ."

"Of course, sir."

She came over to pour it. As she did, the Colonel realized how ludicrous his thoughts of a moment earlier had been. Attractive or not, the woman was a servant, certainly not suitable to be the wife of the President of the United States. She was good enough for cooking and cleaning, as well as caring for an Indian baby. She was even an acceptable, compliant bed partner for those times when the Colonel needed to slake his unavoidable human lusts. But anything else . . . ?

No. Definitely not.

"Thank you, Mrs. Dayton," he muttered as she withdrew from his side after filling his glass.

The sound of a faint cry floated through the open doors into the opulent dining room.

"He's awake," she said. "I had better go see to him."

The Colonel waved a hand negligently.

"Go ahead," he told her. "I'm fine here."

With hooded eyes, he watched her leave the room. Once he got to Washington, he thought, there would be other widows in the city, more suitable widows. Women who had been married to politicians or diplomats, women who knew how things worked in the halls of power and would be content to stay in their place, happy in the luxury and celebrity of being First Lady. He would find a woman who would make no real demands on him and turn a blind eye whenever he paid a nighttime visit to the quarters of his housekeeper. It would all work out. . . .

With enough money and power, everything always worked out, the Colonel thought as he cut off another bite of rare roast beef and popped it into his mouth.

Preacher ate supper in a hash house on Main Street and then drifted back into the Emerald Palace Saloon for another beer to let the hour get a little later before he scouted the Colonel's mansion. He checked by looking over the bat wings first to make sure Randall wasn't in the saloon. Not seeing any sign of the big gunman, he went on inside.

Archibald Ingersoll stood at the bar this time instead of outside trying to drum up business. He lifted a hand in greeting and said, "Hello, old-timer. Did you get your free drink?"

"I sure did," Preacher said. He laid a coin on the bar. "Now I figured on buyin' one."

Ingersoll chuckled.

"That's the idea, my friend." He waved the bartender over. "What are you having?"

"Beer's fine."

"Draw a mug for our amigo here," Ingersoll instructed the bartender, who wasn't the same one Preacher had talked to earlier in the day.

As Preacher sipped the beer, Ingersoll went on, "What do you think of our town so far?"

"It's all right, I reckon."

"Think you might want to settle down here?"

Preacher smiled and said, "You wouldn't want me as a citizen. I ain't the settlin'-down type."

"Too fiddle-footed, eh? I understand. I used to be the same way, always looking for a new place, searching for something better. But I've found it here, I do believe."

"Even though this Colonel fella owns everything in sight?"

The saloonkeeper shrugged and said, "He seems to be a fair man. The rent he charges me for this building is reasonable enough. And he's promised to bring the railroad in, which will make us all rich men."

"It'll make the Colonel rich, all right. I ain't so sure about anybody else." Preacher downed some more of the beer. "You ever been up there to that fancy house of his?"

"As a matter of fact, I have. A while back he ordered some wine from my suppliers, and I delivered it to him. Well, to his housekeeper, Mrs. Dayton. Wonderful woman. Nice as she can be."

"So everybody keeps tellin' me."

"It's the truth. If you ever meet her, I'm sure you'll like her, too."

"Why in the world would I ever meet up with the Colonel's housekeeper?"

"I don't know," Ingersoll said. "I was just saying that she's a fine woman."

"Does he have any other servants?"

"The Colonel? Not really. There are a couple of women who come in and help Mrs. Dayton with the cleaning, I believe, but that's all. Oh, and he has a bookkeeper, but that fellow spends most of his time in the Colonel's office here in town, not up at the house. The Colonel keeps his buggy and his horses at McFarland's livery, so there's no need for him to have a hostler of his own."

None of this chatter was getting Preacher the information he really needed. He said, "I never seen a rich man yet who didn't keep a bunch of bodyguards around."

"I wouldn't know about that. It wouldn't surprise me too much, though, if there were a couple of men patrolling the grounds around the mansion at night." Ingersoll lowered his voice. "You didn't hear it from me, mind you, but some of the men who work for the Colonel are professional gunmen. Tough hombres, too. You wouldn't want to cross them."

"I don't intend to," Preacher said, and he wasn't

lying. Under the circumstances he preferred to avoid the Colonel's gun-wolves. He wasn't scared of the varmints, but he was more interested in getting Little Hawk away from there safely and finding out what had happened to Wildflower. A shoot-out during the rescue would just endanger the tyke.

He took his time with the beer, chatting idly with Ingersoll while he nursed it. He wanted things quiet and settled down before he made his move. When he was finished, he pushed the empty mug across the bar, prompting Ingersoll to ask, "Want another?"

Preacher shook his head and said, "One's my limit, I reckon. I ain't as young as I used to be."

"None of us are, my friend, none of us are."

"I'll see you around," the mountain man said, although he knew that if everything went the way he wanted it to, that wouldn't be the case. He wouldn't see Ingersoll or anybody else in Hammerhead.

At least not for a while. Not until he came back with Smoke and Matt, cleaned out this rats' nest, and settled things with the Colonel.

He left the saloon and turned west, toward the big house on the edge of the settlement. It loomed there on top of the rise, with the yellow glow of lamplight in a couple of windows. Not everyone up there had gone to bed yet, Preacher mused, but he was tired of waiting. He wasn't as patient as he had been when he was a young man.

His steps carried him toward the mansion, and as he walked he slipped into the shadows, disappearing with the practiced ease of a man whose life had often depended on stealth.

* * *

Randall stood in the doorway of a room on the second floor of the Emerald Palace. Behind him, the whore he had just been with was getting dressed. Randall had already given her a couple of silver dollars and had been just about to leave when he spotted the old man in buckskins standing at the bar talking to Archibald Ingersoll.

Even though he couldn't see the old-timer's face from here, something about him was familiar, Randall thought. That puzzling sensation was enough to make him pause in the doorway instead of stepping out onto the balcony that ran around the rear of the barroom. He moved the door so that it was still open but cast a shadow over him.

"Something wrong, honey?" the soiled dove asked.

"No," Randall said. "Be quiet."

"Because if there's anything else you want to do, I reckon a few more minutes wouldn't hurt anything—"

"Shut up," Randall snapped.

He heard her sniff. Even a whore could get her feelings hurt. He didn't care. All the instincts he had developed over the past two decades were telling him it was important to find out more about the man at the bar.

The old-timer finished his beer. Ingersoll said something to him, and the man turned his head slightly as he replied.

Randall stiffened and drew in a deep breath through his nose. He could see enough of the man's face now to know that it was familiar. It took him only a couple of seconds to remember where he had seen those leathery, bearded features before.

In Two Bears's village, on the night of the raid. The old man was the one who had ridden in during the fighting and pursued him. Randall had gotten a fairly good look at the man's face in the firelight, and he was certain this was the same one.

The old man turned and walked out of the saloon.

Randall didn't believe for a second that it was a coincidence the old-timer was here. He had followed them all the way from the Assiniboine village to Hammerhead, and that had to mean he planned to rescue the prisoners. Well, there was only one hostage now, Randall reminded himself, but the old man wouldn't know that.

Had some of the Indians come with him? That seemed likely, Randall decided. The savages would be waiting somewhere outside of town, staying out of sight, while the old man tried to locate Wildflower and Little Hawk.

The Colonel needed to know about this, even though Randall didn't regard either the old-timer or a ragtag bunch of redskins as much of a threat. They could become an annoyance, though, and the Colonel disliked annoyances.

"You gonna stand there all night, honey?" the woman asked. "I got work to do, you know."

Randall restrained the impulse to turn around and slap the whiny bitch. Instead, he said, "I've got work, too."

Killing work.

Chapter 31

Preacher cut through alleys and circled around so that he left the town behind. He aimed to approach the Colonel's mansion from the south. Several clumps of trees in that direction would give him some cover. However, he had noticed earlier that all the trees right around the house had been cleared away, so that it sat in the open on the hilltop.

That was a sure sign of a military man, Preacher reflected. One of the first things the commander of a new fort always did was to make sure the area around it was open. That made it a lot harder for anybody to sneak up on the sentries.

Preacher had the ability to blend into whatever shadows were available, though, and he didn't mind crawling on the ground if he had to.

He still caught glimpses of the front of the mansion through the trees as he approached. The lighted windows went dark. It looked like the Colonel and his housekeeper were turning in, Preacher thought.

Another window on the back of the house, on the second floor, was lit up, though.

Preacher didn't have any idea where Little Hawk was being kept. He was worried that Wildflower wouldn't be here, too. It was possible the Colonel had split up mother and child to make sure that Wildflower followed his orders, and he could be holding her somewhere else.

First things first, he told himself. Get the little boy and take him back to Standing Rock. Then he could figure out what to do next.

He was nearing the edge of the trees, about fifty yards from the back of the house, when he stopped and stood absolutely still. The smell of tobacco smoke drifted to him.

Not far away, someone was smoking a quirly. That meant a guard, and he was likely somewhere in these trees.

The Colonel's men were supposed to be professionals, but it was a pretty sloppy mistake for a guard to give away his position like that. The man probably thought there was no real danger here in Hammerhead, so he had gotten careless.

He was about to find out what a mistake that was.

Preacher moved again, more slowly and quietly than ever. He followed the scent until he spotted the tiny orange glow of the coal at the end of the guard's cigarette. The man stood with his shoulder leaning against a tree trunk, which made his shape blend with that of the tree, but after a moment of studying the patch of darkness Preacher had them sorted out.

His fingertips caressed the handle of the Bowie knife at his waist. He knew the sentry had no idea how close danger was lurking. Preacher could step up behind the man, clap a hand over his mouth to stifle any outcry, and bury a foot of cold steel in his vitals before the hombre ever knew what was going on.

Remembering what had happened in the Assiniboine village, the old mountain man was tempted to do exactly that. If he knew for sure that the guard had taken part in the raid, he would have.

But it was possible that the man hadn't killed anybody, even though he worked for the Colonel. Preacher drew his right-hand gun instead of the knife. He reversed the weapon and struck as swiftly and silently as a snake, bringing the butt crashing down on the guard's head.

The man's hat cushioned the blow a little; otherwise, Preacher would have busted his skull open. As it was, the fella's knees unhinged and dropped him straight down. He toppled forward on his face, out cold. When he wokc up, hc would have one hell of a headache, but if he knew how close he had come to dying, he would have counted himself mighty lucky.

The quirly the man had dropped was still smoldering. Preacher ground it out with the toe of his boot. A fire might have made a good distraction, but it was too risky to take chances with anything like that.

Preacher scouted along the edge of the trees, searching for more guards. He didn't find any, which told him that the Colonel was pretty confident.

Too much confidence could sometimes get a man killed, Preacher thought with a grim smile as he dropped to his belly and started crawling toward the house.

The Colonel stood in front of the door in his dressing gown, frowning as he hesitated. This was his house. He owned everything in it, and no doors were barred to him. Yet he still felt the impulse to knock, as if he had to request permission to enter. He didn't like that feeling. He had always been one to take whatever he wanted.

But he had been raised to be a gentleman, and those lessons learned at an early age were not easily forgotten. He took a deep breath, raised his hand, and knocked.

Mrs. Dayton opened the door almost instantly, as if she had been waiting for him. She wore a dressing gown, too, belted tightly around her waist. With the door open about a foot, she smiled and said, "Yes, Colonel? Is there something I can do for you?"

She knew damned good and well what she could do for him, but despite that there was always this give-and-take, this little game that sought for some pretense for him to be here. It made him impatient sometimes, but he had become accustomed to it, like the steps of a dance.

"You have the redskin child in there with you?" he asked. The brat was as good an excuse as any to get him into her room.

"I do," Mrs. Dayton said, moving back a step and opening the door wider. She gestured toward a crate on the floor next to her bed. "I made a crib out of it."

"I'd like to take a look at him."

She stepped back even more and said, "Of course. Come in."

The Colonel went over to the crate and looked down at the sleeping child. Little Hawk appeared to be resting comfortably.

"You got the Mexican woman to come and nurse him?"

"Yes. She was glad to do anything she could to help you, Colonel."

"I should think so," he said. "After all I've done for

everyone in this town, they should all be eager to assist me."

And too frightened not to, if they knew what was good for them, he added to himself. It never hurt to have people afraid of you, as well as in your debt.

"Is there anything else you need, Colonel Ritchie?" Mrs. Dayton asked softly.

He breathed deeply.

"Yes, there is . . . Irene. I thought perhaps you would . . . enjoy some company for a time."

"I always enjoy your company, Hudson. You know that."

Moments such as these were the only times they used each other's first names. And in the morning, while what happened here tonight might not be forgotten, it would be ignored. Completely, by both of them. That was the way it had to be, and they both knew it.

He moved to take her into his arms, but as he did, the baby began to stir and fret. *Damn the luck!* the Colonel thought. The child had appeared to be sound asleep mere moments earlier. As if it sensed that it would be inconveniencing him, it was waking up now.

Him, the Colonel reminded himself. Him, not it.

"I'll settle him down," Mrs. Dayton said. She bent to lift the baby from the makeshift crib. "It'll only take a few minutes."

Little Hawk's cries weren't the only interruption, however.

At that moment someone started banging on the front door downstairs, and the sound was full of urgency.

Preacher had told Standing Rock that his Ghost Killer days were far behind him. In truth, though, he could still almost match the stealth with which he had crept into Blackfoot villages and slit the throats of his enemies.

He didn't have throat-slitting in mind tonight, but he would do it if he had to. It sure as hell wouldn't break his heart if he had to kill the Colonel in order to get Little Hawk to safety. The law might not be too pleased about that, but it had been a long, long time since Preacher had worried much about what the law liked or didn't like. He did what he knew was right and the devil with everything else.

If there were other guards keeping an eye on the house and the area around it, they never saw him. He reached the back of the mansion and stole toward the nearest window. The house was relatively new, so the window went up without sticking and making any racket. The room beyond was dark, so he threw a leg over and climbed in.

Once he was inside, he stood absolutely still again and listened intently. Somebody was moving around upstairs. One set of fairly heavy footsteps, Preacher judged. The Colonel? That was likely, since the only other person in the mansion was supposed to be the housekeeper, Mrs. Dayton, and he couldn't imagine a lady clomping around like that.

Once his senses had assured him that he was alone in the room and that no one seemed to be nearby, Preacher moved around enough to determine that he was in a kitchen. In most houses people either had a separate cook shack or prepared their meals in the same room where they spent most of their time, but it was becoming the fashion, especially in fancy places like this one, to have an actual kitchen inside the house. It seemed like foolishness to Preacher, but he supposed it was none of his business how people built their houses.

There was usually a set of rear stairs in a mansion like this, too, that would be used mostly by the servants. Once his eyes had adjusted to the even deeper darkness inside the house, he hunted around until he found the narrow staircase and started up to the second floor. He stayed close to the wall and tested each step before he put his full weight down on it, to make sure that none of them creaked underneath him.

He reached the second floor landing and a short hallway that led to what appeared to be a main corridor. It was dimly lit, and Preacher figured the glow came from the open door of the room where he had seen the lighted window. He was a little turned around, but he thought that agreed with the layout of the house. As he moved closer to the main hall, he heard the soft murmur of voices.

A man and woman were talking, he thought as he paused and pressed himself to the wall just short of the corner. It had to be the Colonel and Mrs. Dayton. He couldn't make out the words, but he stiffened as he recognized what he heard next.

The fretful wail of a baby crying.

Little Hawk! Preacher was sure of it. One of the captives he had come all this way to rescue was only a few feet away from him. His fingers closed around the butt of his right-hand revolver. He was about to draw the gun, move around the corner, step into that room, and throw down on the Colonel.

That was when somebody began slamming a fist against the front door downstairs.

Preacher heard those heavy footsteps coming toward him and drew back deeper into the shadows. A bulky, bald-headed man in a dressing gown moved past him. That was Colonel Hudson Ritchie, Preacher thought, the man who had ordered death and destruction delivered to the Assiniboine village. Preacher had to make a physical effort not to step out behind him and brain the son of a bitch.

Little Hawk's safety was his first concern, though, and this was his chance to get the baby and find out from the housekeeper where Wildflower was. If she was like every other housekeeper Preacher had ever seen, she knew all about her employer's business.

Besides, he didn't know who was downstairs, but from the sound of the knocking on the door, the varmint was getting pretty impatient.

Chapter 32

"What the devil do you want?" the Colonel demanded angrily as he jerked the door open.

Randall was glad to see that the Colonel had at least had the sense to pick up a gun before he opened the door. He had a long-barreled, silver-plated Remington in his hand. Randall knew that the Colonel was quite a good shot with the revolver, too.

"I've got news, Colonel," Randall said.

"It had better be important."

The Colonel sounded really annoyed. Randall wondered briefly if he'd been engaged upstairs with Mrs. Dayton. Randall knew good and well the Colonel bedded that housekeeper of his on a regular basis. The Colonel's personal life didn't matter one way or the other to Randall, except when it threatened to have an effect on the way he did his own job.

"I was in the Emerald Palace Saloon a little while ago and saw an old man I recognized. He was in the Assiniboine village the night we carried out our operation."

"An old man?" the Colonel repeated. "You came up here and disturbed me because you saw an old man?"

Randall swallowed the exasperation he felt because the Colonel didn't seem to grasp what he was saying. He went on, "The important thing is that he was with the Indians. He may have tracked us here and brought a war party with him."

"Did you see any Indians in town tonight, Lieutenant?"

"No, sir."

"Just an old man. Are you sure it was the same old man?"

Randall's jaw tightened. The Colonel was making fun of him. He didn't like that, but he would put up with it, of course, as he always had.

"I'm sure," he said. "I think we need to increase the guards. Those savages could try to get into the house."

The Colonel waved the hand that wasn't holding the revolver.

"Fine, go ahead. I trust your judgment in matters like this, Randall, you know that. Now, is that everything?"

Randall said, "I think we should check on the baby."

"The child is fine. I saw it just a few minutes ago."

"No offense, sir, but I'd feel better about that if I saw him for myself."

The Colonel's eyes narrowed angrily.

"Your attitude is bordering on insubordination, Lieutenant, you know that."

"I'm sorry, sir. I just want to be sure."

With an irritated sigh, the Colonel said, "Very well, then. Come on."

Randall stepped into the house, and the two men started toward the wide, curving staircase that led to the second floor.

* * *

Preacher waited until the Colonel reached the bottom of the stairs and then darted around the corner into the main hall. The door of one of the rooms stood open, just as he expected, spilling light into the corridor. The sound of Little Hawk's crying still came from inside that room

Quickly and silently, Preacher cat-footed toward the door. He was nearly there when a figure suddenly moved into the opening. It was a blond, middle-aged woman who had to be Mrs. Dayton, the housekeeper, and she had Little Hawk cradled in her arms, holding him against her shoulder as she tried to quiet his crying.

Her eyes opened wide as she saw the tall, buckskin-clad man moving swiftly toward her. Fear and shock were on her face. She opened her mouth to shout to the Colonel.

Preacher's left hand shot out and clamped around her jaw, silencing her. At the same time he slid his right arm around her and jerked her toward him, trapping her against his body with Little Hawk between them. She tried to twist away from him, but she was no match for his strength.

He put his face close to hers and whispered, "Take it easy, ma'am. I ain't lookin' to hurt you or the child. Fact is, I'm here to save the poor little varmint from whatever the Colonel's got planned for him. I'm good friends with his ma and pa and grandpa."

It was stretching the truth to claim that he and Standing Rock were friends. At the moment, that didn't matter, and anyway, Preacher and Two Bears had indeed been good friends for decades.

"Now, I know you work for Colonel Ritchie," Preacher went on, "but I want you to give Little Hawk to me and not raise a ruckus while I slip back out of here. Before

I go, though, you need to tell me where I can find the little fella's ma. Her name is Wildflower, and I know that wherever she is, she's sure missin' her son."

Preacher didn't like the look that came into the woman's eyes when he said that. Mrs. Dayton stopped fighting. Even though his big hand still covered the lower half of her face, he could see the sorrow that crept into her expression.

That recognition shook Preacher. He leaned even closer and whispered, "Did somethin' happen to Wildflower?" A part of him didn't want to hear the answer, but he had to know the truth.

Mrs. Dayton swallowed and then nodded.

"If I take my hand away, will you promise not to scream?"

Again, she nodded. Preacher didn't know if he could trust her not to yell, but he didn't think she was lying about something happening to Wildflower. The emotion in her eyes was too genuine for that.

He lifted his hand slightly, ready to grab her again if he needed to. She licked her lips and said quietly, "The child's mother . . . the poor woman . . . she was killed. She tried to escape, and one of the men bringing her here . . . shot her."

The words were like a knife in Preacher's guts. His first thoughts were for Two Bears, who would have to find out eventually that his youngest child was dead. Preacher reckoned there was no greater pain possible than that.

But having Little Hawk returned safely to his people might mitigate that loss. Not much, but anything that eased the grief of Wildflower's death would be welcome.

Then there was Standing Rock. When he found out that his wife had been killed, the warrior might well go insane with anger and loss. Preacher wouldn't blame him a bit for feeling that way, either. But somehow, Standing Rock would have to keep his wits about him and not lose control while they tried to get Little Hawk away from here.

"I ain't gonna ask you what-all the Colonel was plannin'," he told the housekeeper. "I don't care right now. I just want the boy. Will you let me take him and give me your word you won't raise the alarm?"

While he was talking, he had been aware of a faint rumble of men's voices downstairs. Now those voices were coming closer, and he thought he heard footsteps at the bottom of the stairs. He had to move fast, even if it meant taking Little Hawk from the woman and letting her yell her fool head off while they got away.

"I'll help you," she whispered with a note of urgency coming into her voice. "Come this way!"

She didn't let go of the baby, but she stepped away from the door and beckoned for Preacher to follow her in the opposite direction from the short hallway that led to the rear stairs. When he hesitated, she added, "There's another set of stairs. You can't go back the way you came!"

She was probably right about that. Preacher started to follow her. She took a quick step aside, and he realized too late that she was double-crossing him. She darted past him, still clutching Little Hawk, and screamed, "Colonel! Colonel, help!"

Preacher grated a curse and reached for her, snagging the collar of her dressing gown. She cried out as he jerked her toward him.

At the same time, Colonel Ritchie appeared at the top of the stairs, shouting angrily. The big gunman called Randall was right behind him. Ritchie had a gun in his hand. He jerked it up and fired, flame stabbing from the revolver's muzzle.

The loco son of a bitch! Preacher thought. Little Hawk and the woman were in the line of fire, but the Colonel obviously didn't care about that. He saw an intruder in his house, and the killing rage that filled him was the only thing that mattered.

The Colonel's first shot missed, whistling past Preacher's ear. The man was already about to fire again, though. Preacher used his left hand to give Mrs. Dayton a hard shove that sent her and Little Hawk tumbling through the doorway into her room, out of the path of any more slugs.

At the same time, the old mountain man's right hand palmed out the holstered Colt on that side. The gun came up fast, spitting flame.

Preacher's shot would have struck the Colonel in the chest, but at that instant Randall drove a shoulder into the Colonel and knocked him aside. The slug from Preacher's gun clipped the upper part of Randall's left arm and knocked him halfway around. He kept his feet, though, and didn't drop the gun in his right hand. It roared deafeningly.

Preacher felt the impact of Randall's bullet as he triggered a second shot. It made him take a step back. He was hit somewhere in the body, and a hot weakness began to spread through him like a rampaging flood.

Many times over the years, he had been wounded in the middle of gunfights. He knew how to stay on his feet and keep those smoke poles working even though he was hit. He drew his left-hand gun and fired at the Colonel, but Randall knocked him all the way down this time. As the Colonel sprawled on the balcony, Randall dropped to a knee beside him and coolly squeezed off another shot.

The man was good in a fracas; Preacher had to give him that. Randall's shot tore along Preacher's left forearm and made him drop that gun.

"Kill him!" the Colonel shrieked, his voice sputtering and almost incoherent with fury.

Preacher reeled to the side, trying desperately to stay upright, but his shoulder hit the wall and caused his balance to desert him even more. His strength was going, too. The gun in his right hand slipped from his fingers.

This was one sorry state of affairs, he thought. Shot up like this at his age. And the worst of it was that he hadn't succeeded in getting Little Hawk away from these polecats before he got ventilated.

He didn't know he was falling until he hit the floor. His eyes were open, but the walls around him were spinning crazily. He heard sounds around him, but they were distorted, indecipherable. Then he recognized heavy footsteps, and a big, ugly shape loomed over him. Colonel Hudson Ritchie stood there pointing a Remington revolver at Preacher's face, and to the mountain man the muzzle looked as big around as a cannon.

The Colonel's face was flushed and twisted. He was about to pull the trigger. Preacher knew that, but there was nothing he could do about it.

Then Randall was at his side, taking hold of the Colonel's wrist and pushing the gun aside.

"Begging your pardon, sir," the man said, his voice hollow and barely human in Preacher's ears but understandable. "It wouldn't be a good idea to kill him before we question him. We need to find out how many men he has with him and where they are."

"Get your hand off me, Randall," the Colonel said

through clenched teeth. "I'll forgive your impudence . . . this time."

Randall let go of the Colonel's gun wrist and stepped back. His words must have gotten through, because the Colonel lowered the weapon and went on, "Take charge of the prisoner, Lieutenant."

"Yes, sir."

Randall kicked Preacher's fallen Colts well out of reach, then bent and got an arm around the mountain man. He lifted Preacher easily.

Preacher was groggy from loss of blood but still conscious. He saw Mrs. Dayton standing in the doorway of her room, still holding Little Hawk. The boy was crying, and she was trying to comfort him. She looked up, and for a second her eyes met Preacher's.

He thought he saw regret there. She had acted on impulse and out of loyalty to the Colonel when she betrayed him, but now she was starting to think she might have made a mistake. He was still aware enough to realize that.

But it was too late for regret. He was wounded, maybe dying, and had been taken prisoner. At the moment, there was nothing more he could do.

But help was on the way, he thought as consciousness began to fade.

Somewhere out there, maybe at this very moment, Smoke and Matt Jensen were riding toward Hammerhead.

BOOK FIVE

Chapter 33

For a week now, Smoke and Matt had been pushing their horses pretty hard. The 'Palouse and Matt's big steel dust were up to the challenge, carrying their riders in a ground-eating lope with seemingly effortless ease for long hours at a time.

Smoke knew that the mounts were nearing the end of their stamina, though. That was why he was glad their destination might be in sight as they reined in and paused at the mouth of the pass overlooking a broad green basin.

Matt let out a low whistle of admiration as he gazed across the landscape.

"Smoke, this is some of the best country I've come across in a long time. It looks like it's danged near as good as the Sugarloaf."

"Yeah, but look how it's situated," Smoke said as he rested his hands on the horn and leaned forward in the saddle. "There are mountains on two sides of it, east and south, and some pretty rugged-looking breaks on the west. The only good route in for freight wagons is to the north, and you'd have to go almost all the way to

Canada before you circled back south into the basin. You'd run into the same problem if you were trying to drive cattle out. They'd have all the fat run off them by the time you got them to market."

"It appears what the folks in these parts really need is a railroad."

Smoke pointed to some stakes driven into the ground in various places.

"Like the one that somebody's already surveying for?" he asked. "It won't be easy building a spur line all the way up to this pass and on through into the basin, but it can be done. And if it is, whoever does it will stand to make a whole heap of money."

Matt pointed, as well, to the town that was visible in the distance.

"Whoever's planning to do that, I'll bet we can find him in that settlement down yonder."

"Bound to be," Smoke agreed as he nodded slowly. "Question is, will we find Preacher down there as well?"

For days now, they had been on the trail of the old mountain man and the raiders who had attacked the Assiniboine village. Smoke had gone there in response to Preacher's telegram, to meet with Chief Two Bears and find out exactly what had happened. After spending the night and enjoying Two Bears's hospitality, Smoke had been getting ready to take up Preacher's trail when Matt rode in. That was good timing, because they were able to travel together and Smoke could fill in his adopted brother on the details of their mission, which was to find Preacher and help him in any way they could.

The trail hadn't been difficult to follow. They could have done so anyway, since both men were expert trackers, but Preacher had made it even easier for them by leaving what amounted to road signs along the way, carving special marks into tree trunks and scratching them onto rocks.

Nothing as crude as arrows pointing the right direction, however, so that to anyone other than Preacher, Smoke, and Matt the marks would have appeared completely random and natural. That was another example of how the three men could communicate by what seemed like supernatural means, when it was really just good planning and common sense.

"It could be that the trail doesn't stop at the settlement," Matt commented. "Maybe whoever kidnapped Wildflower and Little Hawk went around the town and kept going."

"If they did, we'll see signs of it," Smoke said with confidence. He lifted the 'Palouse's reins. "Come on."

They followed the trail down from the pass into the basin, and as they rode, Smoke's experienced eyes looked over the terrain and picked out places where a possible railroad could run. He had been involved in the construction of several rail lines in the past, and while he certainly wasn't an expert on the matter, he knew enough to tell that getting the rails through the pass would be the difficult part. Once they were in the basin, the rest of the job would be relatively easy.

Smoke kept his eyes open as well for more of Preacher's marks. He and Matt spotted some of them on a tree at the same time and brought their mounts to a halt.

"Looks like the trail leads up that little canyon," Matt said as a frown creased his forehead. "It's not going toward the settlement after all. Maybe that's not really Preacher's mark."

Smoke brought the 'Palouse closer to the tree and studied the scratches in the bark.

"Preacher left it there, all right," he said. "I'd know that old-timer's work anywhere. He knew we'd be coming along behind him, and he wanted us to ride up that canyon."

Matt pulled his Winchester from its scabbard and rested the rifle across the saddle in front of him.

"Then I guess we'd better ride up it," he said. "My gut's telling me to be ready for trouble, though."

Smoke drew his Winchester from its sheath as well and said dryly, "No reason for today to be different from any other day."

The canyon wasn't very big, maybe fifty yards across, and its walls were roughly thirty feet tall. A small creek meandered along it and led into some thick stands of cottonwood and aspen. Smoke felt his nerves draw taut as he and Matt rode into the trees. This would be a good spot for an ambush.

Because he was expecting trouble, Smoke wasn't surprised when an Indian suddenly stepped out from behind one of the trees ahead of them and leveled a rifle at them. Matt let out an exclamation and was about to jerk his Winchester to his shoulder when Smoke said, "Hold it!" He added, "Take a look around, Matt."

Matt did so and saw the same thing Smoke had seen from the corner of his eye: About a dozen rifle barrels were pointed at them from behind tree trunks, rocks, and clumps of brush.

"Some tough hombres we are," Matt said disgustedly. "We rode right into a trap."

"Maybe not. Remember, Preacher told us to come this way, and unless I'm mistaken, the markings and decorations on those buckskins those fellas are wearing say that they're Assiniboine."

"You reckon they're Standing Rock and the rest of the warriors who went with Preacher?"

"That's what I'm counting on," Smoke said with a faint smile.

If he was wrong, they might both wind up dead.

There was only one good way to find out. He raised his right hand, palm out in the universal symbol of peaceful greeting, and said, "We're looking for Standing Rock. I'm Smoke Jensen, and this is Matt Jensen."

The warrior who had revealed himself slowly lowered his rifle. He had been glaring at them ever since he stepped out from behind the tree, and his expression didn't get much friendlier as he said in English, "I am Standing Rock. How do I know that you are Preacher's friends?"

"He told you that he sent a telegram asking for me and Matt to help him, didn't he? Actually, he asked Chief Two Bears to have it sent, if you want to get right down to it. Matt and I rendezvoused at Two Bears's village, and we've been on your trail ever since. If you want me to describe Preacher to you, I reckon I can do that. I've known the old pelican for more than fifteen years. The easiest way, though, would be to bring him out here and let him take a look at us."

Even as he spoke, worry was stirring inside Smoke. He had expected Preacher to be with the Assiniboine rescue party. If he wasn't, it meant that something might have happened to the old mountain man, as inconceivable as that was.

Standing Rock's scowl deepened. He said, "I would show you to the one called Preacher if I could, but . . . he is not here. We have not seen him for almost a week, since he went into that white man's town to look for my wife and son."

"He's been missing for a week?" Matt said, sounding every bit as worried as Smoke felt.

"You've got a camp around here somewhere, don't you?" Smoke asked.

"We do," Standing Rock admitted. "Preacher helped us find a good place and told us to remain there, out of sight of the white men, until he came back. But he never did."

"Why don't we go to your camp," Smoke suggested, "and we'll talk about it and figure out our next move?"

That was agreeable to Standing Rock. He motioned for his warriors to put down their guns. Smoke and Matt dismounted. Leading their horses, they walked with Standing Rock around several bends in the creek to a clearing that was concealed by thick growths of trees all around. The remains of a fire and bedrolls spread around showed that this was where the Assiniboine had been making their home for the past several days.

Smoke and Matt let their mounts drink from the creek and graze on the grass that grew along its banks. The horses didn't mix with the Indian ponies that were picketed at the edge of the camp.

"We have food," Standing Rock offered.

"Matt and I brought along plenty of supplies," Smoke said, "but thank you. I want to hear more about Preacher."

"He was going to look for Wildflower and Little Hawk. He believed they had been taken to the settlement to be turned over to a man known as the Colonel."

Smoke and Matt exchanged a glance. Matt said, "That's probably the hombre Preacher thought might be tied up with the Indian Ring. He sounds like somebody who would be."

Smoke nodded in agreement and said to Standing Rock, "Go on."

"Preacher believed that if all of us rode into the settlement and tried to force the whites to tell us where my wife and son are, they would think we were attacking and there would be a battle."

"That's probably right," Smoke said. "So he planned to go in and scout around because nobody would pay any attention to an old geezer like him."

"There aren't any other old geezers just like Preacher," Matt added. "But I guess you can't really tell that by looking at him."

Standing Rock said, "That is what he planned. If he could rescue them and get them out of town without raising an alarm, he planned to do so. Otherwise, he would return here and tell us what he found, so that we could think on what to do."

"But he never came back," Smoke said.

"That is right. And with every day that passes, I become more fearful for Wildflower and Little Hawk."

Smoke couldn't blame the man for feeling that way. He was pretty worried about Preacher right now. The only thing that would have kept him from returning to the Assiniboine as he had promised was if he had been taken prisoner.

Or if he was dead.

Smoke wasn't going to allow himself to think that, at least not yet. He said, "I know it's hard, Standing Rock, but Preacher was right about you and your men staying out of sight. Until we know what's going on, it would just cause more problems than it's worth to have you show up in the town."

"So what will we do?"

"I hate to ask it of you, but I think it would be best

if you stayed right here for a little while longer. Matt and I will ride into the settlement and see if we can find Preacher and your family."

"And if the two of you never return?"

"We'll go in separately," Smoke said. "That'll double our chances of success. And once we've found out what we need to know, we'll come back here and decide how to get them all."

"Do not take too long doing this, Smoke Jensen," Standing Rock warned. "My patience is almost gone. I feel the need to kill my enemies."

"I've got a hunch that it won't be much longer before you get the chance," Smoke said.

Chapter 34

Matt left the Assiniboine camp and headed for the settlement first. Smoke would follow an hour later. Since they weren't brothers by blood, no one in town would notice any family resemblance between them. They could pretend to be complete strangers and pull that off without any trouble.

Standing Rock hadn't been able to tell them what the name of the town was. Matt was a little curious about that as he rode in a short time later. He kept his eyes open for Preacher, but he didn't really expect to see the old mountain man walking down the street. Preacher would have returned to the camp in the canyon as planned if he was able to.

"Hey, young fella! New in town?"

Matt wasn't sure the greeting was directed at him. He turned his head and looked toward the boardwalk. The man who stood there was a burly gent with a derby hat shoved down on his head. A red handlebar mustache adorned his upper lip and gave him a distinctive appearance. He grinned and motioned toward Matt.

"Are you talking to me, mister?" Matt asked as he nudged the stallion over to the side of the street.

"Come on inside and have a drink," the man invited as he waved a hand toward the bat-winged entrance of the saloon in front of which he stood. The Emerald Palace Saloon, Matt noted as he glanced at the sign hanging over the boardwalk. The man continued, "The coldest beer between here and Montana!" He dropped an eyelid in an exaggerated wink. "And the prettiest girls, too!"

Both of those things sounded appealing to Matt, especially after a week on the trail, but he was here to do a job, he reminded himself. He had find out what had happened to Preacher, and if he could locate Wildflower and Little Hawk while he was doing that, so much the better.

On the other hand, he thought, a saloon was often one of the best sources of information in a town.

"Come on," the man with the handlebar mustache prodded. "A young fella like you is bound to have plenty of wild oats that still need sowing!"

"You're right about that, mister," Matt said as he reached a decision. He put a big grin on his face so he would look more like a callow, eager youngster who was no threat to anybody except maybe himself. He swung down from the saddle and tied up the stallion at the hitch rail in front of the saloon.

As he stepped up onto the boardwalk, the man slapped him on the back and said, "Archibald Ingersoll's the name, son, and this is my place. Go right in there and tell the bartender to set up your first drink on the house. Don't worry; it's our policy here at the Emerald Palace."

"I'm much obliged, Mr. Ingersoll."

"And your name is . . . ?"

"Matt Stevens, sir."

He didn't know if there was any need to use a fake name, but it couldn't hurt anything. His name wasn't as well known as Smoke's, but there might be somebody in this settlement who had heard of Matt Jensen and would wonder why he was here. No point in arousing anybody's curiosity when he didn't have to.

"Well, I'm pleased to meet you, Matt," Ingersoll said, catching hold of Matt's hand and pumping it enthusiastically. "Hope you'll stay around for a while. Hammerhead needs all the solid citizens it can get."

"Hammerhead? That's the name of this settlement?"

"That it is. So dubbed by our founder, the illustrious Colonel Hudson Ritchie."

That would be the Colonel Preacher had mentioned. Ingersoll seemed eager to talk, so Matt postponed going into the saloon for a moment and said, "This Colonel Ritchie, he's in the army?"

"He was. A highly decorated cavalry commander in the Union forces during the Late Unpleasantness. I don't take sides in that dispute, by the way. It's over, so I say live and let live, and besides, a good businessman can't afford to make enemies of potentially half his customers, can he?"

"I suppose not. I've never run a business."

"I can tell that by looking at you, son," Ingersoll said. "You're an adventurer; anyone can see that, a bold young cavalier in search of romance and excitement."

This fella sure was in love with the sound of his own voice, thought Matt. But as long as Ingersoll was willing to talk, he was willing to listen.

"So the Colonel's not a military man anymore?"

"Well, once a soldier, always a soldier, I suppose," the saloonkeeper said. "But Colonel Ritchie's a businessman now. He started this town, and he's going to bring in the railroad. The basin's going to boom, son, mark my words!"

"Yes, sir, I don't doubt it. The Colonel sounds like a good man to hitch a wagon to. You think maybe he's hiring?"

For the first time since Matt had met the man, a shadow passed over Ingersoll's face. His eyes took Matt in, head to foot, and he said, "You don't really look like a carpenter or a blacksmith or anything like that. Do you have a trade, Matt?"

Matt shrugged and hooked his thumbs in his gun belt.

"You could say that. It's not hammering nails or shoeing horses, though."

"I don't know. You'd have to talk to a fellow named Randall. He's the Colonel's second-in-command, I guess you could say. Wouldn't surprise me to find out that they rode together during the war, but I don't know that for a fact."

"Where would I find him?"

Ingersoll inclined his head toward the bat wings and said, "He's in there playing billiards. Just got the table in this week, in fact." He paused, then added, "Walk easy around Randall, my young friend. I wouldn't pretend to know the reason, but he's been a mite on edge the past week or so. Might be from that bullet graze on his arm."

That told Matt probably more than Ingersoll intended for it to. It had been about a week since Preacher had ridden into Hammerhead and promptly disappeared. Randall worked for the Colonel, he had a wounded arm, and he'd been edgy for the past week. All that added up to one thing as far as Matt could see.

Preacher had swapped lead with this fella Randall before he'd gone missing. Randall was still alive, so that meant . . .

Matt's jaw tightened. He refused to believe that Preacher was dead. It was hard enough to believe that the old-timer might have come out second-best in a gunfight. Even at his advanced age, Preacher was slicker on the draw than nine out of ten men he might run up against.

But there was always that tenth man to consider, and Randall might be him.

"Are you all right, Matt?" Ingersoll asked, breaking into Matt's grim thoughts. "For a second there, you looked like . . . well, you looked like you were ready to kill somebody."

Matt forced that carefree grin back onto his face.

"Me? Nah, I'm fine, Mr. Ingersoll. Just a mite thirsty for that beer you mentioned, that's all, I reckon."

"Then by all means go ahead and get it, son. Remember, first drink's on the house in the Emerald Palace." He winked again. "But only for special customers, you understand."

Matt didn't figure he was all that special, but he didn't contradict the saloonkeeper. He gave Ingersoll a friendly nod, stepped over to the bat wings, and pushed through them into the barroom.

It took a second for his eyes to adjust to the dimness inside the saloon after being in the bright afternoon sunlight outside, but he heard the click of billiard balls right away and looked in that direction. As his vision sharpened, he saw the felt-covered table in the rear corner of the room, next to a small stage that was empty at the moment. A big man stood alone next to the table, chalking a cue stick. He had pushed his hat back off his head so that it hung from its chin strap around his strong, thick neck. A bulky area under his left shirtsleeve showed where he had a bandage wrapped around his upper arm.

Yep, that had to be Randall, all right. The glare on his face was added proof.

Matt didn't want to pay too much attention to Randall right away, so he turned and ambled over to the bar. When the bartender came up, Matt said, "I'll have a beer, and the fella outside said to set it up on the house."

"Of course, he did," the bartender said with a sigh. "A dozen times a day, he gladhands somebody in here with the promise of a free drink. I suppose that as long as he can pay my wages, though, I shouldn't complain."

The man filled a mug with beer and set it in front of Matt, who picked it up and took a long swallow. It wasn't exactly cold, as Ingersoll had claimed, but it was pleasantly cool and had a smooth taste to it. Matt nodded in appreciation.

"When I finish this one, you can draw me another," he told the bartender.

"You're getting a second one and paying for it? Will wonders never cease!"

Matt chuckled at the acid-tongued bartender. He supposed a man in that line of work saw more than enough to make him cynical.

He turned, resting his right elbow on the bar so that his hand hung fairly close to the butt of the Colt on his hip, while he held the beer mug in his left hand and sipped from it. It was a casual stance, the sort that any man might adopt while enjoying a cool beer on a warm afternoon. But the important thing was that it allowed him to keep an eye on everybody in the saloon except for the bartender.

There were a couple of dozen customers at the moment. Matt's eyes flicked over them, quickly cataloging them. He could pick out the regular townspeople—the clerks, the laborers, the men who owned small businesses—without much trouble.

But there were half a dozen other men, lean, hard-eyed, roughly dressed for the most part. Matt had run into their sort many times in the past, despite his relative youth. He knew he was looking at gunmen, more than likely hired killers who would take any job if the price was right.

Randall fell into that same category. Matt thought it was likely all those men worked for the Colonel, and Randall was the crew's ramrod.

Randall or one of those other men might have killed Preacher, Matt thought. At the very least, they probably knew what had happened to the old mountain man.

That was the information Matt needed to find out. Once he did . . .

Then if there was a score to be settled, he could get started on the settling up.

Finished chalking the cue stick, Randall lined up a shot at one of the balls scattered on the table and sunk it. He moved around to study his next shot. As he did, footsteps sounded on the stairs that led to the second floor. Matt glanced in that direction and saw a man descending. He was sandy-haired, with a pinched, ugly face that was flushed red at the moment. It was clear from the man's face and the slight unsteadiness of his movements that he was drunk.

Randall wasn't paying any attention to the newcomer. As the man reached the bottom of the stairs, he slipped his gun from its holster. Randall's back was turned toward him as he drew.

Matt had seen enough ambushes to know what was about to happen. The newcomer yelled, "All right, Randall, time to pay up for Dwyer!" and thrust his gun out in front of him, ready to commit murder.

Chapter 35

Matt's thoughts worked like lightning. He had no reason to save Randall's life, especially if the man had done something to Preacher.

But there were still too many questions, and Randall might have the answers to some or even all of them. So maybe there *was* a good reason to keep the other man from gunning him down after all.

Even under these circumstances, Matt didn't want to shoot a man in the back. Instead, he threw the half-full beer mug as hard as he could. The heavy glass mug crashed into the back of the would-be killer's head with such force that it knocked him forward a step. The gun in the man's hand roared, but the barrel had dipped and the slug thudded into the floor between him and Randall, kicking up splinters.

With the instincts of the big cat he resembled, Randall reacted with blinding speed and whirled around. The gunman was out of arm's reach, but Randall still held the cue stick. He whipped it across the man's face, shattering the stick. Randall leaped forward and brought the piece he still held down sharply across the man's wrist.

Matt heard something break, but he wasn't sure if it was cue stick or bone. Either way, the man dropped the gun. Randall grabbed the front of his shirt with both hands and heaved, pivoting at the hips as he hauled the man off his feet and flung him like a rag doll through one of the saloon's side windows. Glass shattered and sprayed outward as the man flew through the air for a few feet and then crashed limply to the ground outside the saloon.

The flurry of violent action had taken only seconds. The rest of the people in the saloon had barely had time to lift their heads to see what all the commotion was about.

Randall drew his gun as he looked out the window at the man's huddled shape. Matt had moved forward enough to peer past Randall's shoulder. The man lying on the ground was either out cold or dead. Randall didn't appear to be overly concerned about which one it was as he grunted and holstered his gun.

"Simmons, Quitman, get out there and gather up Page," Randall ordered. "If he's alive, tend to him. If he's dead, haul him to the undertaker."

Two men, who'd been seated at a table, playing poker, threw in their cards without argument and stood up to hurry out of the saloon.

Randall looked over at Matt and said in a cold voice, "Who the hell are you?"

"The name's Stevens," Matt replied.

"You're the one who made Page miss by throwing that beer mug at his head?"

"That's right."

"Pretty quick thinking. But why'd you do it? I never laid eyes on you before, at least not that I remember."

"Nope, you haven't," Matt said. "I just rode in to town less than half an hour ago. As for why I stepped in . . . let's just say I don't cotton to back-shooters."

"Maybe I deserve to be shot in the back. You don't know me."

"That's true," Matt admitted. "But I was willing to take a chance."

Randall studied him for a long moment and then finally nodded.

"I'm obliged to you for the help," he said. "I might've been able to handle him on my own, but you made it easier, Stevens."

"Glad I was in the right place at the right time," Matt said, and in his own way, he meant it. He nodded toward the window. On the other side of it, the two men Randall had sent out there were picking up a groggy and moaning but very much alive ambusher. "That fella must be holding a powerful grudge against you."

"I killed a friend of his," Randall said curtly. "The bastard had it coming."

"What did he do?"

"Shot a woman in the back. She was an Indian woman, but still . . ." Randall's voice trailed off as he looked at Matt with narrowed eyes. "You ask a lot of questions, mister, and you're a stranger, to boot."

Matt held up both hands and said, "I didn't mean to pry. Just curious, that's all."

"Forget it. I reckon you've earned a little curiosity."

Archibald Ingersoll had come into the saloon. He approached Randall cautiously and chose that moment to speak up.

"Mr. Randall, sir . . ."

Randall didn't let him go on.

"The Colonel will pay for the window." Randall reached down and picked up the now-empty beer mug from the floor. He handed it to Ingersoll and added, "At least the mug didn't break."

"I'm not worried about the mug or the window, Mr. Randall," Ingersoll said. "But if you consider me in any way to blame for what happened—"

"Because your bartender sold Page the bottle he got drunk on?" Randall snorted. "Page is a grown man, Ingersoll. He makes his own decisions. Bad ones, usually."

"Yes, sir. Just so we're clear and everything's all right."

"It's fine. Get the window replaced and give me the bill. I'll see that it's paid."

"It won't be cheap," the saloonkeeper warned, "with freight having to go so far around the mountains, and it's a long way to start with to the nearest town with glass like that."

"Just take care of it," Randall said, obviously growing impatient. He kicked the broken cue stick aside, adding that the Colonel would pay for it, too, and then said to Matt, "Come on, Stevens. I'll buy you a beer to replace the one you lost."

Normally, Matt wouldn't think of having a drink with a man he suspected of harming Preacher, but under the circumstances, being friendly with Randall might be the best thing he could do. There were still plenty of things he needed to find out.

Such as the identity of the Indian woman who had been shot in the back. A terrible chill had gone through Matt when he heard those words, but he thought he had been able to keep the reaction from showing on his face.

"I appreciate that," he said. He and Randall turned toward the bar.

When they had their beers, Randall picked up his and nodded toward an empty table.

"Let's sit down," he suggested.

"Sure," Matt agreed.

They took their seats. Matt thumbed back his hat like he didn't have a care in the world and took a long swallow of the cool beer.

"What brings you to Hammerhead, Stevens?" Randall asked.

Matt thought it was more than mere curiosity that prompted the question. Randall was eyeing him speculatively, like he had something else in mind.

"Nothing in particular," Matt replied. "I'm just drifting. I came through the pass in the mountains to the east and thought this basin was mighty pretty. Saw the settlement in the distance and decided to take a walk over here. I've been riding a lot of lonely trails lately."

"Been hearing a lot of owls hoot at night, have you?"

Matt shrugged. If Randall wanted to think that he was on the dodge, that was just fine.

"You're fast with a beer mug," Randall went on. "How are you with a gun?"

"I get by. I'm still alive and kicking, and I've seen my share of gun trouble."

Randall took a long swallow of beer and then nodded.

"There's something to be said for staying alive, all right. You know what I'm thinking, Stevens?"

"That after today you won't ever be able to trust that fella Page again?"

"I can't ride with a man I don't trust to have at my back with a gun in his hand," Randall said with a harsh note in his voice. "You're right. Page is done." That cold, grim smile touched Randall's mouth again. "Anyway, I'm pretty sure I broke his jaw and his wrist with that cue stick. He won't be any good for several weeks. If he's got any sense, he'll slink on out of the basin like the coyote he is as soon as he's able to travel."

"So you're going to need somebody to take his place," Matt said.

"That's right. But you don't even know what the job is."

Matt shrugged and said, "I don't know what the *pay* is. That's the only important thing."

Randall laughed, and there was at least a trace of genuine amusement in the sound.

"The job is doing whatever the Colonel tells us to do, and the pay is a hundred dollars a month for you."

That implied that Randall was making more, which came as no surprise.

"Who's this Colonel fella?"

"The man who runs things around here. He gives the orders, and I make sure they're carried out. The men who work for him do as they're told, without question. Can you handle that?"

"I reckon I can," Matt said. "There's one thing, though."

"Spit it out," Randall snapped.

"You said something about a woman being killed. I don't cotton to that any more than I do to backshooters."

"That wasn't supposed to happen." Randall's face hardened with remembered anger. "We were bringing her here to the Colonel, and she tried to get away. The man who nearly let her escape lost his head. She'd put a knife in him, and I reckon he wasn't thinking straight.

He yanked his gun out and shot her before I could stop him." He took a drink. "I suppose I got carried away, too. The son of a bitch shouldn't have been so careless as to let it happen. So I shot him."

"And he and Page were pards," Matt guessed.

"Yeah. Page claimed he was all right with it, that Dwyer dug his own grave, but I guess the anger just sat there inside him, festering for a week. Earlier this afternoon he took a bottle and a whore upstairs with him. I had a hunch the bottle might finish poisoning him, but I hoped the whore would work it out of him. Reckon that didn't happen."

"That's a shame. Some people get it in their head that they've got to even a score, and they just can't get over it."

Matt kept his tone light, but inside he was seething. He was almost completely convinced that the woman who had been killed was Wildflower, Two Bears's daughter and Standing Rock's wife. He wanted to ask about the little boy, but he couldn't. Matt Stevens, drifting gunman, wouldn't know a damned thing about that.

Randall drank the last of his beer and said, "You never gave me a firm answer, Stevens. Do you want the job?"

Matt said, "Yeah, I do."

Randall scraped his chair back and stood up.

"Good. I'll take you up to the Colonel's house and introduce you. Maybe you can give me a hand with a little chore, too."

"What chore would that be?"

Randall raised his right hand and touched his upper left arm where the bandage was, under his shirtsleeve. He said, "Trying to beat some sense into the stubborn old son of a bitch who shot me last week."

Chapter 36

The rattle of a key in the lock made Preacher's eyes flutter open instinctively. He closed them again almost immediately. He didn't want whoever was coming into this attic room to know he was awake, not until he figured out who it was and what they wanted. The visitor could be Mrs. Dayton, bringing him something to eat and drink. That was good.

Or it could be the Colonel or Randall, and that was bad. Very bad.

As Preacher hung there limply, suspended by a rope slung over an exposed attic beam and tied to his wrists, he smelled the air and caught a whiff of lilac water, as well as the odors of leather and tobacco and sweat. The lilac came from Mrs. Dayton, the other smells from the guard who accompanied her into this makeshift prison. She never came in without having one of the Colonel's gunmen with her, although Preacher wasn't sure what they thought he could do, trussed up the way he was.

His ankles were lashed together. With his arms pulled up over his head the way they were, he had to come up on his toes to keep all his weight from resting on his wrists, arms, and shoulders. That awkward stance caused burning pain to radiate through the muscles of his legs and back.

Thankfully, they didn't leave him strung up like this all the time. If they had, it probably would have killed him by now. As it was, he was only half dead from the torture and from the bullet wounds he had suffered in the shoot-out with Randall and the Colonel on the mansion's second floor.

When he had first come to, lying on a cot with his hands and feet bound, it hadn't taken him long to figure out where he was. A candle burned on a crate beside the cot, and its flickering glow revealed the exposed beams and rafters above his head. He was in a small room in the mansion's attic. Preacher didn't know if it had been built for prisoners or just happened to be here, but for the time being it was his jail, sure enough.

The wounds in his side and arm had been cleaned and bandaged. They hurt like blazes, but Preacher had been shot often enough in his long and perilous life that he could tell how serious the injuries were. They could still fester and kill him, but other than that, he wasn't in any danger of dying from them.

With no windows in the room where he was being held, he couldn't tell at first if it was day or night outside. But eventually he began to see light seeping through the cracks between boards and knew the sun had come up. Since then he had tried to keep track of how many days had gone by, but it was difficult because sometimes he passed out. The number of meals Mrs. Dayton brought him didn't really help, either, because he had no way of knowing how many times a day she was feeding him. But he thought that roughly a week had gone by since he was captured.

A week in hell, for the most part.

He had been there a day or so when the Colonel and his pet gun-wolf Randall came into the attic room. Randall strung Preacher up from the beam, and then the Colonel began to question him, wanting to know how many of the Assiniboine he had brought with him and where to find them. He asked as well who Preacher was and what his connection was with the Indians.

Preacher had the same answer to all the questions: "Go to hell."

He knew he was in for trouble when the Colonel began pulling on a pair of soft doeskin gloves. Ritchie didn't bother with a whip or any other implements of torture. He relied on his fists, putting the weight of his blocky body behind them as he swung blow after blow to Preacher's head and torso. After he had thrown enough punches to wind him slightly, the Colonel paused and asked the same questions again.

Preacher's answer remained the same, too.

Eventually, he passed out, and when he came to, he was back on the cot. Mrs. Dayton was there, with a guard standing behind her. She wiped Preacher's face with cool cloths and pressed hot ones to his body to draw out some of the aches and pains.

She still had that sorrowful look in her eyes, as if she didn't like what was being done to him, but she said, "You should tell the Colonel what he wants to know. You're too old to take this kind of punishment."

"I'm too old and stubborn . . . to give in to the varmint," Preacher husked through dry, cracked lips.

"He'll kill you," the woman warned in a whisper.

"He can try," Preacher said.

The Colonel certainly had tried, visiting the attic room several times a day to pummel the prisoner, sometimes to the point of unconsciousness. Randall took a turn now and then, when the Colonel told him to, although he seemed somewhat less enthusiastic about it.

But Preacher's body was rawhide, leather, and steel. All the softness had been honed away from it decades earlier. And his skull was cast iron, an advantage he'd been blessed with by nature. He absorbed the punishment and maintained his defiant attitude.

Being strung up was actually worse than being beaten. It was a slow, steadily grinding pain that ate away at him. But he withstood it, too. He knew that if he gave away the location of the camp where Standing Rock and the other warriors were waiting for him, Randall would take his crew of hired killers and wipe them out.

Preacher wondered sometimes whether the Assiniboine were still there, or if Standing Rock had lost patience and tried to come into town. He didn't think that was the case because the Colonel was still asking him about the Indians. But Preacher knew Standing Rock wouldn't wait for him forever. He was a little surprised the man hadn't made a move before now.

If Standing Rock ever found out that Wildflower was dead, mercilessly murdered by one of the Colonel's men, that would be the end of it. The Assiniboine would attack Hammerhead and they would all die, most likely along with a number of innocent citizens.

Preacher held out one strong hope: He knew that Smoke and Matt would show up sooner or later. If they followed his sign to Standing Rock's camp and found out what was going on, they would know what to do.

And sooner or later they would unleash all hell on the Colonel and his men.

Now he was strung up again, waiting to see what would happen next since that was all he could do. He kept his eyes closed as Mrs. Dayton told the man with her, "Take him down."

Several times Preacher had considered trying to escape in situations like this, but he knew he was too weak to overpower the guard. If he could get his hands on a gun, it might be a different matter. He believed he was still plenty strong enough to pull a trigger.

But the man untied one of his wrists and then stepped back out of reach quickly before Preacher could even start to lower that arm. The rope slithered over the beam and dropped away from it. Without it to hold him up, Preacher's strength deserted him and he crumpled to the rough floor.

The guard tied his wrists together and picked him up to place him on the cot. Preacher opened his eyes then, because there was no point in continuing to pretend to be asleep.

Mrs. Dayton stepped out into the hall for a moment, then came back carrying a tray with a bowl and a cup on it. Preacher smelled coffee and stew. His belly clenched with hunger. He was a little surprised that the Colonel hadn't tried to starve him into cooperating, but so far he'd been getting fed fairly regularly.

"Help him sit up," Mrs. Dayton told the guard.

Preacher had seen the man before but didn't know his name. He didn't care what the varmint was called. The man took hold of him and lifted him into a sitting position.

"This old coot's nothing but skin and bones," he said.

"I never expected him to be so blasted stubborn. The Colonel's broken bigger, younger men a lot faster than this."

"A man's age and size are no measure of his heart," Mrs. Dayton said. She held the cup to Preacher's lips. He took a swallow of the hot, strong coffee and immediately felt its bracing effect.

For the next few minutes she fed him, spooning beef stew into his mouth and letting him wash it down with the coffee, all the while sitting beside him on the cot while the guard stood by with his arms folded across his chest and a scowl on his hard-bitten face.

"I don't think there *are* any Indians," he said. "If there were, they would have attacked the town by now."

"I don't know anything about that," Mrs. Dayton said. From the sound of her voice, she didn't want to know anything about the Colonel's business.

When Preacher finished the food, he slumped back against the wall behind him. Mrs. Dayton got to her feet and picked up the tray. She looked like she wanted to say something to him, but before she could, footsteps thudded on the stairs leading to the attic room. From the sound of them, a couple of men were headed up here to Preacher's prison.

Randall's broad shoulders filled the doorway. Another man was behind him, but Preacher couldn't make out anything about him except the general impression that he was almost as big as Randall. The gunman gave Mrs. Dayton a curt nod and said, "Are you finished?"

"Yes, he just ate," she said. "You're not going to beat him again, are you?"

"That's none of your affair," Randall told her. His

voice was edged with impatience. "When the Colonel wakes up, let him know I'm here, will you?"

"All right," she murmured. "I'll do as you say, Mr. Randall."

She ducked her head and stepped around Randall and the other man to go out the door.

That left three men in the little room with Preacher, and they just about filled it up. The old mountain man's head rested against the wall. His eyes were slitted and he tried to look like he was only half-conscious, but that wasn't the case. As he had been doing before, he pretended to be worse off than he really was until he had a better idea of what was about to happen.

"Doesn't look like much, does he?" Randall said to the man who had climbed to the attic with him. "He's just about the stubbornest son of a bitch I've ever run into, though."

The other man moved a little to the side to get a better look at Preacher, and as he did so he asked, "Who is the old pelican, anyway, and why are you holding him?"

It took every bit of effort Preacher could muster not to show any reaction to the voice, because he recognized it instantly.

Matt Jensen had come to Hammerhead.

Chapter 37

Matt managed to keep his tone idly curious as he asked his question. He didn't want to betray too much interest in the prisoner, because if he did, Randall might start to wonder if there was some connection between him and the old mountain man.

What Matt really wanted to do was whip out his Colt and blast slugs through both Randall and the other man. The sight of what had been done to Preacher filled him with rage.

Preacher wore only his buckskin trousers. His lean, pale torso was covered with bruises, some of them fresh and angry-looking blotches of blue and purple, others older and turning mottled shades of brown and yellow. His face was the same way, with the addition of brown smears of dried blood from a number of cuts and gashes. Clearly, someone had been beating the hell out of him for days now.

From what Randall had said in the saloon, he was one of the men who'd been dealing out that punishment. But maybe not the only one, because he said, "I see the Colonel's paid you a visit since I've been up here, old-timer."

Preacher opened one eye wider and squinted up at Randall. His swollen lips moved. His words were thick and slightly distorted because of that, but Matt understood them just fine.

"Go to hell."

"You'll be there before me, old man," Randall said.

Matt was starting to get the feeling that they didn't even know Preacher's name. He hadn't told them a blessed thing during his captivity. That was just like him, stubborn as an old mule.

"He's the one who shot you?" Matt asked.

"Yeah," Randall said. "But I winged him a couple of times, too."

Matt chuckled and said, "A fella that old and decrepit, I'm surprised he didn't die right off."

Preacher's squint got even more furious as he glared up at them. He was putting on a good show, thought Matt. Randall shouldn't have any clue that they knew each other.

"Yeah, well, he's tougher than you'd think he would be," Randall said. "We've been questioning him for a week and haven't gotten a damned thing out of him."

"What are you trying to find out?" Matt asked. Again, he tried to sound just idly curious.

Randall glanced over at him and frowned, obviously considering whether he wanted to answer that question. After a few seconds, he said, "If you're going to be working for the Colonel, I suppose you'll need to know what's going on. You know that he's going to build a railroad into this basin, don't you?"

"I heard some talk about it in the saloon," Matt replied vaguely.

"Well, there's one piece of the best route that he doesn't have locked up yet, and it just so happens a bunch of filthy redskins are squatting right on it. It's their traditional hunting grounds or some such."

"Why doesn't he just make them move?" Matt asked. "Folks have never hesitated to push Indians out of the way before if they were standing in the way of progress."

"If it was only up to the Colonel, I'm sure that's what he'd do. But he has some powerful friends in Washington who have made it clear to him that they'll only help him out if he goes about it more . . . discreetly, I guess you'd say."

Raiding Two Bears's village and killing a bunch of innocent men, women, and children in order to kidnap a young woman and her baby wasn't exactly what he would call discreet, Matt thought, but maybe it was in comparison to some of the other things the Colonel could have done.

"The Colonel wanted to get his hands on the chief's daughter and grandson," Randall went on. "He figured if he did that, the Indians would cooperate and do whatever he said, including moving off their land in what everybody else would think was their own decision. It has to *look* good for those spineless weasels in Washington. So he sent a message to the chief explaining what has to be done. The redskin ought to have it by now."

"So the woman you mentioned who was killed . . . ?"

"The chief's daughter." Randall shrugged. "But it doesn't really matter. As far as the savages know, she and her brat are both our prisoners, and that's all that really matters."

With an effort, Matt controlled the anger that threatened to erupt inside him. He nodded and asked, "So how does the old man tie in with all of that?"

"That's what we're not completely sure of," Randall replied with a shake of his head. "As best I can tell, he's a friend of those Indians. You know how a lot of those old squaw men were practically savages themselves."

"That was before my time," Matt said.

"Well, you can take it from me, there were plenty of white men who went west to become fur trappers, and they wound up living with the Indians so much they might as well have been redskins themselves. I figure this old man is one of them. He trailed us here, and what we want to know is if he brought some of the warriors with him. If he did, he needs to tell us where they are so we can deal with them."

"Wipe them out, you mean?"

"You have any objection of that?" Randall asked sharply.

Matt shook his head and said, "I've fought Indians before. Reckon I probably will again."

"I'd say there's a good chance of it if you go to work for the Colonel. As soon as he wakes up from his nap, I'll introduce you to him and make sure it's all right for you to take Page's place. In the meantime . . ." Randall gestured to the other man. "String him up again, Harry. I'll work him over a little, soften him up for when the Colonel visits him later on."

Matt stiffened. He had seen several other gunmen downstairs and hanging around the mansion outside. If he ventilated Randall and Harry and cut Preacher loose, he didn't know if they could shoot their way out of the house. Maybe if they were able to take Colonel Ritchie hostage . . .

But one thing was certain. He couldn't just stand by and watch while Randall hammered his fists into the old mountain man. That was never going to happen. As

Harry bent toward Preacher to haul him off the bunk,
Matt caught Preacher's eye and moved his hand toward
the butt of his Colt, to let Preacher know that he was
about to make his move.

Before any of that could happen, a voice called from
downstairs, saying, "Randall! Are you up there, Lieutenant?"

Randall motioned for Harry to wait. He said, "That's
the Colonel now. Come on, Stevens."

Matt hated to leave Preacher up here, a prisoner in
this cramped, airless little room, but for the moment he
thought his best course was still to play along with their
enemies. That would give Smoke a chance to get into
town, and the three of them would stand a better chance
together.

Besides, even though Wildflower was dead, evidently
Little Hawk was still alive, and rescuing the child was
another reason Matt and Smoke had come here.

Matt glanced at Preacher as he turned to go out. The
mountain man glared at him and Randall with undis-
guised hatred. It was a good job, Matt thought, and only
half of it was acting. But as far as anyone could tell,
Preacher despised him and Randall equally.

Matt followed the big gunman through the door,
wishing that he could tell Preacher he would be back to
help him.

Matt had a hunch Preacher knew that anyway.

Smoke kept an eye out for Matt's big steel dust as he
rode into the settlement, but he didn't see the stallion
tied at any of the hitch rails along the street. That wasn't
necessarily a cause for concern. Matt could have put the
horse in a livery stable, or he could have come across a

clue to Preacher's whereabouts that had led him out of town. One way or another, Matt could take care of himself, and Smoke knew that.

He saw what looked like the biggest and most successful saloon in town, the Emerald Palace, and thought about going in there because such places were good for picking up all the local gossip.

But general mercantile stores were also good for that, so he angled the 'Palouse toward the Hammerhead Emporium instead. Hammerhead had to be the name of the settlement, he decided. He couldn't imagine a businessman using it on a store otherwise.

He dismounted and tied up, then climbed the steps at the end of the high porch that also served as a loading dock. The store's double front doors stood open. Smoke went inside and took a whiff of the various odors that blended together to form the distinctive smell of a general store: tobacco, pepper and other spices, vinegar from the pickle barrel, lilac water, gunpowder, leather, fabric, flour, and a number of other things.

Several customers were browsing in the aisles formed by wooden shelves. Those aisles all led toward a long counter in the rear of the store. A balding man in a gray canvas apron stood behind the counter, talking to another man in a tweed suit and narrow-brimmed black hat. The man in the apron seemed upset about something as Smoke strolled closer, pretending to look at the merchandise on the shelves he passed.

". . . knows I'll pay him as soon as I can," the man was saying. "Business is pickin' up, but it still ain't what it's gonna be once the railroad gets here."

"I assure you, Mr. Springhorn, Colonel Ritchie is aware of that," the man in the suit said. "That's why he's going to give you just as many extensions as he possibly can. You're in no danger of having him foreclose at the moment. I just thought it would be a good idea to alert you to the possibility that such a thing might come to pass at some time in the future."

"Reckon I already knew that," Springhorn said, visibly struggling to contain his temper. "And I know this ain't your fault, Mr. Webster. I'm sure it'll all work out fine."

"As am I," Webster said. He turned to leave the store. As he passed Smoke, he nodded politely. Smoke touched the brim of his hat in return and then moved on to the counter.

"What can I do for you, mister?" Springhorn asked.

"I could use a pound of flour and half a pound of salt," Smoke said. That was actually true. The supplies in his saddlebags were starting to run a little low after the long trail he and Matt had followed to get here.

"Well, I can fix you up, and glad to do it, too."

"Business not very good?" Smoke asked, acting like he was just making idle conversation. Actually, he had heard Webster, the man in the suit, mention Colonel Ritchie, and he wanted to find out more about the man. It was quite likely, thought Smoke, that Ritchie was the mysterious Colonel whom Preacher suspected of being connected to the Indian Ring.

"Business is fine," Springhorn answered crisply. "Just not as good as it will be once things start booming here in the basin."

"It's good-looking range, all right," Smoke said. "If I was looking to start a spread, this would be a fine place, especially if there was a way to get a herd to market without having to make that long drive around the mountains."

Springhorn let out a snort.

"We're workin' on just that, friend, so if you're really lookin' to settle down, you could do a whole lot worse. Once the railroad gets here sometime next year, this basin will be the prime piece of real estate in the whole territory."

"I don't doubt it," Smoke agreed.

"I just hope I'm still here when that day arrives," Springhorn said, his control slipping for a second so that worry showed on his face.

"You don't think you can hang on until then?"

Smoke could put a friendly expression on his face when he wanted to, the sort of expression that prompted people to talk to him. Of course, there were also the times when his face turned grim and his eyes got icy and he looked like he was about to unleash hellfire and hot lead on any varmint who got in his way. That expression made folks who had any sense clear out in a hurry.

Right now, though, Springhorn sighed and said, "I'm sure it'll be all right."

He was middle-aged, with the scrawny, pinched look of a man who had worked hard all his life for not enough reward. His head was mostly bald and he had a sandy mustache under a prominent nose. He took off the spectacles he wore and rubbed at the bridge of that nose as he continued, "The fella who backed me in this business is the salt of the earth. He loaned me enough money to start the store, and he charges me nice reasonable rent on the building. I'm sure the Colonel will give me every chance to make it. That was his bookkeeper I was just talkin' to, fella name of Webster. He was just lettin' me know how I stand on my accounts."

"I see," Smoke said with a nod. "Well, maybe that flour and salt I need will help out a little."

Springhorn started slightly, as if he had forgotten about the things Smoke wanted to buy until that reminder. He said, "I'll get your order ready right now, mister."

While the storekeeper went off to do that, Smoke thought about what he had just learned. Colonel Ritchie had staked Springhorn, and he owned the building in which the general store was housed. It was pure speculation, Smoke knew, but what if the Colonel had interests like that in most of the other businesses in town? He could bide his time, waiting while he built the railroad into the basin—with the help of the Indian Ring, more than likely—and while that was going on, the businesses in Hammerhead would continue to develop. Then, when the railroad arrived and the basin was poised to explode with growth, the Colonel could crack down, force out all the men he had supposedly helped, and take over everything.

It was the sort of power play that could make a man incredibly rich . . . as long as he didn't mind crushing anybody who got in his way. Smoke had a hunch that the Colonel wouldn't mind that at all.

He needed to find out more before he would be convinced his theory was right, but his instincts told him he was on the right track. The Colonel's long-term plans didn't really matter at the moment, though. Finding out what had happened to Preacher and locating Wildflower and Little Hawk were a lot more pressing.

"Here you go, mister," Springhorn said as he put a couple of small bags on the counter. "That'll be six bits."

Smoke slid across a silver dollar and said, "That's close enough."

"I'm obliged to you," Springhorn said. "You gonna be stayin' around Hammerhead for a while?"

Smoke thought about the questions that still needed to be answered and the sinister plans of the Indian Ring that remained to be exposed, and he said, "I've got a hunch I just might be."

Chapter 38

Matt and Randall went down three flights of stairs to the mansion's ground floor. Randall led the way to the Colonel's library, where Ritchie had gone after calling up the stairs to them. The door was open, but Randall stopped in the hall and rapped a knuckle on it anyway.

"Come in, Randall," the Colonel called from inside the big room lined with bookshelves. Matt glanced at the titles and saw that most of the leather-bound volumes were histories, biographies, or books about military tactics. That didn't surprise him. The Colonel didn't strike him as the sort of hombre who read dime novels.

The Colonel stood behind his desk wearing a plain gray suit. He was a big man, although not quite as large as Randall or Matt. His build in the suit said that once he had been a very powerful man physically, but he had started to run to fat. He would probably still be a pretty formidable opponent in a fight, though.

"Who's this?" the Colonel snapped as he looked at Matt. He didn't seem to be too pleased that Randall had brought a stranger into the house.

"His name's Matt Stevens. He gave me a hand a while ago when there was some trouble."

The Colonel didn't greet Matt. Instead, he asked curtly, "What sort of trouble?"

"Page tried to gun me down from behind while we were in the Emerald Palace."

The Colonel's eyes narrowed. He asked, "Did you kill him?"

"I didn't have to. I broke his jaw and his wrist, though."

"I assume he's no longer working for us?"

"You know I leave decisions like that up to you, Colonel. But I'd prefer not to ride with him anymore. I can't trust him. Besides, he's laid up. He's not going to be any good to anybody for a while."

The Colonel's cold gaze flicked over to Matt for a second.

"And you want to hire this man to replace him?"

"Like I said," Randell replied with a shrug, "he gave me a hand. I'm not saying Page would have killed me if Stevens hadn't stepped in, but it made it easier to handle the situation."

"Very well. You're riding for me now, Stevens."

Matt said, "Thank you, Colonel."

The Colonel turned his attention back to Randall and said, "I suppose Page had been drinking, or he never would have attempted such a foolish thing."

"Yeah, he polished off a whole bottle of rotgut. He's lucky that didn't give him the blind staggers and kill him, right there. He's been brooding all week about what happened to Dwyer."

"Dwyer?" The Colonel frowned. "Oh, yes, the man who shot the Indian woman."

"That's right. Page didn't think I should have killed him."

"What else can a man who disobeys orders expect? Whether it was vital that the heathen survive or not, I ordered her brought here. You were right to execute the man, Lieutenant. However, a firing squad would have been more in line with proper military protocol."

"Yes, sir. I'll remember that if the situation ever comes up again."

Matt managed not to frown in confusion. The way the Colonel addressed Randall as "Lieutenant" and the mention of a firing squad made it seem almost like Ritchie believed they still held their ranks and were back in the war.

Matt had heard of men who lived in the past and sometimes had trouble distinguishing the present from days gone by. Was it possible that the Colonel could suffer from such an affliction and still be able to come up with elaborate plans involving murder and kidnapping?

Matt supposed it was. In the past, he had run up against men who were both dangerously intelligent and downright loco. One thing didn't rule out the other.

The Colonel stepped over to a sideboard, pulled the stopper from a decanter that contained amber liquid, and poured some of it into a snifter. Matt assumed it was brandy. The Colonel didn't offer either of them a drink. Instead, he turned to face them, holding the snifter and moving it in little circles so that the brandy swirled a little inside it.

"What about the old man?" he asked.

"I was just about to have another go at him when you called, Colonel," Randall said. "I can go up and do it now if you like."

The Colonel shook his head and said, "No. I've decided that it's not worth the effort. We're not going to attempt to beat any information out of him anymore. I don't believe he brought any of the savages with him. If he had, we would have seen some sign of them by now."

"Maybe," Randall said. He sounded like he wasn't sure he agreed that it was time to stop questioning Preacher. "I've had men searching the basin, but they haven't found anything so far. Redskins are pretty good at hiding."

Matt was relieved that Preacher wasn't going to have to suffer any more beatings, as well as grateful that he wouldn't have to reveal his true identity in order to stop that from happening. That was good news . . . maybe.

It wasn't long before that hope was dashed. The Colonel said, "I think we can safely dispose of him now. Take care of that, Lieutenant."

"Yes, sir. Right away?"

Matt waited tensely for the Colonel to finish pronouncing a death sentence on Preacher. If the madman told Randall to go up and kill Preacher right away, Matt would have to act. He thought he could get both of them, go upstairs to free Preacher, and then try to fight their way to safety. It would be a long shot, but he had gambled his life plenty of times before.

Those thoughts flashed through his head in the couple of seconds the Colonel took to ponder Randall's question. Then the Colonel shook his head and said, "No, it can wait until tonight, after Mrs. Dayton goes to bed. She's been taking care of the old man, you know, and I believe she's grown a bit fond of him. I'd rather it was done while she's asleep, so that in the morning when she gets up, he'll simply be gone and I can tell her not to trouble herself about him any longer."

"Yes, sir," Randall said. "That's fine with me."

"In the meantime, I have nothing else for you to do. In a few days I should receive a response from Two Bears. Until then, all we can do is wait. If the man has any sense, he'll agree to my demands and move his filthy tribe off that land so I can give the order to commence construction on the rail line."

Randall nodded and said again, "Yes, sir." He jerked his head at Matt. "Come on. We'll get some supper, and I'll fill you in on the way we work guard details around here. You'll be handling some of those."

"Fine by me," Matt said as he followed Randall out of the Colonel's library. A glance back told him that the man was standing there by the desk, sipping the brandy and looking pleased with himself.

Matt had seldom felt a stronger urge to put a bullet through somebody's brain.

He had to wait, though. He had been lucky. Preacher's execution had been postponed until sometime tonight. That gave Matt some time to come up with a plan to rescue the old mountain man.

More importantly, it gave him a chance to find Smoke and let him know what was going to happen if they didn't move fast. Matt had a hunch it was going to take blazing guns from both of them to free Preacher and put a stop to the Colonel's plans.

By the time night was beginning to settle over Hammerhead, Smoke had visited a number of the businesses in town. He had stopped at the blacksmith shop to have the smith take a look at one of the shoes on the 'Palouse and see if he thought it needed to be tightened. It didn't, of course, but that gave Smoke the chance to engage the man in conversation and find out that not only did he rent the shop from Colonel Ritchie, the Colonel had loaned him money to start the business. The same was true at the livery stable where Smoke rented a stall for the big Appaloosa, and at the gunsmith's where he asked about a busted sear, and at the apothecary where he picked up a bottle of rejuvenating tonic that he didn't intend to drink. In fact, the story was the same everywhere he went: Business was all right and slowly getting better, but the owners faced a precarious future that was largely dependent on Colonel Hudson Ritchie giving them time to build up their establishments.

They would get that time, Smoke thought . . . and then the Colonel would take everything away from them.

In his wanderings around town, he still hadn't seen Matt. He hoped that whatever mysterious fate had befallen Preacher hadn't claimed Matt as a victim, too.

So far Smoke hadn't visited the Emerald Palace Saloon. After leaving the small café where he had eaten supper, he looked across the street at the saloon and decided to get a beer. If he got a chance to talk much with the bartender, he would try to find out if the Emerald Palace might also be one of the Colonel's targets for a takeover when the railroad arrived in the basin.

As Smoke angled across the street, he spotted two men striding toward the saloon on the opposite boardwalk. One of them was instantly familiar to him. A feeling of relief went through him as he recognized Matt's tall, broad-shouldered figure.

The other man was even bigger than Matt. Smoke could tell that even in the shadows on the boardwalk. As they passed a lighted window, Smoke got a glimpse of the man's face. He had never seen him before, but he knew a cold-blooded, ruthless killer when he saw one.

Matt seemed friendly with the stranger, so Smoke knew he was carrying on some sort of pose. The younger man had adopted a swaggering, arrogant gait, and that told Smoke he was probably pretending to be a hired gunman. From the looks of it, Matt had worked his way into the Colonel's good graces in a matter of a few hours.

Smoke increased his pace a little, timing it so that he stepped up onto the boardwalk in front of the saloon's entrance at the same moment as Matt and the other man. To a casual observer it would have seemed that Smoke wasn't watching where he was going, but in reality he knew exactly what he was doing as he rammed his shoulder into Matt's.

The collision staggered both of them. As Matt took a step back, he exclaimed, "Hey! Watch where you're going, mister."

"I could say the same thing to you, amigo," Smoke responded, standing tensely like he was ready for trouble.

"All right, back off, both of you," the big gunman snapped. "Come on, Stevens, we've got enough to do tonight without you hunting up another ruckus."

"Yeah, I guess you're right, boss." Matt followed as the big man headed for the bat wings. He looked back over his shoulder at Smoke and added with a sneer, "You're lucky. If we didn't have a bothersome old geezer to deal with for the Colonel tonight, I'd have time to see about handing you your needings."

"Didn't you hear me?" the other man snapped. "Come on."

Smoke kept the hostile expression on his face, too, until Matt and the other man disappeared into the saloon. He didn't follow them inside, despite his earlier intention to get a drink in the Emerald Palace. What Matt had managed to tell him made all of that unimportant.

Smoke still didn't know all the details, but somehow Matt had infiltrated their enemies, and the message he had just delivered was clear.

They were going to "deal with" an old man tonight, and the only old man Matt would be interested in was Preacher. That meant the mountain man was still alive.

But unless Smoke was mistaken about Matt's meaning, Preacher was marked for death . . . and soon.

Chapter 39

Smoke knew from his conversations with the various businessmen in town that Colonel Ritchie lived in the big house on the slight rise at the western end of town. That's what Smoke would have guessed anyway, but it was nice to have that confirmation.

If Preacher was the Colonel's prisoner, chances were that he was locked up somewhere in that mansion. The Colonel could be holding him somewhere else, but Smoke had a hunch the man would want to keep Preacher close.

At least the old mountain man wasn't dead. That was a relief. Smoke headed for the Colonel's house to do some scouting.

When it came to stealth, Preacher was probably the only man alive who could beat Smoke at that game. Smoke blended into the shadows, and anybody who happened to be watching might have sworn that he disappeared into thin air.

Hammerhead wasn't that big yet, so it didn't take him long to reach the mansion. He paused in the trees to one side of the place to have a good look at it. The house had three stories, with a broad, porticoed verandah in front of it. Smoke had no idea where in the mansion Preacher was being held, but he figured that if he got a chance, he could find his old friend.

A couple of men stood on the verandah, smoking. Guards, Smoke thought. That made him look more closely at the area around the house that he could see from where he was, and sure enough, over the next few minutes he spotted several dark shapes that he recognized as men standing watch.

He would have to get past them, and for that he might need a distraction. But the first thing he really needed was to talk to Matt and find out what was going on here, so he blended back into the shadows and returned to the settlement.

Because some time had passed since his phony run-in with Matt, he thought he could go into the Emerald Palace without it appearing that he was looking for more trouble. He pushed the bat wings aside and walked casually toward the bar, and as he did so, he looked out of the corner of his eye and saw Matt and the big man playing pool at a table in the rear corner.

"What'll it be for you, mister?" the bartender asked Smoke.

"Beer will do fine," Smoke replied. "Is it cold?"

"The coldest you'll find in the whole blamed territory." The bartender rolled his eyes. "That's what the boss always tells people, anyway."

Smoke chuckled and said, "Sounds good. I'll take my chances on how cold it is."

The man drew the beer and placed it in front of him. It was cool and good, and drinking it gave Smoke an excuse to stand there and keep an eye on Matt and his companion in the mirror.

Smoke was sure that Matt had seen him come in. After a few minutes, when they had finished the game they were playing, Matt set his cue stick aside and said, "Reckon I'd better go check on my horse."

"Don't take too long," the other man said as he started to rack up the balls again, evidently planning to run some shots by himself. "We've still got that other chore to take care of."

"I'm not likely to forget," Matt said. "I feel kind of sorry for the old coot."

"Don't," the big gunman snapped. "It was his choice not to cooperate."

That was Preacher, all right, Smoke thought, smiling to himself. Anybody who tried to force Preacher to do something he didn't want to do was going to discover whole new levels of stubborn.

Matt ambled out. Smoke waited until the man at the pool table was concentrating on his shots and not paying attention to what else was going on in the saloon, then he paid for his beer and left the place as well. He paused on the boardwalk outside the bat wings and heard a faint hiss from the black mouth of the alley to his left.

Smoke walked in that direction, apparently aimlessly, and turned to enter the alley. As he did, someone lightly touched his arm.

"It's me," Matt said.

"I know that," Smoke replied quietly. "I wouldn't let anybody else slip up on me like that."

"You heard what they're going to do? They're gonna kill Preacher tonight!"

"No, they're not," Smoke said. "They may try, but we'll have something to say about that. Where is he?"

"In an attic room above the third floor in the Colonel's mansion. You take the main staircase to the third floor, and then there's a door to the right with a smaller set of stairs that leads up into the attic."

Smoke nodded, even though Matt couldn't see the movement in the darkness, and asked, "How bad is he hurt?"

"A couple of bullet grazes, one in his side and one on his arm, but the worst of it is that they've been beating him for the past week, trying to get him to tell them where Standing Rock and the rest of the warriors are."

"I don't reckon they had any luck with that," Smoke said.

"Not a bit. But he's covered with bruises. I don't see how he stood up to that much punishment."

"People have written Preacher off for dead plenty of times. I did it myself once, before I knew better. But that old man will always surprise you. He can stand up to just about anything."

"Maybe not what they've got planned for him," Matt said. "The Colonel's decided none of the Indians came here with Preacher, so he figures it's all right to go ahead and get rid of him."

"They're going to find out different."

Anger filled Smoke at the thought of the beatings Preacher had been forced to endure. They had even more of a score to settle with the Colonel now, he thought.

Matt's hand gripped Smoke's arm.

"That may not be the worst of it, Smoke," he said. "Wildflower is dead."

That terrible, unexpected news made Smoke catch his breath. He stiffened, his hand instinctively going to the butt of his gun as he asked, "Are you sure?"

"I heard all about it from Randall. He's the ramrod of

the Colonel's crew of gun-wolves. While they were bringing Wildflower and Little Hawk here after they kidnapped them from Two Bears's village, she tried to get away. She got hold of a knife and stabbed one of the men, and he lost his head and shot her. Then Randall killed him for disobeying orders." Matt paused. "I get the feeling that Randall and the Colonel are both a little loco, Smoke. They rode together in the Union cavalry during the war, and the Colonel especially seems to think he's still commanding an army unit about half the time."

"Just because a man's loco doesn't mean he's not dangerous."

"I thought the same thing," Matt said.

"What about Little Hawk?"

"He's in the mansion, too. The Colonel's housekeeper has been taking care of him. As far as I've been able to find out, he's doing fine. He's too young to understand that his ma is dead."

"Poor little varmint," Smoke muttered. "When we take Preacher out of there, we'll have to bring Little Hawk with us, too."

"A shootout with a baby in the middle of it?" Matt sounded pretty doubtful about that.

"Maybe there won't be a shootout."

"The Colonel's got a dozen men standing guard. I don't see how we'll get in and out without swapping lead with them."

Smoke rubbed his chin in the darkness and said, "Those hombres need something else to keep them busy. Maybe I can come up with something to accomplish that."

"What do you want me to do?"

"Since they know you already, stick close to the house. I'm going to head back out to Standing Rock's camp and break the bad news to him. Then he and his men are going to pretend to attack the town in order to draw off the Colonel's guards. When that happens, you and I will get Preacher and the little boy." Smoke paused, then asked, "How'd you get in good with them so quickly, anyway?"

"I pitched in to help Randall when one of his own men tried to bushwhack him. The fella was a friend of the man who killed Wildflower. He'd been nursing a grudge against Randall ever since that happened."

"That was a lucky break for us," Smoke said, "but bad luck all around for everybody else. This whole thing is about the railroad, isn't it?"

"Yep. The Colonel sent a message to Two Bears saying that he has both Wildflower and Little Hawk, and if Two Bears wants them back he and his people have to get off the land the Colonel wants."

Smoke's eyes narrowed as he said, "If the Colonel and this fella Randall happen to get in our way when we go in there . . ."

"I'm sort of hoping they do," Matt said. "We need to hurry, though, Smoke. The Colonel told Randall to wait until after the housekeeper had gone to bed to kill Preacher. She's been taking care of him, and the Colonel didn't want her to find out about it until after everything was over. I don't have any idea what time she turns in, but it might be soon."

"I'm on my way to fetch Standing Rock right now. Good luck, Matt."

"Reckon we can use all of that we can get," Matt said.

If the hostler at the livery stable thought it was odd that Smoke was taking the 'Palouse back out only a couple of hours after bringing him in, he didn't say anything. Smoke handled the saddling up himself and rode out of town at a leisurely pace so as not to draw attention, and then put the big horse into a gallop toward Standing Rock's camp as soon as he was clear of the settlement.

Even though Smoke had been over the route only once, and that during the day, he didn't have any trouble finding the place he was looking for. Once he had been over a trail, he was always able to retrace it. He turned up the canyon and began following the little creek.

He expected Standing Rock to have sentries out, so when he came close to the camp he called softly, "It's Smoke Jensen. Hold your fire."

Standing Rock himself was standing guard. Smoke recognized the warrior's voice when he said, "Jensen. Come ahead."

Smoke wasn't looking forward to telling the man that his wife was dead. Even after all these years, he remembered how hearing about the tragic fate of his first wife, Nicole, had been like a knife in his guts. For a long time, he had been almost consumed by grief and the hatred for her murderers that gripped him. The fact that their son, Arthur, had been killed, too, had just made it worse.

At least Standing Rock would still have his son, once they succeeded in rescuing Little Hawk from the Colonel. That would be scant comfort for Standing Rock at first, but any comfort was better than nothing.

Smoke dismounted and led the 'Palouse forward into the trees. He said, "Standing Rock, I have to talk to you."

Standing Rock came out of the shadows. He asked, "Have you found my wife and son, Jensen?"

There was no good way to do this. Smoke said, "I know where Little Hawk is. He's all right. But I'm sorry, Standing Rock, Wildflower is dead."

He heard the hiss of breath through Standing Rock's clenched teeth. Other than that there was silence for a second. Then the warrior said in a low, intense voice, "No! You lie!"

Standing Rock took a step forward, and Smoke knew that the man's first instinct was to strike out at him. He was ready to stop Standing Rock without hurting him too much, if he had to.

"I'm sorry, but it's true. She was killed while they were bringing her here to use her as a hostage to force your people to move. For what it's worth, the man who shot her when she tried to escape is dead, too. And your son is alive and unharmed, Standing Rock. Remember that."

Smoke heard the harsh rasp of the warror's breathing as Standing Rock struggled to come to grips with the awful news he had just heard. Minutes went by. Smoke didn't want to rush him because he knew how much Standing Rock was hurting right now, but Preacher still had that death sentence hanging over his head.

Finally, Standing Rock said, "My son . . . where is he?"

"Little Hawk is in the house of the man responsible for everything, the man who owns that settlement and almost everything in it. And Preacher is there, too, being held prisoner. He was captured when he tried to rescue Little Hawk. That's why he never came back from scouting the town."

"We will ride in and free both of them. And anyone who tries to stop us, we will kill!"

"I understand why you feel that way, Standing Rock," Smoke said.

"You do not know!"

"The hell I don't," Smoke replied with a hard edge in his voice. "I was married to a woman who was killed by evil men, too. They murdered my child as well. So I know good and well why you feel like riding in there and shooting everybody you see. But most of the people in the settlement are innocent. They don't have anything to do with the Colonel and his plans." Smoke paused. "Anyway, you ride in on a rampage like that and you'll just get yourself killed along with all your men, and the Colonel will still have Little Hawk. Matt and I have a plan, though, and we need your help to carry it out."

Again Standing Rock didn't say anything while precious time slipped past. But then he asked, "If this plan of yours succeeds, my son will be free? He will be returned to me?"

"That's right."

"And the men responsible for this evil? They will pay with their lives?"

"I reckon you can count on that," Smoke said.

Chapter 40

Mrs. Dayton brought Preacher more stew for supper, along with a cup of hot tea this time. He didn't know why Randall hadn't come back up to the attic to carry out another beating, but he was grateful for the respite.

The housekeeper had brought a blanket with her, too. After she finished feeding Preacher, she said, "Here, let me drape this around you."

"That's all right, ma'am," he told her. "I know I ain't got no shirt on, but it stays pretty warm up here."

That was an understatement. During the day, depending on how brightly the sun was shining, the little windowless chamber right under the roof could get almost unbearably hot. When Preacher was strung up from the beam, sweat sometimes rolled off his torso.

"Nonsense," Mrs. Dayton insisted. "It's going to get pretty chilly tonight. I can feel it in my bones. You wouldn't argue with a woman's intuition, would you?"

"I learned a long time ago not to argue with a woman, period," Preacher said as he summoned up a grin. "It's a plumb waste of time and energy."

"That's right," she said. She put the blanket around his shoulders and tucked the trailing ends into his lap.

"Careful, ma'am," the guard warned her. "You shouldn't be gettin' that close to the old varmint."

She gave him a scornful look as she straightened.

"The poor man is tied hand and foot," she pointed out. "About the only thing he could do is bite me, and I hardly think that he's going to do that."

"No, ma'am," Preacher said. "I'm a heap too chivalrous to go around bitin' ladies . . . less'n they want me to, and at my age, that ain't too likely to happen."

She laughed as she picked up the tray with his empty bowl and cup on it.

"I hope you can at least draw a little comfort from that blanket tonight," she said.

"Yes'm, I'll try," Preacher promised, although he still didn't think that he needed the blanket.

Then he moved his bound hands slightly and realized he was wrong about that.

Very wrong.

Mrs. Dayton nodded to him and went out. Preacher kept his face expressionless and let his head droop forward a little in an attitude of despair that was far from what he was really feeling.

With a little careful exploration, moving his fingers so slowly the guard wouldn't notice, Preacher was able to determine that a fold of fabric on the inside of the blanket had been pinned closed, forming a small pocket. Preacher felt a small, hard object inside that crude pocket. He wasn't sure what it was, but it had to be something Mrs. Dayton knew she shouldn't be giving him, otherwise she wouldn't have concealed it like this.

Carefully, Preacher removed the pins and dropped

them between his legs onto the cot. The hidden object slid out into the palm of his hand. It was a small shaving razor, closed at the moment.

Was she trying to help him escape? That was sure what it seemed like. He didn't think she had smuggled the razor to him so he could shave off his whiskers.

The guard usually went out of the room with Mrs. Dayton, but this hombre had lingered. He leered at Preacher and said, "You think you're a tough old bird, don't you?"

"I been alive a hell of a long time," the mountain man replied. "I must've been doin' somethin' right all these years."

"Or maybe you're just a lucky son of a bitch."

"I've had my share of luck," Preacher admitted as he eased the razor out of its handle. "The thing of it is, you got to be prepared to take advantage of that luck when it comes along."

"It's not coming along for you," the man said, still sneering. "You're done, mister. The Colonel's tired of messin' with you. And when the Colonel gets tired of something, you know what he does with it? He gets rid of it! Haw, haw!"

"Is that so?" Preacher tested the razor's keenness with his thumb, and then pressed it against the ropes around his wrists. He began to saw back and forth with slow, short strokes. "Are you sayin' I ought to be worried?"

"No, it's too late for that. You ought to be prayin' instead of worryin'."

Preacher's eyes narrowed.

"There's an old sayin' about how the Good Lord helps those who help themselves."

"Yeah, but there's not a blasted thing you can do to help yourself, old man."

The guard turned toward the door, and Preacher knew he was about to leave. He said, "Hold on, hold on."

Looking annoyed now, the guard glanced around and asked, "What do you want?"

Preacher felt some of the strands of rope part. He said, "If this is gonna be my last night on earth, the way you're actin' like, I, uh . . . well, I don't really want to spend it by myself."

The razor cut through another strand.

"What the devil do you want out of me?" the guard demanded. "I'm not gonna sit around and sing hymns with you, if that's what you've got in mind!"

"Hell, no!" Preacher exclaimed, and he hoped his voice was loud enough to cover the small sound the rope made when he tensed his arms and broke the last strands binding his wrists. While he was tied he had kept working his fingers a little from time to time so his hands wouldn't go completely numb, and that effort paid off now because he was able to grasp the razor's handle. He went on, "I was hopin' you'd go to the saloon and bring back one of the gals who work there."

"You want me to fetch you a whore? An old buzzard like you?" The guard threw his head back and laughed. "Why, you crazy old coot! What do you think you could do with a whore?"

"More than you," Preacher said he lunged up off the cot and slashed the razor across the guard's throat. Blood spurted out of the gaping wound in a grisly fountain.

The gunman's eyes bulged out in shock, pain, and horror. He made a gurgling sound, but he wasn't able to scream. As he reeled back, he clawed at the gun on his hip. He got his hand on the revolver's butt, but wasn't able to draw it before Preacher grabbed him in a bear hug, pinning his arms to his sides. They swayed there, both men struggling desperately even though they moved very little, as blood continued to bubble from the guard's severed arteries and veins. It flowed down between them and coated Preacher's bare chest like a crimson beard.

After a moment, the guard's efforts weakened. From a distance of a few inches, Preacher watched as life faded from the man's eyes. He didn't let go, though, until he was sure the guard was dead. Then he carefully lowered the man onto the cot. The heavy thump of a body falling on the floor might attract attention downstairs, and Preacher didn't want that.

A wave of dizziness and weakness went through him as he bent to cut the ropes around his ankles with the razor. He had to put his free hand on the cot to steady himself.

"You ain't as young as you used to be, old son," he muttered to himself.

When his arms and legs were free, he straightened and looked down at himself with distaste. He was covered with blood and looked like a particularly stringy carcass ready to be strung up in a butcher's shop.

That couldn't be helped. He closed the razor and tucked it in the waistband of his trousers. Then he pulled the guard's revolver from its holster and checked the cylinder. There were five rounds, with the hammer resting on an empty chamber. The gunman had been smart in that respect, even though he was dumb as a rock in others. Preacher took another half-dozen cartridges from the loops on the man's gun belt and clutched them in his left hand, since he didn't have any other way to carry them.

A creaking stair step made him whirl around in that direction. The gun in his hand came up, ready to fire with his finger tense on the trigger.

Mrs. Dayton gasped and flinched back, her eyes widening as she found herself staring down the barrel of the weapon.

"Oh, my God," she whispered as she stood there in the opening at the top of the stairs. "So much blood."

"None of it's mine," Preacher said as he lowered the revolver. "I put that razor you hid in the blanket to good use."

A shudder went through her as she glanced at the dead guard on the cot. She averted her eyes and said, "When the guard didn't follow me downstairs I knew something had happened. I came back to tell you that you have to get out of here. The Colonel plans to have you killed tonight!"

"I ain't surprised. I'm obliged to you for your help, but I sure didn't expect it."

She drew in a deep, ragged breath and said, "I . . . I just couldn't let it go on. I was outside the door of the library when I heard him tell Randall and that other man to get rid of you and dispose of the body after I went to bed tonight. There have been so many things he's done over the years . . . such terrible things . . . and I always turned a blind eye to them because he was kind to me and I . . . I had grown to care for him. But it's finally too much. To have a woman and her child kidnapped . . . to bear the ultimate responsibility for her death and for that baby growing up without a mother . . . you see, I had a child once . . . I doubt if

Hudson even remembers . . . and then to order you killed like that, so coldly, so casually . . . it was just one murder too many. . . ."

The words spilled erratically from her mouth, and Preacher knew she was edging toward hysteria. He reached out and put a hand on her shoulder. She flinched, but didn't pull away from his bloodstained grip.

"You done the right thing," he told her. "I'm sorry the Colonel maybe ain't the same man he once was, but you got to look at things the way they are, and he's got to be stopped."

"I know," she whispered. "Right now, though, I want you to leave. Get away while you can, before they kill you."

"Not without the little boy," Preacher said.

She stared at him for a second before saying, "You want to take Little Hawk with you?"

"I got to," Preacher said. "That's what I come all this way for, to take that young'un back to his family. His ma may be gone, but he's got a pa and a grandpa and plenty o' aunts and uncles and cousins who love him and want him back safe and sound."

"You can't. It's too dangerous. If the guards see you trying to escape, they'll shoot. And if you have Little Hawk with you . . ." She shook her head. "I can't give him up."

Preacher could tell by the light in her eyes that she might be a little loco, too. Not kill-crazy like the Colonel, but she was acting almost like that baby was hers. He wondered if something happened to the child she had mentioned earlier. That seemed pretty likely to him.

"I don't want to argue with you," he said, "but I ain't leavin' without the kid." He took hold of her arm, hoping that she wouldn't scream, and turned her toward the door. "Let's go—"

What he heard then rendered the argument pointless. Heavy footsteps were coming up the stairs.

Somebody was on their way to kill him, Preacher knew.

Chapter 41

After his conversation with Smoke in the alley next to the Emerald Palace, Matt returned to the saloon and found Randall still at the billiard table.

"Your horse was all right?" the big gunman asked without looking up from the shot he was lining up.

"Yeah, just fine," Matt replied. "He gets a little skittish sometimes, especially in strange places."

Randall made the shot and carelessly tossed the cue stick onto the table.

"Let's go take care of that job," he said.

"Are you sure it's late enough?" Matt asked.

Randall gave him a chilly stare and said, "Are you questioning my orders, Stevens?"

"Not at all," Matt said. "I just know the Colonel wanted us to wait until his housekeeper was asleep." He shrugged. "For all I know, she might be. Maybe she goes to bed with the chickens."

Randall's eyes narrowed in thought. After a moment, he said, "I don't guess it would hurt anything to wait a while longer, just to be sure. I'm tired of shooting pool, though."

"Maybe you should get you one of those painted gals and take her upstairs?" Matt said. He closed one eye in a suggestive wink. "When I've got an unpleasant chore coming up, sometimes that helps take the edge off it."

"Who said this chore was unpleasant?" Randall asked. "Anyway, I'm not in the mood for a girl, but I reckon I could use a drink."

"Sounds good," Matt said with a smile. "I'm buying."

"I won't argue with that."

They walked over to the bar. Matt signaled the bartender to bring them two beers. He intended to nurse his mug along as much as he could. The more time Smoke had to reach Standing Rock's camp and set up a diversion with the Assiniboine warriors, the better.

"You've been with the Colonel a long time, haven't you?" he asked. If he could get Randall talking, it might help.

"Since the war," Randall replied. "Antietam was the first action we saw together. That was a long, bloody day."

"So I've heard."

Randall grunted and said, "Yeah, that was before your time, too. You didn't miss much except a lot of killing and dying. It really bothered the Colonel. He was a good man. A kind man."

That hardly seemed possible to Matt, but he said, "War can change a man, I've been told."

"Yeah. Not me, though." Randall's smile was like ice. "Killing never bothered me all that much. As for dying . . . well, I haven't done that yet."

"How did the Colonel get the money to set up this

deal with the railroad?" Matt asked. "He must have been successful in some other business."

"Not really. He comes from money. His family's rich. Got more money than they'll ever need."

Matt frowned.

"Then why go to so much trouble to take over this basin and bring in the railroad?"

"Well . . ." Randall lifted his mug and swallowed the rest of his beer. He wiped the back of his other hand across his mouth and smiled humorlessly. "You can never have enough money, can you?"

"Maybe some men can't," Matt answered honestly without thinking about it.

"I wouldn't let the Colonel hear you talking like that. More money means more power, and those are the only two things that mean anything to him."

Matt was even more disgusted now. Colonel Ritchie had unleashed a killing spree out of sheer greed. As far as Matt was concerned, the man was an animal.

No, worse than an animal, Matt corrected himself. With rare exceptions, animals killed only for food or to protect themselves or their young. That was a matter of sheer survival. Greed had no place in nature . . . except in man.

Randall shoved the empty mug across the bar and said, "Let's go. We've waited long enough to get this done. You're going to give me a hand, Stevens. That'll be a good way to break you in, now that you're working for the Colonel."

"Lead the way," Matt said, hoping his voice didn't sound as hollow as he felt inside.

* * *

Matt still thought taking the Colonel hostage might be a good idea, but when they got to the big house, Randall went straight to the staircase and started up.

"Shouldn't we tell the Colonel we're here?" Matt suggested.

Randall paused on the second step and looked back at him.

"The Colonel gave an order, and he expects it to be carried out. There's no need to tell him that we're going to do what he told us to do in the first place. Now come on and stop stalling." Randall got a curious look on his face. "Unless you don't want to work for the Colonel after all if it means doing things like this."

"I never said that," Matt replied without hesitation. He bounded past Randall on the stairs. "Come on, let's go take care of the old coot."

"That's more like it," Randall said behind him.

Matt grimaced since Randall couldn't see him. His brain worked quickly. If there was no other guard in the attic room where Preacher was being held, he ought to be able to get the drop on Randall. He could free Preacher, and then the old mountain man could hold a gun on Randall while Matt tied and gagged him. Then they would have to get Little Hawk and find a way out.

Their chances that way would be slim, but certainly better than nothing.

They reached the third floor with Matt in the lead. He hung back so that Randall could go first up the narrow staircase leading to the attic. But Randall nodded toward the door and said, "Go ahead."

Matt couldn't think of a way to refuse without arousing the hired killer's suspicions, so he opened the door. Light from the candle in Preacher's prison reached into the stairwell since there was no door at the top, just an opening for one, but it left the stairs shadowy.

Matt took a deep breath and started up. He was halfway there when he realized that he smelled something odd. It was a metallic odor, like sheared copper, and it set his teeth on edge and caused his nerves to draw taut. He had smelled that odor before, and he didn't like it.

It was the smell of freshly spilled blood, and a lot of it.

Matt's step faltered for a second when he spotted the edge of the dark red puddle dripping over the top step.

"Something wrong?" Randall asked, close behind him.

"Nope," Matt said. "Not a thing."

"Keep going, then. I want to get this over with."

Cold horror pawed at Matt's vitals like a dead but somehow animated hand. Nobody who lost that much blood could still be alive, and since the room just above him was where he had last seen Preacher . . .

Matt's head rose above the level of the top step so he could see into the room. A body was propped up on the cot, but it didn't belong to the mountain man. It was one of the guards, and the front of his shirt was sodden with blood that had spilled from the slash in his throat.

That was Preacher's work. Matt was sure of it. But where *was* Preacher?

He had to be waiting up there, hiding around the corner by the opening so that he couldn't be seen by anyone on the stairs. Realizing that, Matt knew he had to get Randall up there in a hurry, before the gunman had time to think. He made himself sound startled—that didn't take much of an effort—as he exclaimed, "Randall, there's something wrong! Come on!"

He drew his gun and charged the rest of the way up

the stairs, taking a big step over the pool of blood so he wouldn't slip in it. Randall was right behind him, booted feet thudding heavily on the stairs. Randall said, "Careful, Stevens, you damned fool! It could be a trap!"

From the corner of his eye Matt saw Preacher in the corner with the housekeeper huddled behind him. The old mountain man had the guard's gun in his hand. As Randall reached the top of the stairs, Preacher thrust the revolver at him and said, "Don't stop now, mister. Step right on in here and say howdy to a man whose hands ain't tied no more!"

Remembering all the times Randall's fists had smashed brutally into him, Preacher wanted to pull the trigger and blow the varmint's brains out. He wanted it so bad he could feel his muscles twitching a little with the desire for vengeance.

Instead, he held his fire. A shot would draw the other guards in and around the house, and that could ruin everything.

Matt had whirled around, and he covered Randall, too. The gunman's eyes darted back and forth between the two of them, and he growled, "You're a damned traitor, Stevens. I should've known better than to trust you."

"The name's Jensen," Matt said. "Matt Jensen."

"And they call me Preacher," the old mountain man said. "You been tryin' to get my name outta me all week, Randall, and now you finally got it."

Matt said, "Preacher, I hope all that blood isn't yours."

"None of it is," Preacher told him. "I'm near fit as a fiddle now that I got a gun in my hand and this here polecat in my sights. Come on in, Randall. Don't you know it's impolite not to accept an invitation?"

Randall was poised there at the edge of the stairs. His right hand rested on the butt of his gun, but he hadn't tried to draw the revolver with two Colts pointing at him.

Now a smile spread slowly across his face.

"Jensen," he said. "I've heard the name. Seems like there's another one of you. Is he around, too?"

"Never mind about that," Matt told him. "Get on in here."

"So you can tie me up and shove a gag in my mouth? I don't think so."

With no more warning than that, Randall threw himself backwards down the stairs, whipping out his gun as he fell and blazing away at Matt as fast as he could pull the trigger.

Smoke reined the 'Palouse to a halt in the trees to the side of the mansion. Standing Rock and the rest of the Assiniboine warriors ought to be in position by now. When they were ready, they would charge down Hammerhead's main street, firing their rifles into the air and howling war cries and generally making it sound like the Battle of the Little Big Horn all over again. One fast charge, straight toward the Colonel's house, to draw out the guards and make them rush to defend against what would look and sound like an all-out frontal attack.

But when they reached the last cross street, the rescue party would split up and gallop along it in both directions, away from Main Street, before circling to close in on the mansion and the Colonel's hired killers in a classic pincer movement. Even if they were outnumbered, that flanking maneuver ought to give the Assiniboine at least a momentary advantage.

Smoke had made it clear to Standing Rock that they weren't to gun down any of the townspeople on their charge through the settlement. Standing Rock had agreed, reluctantly, and made sure that his men understood. Their battle was with Colonel Ritchie's hired killers, not with the innocent settlers who were unknowing pawns in the Colonel's grand scheme.

Smoke swung down from the saddle and left the 'Palouse's reins dangling. As soon as the shooting started and the Colonel's men rushed out, he was going to perform a little flanking move of his own, racing to the house behind them and getting inside to find Preacher and possibly Matt. If Randall had already returned to the mansion to carry out Preacher's execution, Matt would be with him to put a stop to those plans.

That was what Smoke hoped, anyway.

He stiffened as he heard shots ring out suddenly, but they didn't come from the far end of town like they were supposed to. Instead, they were slightly muffled, and Smoke could tell they came from *inside* the house. The guards on the verandah and the ones scattered around the grounds heard the gunfire, too, and jerked around toward the mansion, ready to charge inside and find out what was going on.

At that moment, more shots erupted, these coming from the other end of Main Street. Smoke heard the yips and cries and shouts that followed them instantly. The Assiniboine "attack" on the settlement was underway.

Some of the men started toward town, just as Smoke hoped they would. But others hung back, and one of them yelled, "Don't let those crazy redskins reach the house!

With that, he and several of his companions ran into the mansion.

Well, thought Smoke, the odds had just gotten a little longer. But that had never stopped him before, and with the lives of Preacher and Matt at stake, not to mention Little Hawk, it wasn't going to stop him now.

Smoke broke into a run toward the Colonel's house.

Chapter 42

Matt's Colt roared as he crouched and returned Randall's fire. Bullets from Randall's gun whined over his head as he heard the big gunman crashing and tumbling down the narrow staircase. Randall risked a broken neck by recklessly throwing himself down the stairs that way, but he must have preferred that to letting himself be taken prisoner.

Matt couldn't see Randall anymore. The man must have rolled all the way to the landing. Preacher started to rush forward into the opening, but Matt motioned him back.

Another slug snapped through the air and thudded into the roof. Obviously, Randall hadn't broken his neck. And he had them trapped up here, Matt realized. If they tried to make it down those stairs, they would be easy targets.

Randall's gun fell silent, and as it did, Matt heard the faint crackling of shots coming from somewhere outside. He glanced over at Preacher and saw the old mountain man frowning in confusion at the sound.

"That's Standing Rock and the other warriors, more

than likely," Matt explained. "Smoke was going to get them to stage a diversion so we could get out of the mansion. It would have worked if Randall hadn't pinned us down up here."

"What we need is a diversion of our own, I reckon," Preacher said. "Grab that fella on the bunk."

Matt looked at the bloody corpse, not sure what Preacher intended for him to do.

"Heave him down the stairs," Preacher went on. "I'll be right behind him."

"No, I will be," Matt said. "I can move faster than you, stove up like you are."

"Stove up! Maybe I ain't as young as I used to be, but I'm still faster than you, you big ol' muscle-bound galoot!"

Matt ignored Preacher's outburst and said, "Throw some lead down the stairs to cover me."

He bent and took hold of the dead man, turning the body so that he could slide his arms under the guard's arms and lock them around the corpse's sticky, blood-soaked chest. It was a grisly task and made a wave of revulsion go through him, but with his great strength Matt was able to lift the dead man and hold the body in front of him like a grotesque shield.

Preacher stuck the guard's gun around the corner and triggered three swift shots down the stairs. The racket in those narrow confines was deafening. Hoping that Preacher's shots had made Randall duck back momentarily from the bottom of the stairs, Matt lunged down them.

He heard a gun roar twice and felt the shock of bullets striking the body he held in front of him. Halfway down the stairs, the guard's dead weight threatened to make him lose his balance, so Matt gave the corpse a shove and sent it plummeting the rest of the way. He caught himself by bracing a shoulder against the wall and palmed out his revolver. Flame licked from the muzzle as he triggered.

The echoes made it hard to hear, but Matt thought he detected running footsteps from the third floor hall. He bounded down the rest of the stairs and dropped into a roll that carried him through the door at the bottom.

As he came to a stop and raised his gun, he caught a glimpse of Randall ducking away from the main staircase's third-floor landing. The gunman snapped a shot that tore up the flower-patterened wallpaper a couple of feet from Matt's head. Matt triggered again, but knew he had missed as Randall continued to flee downstairs.

"Come on!" Matt called to Preacher and Mrs. Dayton as he scrambled to his feet. Now that they weren't trapped in the little attic room anymore, they had a chance to fight their way clear of the mansion.

That chance improved with every minute that passed, since Matt knew that Smoke was on his way by now.

While the diversion staged by the Assiniboine hadn't been completely successful, it had partially served its purpose by drawing away some of the guards from the front of the mansion. And since the other gunmen had rushed inside to see what the shooting was about in there, the front door was unguarded at the moment. That was the easiest way in, so Smoke took it.

When he rushed into the foyer, a couple of the guards were halfway up a broad, curving staircase. They must have heard him come in, because they stopped and whirled around. Recognizing him as an intruder, one of the men yelled, "Get that son of a bitch!" Both guards jerked up their guns.

They never had a chance. Smoke drilled both of them, each with a single shot. One man fell backwards on the stairs with blood welling from the hole in his chest. The other doubled over from the slug in his guts and fell against the fancy banister running along the edge of the staircase. He tumbled over it and crashed to the parquet floor of the entrance hall.

Smoke bounded up the stairs, stepping over the dead man who still lay there, eyes glassy and staring at nothing.

A slug whipped past his head when he reached the second-floor landing. The other guards who had charged into the mansion must have doubled back when they heard the shots break out behind them.

Smoke dropped to one knee as he saw a muzzle flash to his right. A gunman had taken cover behind a spindly-legged little table. It didn't offer him enough protection, though. Smoke's next bullet smashed one of the table legs and knocked it out of the way. The slug after that ripped through the man's spine and sent him rolling across the floor.

A bullet chewed splinters from the wall near Smoke's head. He twisted and fired the other way at a man standing in an open doorway. The man jerked back out of sight as the bullet smashed into the doorjamb beside his ear.

Smoke didn't like leaving a threat behind him, but according to Matt, Preacher was being held in the attic so Smoke wanted to keep going in that direction. His gun was empty, though, so before starting up to the third floor, he ducked into an alcove to thumb fresh cartridges into the Colt's cylinder.

"What's going on out there?" a man's voice bellowed from down the hallway. "By God, what's all that shooting? Somebody answer me!"

The man's tone told Smoke he was used to giving orders and to being obeyed. That probably meant it was Colonel Hudson Ritchie doing the yelling. As he thought about all the death and destruction the Colonel was responsible for, either directly or indirectly, Smoke wanted to go after him and deliver some hot lead justice to the man, but saving Preacher and Little Hawk had to come first. He leaped for the stairs that led to the third floor. A bullet whined past his head as he dashed across the open space between the alcove and the staircase.

Shots had been ringing out above him. Just as Smoke started up the stairs, the big man he had seen earlier with Matt lunged onto the staircase at the top. For a split-second the two men froze as they looked at each other.

The shot that crashed in the next instant didn't come from either of their guns. Smoke felt the bullet's impact. It twisted him halfway around. He kept moving, spinning out of the way as the man at the top of the stairs opened fire. More shots came from the other end of the corridor, where the man Smoke took to be the Colonel was firing around the corner of an open doorway. He was the one Smoke's shot had chased back into the room a moment earlier.

Smoke had to take cover in the alcove again. He looked down at his right side where the bullet had hit him and saw that the slug had torn along the thick leather of his gun belt at an angle instead of penetrating his body. It had been enough to knock him off-balance for a moment, but hadn't done any real damage.

That was a stroke of luck, but Smoke knew he couldn't count on that happening again.

He heard movement on the stairs. More shots blasted, tearing up the wall at the corner of the alcove. As the gun fell silent, he risked a look and saw the big man, who had to be Randall, lunge past, dragging a man in a gray suit. That would be Colonel Ritchie. Smoke threw a shot at them, but he missed and the bullet exploded the newel post on the staircase's top baluster.

Another figure suddenly appeared at the bottom of the stairs from the third floor. Smoke held off on the trigger at the last second as he recognized Matt.

Matt had almost fired as well. They stared at each other over their gun barrels for a heartbeat, and then Matt grinned. He waved at someone up the stairs and said, "Come on! Smoke's here!"

That was encouraging. Sure enough, Preacher appeared at Matt's side a moment later, although Smoke had a little trouble recognizing the old mountain man at first. Preacher looked like he had taken a bath in blood.

A fair-haired woman hesitantly came down the stairs behind Preacher as Smoke hurried to join them. Preacher looked at her and asked, "Where's the young'un?"

"In my room," she answered. "He must be terribly frightened with all this shooting going on."

"He comes from good stock," Preacher told her. "He'll be all right. Best fetch him, though."

As the woman hurried down the corridor away from the stairs, Smoke asked, "Preacher, are you all right? You look like you just crawled out of a slaughterhouse."

"It ain't my blood," Preacher assured him. "I'll be a mite stiff and sore for a while, but I'm fine. Better now that the three of us are together again."

Smoke felt the same way. They were still in great

danger, but as long as they were together, he liked their chances.

"Where are Randall and the Colonel?" Matt asked.

"Randall made it past me," Smoke said. "He hustled a fella I took to be the Colonel downstairs."

"Big man, bald, forehead sort of bulges?"

"I didn't get a real good look at him," Smoke said, "but I think that's him."

Matt nodded and said, "That's the Colonel, all right. And if there are any guards left alive downstairs, Randall will rally them and try to keep us trapped up here."

"He's liable to have his hands full with other things if Standing Rock and his warriors are able to fight their way through the Colonel's men outside."

The woman came back up the hall with a blanket-wrapped bundle in her arms.

"Here he is," she said.

Preacher said, "Smoke, Matt, this here's Miz Dayton. She helped me get loose. She works for the Colonel, but she wants Little Hawk to get back to his pa where he belongs."

Smoke tugged on his hat brim and said, "Smoke Jensen, ma'am. I'm pleased to meet you. I just wish it was under better circumstances."

"Please, Mr. Jensen . . . if it's possible . . . if you could spare Hudson's life . . ."

"Ma'am, I'm afraid that's going to be entirely up to him," Smoke told her. "But one way or another, we're taking this baby home."

Mrs. Dayton swallowed hard and nodded.

"I know. Little Hawk should go home. It . . . it's the only right thing—"

A shot roared. She cried out and staggered. Little

Hawk was about to slip from her arms and fall when Preacher caught the child, using his free arm to pull Little Hawk against his bloodstained chest.

"You bitch!" a man roared. "You betrayed me!"

Smoke, Matt, and Preacher whirled toward the far end of the hall. The Colonel stood there, smoke curling from the barrel of the pistol in his hand. He knew this house much better than they did, and Smoke realized he must have slipped up a rear set of stairs to reach the second-floor corridor and get behind them.

Shooting Mrs. Dayton was the last thing he was going to do. Smoke, Matt, and Preacher all fired at the same time, the three shots blending into a thunderous explosion. The slugs hammered into the Colonel's chest and threw him back against the wall behind him. He hung there for a second, his gun hand sagging and blood bubbling from the bullet holes in his chest.

"You . . . you can't do this," he said, his voice weak. "That's . . . an order. . . ."

He pitched forward, already dead by the time his face smacked into the carpet runner.

"That just leaves Randall," Matt said.

"And whoever he's still got with him," Smoke added. He turned to Preacher. "Is Little Hawk all right?"

"Yeah, the little feller don't appear to be hit," the mountain man said. "Better see about Miz Dayton, though."

The woman had collapsed after being shot by the Colonel. Smoke holstered his gun and knelt beside her, carefully lifting her so that she was propped against his leg. Blood stained the front of her dress. Her eyes fluttered open. She peered up at Smoke and whispered, "The . . . the baby?"

"He's fine," Smoke assured her. "The Colonel missed him."

"No . . . he never meant to hurt Little Hawk. . . . He was trying to kill me. . . . I gave him . . . everything . . . but none of that mattered. He didn't care . . . didn't care who he hurt . . . as long as he . . . got what he wanted. . . ." Her eyes widened, and she had even more trouble talking as she said, "You'll keep the little one . . . safe . . . take him home . . ."

"You got our word on it, ma'am," Preacher said as he held Little Hawk. "This little varmint's gonna be fine."

"Thank you . . . I . . ." A spasm shook her. In a clear, amazed voice, she said, "Oh, my."

Then her head fell back against Smoke's knee as death claimed her.

He lowered her gently to the floor and then stood up. His face was grim as he said, "The Colonel got what was coming to him."

"You won't get any argument from us," Matt replied. "What now?"

The shooting had stopped outside. Smoke moved closer to the landing and called downstairs, "Randall! Randall, do you hear me?"

"I hear you," Randall said. "Who are you, and what do you want?"

"Name's Smoke Jensen," Smoke told him. "Colonel Ritchie is dead. You don't have anything to fight for anymore. You might as well throw down your gun."

Randall's answer came back immediately.

"The hell with that! The Colonel died fighting, didn't he?"

"He died with a gun in his hand . . . after he killed a poor woman who never did anything except love him when he didn't deserve it!"

Randall was silent for a moment after that. When he spoke again there was a trace of regret in his voice.

"Mrs. Dayton was a good woman, all right, and maybe the Colonel was a little loco. But he was my commanding officer."

"The war's been over for a long time!"

"The war's never over. Not for some of us . . ."

Randall's voice trailed off. After a moment, he went on, "Looks like I'm the only one still alive down here. From the sound of it, all the Colonel's men who were outside are dead, too, or at least wounded bad enough to be out of the fight. That leaves me to carry on."

"Randall, what are you—" Smoke began.

The sound of the front door opening interrupted him. A second later, it slammed.

"He's gone out to face down Standing Rock and the rest of the Assiniboine!" Matt exclaimed.

Shots began to roar outside.

The battle, if it could be called that, lasted only a few seconds. Then silence settled down again.

"Come on," Smoke said.

The three men, with Preacher carrying the baby and staying back a little, walked down the stairs. They had their guns in their hands, just in case. But as they stepped out of the mansion onto the verandah, they saw the weapons wouldn't be necessary. Randall's body lay crumpled on the flagstone path leading to the arched entrance. He had been shot to pieces. A soldier's death, thought Smoke . . . but still senseless.

Standing Rock and the rest of the Assiniboine came out of the shadows in front of the mansion. It looked like the rescue party had lost a few men in the fighting. Standing Rock had blood on his buckskins, but didn't seem to be badly wounded. He glanced contemptuously at Randall's body, and then hurried forward.

"My son . . . ?" he asked.

Smoke and Matt stepped aside and let Preacher move forward with Little Hawk cradled in his left arm. Standing Rock stopped short. Anybody who thought all Indians were stoic should have seen the tears of joy and relief on Standing Rock's face at that moment, Smoke thought. Carefully, he took his son from the old mountain man and hugged him.

"We will go home now," he said, his voice choked with emotion.

"Soon," Preacher said. "First, though, I reckon we better let the folks in the settlement know they ain't all about to be massa-creed."

Chapter 43

"I swear, none of us knew a blessed thing about any kidnapping," Archibald Ingersoll said.

"Or about raiding some Indian village," the storekeeper, Fred Springhorn, added.

The men were in the Emerald Palace Saloon, gathered there with most of the other business owners in Hammerhead, as Smoke and Matt explained what had happened tonight at the big house on the western edge of the settlement.

Smoke nodded and said, "We know that. The Colonel kept his real plans secret from everybody except Randall and the other gunmen who worked for him."

Matt said, "Not even that fella Webster who kept books for him knew everything that was going on. When he found out the truth, he opened the office and let us go through all the files. It's pretty clear from the documents we found that Colonel Ritchie planned to take over everything, including all of your businesses, as soon as the railroad came in."

"But what are we going to do now?" one of the men

asked. "If the railroad *doesn't* come in, the town can't make it! We'll still lose everything!"

"Maybe not," Smoke said. "I know some men who are involved with the railroads. If I tell them about this basin and how it's just sitting here waiting to boom, I've got a hunch some of them will want to come in and do it right this time, so that all of you have a chance to get rich."

"But the Colonel's heirs will still own all the land," Ingersoll pointed out. "We'll have to deal with them."

Matt said, "From what we've been able to find out, the Colonel's family back East is pretty proper and respectable. Chances are, when they hear how loco he had gone, they'll want to keep the whole thing as quiet as they can. The easiest way to sweep it all under the rug will be to cooperate with you folks."

"You're going to need some law in here as the town continues to grow, too," Smoke said. "You'll need to hire a marshal, maybe even try to form your own county here in the basin and elect a sheriff."

"How about one of you fellas?" Springhorn asked. "You're the ones who found out what was really goin' on and put a stop to it."

Ingersoll nodded enthusiastically and said, "One of you can be the marshal and the other can be the sheriff!"

Smoke laughed and shook his head.

"Sorry, but I've got a wife and a ranch waiting for me down in Colorado, and I'm ready to get back to them," he said.

"And I, uh, never stay in one place long enough to do something like that," Matt said. He grinned. "But maybe you could get Preacher—"

"Who's talkin' about me? Get Preacher to do what?" the old mountain man asked as he came into the saloon. He had gone to the hotel to soak all the blood off in a tub of hot water, and now he was dressed in baggy trousers, a white homespun shirt, and a cowhide vest instead of his usual buckskins. The clothes were borrowed, but he had found his battered old hat in the mansion and had it perched on his head.

Matt waved a hand at Hammerhead's civic leaders and said, "These fellas are looking for a star packer, Preacher. I thought you might like to retire and take the job."

"Retire? Pin on some tin star and strut around like I'm some sort o' highfalutin' muckety-muck? Have you done lost all the sense you was borned with? I know it weren't much to start with, but good Lord, son!"

Smoke and Matt each took hold of one of Preacher's arms and steered him toward the bat wings. Smoke smiled back over his shoulder and told the townspeople, "I reckon you can assume he's not interested in the job, either."

Once they were outside, Preacher stopped ranting and muttering. He pulled loose from Smoke and Matt and said, "What about that goldurned Indian Ring? The Colonel was mixed up with them, and they ain't gonna like it when they hear how his plans fell through."

"They won't be able to do anything about it," Smoke said. "I'm going to make sure the U.S. Marshal for this territory gets the whole story. He'll see to it that nobody bothers Two Bears and his people again. As for the Ring . . ." Smoke shrugged. "I guess this is one more grudge they can hold against us. It probably won't be the last one."

Matt said, "One of these days they're liable to decide to settle all those scores."

"Let 'em," Preacher said. "Let those buzzards come after us and we'll hand 'em their needin's. We'll burn powder all the way to dadgum Washington if we have to!"

A Little Bit of William W. Johnstone
by J. A. Johnstone

William W. Johnstone was born in southern Missouri, the youngest of four children. He was raised with strong moral and family values by his minister father, and tutored by his schoolteacher mother. Despite this, he quit school at age fifteen.

"I have the highest respect for education," he says, "but such is the folly of youth, and wanting to see the world beyond the four walls and the blackboard." True to this vow, Bill attempted to enlist in the French Foreign Legion ("I saw Gary Cooper in *Beau Geste* when I was a kid and I thought the French Foreign Legion would be fun") but was rejected, thankfully, for being underage. Instead, he joined a traveling carnival and did all kinds of odd jobs. It was listening to the veteran carny folk, some of whom had been on the circuit since the late 1800s, telling amazing tales about their experiences which planted the storytelling seed in Bill's imagination.

"They were honest people, despite the bad reputation traveling carny shows had back then," Bill remembers. "Of course, there were exceptions. There was one guy named Picky, who got that name because he was a master pickpocket. He could steal a man's socks right off his feet without him knowing. Believe me, Picky got us chased out of more than a few towns."

After a few months of this grueling existence, Bill returned home and finished high school. Next came stints as a deputy sheriff in the Tallulah, Louisiana, Sheriff's Department, followed by a hitch in the U.S. Army. Then he began a career in radio broadcasting at KTLD in Tallulah, Louisiana, that would last sixteen years. It was here that he fine-tuned his storytelling skills. He turned to writing in 1970, but it wouldn't be until 1979 that his first novel, *The Devil's Kiss*, was published. Thus began the full-time writing career of William W. Johnstone. He wrote horror (*The Uninvited*), thrillers (*The Last of the Dog Team*), even a romance novel or two. Then, in February 1983, *Out of the Ashes* was published. Searching for his missing family in the aftermath of a post-apocalyptic America, rebel mercenary and patriot Ben Raines is united with the civilians of the Resistance forces and moves to the forefront of a revolution for the nation's future.

Out of the Ashes was a smash. The series would continue for the next twenty years, winning Bill three generations of fans all over the world. The series was often imitated but never duplicated. "We all tried to copy *The Ashes* series," said one publishing executive, "but Bill's uncanny ability, both then and now, to predict in which direction the political winds were blowing, brought a dead-on timeliness to the table no one else could capture." *The Ashes* series would end its run with more than thirty-four books and twenty million copies in print, making it one of the most successful men's action series in American book publishing. (*The Ashes* series also, Bill notes with a touch of pride, got him on the FBI's Watch List for its less than flattering

ortrayal of spineless politicians and the growing
ower of big government over our lives, among other
hings. "In that respect," says collaborator J. A. John-
tone, "Bill was years ahead of his time.")

Always steps ahead of the political curve, Bill's
ecent thrillers, written with J. A. Johnstone, include
*engeance Is Mine, Invasion USA, Border War, Jack-
nife, Remember the Alamo, Home Invasion, Phoenix
tising, The Blood of Patriots, The Bleeding Edge,* and
he upcoming *Suicide Mission.*

It is with the western, though, that Bill found his
greatest success and propelled him onto both the *USA
oday* and the *New York Times* bestseller lists.

Bill's western series, co-authored by J. A. Johnstone,
nclude *The Mountain Man, Matt Jensen the Last
Mountain Man, Preacher, The Family Jensen, Luke
ensen Bounty Hunter, Eagles, MacCallister* (an
Eagles spin-off), *Sidewinders, The Brothers O'Brien,
iixkiller, Blood Bond, The Last Gunfighter,* and the up-
oming new series *Flintlock* and *The Trail West.*
Coming in May 2013 is the hardcover western *Butch
Cassidy, The Lost Years.*

"The Western," Bill says, "is one of the few true art
orms that is one hundred percent American. I liken the
Western as America's version of England's Arthurian
egends, like the Knights of the Round Table, or Robin
Hood and his Merry Men. Starting with the 1902 pub-
ication of *The Virginian* by Owen Wister, and followed
y the greats like Zane Grey, Max Brand, Ernest
Haycox, and of course Louis L'Amour, the Western
as helped to shape the cultural landscape of America.

"I'm no goggle-eyed college academic, so when my
ans ask me why the Western is as popular now as it was
century ago, I don't offer a 200-page thesis. Instead,

I can only offer this: The Western is honest. In this grea country, which is suffering under the yoke of political cor rectness, the Western harks back to an era when justice was sure and swift. Steal a man's horse, rustle his cattle rob a bank, a stagecoach, or a train, you were hunted down and fitted with a hangman's noose. One size fit all

"Sure, we westerners are prone to a little embellish ment and exaggeration and, I admit it, occasionally play a little fast and loose with the facts. But we do so for a very good reason—to enhance the enjoyment of readers

"It was Owen Wister, in *The Virginian* who first coined the phrase '*When you call me that, smile.*' Legend has i that Wister actually heard those words spoken by a deputy sheriff in Medicine Bow, Wyoming, when an other poker player called him a son-of-a-bitch.

"Did it really happen, or is it one of those myths tha have passed down from one generation to the next? I hon estly don't know. But there's a line in one of my favorite Westerns of all time, *The Man who Shot Liberty Valance* where the newspaper editor tells the young reporter 'When the truth becomes legend, print the legend.'

"These are the words I live by."

GREAT BOOKS, GREAT SAVINGS!

When You Visit Our Website:
www.kensingtonbooks.com
You Can Save Money Off The Retail Price
Of Any Book You Purchase!

- **All Your Favorite Kensington Authors**
- **New Releases & Timeless Classics**
- **Overnight Shipping Available**
- **eBooks Available For Many Titles**
- **All Major Credit Cards Accepted**

Visit Us Today To Start Saving!
www.kensingtonbooks.com

All Orders Are Subject To Availability.
Shipping and Handling Charges Apply.
Offers and Prices Subject To Change Without Notice.

THE LAST GUNFIGHTER SERIES BY
WILLIAM W. JOHNSTONE

__The Drifter
0-8217-6476-4 $4.99US/$6.99CA

__Reprisal
0-7860-1295-1 $5.99US/$7.99CA

__Ghost Valley
0-7860-1324-9 $5.99US/$7.99CA

__The Forbidden
0-7860-1325-7 $5.99US/$7.99CA

__Showdown
0-7860-1326-5 $5.99US/$7.99CA

__Imposter
0-7860-1443-1 $5.99US/$7.99CA

__Rescue
0-7860-1444-X $5.99US/$7.99CA

__The Burning
0-7860-1445-8 $5.99US/$7.99CA

Available Wherever Books Are Sold!

Visit our website at **www.kensingtonbooks.com**